*The v___ ___ of Elliot's hand*
on her shoulder brought Julianna out of her reverie. "Please don't go," he begged softly. "Be here when I come back. For right now, that's all I ask, darlin'."

"You ask too much, Elliot," she answered quietly. "I need more."

"More?" His voice was like black velvet, caressing her in the twilight's gloom. "More than this?" he whispered, stroking her neck. "Or this?" he murmured, drawing her close to capture her lips with his.

With enormous effort, she pushed out of his arms. "Please, Elliot, don't make this more difficult than it already is. Let me go. I have to pack." "All right, then I'll let you pack." She heard a gentle note of persuasive scheming in his tone, then he swept her up in his arms, and with a determined stride, turned toward her bedroom.

"No!" she exclaimed. He paused for an instant, smiling down into her eyes, a shock of oak brown hair falling into his. "You said you had to pack. I'll help." He undid the top two buttons at the high collar of her gingham frock. Without allowing further argument, he strode boldly down the short hallway and through her bedroom door.

All Julianna's thoughts of resisting vanished as soon as Elliot bent over her and touched his lips to hers.

# BECKY LEE WEYRICH

# SWEET FOREVER

PINNACLE BOOKS
WINDSOR PUBLISHING CORP.

*To BELLE*
*She was the sweetest, the dearest, the best!*
*July 10, 1991*

PINNACLE BOOKS

are published by

Windsor Publishing Corp.
475 Park Avenue South
New York, NY 10016

First printing: May, 1992

Printed in the United States of America

# Prologue

Rain lashed the old Dutch cottage, Netherwood, rattling against the tall windows of the girls' bedroom. A deafening boom of thunder brought a trio of shrieks, then a burst of nervous giggles from Lettie and Sarah Worthington and their visiting cousin—tall, copper-haired, emerald-eyed Julianna Doran.

From the shadows on the far side of the room a hoarse whisper drew their attention. "Tis only Hendrick Hudson playing at ninepins with his goblin crew."

The three girls stared at old Maeyken Huyberton, who had been nurse to Worthington offspring for as far back as anyone remembered. The ancient soul knew more tales about Netherwood, the Hudson River, and the legends of the

5

valley and the mountains than any person alive, it seemed. Perhaps she was in a storytelling mood tonight.

But instead of weaving one of her magical tales, Maeyken cocked her gray head and put one gnarled finger to her thin lips. Her eyes seemed to glimmer in the shadows.

"Listen," she whispered, "and you'll likely hear the spirit of Storm King Mountain roaming about tonight. Restless, this weather makes him. I'd be abed, if I were you. 'Tis not a safe time for helpless little girls like yourselves. A good night to you, misses, and do not forget to pull the covers up over your heads. Mind what I tell you."

A few moments of tense stillness followed old Maeyken's departure. Then another clap of thunder brought screams from the two younger girls, Sarah and Julianna, who clutched each other in only partly feigned terror.

Sh-h-h!" Sixteen-year-old Lettie cast a stern look toward the pair. "We have to be quiet or we'll wake Mother. Now that Maeyken's finally gone, we can turn out the lamp and light the candles. Julianna, you do that. Sarah, you get the Ouija board out from under the bed so we can get started."

When neither of the younger girls made a move, Lettie clapped her hands sharply. "Do what I say, both of you!"

Julianna and little Sarah exchanged doubtful glances, but neither was willing to disobey Lettie's imperious commands. Besides, they had made a solemn pact, the three of them, to hold this séance and to keep it a secret among themselves. Lettie had even insisted earlier, when the day was still fine, with no threat of frightening weather, that they all prick their fingers with a darning needle and swear a blood oath to keep silent about their ghost-stalking plans.

Julianna shuddered slightly, glancing down at the sore little wound on the tip of her right forefinger. This had all seemed a grand adventure by the buttery-warm light of day. But now, near midnight, with her aunt and the servants all sleeping and a storm raging outside, it was quite a different matter. At fifteen, Julianna prided herself on her courage. She craved adventure and was always eager to join Lettie in her daring schemes. But this—this tampering with spirits from beyond the grave—was something far different. The very thought of it was enough to scare the curl out of Juli's long red-gold hair.

Another clap of thunder brought Sarah scurrying out from under the bed, her blond hair mussed and her long night-gown hiked up around her plump thighs.

"Lettie," she cried, "it's dark under there . . . and scary. And I couldn't find the board. Can't we wait till it stops thundering?"

"You're such a goose," Lettie scolded, tossing her pale-yellow curls impatiently. "The storm's the best part. You heard what Maeyken said. The thunder and lightning will stir up the spirits so it will be easier for them to get through to me."

Julianna watched twelve-year-old Sarah's lower lip start to tremble, presaging a childish tantrum.

"I wanted to do the trance part," Sarah insisted for the dozenth time that evening. The argument over which sister would act as medium had raged all day. Of course, Julianna, being only a cousin, a visitor, and a poor relation at that, had never been considered for this important role.

"I told you, Sarah, you're too little," Lettie replied. "No serious, self-respecting spirit is going to talk to a *child*. Why, you can't even do what I tell you. Where's the Ouija board?"

"I'll get it," Julianna offered, determined to hide her fear from herself as well as from her cousins.

Moments later, the three girls were seated in the middle of the room at a white wicker table. Flickering candlelight cast grotesque shadows about the walls, making the younger girls glance about fearfully, wondering if some restless spirits were already gathering for this midnight tête-à-tête. Lettie placed her hands on the Ouija board's pointer. Julianna held a pencil poised to write down any messages the spirits might impart. Sarah's job was to watch for apparitions that, according to the all-knowing Lettie, could materialize at any moment from the dusky corners of the large room.

Julianna had to admit that she felt a certain electricity in the air, but she blamed that on the storm alone. She hadn't had much faith in this séance since the moment Lettie suggested it. Granted, the spooky old house—built on the heights overlooking Tappan Bay nearly two centuries ago by some long-dead Dutchman—had sheltered enough beings over the decades to provide spirits a-plenty. But Julianna wasn't sure she believed in ghosts, and she certainly had her doubts about Lettie's ability to summon them. Yet, as her left palm rested flat on the table, her little finger touching Sarah's, she sensed a certain energy starting to kindle. It quickly spread over her body, like tiny sparks bubbling through her veins.

"Oh, spirits from beyond the grave," Lettie intoned, eyes closed, head back, "hear me and come. Speak to me from the other side."

The table jumped suddenly and both Lettie and Julianna cried out.

"Sarah, what are you doing?" Lettie demanded in a harsh whisper.

"Scratching my leg. A mosquito bit me."

"Well, do hold still! You broke my trance."

"You weren't in any trance," Sarah countered, still pouting.

"If I wasn't, it's all your fault. Now, hush!"

Julianna experienced several odd sensations suddenly. She heard the testy exchange between the two sisters, but it seemed as if their voices came from far away. She was aware of the table growing hotter and hotter beneath her

8

hands. Her head felt light. The glow of the candles hurt her eyes. Reluctantly, she let her lids droop shut.

"Go on, ask the board a question." Sarah's voice sounded to Julianna as if it came through a long, black tunnel.

"Can . . . you . . . hear . . . me . . . spirits?" Lettie drew the words out, or was she, too, in the dark tunnel with her little sister? Julianna couldn't be sure.

"It's moving!" came an excited whisper from one of the other girls, Julianna couldn't tell which.

"Hey, what's going on?" This was definitely Lettie.

Suddenly, Julianna felt cool wood nudge her fingertips.

"The pointer wants Julianna to operate it," announced Sarah triumphantly.

Hardly conscious of what she was doing, Julianna let her fingers rest lightly on the pointer. "Who are you?" she asked, fully expecting an answer from the presence she sensed very near—a presence that prickled the hair on her arms and sent a shiver down her spine.

Juli was barely touching the smooth wood when she felt it jerk to life beneath her fingers.

After only moments, Julianna heard Lettie slowly spelling out a series of letters: "B-R-O-M. *Brom!*" the oldest girl cried excitedly. "Why, that's the old Dutch nickname for Abraham." Then she turned on her cousin accusingly, demanding in a harsh whisper, "You did that on purpose, didn't you, Juli? Are you trying to scare us?"

Julianna attempted to deny her cousin's accusation, but no words came from her dry mouth. Lettie's voice was fading again. Julianna found she was conscious only of the movement of the pointer and a sensation of weightlessness spreading through her limbs.

"I don't like this. Not one bit!" Sarah's high-pitched, hysterical whimper was the last sound Julianna heard from either of her cousins.

The light suddenly glowed brightly. Even though Julianna's eyes were closed, she twisted this way and that in her chair trying to avoid the burning glare. Then something touched her shoulder. A male voice urged, "Come. Don't be afraid."

Julianna rose—floating, it seemed—letting the unseen spirit lead her away from the table. The bright light still hurt too much to open her eyes. Slowly, ever so slowly, it began to fade. She sighed with relief and blinked. She was no longer in the bedroom. In fact, she wasn't sure where she was. Before her was a small arched door she'd never seen before.

"Come in," the ethereal voice invited.

Julianna glanced about, but saw no one, only bare, windowless walls and the door with the shining glass knob. Slowly, she turned it. She eased the door open, her heart pounding in her breast. A flash like green fire burst from the opening, then vanished in an instant.

When Julianna stepped over the threshold, she found herself once again in her cousins' bedroom, but it looked so different. Lettie and Sarah were gone. Gone, too, were the brass bedstead, the white wicker, the chintz curtains. No dolls rested on the window seat. No toys and games filled the inglenook beside the fireplace. The flower-papered walls were now painted forest-green, the floor covered in a jewel-hued Persian carpet. A pair of ornate Chinese urns sat on the mantelpiece where a set of Staffordshire dogs had been only moments before. The chairs, upholstered in Russian leather, looked solid and masculine. She sniffed the air. Tobacco, bay rum, brandy. She caught her breath as another distinctive odor assaulted her senses. *Blood!*

"Lettie? Sarah?" she called in a ragged whisper. "Where are you?"

Julianna turned toward the massive oak bed. Heavy velvet

10

drapes were drawn all around. They'd be hiding in there, of course, she thought. With a feeling of triumph for having outfoxed the pair, Julianna tiptoed to the bed and threw back the curtains with a loud, "Aha!"

She froze where she stood as her wide green eyes met the smoldering, heavy-lidded gaze of a strange man. Stretched out on the bed, he wore only purple velvet breeches and high, spurred boots of yellow tooled leather. Long black curls swept his shoulders, and through his thick jet hair, Julianna could see the gleam of a single golden earring. His face—familiar and yet not so—was all planes and angles, seeming hewn by wind, sun, and sea. His flesh was deeply bronzed and he wore a trim mustache and short, pointed beard. His broad chest, furred with a thick matting of black hair, was crisscrossed by a wide, white bandage—a bandage stained crimson with blood.

All Julianna's fear fled suddenly. She experienced a sense of truly belonging to someone for the first time in her life. She had no idea who this man was, yet she knew instinctively that he was hers and she was his. Some invisible force linked their very souls. Awestruck by what she was feeling for him, it took a moment for Juli to express her deep concern.

"You're hurt!" she cried, wanting to weep. Julianna could actually feel the burning pain of his wound as if it were in her own flesh. She tried to reach out to him, but she found herself unable to move.

Slowly, the man raised himself on one elbow and held out a hand to her. Her gaze focused on the emerald-studded gold ring on his little finger—a dragon with fiery scales. Again, the flash of green fire blinded her for an instant.

"I've been waiting for you," he said in a husky, pain-filled whisper. "So long. So *very* long."

His hand gripped hers, drawing her closer. Julianna felt

11

an instant of warm tingling all over. When he leaned toward her, letting his lips brush her forehead, his kiss was a hot brand against her cool flesh.

"But you must go back before it's too late," he warned. "You should not be here now. It isn't time yet."

Julianna lowered her eyes, trying to hide the sudden wave of sadness and the sense of deep loss that his warning caused. When she looked down, a soft gasp escaped her lips. The pristine white of her linen gown was stained with his blood. Again, she felt the sharp stab of his pain.

"Please, let me stay and help you." She gripped his hand more tightly, trying to grasp the meaning of this mysterious magic between them. But mists seemed to be closing around her, forcing her away from him. Ever farther, ever faster.

"Go now!" His voice held a gentle but urgent command. "We shall meet again. I promise you."

"Please?" she begged, trying desperately to hold on to this feeling, this moment, this man.

But the instant his hand slipped from hers, Julianna moaned and collapsed to the floor.

"Julianna? Juli, what's wrong with you? Are you ill?" Lettie sounded frantic.

Julianna opened her eyes and stared up. Lettie was fanning her furiously with a picture book. Chubby Sarah stood next to her tall, slender sister, blubbering and hiccoughing, her blue eyes wide with fear.

"I'm all right. Really, I am," Julianna assured them. "What happened?" She glanced about the room quickly, taking stock. Brass bed, wicker furniture, dolls, toys . . . Ouija board.

"Well, it was just the oddest thing!" Lettie exclaimed. "First, you took the pointer from me."

"No, she didn't," Sarah interrupted with some force.

"The pointer went to Juli. It wanted *her* to be the medium, not *you*."

"Don't be ridiculous! You talk as if the thing has a mind of its own."

"It does!" Sarah insisted.

"After you spelled out that name, Brom, numbers started coming. Don't you remember anything, Juli?" Lettie demanded in exasperation.

"My head is still swimming," Juli answered, touching the heel of her palm to her forehead—the very spot where the stranger had kissed her. "You say the pointer went to the numbers?"

Lettie nodded. "I think it must have been a date, 1699, it was. But before I could find out anything else, the storm blew a window open and all the candles went out. By the time I could light them again, you were lying on the floor here by the bed."

"Sixteen ninety-nine?" Julianna repeated. "What could that mean?"

"I haven't a notion," Lettie admitted. "Don't you know?"

Julianna shook her head. She glanced again toward the bed. Should she tell her cousins about the man who had been there? No, she decided. She'd probably imagined the whole thing anyway. Besides, they'd all had enough excitement for one night, and she needed to think everything through before she'd be ready to talk about it. She still felt quite weak and dizzy and very confused.

The door to the room flew open just then. All three girls turned simultaneously to see Martha Worthington glaring at them. "Just what are you young ladies up to this time?" she demanded.

"Nothing, Mother!" Lettie and Sarah chorused.

"Do you know it's past midnight?"

All three nodded silently.

"Well? What are you doing still up?"

Mrs. Worthington's sharp eyes roamed the room, searching for something amiss. All year her daughters were proper young ladies. When their cousin came for her annual summer visit, however, she never knew what to expect from them next. But whatever it was, Julianna could be blamed, Martha Worthington was sure. Her gaze lit upon the Ouija board and she gasped. "Where did you get that instrument of the devil?"

The girls exchanged glances, tacit understanding on their faces that they would not tell on old Maeyken, the one who had put this whole idea in their heads by giving them the Ouija board and explaining its mysterious powers.

When Mrs. Worthington received no answer, she took the board and broke it across the bed rail. Then, throwing the pieces into the fireplace, she used one of the lighted candles to set them ablaze. She watched closely until only ashes remained.

"That will be the end of that, young ladies. You haven't heard the last of this incident, however. Your father will be here from New York tomorrow to spend the weekend. I'll let him deal with this matter." She turned her angry gaze on her niece. "And be assured, Julianna, that your father, too, will hear about this. Now, go to sleep, all of you."

So saying, Martha Worthington, her silk dressing gown swishing in her broad wake, shut the door firmly and went to her own bed.

"I'll blow out the candles," Julianna offered, feeling a sinking sensation in the pit of her stomach. She knew her aunt disliked her. She couldn't figure out why.

Only when Juli drew near the bright flame did she notice the smear of blood hidden in the folds of her nightgown. A chill ran through her. Could it all have been real, then? If so, who was the man and how had he been injured? Why did he tell her he'd been waiting for her? And, most curious of all, why had neither Lettie nor Sarah seen him? Or were her cousins only denying the truth, frightened by what they had *all* witnessed?

The candles out, Lettie, Sarah, and Julianna crept under the covers without another word to one another. Soon, her cousins were breathing heavily on either side of her. But Julianna remained awake, memorizing every detail of what she had seen and heard and felt that night.

Brom, his name was. But where was the door that had led her to him? And would he be waiting again if ever she tried to return to him? Somehow she knew she must see him again. Her whole future depended on her being with him, on their coming together to share some bond that Julianna could not quite define as yet. But Brom had promised, and she meant to find him and hold him to his pledge.

She whispered a vow of her own in the darkness before she fell asleep. "I *will* find you again, Brom. Sometime. Somewhere. And I won't leave you the next time." Tears of loneliness, emptiness, and need coursed down her cheeks as she spoke the words.

Julianna's last memory of that night would ever remain the sound of distant, rumbling thunder—Henry Hudson's ghostly crew, playing at ninepins on Storm King—and her own heart softly thudding in her breast, aching for something . . . for someone.


The strange dream remained with Julianna for many years. But everything else in her life changed, including her hopes and goals for the future. She had always assumed that when she grew up she would be content to follow her mother's life pattern—marry a good man who loved her and raise children born of that love. But from her first meeting with the man named Brom, she knew that through him—whoever he was—some curious and exotic fate awaited her.

15

But what could it be and which path must she travel in order to discover the secret behind such a mystery? Through the coming years, these questions became an obsession. Returning to Netherwood seemed the only sensible route to follow.

The immediate changes wrought by Julianna's vision took a more concrete form. Instead of spending the rest of the summer with her cousins as had been the plan, she was packed off to her father's small farm in Pennsylvania the very next morning, after a sharp reprimand from her uncle. Nor was she ever again invited to visit at the Worthingtons' summer house in Tarrytown, New York. The close bond between Juli and her rich relations dissolved with the passing of time.

It would be ten years before Julianna Doran returned to Netherwood to search for Brom. When she did, all the others would be gone, and "Brom's house," as she came to think of the place, would be hers alone.

*Or would it?*

# Chapter One

Elliot Creighton wanted to marry Julianna Doran. He really, truly did! He wanted it more than anything else in the world, even more than he wanted top billing at New York's Majestic Theater or a reserved table on the main floor at Rector's Champagne and Lobster Palace where he could rub elbows with the celebrities of the Gay White Way. However, the sweet but bull-headed letter from Juli in his pocket seemed to dash any hopes of their chances at marriage, at least for the present.

"Dammit, not if I have my way!" the extremely tall, extremely handsome, extremely distraught actor shouted into the brisk autumn wind as he doggedly galloped his hired horse over the fertile Pennsylvania countryside—destination: Julianna.

17

He could understand her reticence in the beginning, back two years ago when they had first met. He had swooped down on her that night at the Opera House in Lancaster like a hungry hawk after a particularly juicy morsel. She'd been of an age to marry. Twenty-three. But she had led a sheltered life on her father's farm, so, of course, she'd been taken aback by his forward approach. He could kick himself now for having rushed things, but he'd been thunderstruck the moment he spied her out in the audience. All evening, he'd been unable to see any other face but hers. Those glittery-green eyes staring up at him, wide with innocence and a touch of mystery. Her lovely pale skin with the slightest hint of freckles sprinkled across her pert nose like pixie kisses. And her long, thick hair the color of . . . The color of what? Elliot squinted up into the last rays of sunlight, trying to decide.

"The color of goldenrod honey finely dusted with cinnamon!" Had he been on stage, he would have been heard to the farthest reaches of the balcony when he cried out the words on one long, pent-up breath.

Then he sighed, still remembering. Juli, when he first saw her, had been like a vision out of some painting by an old master, one of those mystically gifted artists of ancient times who had been endowed with the ability to see auras radiating from special ladies and had painted those subjects accordingly. Indeed, Elliot had seen a heavenly glow crowning Julianna's beauty that first night.

"But it wasn't simply her beauty that attracted me," he mused aloud, frowning. The rest of the thought seemed too incredible to speak aloud. The moment he first set eyes on her, he'd experienced the oddest feeling—as if he had finally found something or someone he had been searching for all his life. He'd felt as if he knew her, had always known her, and had been waiting for her a long, long time.

18

Except for meeting Julianna, that particular evening had been a total flop. Because of her, he'd muffed lines, missed cues, played Mark Antony like a lovesick schoolboy. There had been many women in his life before Julianna, but never had he allowed any other to affect his acting that way.

After the performance, what else could he do? He had to invite her backstage before she got away. He had to declare himself then and there, for she might never come back to the Opera House or back into his life, if he let her escape. He had to kiss those full, soft lips, to taste their sweetness, even though his actions had shocked and embarrassed her.

"Creighton, you were ever a forward damn bastard!" he snarled at himself. But he was grinning as he said it.

Still, if he had only held off for a bit and played the suitor's role by the script, perhaps he wouldn't be pounding leather right now in this hell-bent dash to keep her from leaving him.

He had been as astounded as he was distressed when he read her letter. A frown etched itself deep into his smooth forehead and he squinted his gun-metal eyes as he thought back over the gist of it. "I'm selling the farm . . . I moving to Tarrytown, New York . . . unfinished business there at Netherwood . . . remember the séance I told you about . . ."

*The séance!* Elliot almost laughed aloud, but it would have been a bitter laugh. Yes, she had told him all about that childish prank and the vision of some ghostly, wounded stranger from another time. She had felt the swarthy shade needed her help.

"But, dammit, that fellow wasn't *real!*" he cursed. "I *am*, Julianna, and I need you! I *love* you, darlin'!"

His emotions raging, Elliot whipped his weary mount to more speed as if haste might make some difference. But he knew better. Julianna was a strong-willed, stubborn woman.

If she was set on this plan, neither his love for her nor hers for him would make her change her mind. Still, he had to attempt this last-ditch effort.

New determination swept over him in a scalding wave.. "I *will* have you for my wife, Julianna Doran!" He flung his furious wail to the darkening sky. Then in a softer voice, he added, "Please, darlin', just give me a chance."

The green hills and waving fields of late corn sped past, but Elliot Creighton never noticed the loveliness of the September twilight gilding the fertile land. All his concentration centered on Julianna—reaching her in time and making her love *him* above all else.


Julianna told herself she should feel sad, but all she could feel was relief. She stood on the porch of the three-room farmhouse where she had been raised, surveying the expanse of the once-fertile fields now parched and brown. The stubby cornstalks leaned this way and that while milkweed and beggar's-lice plants reigned supreme over the ruined acreage.

"Juli girl, you're no farmer," she said aloud with more than a touch of irony in her voice. "You should have admitted it long ago."

Thinking back to more prosperous times, she could almost see her father, his work-hardened hands guiding the plow, as he moved between his long, straight rows of tall corn while her mother hummed at her tasks, hanging clothes from the black boiling pot onto the line to dry in the warm, clean Pennsylvania air. The well-remembered images stirred an ache of loneliness in Julianna's heart. She missed them both; she always would. She realized suddenly that she would miss this place, too.

"Almost as badly as I miss Elliot," she mused with a sigh. But he was gone so often, for so long at a time, that she had almost become accustomed to the dull ache of longing that lived in her heart, her constant companion.

Why, she wondered, when she finally, truly fell in love, had she chosen an actor as the object of her passion?

"Because I had no choice," she stated matter-of-factly. The fact still amazed her that from the first moment their eyes met, she had known with some inner certainty that she and Elliot were meant to be together—to love each other forevermore. But loving was difficult with the great distances that separated them.

"Never mind that for now," she murmured, then she closed her eyes and sighed again. "At last the chance I've been waiting for has come. If only Brom—whoever he is— is still waiting after all these years. I mean to settle that matter once and for all, then I'll be able to get on with my life with Elliot."

Of course, Elliot Creighton *was* her life, Julianna reminded herself silently.

Squaring her shoulders, she walked down the steps and out into the dooryard. With a resolute yank, she pulled the wooden, handpainted For Sale sign out of the ground. No more need for it. The homeplace was sold to a young couple with dreams far different from Julianna's. Tomorrow she would finalize the papers, collect her money, and leave her old home forever. She realized suddenly that more excitement than sadness filled her heart when she thought of the adventure awaiting her. She felt like a child again, returning to Netherwood for a summer's romp with Lettie and Sarah. But, of course, she reminded herself, they were both gone now.

She stared down at the crude sign in her hands, thinking how difficult it had been for her to make this decision, but how easy it seemed now that the deed was done. After her father's death she had made a determined effort to keep the place up, more for the sake of her parents' memory than for any agrarian instinct on her part. But Julianna Doran, unlike her father's people, who had tilled the earth productively for generations, seemed to be cursed with a black thumb. She took more after her mother's aesthetic stock, with her love of art and music, her tendency to dream and to hope for those dreams to come true. Now, one dream finally had come true. When Juli left tomorrow, she would return at last to Tarrytown, New York.

"To Netherwood!" she reminded herself a bit breathlessly.

The sound of a horse pounding up the dirt lane that divided the ragged cornfields drew Juli's attention. She shaded her eyes against the orange glow of the setting sun.

"Who could be coming for a visit this late in the day?" she wondered aloud.

She propped the sign against the sagging porch steps and walked toward the gate to open it, still staring hard at the dark shape of the oncoming rider.

Suddenly, Julianna gave a short, sharp cry of pure delight. "Elliot?" she shouted. "What on earth? Is that really you?"

Flinging the gate open, she ran down the lane to meet him, her arms spread wide as if she meant to embrace horse and rider in one jubilant hug. It had been months!

She had written him that she was leaving, but knowing his hectic schedule, she had never expected him to come all the way from Philadelphia to see her before she left for New York.

Elliot Creighton sat tall in the saddle, his long legs dangling down past the horse's belly. His dark-brown hair, tousled by the wind, fell over his high forehead. As he drew close and reined in, Julianna saw that he was not smiling. His square jaw was tense and his handsome face etched with lines of anguish. Only his slate-gray eyes softened when he looked at her.

"Thank God you're still here!" he said breathlessly, slid-

22

ing out of the saddle to fold her in his arms. "When I got your letter, I jumped on the first train, then hired this nag in Lancaster to bring me the rest of the way. I was so afraid I wouldn't get here in time, darlin'."

"In time for what?" Juli asked. But Elliot gave her no answer. Instead, he leaned down, kissing her with a hunger heightened by months of longing, a hunger that she returned in kind.

When they parted at last, he said, "You can't go, darlin'. I won't let you leave me."

Julianna stood in the gathering twilight, staring up into his handsome, well-loved face. Elliot, with his sweet smile and soft southern accent, had come into her life two years ago one magical night at the Lancaster Opera House. All through the performance, he had kept staring at her from the stage. She had squirmed in her front-row seat, uncomfortable under his close scrutiny. But it had been a pleasant discomfort. Never before had any man looked at her that way. It was as if some magical link formed between them during the performance, as if they had been searching for each other all their lives. Julianna found it difficult to explain her feelings that night even to herself. But the bond between them was as strong as if they had loved each other through a lifetime . . . several lifetimes.

After the final curtain, he had sent a message, inviting her backstage to meet the cast. She had met only Elliot, but that was enough. Raised strictly by her down-to-earth father and her proper New England mother, Julianna had never believed in anything so romantic as love at first sight—at least, not until that night, not until Elliot kissed her.

In the relatively short time they had known each other, her whole life had changed. If this man she loved led anything close to a normal existence, they would probably be married by now. But Elliot Creighton was married already—to the stage. She could no more take away his dream of becoming a famous actor than she could allow him to take away her dream of returning to Netherwood, of uncovering the greatest mystery of her life—her connection with the man named Brom. Was he real or phantom? She still had no idea. She knew only that he had made her a pledge and she had returned his vow in kind. Until she sorted out truth from fantasy, she could make no binding commitment to any other man. Not even Elliot.

"You'll stay, won't you, darlin'?" Elliot persisted.

As they stood gazing into each other's eyes, Julianna felt torn, but she knew she must stand her ground. She gave him her answer even without words. The very jut of her dimpled chin and stubborn tilt of her head spoke volumes on her determination to do what she knew she must—despite what he said, despite how she loved him.

"I've made up my mind, Elliot. I have to go back to Tarrytown, back to Netherwood."

"Back to your ghost, you mean," he answered, scowling.

Juli winced at his expression and his tone. She should never have told Elliot about her strange experience years ago. He didn't understand. He never could. She didn't understand herself how such a brief encounter could have changed the course of her life. But she knew what she had seen and heard, she knew how different she was after that night. And somehow it almost seemed to her that the experience had something to do with her love for Elliot and their future together.

"I'm going," she answered quietly, resolutely. "I must!"

"Forget all that and marry me, Juli!"

Julianna felt tears pooling in her eyes. They had been all through this before. She shook her head firmly. "I intend to, Elliot, but not just yet. You have things to do before you'll be ready to settle down. So do I."

Elliot gave up the argument for the moment. With a shrug

of his broad shoulders, he turned from her and tethered his horse to the fence rail. Never in his life had he felt so frustrated, so helpless in any situation. Julianna Doran was meant to be his. He had known it from the first time he saw her. There was something in the depths of her so-green eyes that had spoken directly to his heart that night. Since that moment, every other woman in the world had ceased to exist for him. But Juli lived in her own world, a world cluttered with dreams and ghosts and fantasies far more real to her than the here and now could ever be. Somehow he had to make her realize that their love was the only thing that truly mattered, that they had been born to be together always, as if some ancient sage had scribbled down their entwined fates in the Great Book of Time eons ago.

Elliot sighed, patted his weary horse's neck, then followed Juli up to the house.

"It's now or never," he murmured to himself.

Once they were inside the cozy front room, he moved toward her, his dusty boots thudding heavily on the plank floor. When he came to a halt, he stood barely a foot away from her, so close that Julianna, who was tall for a woman, was forced to tilt her head back in order to look up into his face.

"This doesn't make any sense, Juli," he said quietly. "You love me, don't you?"

She nodded, too choked up with warring emotions to answer.

"Then why are you leaving me?"

"*I'm* not leaving *you*, Elliot. You'll be going to New York soon, then on out West in a few weeks. I'll be all alone after you go. Besides, I need to go back to Tarrytown to settle my aunt and uncle's estate. It won't take long. I'll come to New York when I've finished and we'll decide what we want to do then."

"I know what I want to do *now*," he persisted.

25

Julianna could feel his dark eyes on her. She tried not to look at him, not to feel what his nearness was doing to her. She took a deep breath, trying to steady her emotions.

"You know I've wanted to sell the farm, but I could never leave before," she continued, "because I had nowhere else to go. It's different now. I don't think my mother's brother and his wife were ever particularly fond of me. They certainly resented the fact that my mother, in their estimation, married beneath her station. But since there were no other relatives to inherit, I've become the new owner of Netherwood." She smiled, picturing the place. "It's a lovely old home on a hill overlooking the Hudson River. I know I'll be happier there than I am here. I'm sure of it."

Elliot caressed her cheek with the back of his right hand, then touched the dimple in her chin. "Admit it, Juli. You and I will only be truly happy when we can be together. That's the way it is when two people love each other."

He spoke the truth, of course. Julianna loved him. She had always loved him, it seemed, even as he loved her. But there any common ground between them ended. She was a woman who needed a home, who cherished the memory of her parents and longed for a family of her own. He had no roots, no home, no anchor. Elliot Creighton, actor, was born to vanish from the stage of her life at a moment's notice. Chicago, San Francisco, New Orleans, New York. As long as she had known him, he went and did and saw and played, while Julianna was forced by circumstances to stay in this musty old cabin, trying to eke out a living from the poor farm her father had left her.

She almost smiled at the irony of her observations. *Her father*. She still thought of Ephraim Doran that way even after he'd confessed the truth to her as he lay dying three years ago.

"You ain't really blood kin of mine, child, though I feel

26

a right smart affection for you," he'd told her. "Your dear mama—God rest her—loved you like her own right from the start. We wasn't blessed with any younguns of our own, your ma and me. But one day when we was visiting her brother and his stuck-up wife up to Tarrytown, my Ruthie come home bringing this baby in her arms, begging me to let her keep it like it was no more than a stray kitten. Said she found you by the side of the road, near the stream that fed the spring. You was just lying there all alone in the woods and you not more than a few days old. So, it's a foundling you was. But a better daughter no man ever had."

*A foundling*! Julianna thought. The word still caused her pain. Who were her real parents? Hadn't they wanted her? Where had she come from? Still, she'd had as good a life as Ruth and Epharim Doran could give her. They might have been dirt-poor, but she'd been loved, at least. That was better than some could say. Better than Elliot, who had been raised in an orphange down in Richmond with no one to care what became of him.

She glanced up at Elliot's sad-sweet eyes. *No one but me*, she mused. Still, she could not bring herself to total commitment. Not yet. Not until she had returned to Netherwood to sort out her past.

Now that both her parents were gone, it seemed right that she should go back to the place where Ruth Doran had found her. Maybe she would be able to uncover her true background. Her past was like a jigsaw puzzle with one essential piece missing. Perhaps when she returned she would be able to locate that piece—her natural parents.

She almost laughed at her own hypocrisy. There was a driving force pulling her back to Netherwood all right, but bloodlines had little to do with this obsession of hers. The stranger named Brom, was the beginning and the end of it.

The warm touch of Elliot's hand on her shoulder brought

Julianna out of her reverie. "Please don't go," he begged softly. "Be here when I come back. For right now, that's all I ask, darlin'."

"You ask too much, Elliot," she answered quietly. "I need more."

"More?" His voice was like black velvet, caressing her in the twilight's gloom. "More than this?" he whispered, stroking her neck. "Or this?" he murmured, drawing her close to capture her lips with his.

Julianna tried to resist, but her struggle lacked conviction. There was no denying their mutual desire at the moment. Elliot had been on the road touring with a new play for three long months. Three long, lonely months!

"Come with me, back to Philadelphia," he begged. "Right now! Tonight!"

Elliot's desperate plea might have convinced her a few weeks back. But not now. Not when the deed to Netherwood was firmly in her grasp along with her train ticket to New York. She had to go or she would wonder for the rest of her life what might have been.

Still, it had been so long since she'd felt Elliot's touch, tasted his lips. Her very soul ached for his embrace.

With enormous effort, she pushed out of his arms. "Please, Elliot, don't make this more difficult than it is. Let me go. I have to pack."

"All right, then. I'll let you pack." She heard a gentle note of persuasive scheming in his tone, and the silvery glint in his eyes warned her that he was up to something. "I'll even help you pack. But first . . ."

It was useless to fight him, especially when she desperately longed for what he offered. His arms felt good and solid around her. She was so tired of fending for herself, of being strong and capable and responsible. She longed to be protected, to be loved.

Again, he sought her lips, teasing the corners of her mouth

28

with the very tip of his tongue, making her sigh and part a way for his intimate exploration. By the time he finished with her, the strong-willed Julianna lay weak and trembling against his chest, aching for more.

"Why do you do this to me?" she whimpered.

"Because I love you, darlin'."

She sighed deeply. "Why must love present such problems?"

"It doesn't have to, Juli. If you must go, at least let me love you," he pleaded in a whisper. "Now."

Before Julianna could reply, Elliot swept her up in his arms, holding her close for a moment, letting his warm breath kiss her face. Then, with a determined stride, he turned toward her bedroom.

"No!" she exclaimed, embarrassed, not so much by his obvious intent as by the thought of his seeing her poor quarters.

He paused for an instant, smiling down into her eyes, a shock of oak-brown hair falling into his. "You said you had to pack. I'll help." He undid the top two buttons at the high collar of her blue gingham frock. Without allowing further argument, Elliot strode boldly down the short hallway and through her bedroom door.

Julianna had made the room as pretty and feminine as she could, but, despite the wealth of her mother's family, her father had been a poor man. The best furniture he could afford, he had made himself. The curtains and bedspread were patchwork, fashioned by Juli's own hands from worn-out frocks or feedsack cloth. She had been so careful never to let Elliot see her plain, dull room. She felt a woman's boudoir should mirror her personality. She knew the kind of sophisticated women Elliot traveled with in the troupe. She wanted him to think of her as equally exciting, glowing, exotic, even if he had to imagine these qualities. Now she felt exposed and vulnerable. He would know from seeing her room that she was homespun-plain, patchwork-poor, and dishwater-dull.

Amazingly, he seemed not to notice or not to care. The sun had gone down. The room was dark. For that she was thankful. Carefully, Elliot placed her on the bed. The mattress rustled, betraying its cornhusk stuffing. Julianna cringed. But her embarrassingly humble surroundings vanished from her thoughts as soon as Elliot bent over her. He touched his lips softly to hers, letting his slender, sensitive hands slide up her arms. He kneaded her shoulders gently. Julianna began to relax.

"Do you know how long I've been aching for this moment, darlin'?" He kissed her temple, her forehead, her eyelids. "I've left dreams of you scattered in lonely hotel rooms all over this country. When I play a love scene before the footlights, it's always your face and form I visualize for inspiration." His lips trailed down her cheek to press the quivering corner of her mouth, then he sighed deeply. "It's time to find out if we are really as wonderful together as I've imagined we could be. I've tried to be patient and understanding, but, Juli darlin', I can't wait any longer. If you won't have me as your husband, then let me be your lover. Please, darlin'! There's joy here for the taking, and I'm longin' to partake of it . . . right here, right now, sweet woman."

His dramatically emotional words fanned Juli's senses to flame. She wanted to admit that she had shared his fantasies, that she had lain awake night after night in this very bed, thinking of what it would be like to make love for the first time with Elliot. But modesty sealed her lips.

"Oh, Juli darlin', I need you so!" he pleaded, hugging her tightly.

Julianna murmured something, but the sound was unintelligible even to her own ears. She felt caught in a trap between wanting him with a madness that burned deep in her soul and knowing that this was wrong and she would probably be sorry later if she gave in to Elliot and to her own desires. Hadn't Maeyken, her cousins' old nurse, lectured all three girls often enough on the evils of men and how they'd steal a girl's heart, then her virtue, before leaving her to weep all alone? But this wasn't just any man. This was Elliot—*her* Elliot.

He leaned down over her once more, kissing her honey-red hair, her delicately shaped nose, and the dimple in her chin. When his tongue flicked at her lips, Julianna tried to hold perfectly still, but his kisses were spawning a cyclone of emotions and sensations that twisted her this way and that.

"Elliot please, we shouldn't," she begged lamely. "Until we're married, we have no right . . ."

"We have *every* right, darlin'. We love each other."

His lips captured hers, silencing any further objections.

Julianna lay still now—still, but burning with a desire so deep it seemed unquenchable. She felt him ease onto the bed beside her while their kiss went on and on. Then his arms slid down to her slender waist, pressing gently.

Julianna could resist no longer. Her arms encircled his broad shoulders. She kneaded the bands of muscle beneath the silk of his shirt, marveling at his powerful limbs. She let her fingertips roam over his body with the same light touch he used exploring hers. How wonderful it felt to hold him—to have him holding her!

Suddenly, his hands went to the buttons at the neck of her gingham dress, resuming the task he had begun earlier. His work was soon rewarded. Juli shivered as his fingertips trailed down the bare flesh of her throat, threatening to stray farther afield to even more intimate territory.

"Oh, Elliot!" she moaned. "What are you doing to me?"

He leaned down close to her ear, easing her hair aside until his lips pressed her delicate flesh. His whisper seemed

31

to flow all through her aching body. "I want to touch you, darlin'. I want to feel your soft skin, to learn all your sweetest secrets. I *need* to love you, Juli. And you need to be loved."

She was beyond protesting. When the rest of the buttons gave way under his urgent manipulation and she felt his cool fingertips on her warm, bare breasts, she trembled with anticipation. A moment later, his mouth was there. Julianna's eyes closed. She drew in a sharp breath and dug her fingernails into the counterpane. His lips moved over her flesh, sending thrills all through her. Was anything ever so glorious?

Julianna knew she should make him stop before it was too late to turn back. This was madness, pure and simple. But who, after all, did she have to account to? Never mind old Maeyken's warnings. She was now alone in the world. Alone, but *alive*. And what Elliot was doing to her made her feel more alive than she had ever felt in her twenty-five years. She wanted him—here, now, with all her heart, soul, and body. The devil take yesterday's dreams and tomorrow's uncertainties!

"Oh, make me yours, Elliot. Yes, *please*, do!" she whispered, circling her arms tightly around him.

"I love you so much, darlin'," he murmured against her breast. "I don't want you to leave me. Not ever!"

"I won't leave you," Julianna promised. "Not tonight, I won't."

Soon her gingham frock and whalebone-stiffened corset lay on the rag rug beside the bed, tangled with Elliot's trousers, linens, silk shirt, and boots. Julianna marveled at the tingling electricity of her lover's flesh against her own. It was wonderful, too, to finally give up her guise of the strong, independent, self-sufficient woman. How lovely it was to languish in Elliot's embrace, feeling each kiss, each touch, a thousand times through and through. If only this

32

night could go on forever. If only they could shut out the rest of the world and be together always. But never mind, she thought. Tomorrow would take care of itself. Right now, this moment was all that mattered to her mind, her heart, her very soul.

Julianna let her hands slide down his back, feeling the muscle, bone, and taut flesh. Then pressing down on his hips, she raised her own. Slowly, he slid—long and hot and throbbing—into her waiting depths. A flicker of pain, then all was pleasure. The night seemed to turn liquid about them. She was swimming in a dark pool with only this man as her guide, her protector, her love. Deeply, he plunged, then surfaced to dive again. On and on he probed, each new thrust heightening her delirious bliss.

It seemed that suddenly all the years that she had waited and yearned for something—she'd had no idea what—vanished in an explosion of euphoria so intense, so fulfilling, that nothing else mattered, not even life itself. She had to concentrate to keep breathing after such a total, heart-stopping, and lovingly shared release.

After a time, Elliot rolled on his side, but kept her with him. They clung to each other, feeling the sensations subside to a bearable degree.

"My God," he murmured. "My God, Juli darlin'! I *do* love you so!"

She let her fingers twine through his dense, straight locks. How odd! She'd never guessed it would be this way. Even her sense of touch seemed heightened by their shared experience. Had his hair ever been so silky, so thick and luxuriant? She kissed him slowly, deeply, and felt him throb to life again inside her.

"You'll drive me mad," he moaned.

"But this is such sweet madness," she murmured, matching his renewed rhythm with her own.

Much later, dawn crept into the room, gilding their naked

bodies. They slept entwined, legs, arms, and hair atangle. Julianna was the first to wake. She lay very still, memorizing his face—the strong, hard plane of his brow, the square jaw, the aquiline nose. How she loved this man. How difficult it would be to let him go!

A sudden thought struck her. Perhaps now, after their night together, Elliot would decide not to go back to the stage. He would stay with her forever. How could he bear to leave her, if their loving had stirred him as deeply as she had been moved? She smiled. Yes! Now, their lives would work. Now, he would never be able to part from her. Their loving had formed a new bond between them, a bond much too strong ever to be severed. They would go to Netherwood together as man and wife. What a glorious life it would be!

Lost in her lovely thoughts, Julianna wasn't aware he'd awakened until she felt his fingers touch her smiling lips.

"I've made you happy?" he asked hopefully.

She flicked at his fingers with the tip of her tongue. "Supremely," she purred. "Last night was everything— and more—that I ever dreamed it could be." She pouted suddenly, but her green eyes held a merry light. "And you made me wait *so* long!"

He laughed. "*Me?* Seems I remember trying to press the issue—and the lady—these past two years, since the very night we met. She'd have none of it, thank you!"

Julianna snuggled close, kissing his chest, sliding her tongue over his nipple until it puckered. He shuddered and moaned.

"Well, the lady was wrong," she whispered. "The lady, it seems, was overcautious, overmodest, overinhibited."

"And what is she now?"

"Overwhelmed!" she sighed, letting her hand slide down to stroke his maleness.

He laughed with a mixture of pleasure and reviving lust. "Overzealous, I'd say."

But it wasn't a complaint. Another hour of lovemaking ensued, at the end of which they both fell back exhausted, too tired and drained even to talk for a while.

Finally, Elliot spoke. "You make this very hard, Julianna."

She giggled, something she hadn't done since she was a girl. "I certainly hope so!"

One glance at his face told her that he was serious. She guessed what was coming. Pulling the sheet free to cover her nakedness, she rose from the bed, turning her back to him. She couldn't bear for him to see her face just now— smile gone, tears threatening.

"It's late," she said, forcing all emotions from her voice. "I'd meant to get an early start this morning. I have to sign the sale papers on the farm before I catch my train."

Elliot raised up on one elbow, a scowl marring his wonderfully handsome face. "You don't mean you're still leaving?"

"Aren't *you*?" she accused, turning dewy eyes on him. "I'd rather be the first to go than be left behind again, Elliot. I don't think I could bear that."

"You could come with me to Philadelphia, darlin'."

"You could come with me to Netherwood," she countered.

He answered her with a silent, almost imperceptible shake of his head. Julianna wasn't surprised, but she did feel puzzled by her own intractablity. Granted, they were two stubborn people. They both admitted that. But how simple it would be for her to give in to him—to give in to her own needs and desires, actually. Would life on the road be so terrible? Trains and coaches and the best hotels and making love to this marvelous, incredibly handsome and talented man whenever she wished? It seemed almost a dream come true. What woman in her right mind wouldn't want such a life?

She knew Elliot would never give up acting; she didn't want him to. It was the only thing that had ever really been his in all his life. And he was excellent at it, with a bright and promising future ahead. But she, on the other hand, had nothing to leave behind. Not only was her whole family gone now, she hadn't even a cat or a dog to tie her down. No one. Nothing!

She had almost convinced herself to give up her plans— to go to Philadelphia, to marry Elliot, and to live happily ever after—when a strange sense of rebellion mingled with longing overcame her. It was almost as if another voice spoke inside her head.

*You have nothing but Netherwood*, she heard it say, *and Brom*.

The dream, the vision, whatever she had experienced in that house years ago, remained with her to this day. It tugged at her heart like a silken thread, drawing her back time after time. These past ten years, she had been able to make that journey only in her thoughts and dreams. Now, she was about to return in person. She could no more deny herself that opportunity than Elliot could deny himself the chance to become a famous actor. Something far stronger than her own will seemed to be forcing her decision. It was as if her life would remain ever incomplete until she had returned. Julianna realized that there was no need for the debate to continue.

They dressed without further conversation. There was no anger between them. Their night together had meant far too much to them for that. But there the melding ended. Elliot Creighton was not a man to bend to another's will. Nor was Julianna Doran a typical Victorian lady, birthed and bred only to serve a man's desires. She knew what she must do. Her return to Netherwood seemed as inevitable as the next breath she would draw.

A short while later, they paused at the doorway of the old

cabin, gazing, unsmiling, into each other's eyes for a small eternity. Then slowly, Elliot bent down. Julianna raised on tiptoe to meet him halfway. They kissed—a long, deep kiss that was a promise, attesting to their abiding love and their shared hopes for the future.

"I'll see you again soon?" Elliot asked.

"You know where I'll be. Only twenty-seven miles up the Hudson from New York. There's a train from the city. I'll be there, waiting for you."

"I love you, Juli darlin'."

"And I love you, Elliot, with all my heart."

As she drove away in her father's creaking wagon, Julianna felt hot tears stream down her cheeks. She glanced back over her shoulder and waved. Elliot blew her a kiss, allowing her to leave before he departed as she had wished.

With each rotation of the wagon wheels taking her farther and farther away from him, it seemed Julianna's heart would break. Had she, indeed, lost her senses, to be leaving such a man? And what was this force that seemed to will her back to Netherwood even when she might have stayed with Elliot?

She glanced back one last time to catch a final blurred vision of her lover through her tears. Never could Julianna Doran have imagined a sweeter, a more loving, a more devastating farewell.

# Chapter Two

Julianna felt she had recovered some of her sanity and equlibrium during the journey north. The miles and days had dulled the ache of farewell, but none of her longing for Elliot. Marriage would have been so easy, so right. But she knew she had to settle the nagging questions from her past before she could be a proper wife to Elliot. She had no regrets—neither for having given herself to the man she loved nor for daring to pursue her own dreams. Still, an unsettling feeling of doubt had shadowed her all during the trip.

Now, as she bounced along in a hired wagon headed for Netherwood from the train station at the tiny hamlet of Tarrytown, she wondered if she was really doing the right thing. Near-panic seemed to be her constant traveling companion.

"Pocantico Kill up ahead," her driver and self-appointed

tour guide announced. "Feeds out from the Netherwood spring."

Julianna's interest immediately came alive. She looked up to see the weathered covered bridge—the "kissing bridge," her cousins had always called it—spanning the narrow stream. In the fading afternoon light, skeletal black fingers groped across the dirt road—long shadows of the elms that lined the pike. The moment they entered the bridge, all warmth from the fading sun died completely. Juli felt herself wrapped in cool, humid darkness. The only sounds were the horse's hoofbeats ringing hollowly on the wooden planks and the rush of water below.

As echoes rang in her ears, a strange sensation washed over Juli. All her anxieties seemed to take flight in the darkness. She expelled a long breath, at the same time releasing the tight knot she had felt in her chest for days. The murmur of the water rushing over rocks soothed her like a lullaby. When they emerged into the light once more, Julianna experienced a rush of excitement, then a sense of rightness about everything in her life. It was as if she had passed over some invisible threshold from what had been to what could be.

"There she is," announced her grinning driver, pointing one gnarled finger.

Julianna looked in that direction. High up on the wooded hill she spied the old Dutch manse of fieldstone, brick, and timber, with its crow-stepped gables and twin chimneys at either end. A new thrill coursed through her. She kept her eyes trained on the place as they turned into the long drive and drew ever nearer.

Netherwood looked the same as she remembered from her childhood visits, though a bit worse for wear from its years of neglect. Julianna noted its sagging shutters, peeling paint, and the overgrown condition of the rose garden as the wagon plodded up the steep, elm-bordered lane from the post road.

"Plan to live here, do you?" the wizened old driver asked.

"I do." Julianna was too absorbed in mentally listing the needed house repairs to be much inclined toward conversation.

"All alone?"

"Not alone," she replied. "I hear old Maeyken Huyberton is still about. My uncle's will guaranteed her wages for life and stated that she would have a home at Netherwood for as long as she wished to remain."

The driver laughed derisively. "A lot of help that one will be! Ancient as the Catskills she is, and crazy to boot."

Julianna turned a sharp look his way. "Do you know Maeyken or are you only carrying tales?"

"Aye, know her, I do. Wanted to marry her a long time ago. Can you believe she was quite a comely and buxom wench once?" He turned toward Julianna and winked, cocking back his cap as if making ready to tell a long, sad tale. "She wouldn't have me, though. Said I wasn't the one for her . . . like there was another special someone she was waiting for."

"And was there?" As hard as she tried, Julianna couldn't recall if Maeyken had ever had a husband. But then, the Worthingtons' nurse had been an ancient soul the first time Julianna met her.

"Another man?" the driver, who had announced earlier that his name was Ezekiel Scudder but that everyone called him "Zeke," sounded incredulous. "Not in this lifetime! Maeyken was always an odd one. Here today, gone tomorrow. I never could figure where she ran off to, but she'd disappear and then turn back up in a week or a month. Never no explanation, mind you. She figured I'd be there waitin', and I always was. Reckon I was the only beau she ever give a second look to. But then when I thought we was near 'bout to the altar, it all unraveled between us for no reason I could ever figure.''

''That's sad,'' Julianna replied, hoping her own love life was not doomed to a similar fate. Suddenly, Elliot Creighton seemed far, far away.

''Maybe you'll come up to visit with us sometime,'' Julianna invited.

''Maybe,'' Zeke answered, ''maybe not. All depends.''

As they pulled into the circular drive in front of Netherwood, Julianna found herself too excited to ask the man upon what his visits might depend. But Zeke gave her more time, pulling up short of the stoop.

''You *sure* you want to stay in this place, Miss Doran?''

Juli nodded firmly. ''My mother grew up here and now I've inherited the old homeplace. It's *my* property, all I own in the world since I sold my father's farm,'' she answered. ''I intend to set Netherwood to rights and make it my home.''

''You know about the Worthingtons, I reckon.'' Just in case she didn't, Zeke went on to tell her his embroidered facts. ''The whole mess started with trouble over a man.''

''That's usually the case,'' Julianna murmured, as much to herself as to Zeke.

''Miss Lettie was set on marrying a feller her pa thought was no good. See that window up yonder?'' Zeke pointed toward the very second-story room where the three girls had held their séance ten years before. ''Miss Lettie was climbing down from there, bent on eloping, when the ladder just purely fell apart under them. Her feller came out of it with a busted arm and some cuts and bruises. But poor Miss Lettie broke her neck and died on the spot. Right yonder in the middle of that lilac bush. See, it's still all broke apart.''

Julianna shivered as she stared up at the window, thinking that was just the sort of impulsive thing Lettie would have done. Of course, she'd heard of her cousin's death nearly

41

seven years ago, but to be at the scene and have it described in such detail came as a new and tragic shock.

When another shudder ran through her, she looked away from the house, out over that part of the Hudson River known as the Tappan Zee. The view there was equally chilling. The sky, blue and coral with the setting sun only moments before, had gone black now with an approaching storm. Destructive squalls were known to sweep down on the Hudson Valley from the highlands with an appalling suddenness that often proved fatal. While out for a Sunday afternoon cruise in their single-masted, sixty-five-foot Hudson River sloop, her aunt and uncle and little cousin Sarah had been lost shortly after Lettie's tragic death in just such a sudden gale. Now they were all buried in Sleepy Hollow Cemetery. All but Sarah. Her body was never recovered.

"Best be getting you inside before this weather blows in." Scudder's voice interrupted Julianna's grim thoughts. "That is, if you're still bent on staying. There's a comfortable inn on up the pike a ways. I don't mind driving you there."

"No, thank you, Mr. Scudder. Netherwood is as far as I go."

If nothing else, Julianna Doran was a determined young woman. She had stood her ground with Elliot over this decision to come to Netherwood. Now that she had finally arrived, *nothing*, she told herself, could drive her away.

"I mean to spend this night in my new home," she declared, heading for the front door. "I'm looking forward to it."

Zeke, wagging his shaggy gray head, shrugged and sucked noisily at a tooth as he began unloading her trunks.

Just as the first fat raindrops plopped into the dust of the drive, a hunched figure darted out of the front door, broom in hand as if she meant to sweep the both of them off Netherwood's stoop.

42

"Maeyken?" Julianna called. "Can that be you?"

The old nurse stopped in her tracks, her brush broom poised in midsweep. She was dressed in a rusty-black uniform, her once-white apron smudged and rumpled.

"'Tis me!" she cried in a voice cracked with age. "But who're you?" she demanded. "Strangers got no call to come nosing around this place. 'Tis in my charge now that the master and mistress are gone."

"Watch your tongue, old woman!" Zeke bellowed. "You're looking at your new mistress, so show some respect. And, as for me, I just might be the last friend you got left in this world, so you best be nice to me, too."

The old woman cocked her head to one side and squinted hard at him. "Zeke Scudder? That you?"

Zeke leaned toward Julianna to shield his words with one hand. "She don't see too good no more, you understand."

Julianna nodded.

"Hell, yeah, it's me," he hollered back. Then he added for Julianna's further enlightenment, "She ain't long on hearing, neither."

"Poor old thing," Julianna murmured, recalling years back when nothing her charges did escaped the sharp ears and eagle eye of their nurse.

"Yeah," Zeke said with a sigh of resignation. "I reckon, if you're bound to stay here, I'll have to be hanging around a good bit to help out."

A cloudburst just then sent them hurrying indoors. The moment Juli walked into the flagged entryway, she experienced once again that same feeling of well-being, of returning home that she had known when crossing the bridge.

Maeyken shuffled about lighting candles and lamps until the front parlor and dining room to either side of the entry hall glowed with warm invitation. The oak-paneled walls returned the light with a mellow richness born of age. The smoky essence of long winters before huge fireplaces filled

43

Julianna's senses. Netherwood smelled of home and safety and childhood memories. Suddenly, she realized, she had keened an ear, listening for the bright chatter of her cousins rushing to greet her. But there was no sound from above. A moment of sadness caused tears to threaten.

"Well, Miss Julianna, if you ain't a sight for sore eyes," Maeyken said, opening her arms to embrace her former charge. "Growed you have, and filled out real nice. Don't you think, Zeke?"

The old man shuffled over and looked Julianna up and down appraisingly. "Ain't never set eyes on her before this very day. But there's no denying, Maeyken, that she's a right handsome woman. Strong, too, from the looks of her. And *stubborn*? You wouldn't believe how much so, was I to tell you the whole truth of the matter."

Julianna laughed, not angered in the least by Zeke's frank evaluation.

"Maeyken, you've done a fine job of keeping the place tidy," Julianna said, glancing about at the spotless dining room with its long Spanish table and snowy-white linens, the cozy parlor, and the gleaming mirror that had always hung in the hallway. "But there seems to be more repair work around here than you and I can handle together."

The old woman nodded her head, agreeing with a weary sigh.

"What would you think of my hiring Zeke to help us put Netherwood back to rights? His wages would be money well spent, don't you think?"

Maeyken squinted an eye at the man and waited so long to answer that Zeke cleared his throat in discomfort.

"Well," she finally answered, "he's seen better years, you know."

"I ain't the only one!" Zeke snapped.

Maeyken ignored his outburst and went on with what she

had to say. "I reckon we could use his strong back even if his brain's gone a mite soft."

"Why, you old witch! I ought to . . ."

Maeyken cackled with delight at bringing a rise out of Zeke. She danced a little jig of pleasure and slapped him on the shoulder.

"I always could get your dander up, Zeke Scudder." Then turning to her new mistress, Maeyken said, "You couldn't find a finer man in these here parts, Miss Juli."

The two old people exchanged smiles—a secret look of long familiarity.

"Zeke?" Juli asked him directly.

"I reckon I could help out," he answered.

"Fine! We'll discuss your wages this very night and you can start work tomorrow."

"He can start right now, Miss Juli," Maeyken declared. "Come on, Zeke. Let's the two of us get these bags up to the bedroom."

Only after the pair had disappeared up the stairs did Juli-anna remember that she hadn't told them she wanted to sleep in what had been her cousins' room—the room where she had seen the man named Brom so long ago. Oh, well, she thought, she could always move her things from the master suite later.

Alone downstairs, Julianna walked about, exploring her surroundings. Maeyken had kept everything just as Juli remembered it from the summer of 1889. It seemed almost as if she'd suddenly stepped back in time, as if her cousins might still come bounding down the stairs with some new adventure planned.

"A new adventure," she murmured, smiling to herself as she glanced toward the parlor.

Julianna had never been in the parlor before. Her aunt hadn't allowed the children to cross that threshold. Now,

45

she strode boldly into the room, experiencing a feeling of triumph and possession. Over the delft-tiled fireplace, Bohemian glass mantel lustres glowed a deep red, their delicate crystal prisms flashing rainbows in the light. Tapestries hung on the painted Dutch brick walls. A rosewood étagère seemed to groan under the weight of Aunt Martha's collection of fragile porcelain bric-a-brac. The parlor, she decided, was a marvelous room. She couldn't blame the elder Worthingtons for having kept their treasures safe from the clumsy hands of children.

The gleam of old gold stamped into soft leather bindings on the bookshelves beside the fireplace caught Julianna's eye. Rows of bound manuscripts and folio volumes lined the shelves of one entire wall. Most were in foreign languages unfamiliar to Juli. Then she spied one that seemed to be in English, although the flowing script on the cover was difficult to decipher. Carefully, she pulled the thick tome out from between two others, then stared down at the bold lettering on the front cover. Her breath caught in her throat and her heart pounded furiously as she made out the words.

Julianna read aloud: *"BROM VANDERZEE—His Sea Charts."*

Quickly, she opened the leather binding to find a collection of beautifully executed maps. His name was penned with a flourish on each page.

So he really lived! "Vanderzee," she murmured. " 'Of the sea,' it means."

Julianna's mind was awash with overlapping thoughts. She moved toward the front window, still holding Brom's charts. Her eyes focused on nothing in particular, only the rain. As she stood before the old, bubbled panes, hugging Brom's book to her breasts, an odd sensation crept down along her spine. She turned quickly, sure that Zeke or Maeyken had entered the room, but she was all alone.

46

Looking back to the window, she caught her breath once more. Gone was the pounding rain. Gone, too, was the curving drive. Down beyond the green slope in front of the house she could see the river. No lofty elms blocked the view. And there, riding at anchor, was a tall-masted sailing ship, a kind not seen on the river for many a year.

"Maeyken!" Juli cried, eager for someone else to confirm what she saw. She stared, not daring to blink, until she heard the other woman shuffle into the room.

"You called, Miss Juli?"

Never taking her eyes off the ship, Julianna whispered, "Come here and look out toward the river. Tell me what you see. Quickly!"

Maeyken saw it; Julianna was certain she did. She felt the old woman stiffen beside her.

"You see the ship, too, don't you?"

Maeyken only chuckled and said, "Ah, Miss Juli, a body's liable to see anything now and again in these parts. You'll have to get used to it. Could be you glimpsed old Rambout Van Dam and his ghostly vessel, with her faded colors still flying from the jackstaff. It's said he's sailed these waters for nigh on to three centuries, trying to get home to Spuyten Duyvil. Many a *sloep* captain's spied him, so they vow."

"No!" Julianna said emphatically. "This ship is at anchor and it's no ghost ship."

"Well, it's been my experience that a person most often sees what she wants to see, no matter what's really there."

"But you *do* see it, too, don't you, Maeyken?"

"I reckon. If that's what you want me to see," the old woman answered with a wistful smile.

"Do you know the name Brom Vanderzee?"

For a long time, Maeyken gave her no answer. Finally, shaking her head, she replied, "My memory ain't what it used to be, Miss Juli."

Once again, Julianna had the feeling that the old nurse was simply sidestepping her question.

"You've lived here at Netherwood most of your life. Surely you must have heard my uncle speak of him."

Maeyken's head jerked up suddenly and she looked Julianna straight in the eye. "What call would Mr. Worthington have had to mention the likes of Brom Vanderzee? That pirate scoundrel died long before any Worthingtons ever came here."

"A pirate?" Julianna was intrigued. "Then you *do* know of him."

"I heard tales about the man. Born hereabouts of Dutch parents, he was. His ma died right tragic in a fire, so I've heard. After that, his pa took up pirating. Like father like son, I reckon, though they say Brom Vanderzee started out honest enough. But then there was that dirty business with Captain Kidd." Maeyken glanced at Juli and rolled her eyes. "Here, now! Don't get me started when I got supper to cook. I already told you more than you need to know. How did you come by his name?"

Now it was Julianna's turn to skirt the full truth. She made no mention of her vision years ago, but showed Maeyken the book of charts. "I found this on the shelf. The maps are beautifully done—all by hand. He may have been a pirate, but he was a first-rate artist as well."

"One of his *many* talents," Maeyken answered rather sarcastically.

"You sound as if you knew him personally. Tell me more."

Maeyken shook her head. "As I done said, I know all the tales people tell. But *know* him? Me?" She laughed dryly. "Miss Juli, Captain Brom Vanderzee built this house."

Julianna understood Maeyken's meaning. Netherwood had been erected in the late 1600's. So, if Brom did the building, there was no way that Maeyken, ancient as she was, could have known the man.

"Are any of his things still here in the house?" Suddenly, Julianna's pulse was racing. If she could find a likeness of Captain Vanderzee, she would know for sure if the man she remembered so vividly from the night of the séance was indeed the Dutch pirate.

Maeyken muttered something under her breath, then said aloud, "I suppose you'll be wanting to see up in the attic. If there's anything left of his, that's where you'd find it. There's piles of old junk up there."

"The attic, of course," Juli mumured.

Julianna fell silent, her mind whirling again. A moment later when she looked around, Maeyken was gone. She turned back to the window. The ship, too, had vanished.

A short time later when Julianna went upstairs, to freshen up before supper, she found to her surprise that Zeke and Maeyken had put her trunks in the old nursery at the head of the stairs, exactly where she'd meant them to. Lighting a lamp, she looked about. The girls' room had not fared as well as the rest of the house. She noticed a broken pane of glass in one of the tall windows, through which rain had poured in over the years. The walls were damp, causing the flowered wallpaper to sag down. Paint flecks littered the floor.

Curious, Julianna held her lamp close to the water-damaged wall. The room had been decorated and redecorated many times over the years. Once, long ago, some capricious soul had even painted the bedroom walls a flaming scarlet. But to Julianna's satisfaction, she saw that the original color had been the deep green she remembered so well from her vision.

A knock at her door made her turn. "Yes?"

"Supper's ready, Miss Juli, *erwten, olykoeks*, and *bier*, we got."

Julianna felt a sudden pang of guilt at having made the old woman climb the stairs to announce the evening's menu and summon her.

"Coming, Maeyken."

The least Juli could do was lend the servant a hand going down again, and Maeyken accepted her offered arm on the steep, narrow stairs, but she seemed disinclined toward conversation. The two women found Zeke waiting for them in the kitchen.

Julianna insisted that both Maeyken and Zeke join her in the dining room for their hot supper of thick pea soup, doughnut-shaped rolls, and homemade beer to wash it all down. Juli told the two of them that she wanted to discuss her plans for Netherwood. That was partly the truth, but, too, she felt terribly alone suddenly. Now that it was dark outside, ghosts seemed to lurk in every shadowy corner. Truth be told, Julianna craved company.

"Maeyken, there's so much to do here that I hardly know where to begin," Julianna explained between spoonfuls of the rich pea soup. "I suppose I should start with my bedroom. How long has the rain been pouring in?"

A flicker of something—possibly fear, Julianna thought—crossed the old woman's face. "Happened the night poor Miss Lettie . . ."

"Seven years ago and the pane hasn't been replaced? Surely my uncle would have taken care of that immediately."

Maeyken nodded, but it was Zeke who explained. "Mr. Worthington did have it fixed, over and over again. Always called me in to do the job. Every time I put in a new glass it'd be busted out within the week."

"Was there a tree limb outside hitting the window?" Julianna asked. "I don't understand."

"No limb," Zeke replied. "Just busted by its ownself, like something wanted that room closed off to crumble."

"Then why did you put me in there?" Julianna directed her question to Maeyken.

The woman smiled knowingly, and her pale-blue eyes seemed to glow with reflected candlelight. "Ain't that where you wanted to be, Miss Juli?"

Avoiding a direct answer, Julianna said, "I want the window fixed tomorrow, Zeke. If it blows out again, we'll board over that pane. I also mean to start stripping off the old paper. I think I'd like the walls painted dark green."

"Like they was to begin with," Maeyken muttered, concentrating on her soup and not looking at Juli.

"What?" Julianna asked.

"Oh, nothing, Miss Juli. Just thinking out loud to myself."

An uncomfortable silence fell over the group suddenly. Only the howl of the storm outside filled the void.

Julianna went to bed that night with an uneasy feeling. Maybe she would have fared better if she'd dined alone. Maeyken and Zeke certainly had not gone out of their way to put her at ease. Maeyken's remarks in particular gnawed at Juli's nerves.

Finally, she blew out the candle beside the bed and settled herself to go to sleep. But her mind refused to be still. She wondered what Elliot was doing tonight. Was he still in Philadelphia? Was he with someone else? Had she made a mistake leaving him to come here?

"Stop it!" she told herself, pounding her pillow in frustration. "If you can't sleep, make plans for tomorrow."

51

She felt easier as she let her thoughts drift to the work that lay ahead of her. First thing tomorrow, she would go up to the attic. She had never been there before, but Lettie had told her tales of the wonderful treasures hidden away on the third floor—locked trunks, old love letters, books, papers, and antique furniture. Most importantly, she meant to search for anything that had belonged to Captain Brom Vanderzee.

Julianna began to relax. As she did, her mind drifted back to Elliot. She sighed and shifted, recalling the touch of his lips on hers, the feel of his hands caressing her body. But try as she might, total recall of their shared ecstasy eluded her. It was almost as if they had never made love at all. She tossed fretfully, annoyed by her weary mind's sudden lapse.

Drifting in that netherworld of half sleep, half wakefulness, Julianna thought she heard a voice in the darkness. Or was it only part of a dream?

"Enough, madam!" The man's tone was stern. "Be done with him now. You be home."

Her thoughts of Elliot changed instantly. She was still caught up in an illusion of love, but now it seemed other arms were holding her. Other lips kissing hers. She felt the man's long hair draped like a raw silk curtain over her shoulder. His mustache and beard scraped her soft flesh. His hands on her were hard and hot and eager. She moaned and clung to him, frightened—not *of* him, but *for* him.

Suddenly, a deeper sleep descended. The last thing Julianna recalled was the man's husky whisper—words of love—and a soft green cloud closing in around her. She was floating on it, her senses smothered in its hot, musky scent. He was holding her, kissing her, making her ache with longing.

"Brom, I've come back," she moaned softly.

She clutched her pillow to her breasts, then the warm solace of total blackness folded her in its protective arms.

# Chapter Three

The last time Julianna had awakened in such a twisted and tangled bed had been the morning after making love with Elliot. As she opened her eyes, she spied both pillows on the floor, the quilted counterpane half under the bed, and the sheets all torn loose and in a muddle at the foot. Oddest of all, sometime during the night she had stripped off her long linen gown. She lay naked as a babe.

Quickly, Juli jumped out of bed, dressed, and set the covers to rights. It wouldn't do for Maeyken to come in and find such a mess. What would she think?

As for what Julianna herself thought, all she could remember were bits and snatches of dreams. *Quite lovely dreams*, she mused as she straightened the tumbled bed.

The morning proved bright and shining, with brilliant sunshine and a delicious hint of autumn in the air. Juli felt marvelous. But, as she surveyed the bedroom by the morning light, she saw that it really was a shambles. Dampness had rotted the wicker furniture. The bright, flowered rug was ruined—black with mold. And her cousins' big brass bedstead was tarnished beyond all hope of making it shine ever again.

For a moment she thought of moving into the master suite across the hall. As quickly as that idea occurred to her, she brushed it aside. It was crazy, she knew, but if Brom Vanderzee did decide to put in another appearance, he would come to her here in the room that had been his. She meant to be right here waiting. Once and for all, she would find out why he had appeared to her in the first place. Then she could get on with the rest of her life.

"My life with Elliot," she told the glowing image in her mirror. Then she stopped brushing her hair and stared at her reflection sternly for a moment. What in the world was happening to her? Had she gone quite mad? This obsession with Captain Brom Vanderzee had to end. She could not plan her whole life around a man who had been dead since . . . Since when? She had no idea, she realized. As she resumed braiding her hair, then tied on a work apron over her frock, she made a mental note to search out that date.

Suddenly, the fragmented pieces of her dreams from last night returned in sharper focus. She had been thinking of Elliot, then everything had changed. Elliot was clean-shaven. The man she remembered from her dreams had a short, pointed beard, a mustache, and long, flowing hair.

"Captain Vanderzee, I presume." She shook her head, bewildered. "It's the trip," she told herself. She always had strange dreams when she was overtired.

But this morning she felt rested and wonderful, ready to face a busy and exciting day. "Netherwood," she cried aloud, holding her arms up and turning to look around her. "You're all mine. I'm home at last."

Julianna hurried out of the bedroom and down the stairs. She decided she wouldn't waste time on a sit-down breakfast. On her way to the attic, she paused only briefly in the kitchen. Refusing Maeyken's offer of *suppawn and malk*— a thick concoction of corn mush and hot milk—she poured herself a steaming cup of coffee and snatched an apple fritter, which was sizzling in the huge black frying pan.

"Mornin', Miss Juli. Sleep well, did you?" Maeyken's tone suggested that she suspected otherwise.

Julianna decided to keep her dreams to herself. "I slept wonderfully, thank you. Now I'm ready to get to work."

"Zeke and me'll be going to market soon, Miss Juli. Got to lay in some supplies now you're here. You best wait on the heavy work till we get back. Won't be too long, I reckon."

"Take your time, Maeyken. I'll be in the attic," Julianna told her. "I want to get a good start this morning."

"You're going up there *alone*?" Maeyken sounded horrified at the very idea.

Julianna turned and stared at the woman who stood, arms akimbo, beside the ancient black cookstove. "Is there any reason I shouldn't go up there by myself?"

Maeyken shook her head and picked up her market basket. "I reckon not. Just you be careful, Miss Juli." Then she plopped a shapeless straw hat on her gray head and hurried out the kitchen door.

The warning bothered Julianna. She never knew quite what to make of anything Maeyken said to her. But the moment the attic door creaked open, she could see by the light of her lantern that the old woman's exhortation had been straightforward this time. To its farthest reaches, the third-floor storage room was piled high with the trash and treasures of many past generations. If she weren't careful, she could get buried under an avalanche of antiques. She could see why she and her cousins had never been allowed to play up here. Julianna had figured this job for a good morning's task. But it would clearly take days, possibly weeks, to go through everything.

Dodging spiderwebs and streamers of ancient dust, Julianna worked her way through the more recent rejected furnishings to one of the back eaves. A high-domed trunk caught her eyes. Fancifully tooled leather and brass studs covered the outside. With some effort she managed to pull the massive thing out from under a rusted birdcage, a broken windowframe, and a stack of old curtains and bedclothes that had been thrown haphazardly over the whole pile. Julianna's heart was pounding as much from exertion as from excitement when she finally got the trunk out in the open.

"No lock," she murmured. "Thank goodness for small favors."

Carefully, inch by inch, she lifted the heavy lid. The wavering light from her lantern cast its glow on a rainbow of colors and the glint of gold and silver threads. Julianna cried out with delight as she reached inside, her fingertips touching cool, soft folds of antique silks and velvets.

Work would simply have to wait for now. She wouldn't be able to keep her mind on another thing until she had examined the entire contents of this treasure trove. Her aahs and oohs echoed through the silent attic as she pulled forth one wondrous find after another.

When Maeyken and Zeke returned two hours later, Julianna was waiting for them in the parlor, smiling to herself in anticipation. Gone were her heavy cotton work dress and long apron. Instead, she wore the richly embroidered purple velvet gown she had found in the trunk. The bodice was immodestly daring, with only a froth of silver lace to hide the swell of her breasts. The puffed sleeves came just to her elbows, with more gleaming fancy tatting ruffled there. The waist hugged her figure, dipping to a point at the top of the full skirt. Over her shoulders, Julianna had draped another prize from the chest, a fringed, purple silk shawl stitched all over with shiny glass beads. To further the exotic effect, Juli had unbraided her hair, freeing her long red-gold curls to sweep to her waist and crowning them with a tiara of silver filigree. As a finishing touch, about her neck she wore a single strand of pearls the size of partridge eggs.

"Miss Juli, we're back," Maeyken called from the kitchen.

"Come into the parlor, please, both of you."

Julianna felt decidedly devilish as she waited to see their reaction to her exotic transformation. She knew she looked as if she had just stepped out of another century. How she'd love to know who wore these clothes! When? And where?

Maeyken at least did not disappoint Julianna. When the old woman entered the room, she took one look, stumbled, turned pale, and grabbed for Zeke's arm.

Julianna rushed toward her. "Are you all right? I didn't mean to startle you so."

"Lord help us!" Maeyken mumbled, fanning herself with her hand. "You could have been *her*, standing there by the fireplace."

"Who?" Julianna demanded.

"That woman! That *bad* woman, Katrina Rhinehart!"

"Who was she?" Julianna felt her excitement rising. "Did she live here once? Tell me, Maeyken. Please!"

"Mayhap a touch of brandy," Maeyken said, rolling her eyes toward Zeke.

Once the man had left to fetch her restorative drink, Maeyken leaned close to Julianna. "You ought not to be messing with Kat's stuff, Miss Juli. She ain't a woman to take kindly to you wearing her things."

"*Who* is Katrina?" Julianna demanded. "You need to explain to me, Maeyken."

A hard look came over the old woman's face and her pale-blue eyes turned cold. "She was a slut, that one, pure and simple. Her man was no beauty, neither."

57

Julianna felt a sudden ache in her breast. "You don't mean she was Captain Vanderzee's . . . ?"

Maeyken shook her head. "Neither his wife nor his woman. She'd of liked it either way. But, no. Thomas Tew was Katrina's lover. He was a blackguard of the first order— a murderer, too. On top of killing three men, he made Kat do away with her own child. Not that she had no love for her baby, mind you. It was Tew's all right, but he refused to claim it. Vowed it was spawned in a gutter somewhere by one of Kat's other men." Maeyken snorted a humorless laugh. "Can't say as I blame him for doubting her word, sleeping around like she did. Still, she had no right to do what she done. That poor little child!"

"But who are these people, Maeyken? How do you know about them?"

Maeyken glanced about furtively, then lowered her voice to a whisper. "I know what I know, Miss Juli. And I tell you now, you best leave them be—the whole lot of them, Captain Brom Vanderzee included! He might not of been a bad sort, but 'twas the ones he hung with caused all the trouble."

Once Zeke returned with the brandy, Maeyken refused to say another word. What she had said only served to make Julianna more curious.

"I'm going back up to the attic," Juli told them. "If you're feeling up to it, Maeyken, I could use your help. Yours, too, Zeke."

A short while later, after Julianna had changed back into her work clothes, all three of them were in the midst of the chaos on the low-ceilinged third floor. Maeyken was still too nervous to be of much help, but Zeke pitched right in.

"Oh, look!" Julianna cried suddenly. "It's his bed!"

Brom's great oak four-poster loomed in the shadows like some ancient bark.

"I want that for my bedroom, Zeke."

A thought struck Julianna out of the blue. What if she redid Brom's bedroom exactly as it was when she imagined him there? Quickly, her eyes took stock of the things stacked around the bedframe. There were the Chinese urns she had seen on his mantelpiece, the Persian rug from the floor, the wine velvet bed curtains, hardly faded at all.

"Everything, Zeke," she said. "I want all of this brought downstairs."

"Lord help us!" Maeyken muttered, casting a forlorn look toward heaven. "There just ain't no sense to all this, Miss Juli."

"Be patient with me, Maeyken," Juli begged gently. "I know what I'm doing."

"Tain't likely," the old woman stated flatly. But she punctuated her statement with a deep sigh of resignation.

Two weeks later, Julianna and Maeyken were still searching through the attic, sorting trash from treasure—a seemingly endless task—while Zeke had been busy elsewhere.

"It's done, Miss Juli," the old man called up the attic stairs, that crisp afternoon in early October. "Just like you told me."

"Oh, Maeyken!" Juli cried, helping the old woman up from the floor, where she'd been sorting through papers and letters. "Let's go see. I can't wait a minute longer."

"Waited nigh on to two hundred years," Maeyken muttered under her breath. "A mite longer won't make no difference."

But Juli never heard. She was already down the stairs.

Julianna could hardly believe her eyes when she reached the bedroom. It was almost as if she had turned the shiny glass knob and stepped through the arched doorway again. Gone were the moldy carpet, the wicker furniture, the peeling wallpaper, the dull brass bedstead. The afternoon sun glowed like a newly-cut emerald on the forest-green walls, picking up the brilliant hues of the Persian carpet and the dark, blood-red bed curtains. Lamps, tables, chests, the Russian leather chairs, everything she could find of Brom's, had been put back in his room. Even his chartbook lay open on the large captain's desk near the tall windows.

"Oh, Zeke, it's perfect!" Julianna cried, giving him a hug.

The old fellow blushed and shuffled his feet. Entering the room at that moment, Maeyken frowned deeply, and not because Miss Juli was hugging the old woman's beau.

"Zeke," Maeyken said, "I baked some gingerbread this morning. Why don't you go down and treat yourself, you done so good up here?"

He was gone in a flash, leaving the two women alone. Julianna waited, knowing that Maeyken had something on her mind. Juli knew, too, that she was about to hear it whether she wanted to or not.

"I reckon you know what you're doing, Miss Juli, but I don't like it one bit."

Julianna tried to force a smile of innocence. "Just what do you think I'm doing?"

"Trying to get at *him* again, that's what. I'm warning you once and for all, Brom Vanderzee can bring you naught but pain and tears."

"What on earth can you be thinking, Maeyken?" Juli knew she was blushing from the woman's directness, but still tried to act all innocence. "He's been dead for two hundred years. How could I possibly 'get at him,' as you put it? And what makes you think I'd want to?"

Maeyken chuckled, but there was little humor in the sound. "You girls always figured you could outsmart your old nurse. But I know what went on here that night. I peeked through the door and saw every last thing that happened— him on the bed, his blood on your gown."

Julianna gasped. She could hardly believe her ears. "What door are you talking about? The bedroom door was shut tight the whole time."

"You know the one," Maeyken whispered. "The little arched door with the shiny glass knob. I watched through there."

Juli's heart was racing now. "Can you show me where that door is? I've searched the whole house, but I can't find it."

"No," Maeyken answered. "Even if I knew where it was, I ain't sure I'd tell you. You're messing with something that needs leaving alone, Miss Juli. I seen what I seen that night, but I don't crave to see no more. And you shouldn't, neither. You best leave it be!"

Julianna felt almost relieved that Maeyken knew, even if she didn't approve. At least Julianna wasn't the only one who had seen Brom.

"And you think I want to be with him again?" Juli asked.

"You reckon you'd have come back to the here and now the first time, Miss Juli, if he hadn't told you to?"

Suddenly, Brom's words echoed in Julianna's memory: "You must go back."

"Frankly, I don't understand any of this, Maeyken," Julianna confessed. "Do you know what's going on?"

"I dread to think," Maeyken replied, shaking her head sadly. "But I suppose if you're determined to stir things up, there's no way I can stop you."

Julianna reached out and put her hand on the woman's thin arm. "I don't want you to stop me," she murmured. "If you can, I'd like you to help me."

Maeyken sighed deeply, but Julianna could tell her battle was won.

"You'll be needing the Ouija board," Maeyken said.

Julianna's surprise registered in her wide green eyes. "Aunt Martha burned it years ago."

"I think not." Maeyken went to the bed, leaned down with an audible creaking of bones, and pulled out the well-remembered board. She handed it to Julianna.

"But how can this be? I don't understand," she said, staring down at the faded letters and numbers.

"It ain't the last thing you won't understand before this is done," Maeyken muttered.

"Won't you please tell me what this is all about, Maeyken?" Julianna begged. "I know there's more to it than you're willing to admit. How could I have seen Brom Vanderzee? And the ship—we both saw it, too. Then there's the woman named Katrina. Why won't you tell me who she really was? If she never lived here, what were her clothes doing in the attic? You know the answers to all these questions. I'm sure you do."

Maeyken stood before Juli, her watery blue eyes unflinching, her face set like stone. "Don't see as how it would do no good to tell you nothing, child. You was never one to believe till you'd seen with them eyes of yours. Anyways, fairytales is the best I could do." She nodded, then smiled sadly. "Fairytales and ghost stories. That'd be it, I'm afraid."

Julianna gave up. Maeyken refused to do anything but talk in riddles. If Juli meant to find out about Brom Vanderzee, she would have to do it all by herself, it seemed.

Taking the Ouija board, Julianna placed it gently on the desk. Her mind was already busy, plotting her next move.


Late that night, Julianna stood at the bedroom window, glancing every few moments at the antique clock on a nearby chest.

"Almost midnight," she said impatiently. She had decided to follow the details of the previous séance as closely as she could remember them. She would not touch the Ouija board until the clock struck twelve.

She ran her fingertips over the smooth new glass in the window, the same window through which her cousin had eloped to her death. Zeke had replaced the pane two weeks ago. It had been his first task after her arrival at Netherwood. It remained in one piece, almost as if it had broken repeatedly over the years, purposely ruining the room so that she would be forced to redecorate it. She had done that now, and all was ready.

Glancing about, she felt a shiver run through her. Again, she had the feeling that she was not alone in the room. She was almost getting used to the sensation of being watched all the time.

"Brom, are you here?" she asked quietly, feeling only slightly foolish.

She moved silently about, touching his things—his book of maps, a straight razor she had found in the attic with the initials B.V. engraved in the stag-horn handle, the urns, the bed, a jewel-hilted dagger that must have been his . . .

The clock chimed, shattering the silence. Julianna nearly jumped out of her skin. Suddenly, she felt acutely fearful of the unknown. What right had she to try to summon a ghost? And that's all Brom Vanderzee was—all he could be after two hundred years, she reminded herself. Gooseflesh covered her arms. Her palms grew sweaty. She steadied herself, thinking back over all the work that had gone into the preparation for this night. She forced herself to be calm as she moved toward the table in the center of the room.

"So," she murmured in a shaky whisper, "the hour is now."

She sat down at the table slowly, careful of the fragile antique silk of her skirt—another of Katrina's gowns. Leaning slightly forward, she placed her fingertips on the Ouija board's pointer, then closed her eyes. She concentrated on conjuring up Brom's image in her mind—his tanned, weather-toughened face, his long black hair, his

63

beard and mustache, the sensual heat of his obsidian eyes, his big square hands, and the emerald dragon ring flashing on his finger.

"Brom," she murmured, "Brom Vanderzee. It's Julianna. Can you hear me?"

Off in the distance, far up the river, Julianna could hear thunder rumbling. A chilling wind moaned at the eaves, blowing stronger by the minute. Suddenly, the window flew open, threatening the candle's dim glow.

"Is it you?" Julianna's voice was only a wisp of thin sound. "Brom?"

For a time, she was conscious only of the smooth wood beneath her fingertips gliding across the board. Then she felt it, she knew it! A presence had joined her. There was no need to open her eyes. The letters—formed by some unseen hand—shaped themselves in her mind.

"B-E-G-O-N-E . . . K-A-T"

"*Kat!*" Juli cried. "Why, that would be Katrina Rhinehart!" She opened her eyes and glanced about, then asked in a louder voice, "Katrina, are you here?"

Even as she spoke, the pointer jerked away from her fingers. It skidded dizzily across the board and back several times before returning to her hands. Her fingertips once more in place, it moved again, slowly and smoothly.

"B-R-O-M," the pointer spelled out. Then: "B-E-D."

The words, like a command, cast a strange spell over Julianna. Slowly, her eyes closed again. Her body seemed weightless and with no will of its own. Julianna felt herself rise from the chair. It seemed her feet hardly touched the Persian carpet as she floated toward Brom's huge bed. A moment later, she was stretched out, the amber-colored silk of her gown fanned about her. Her breasts, nestled in creamy lace, rose and fell as she breathed evenly. She was deeply entranced.

"Brom," she murmured, "I am here."

Silence closed around her.

Suddenly, out of nowhere, voices boomed in Julianna's head, seeming to fill the whole room. A man and a woman, both invisible to Julianna, were locked in pitched verbal battle.

"Damn your eyes and your lusting prick!" the woman shrilled. "I'll see you in hell for this."

The man bellowed a deep, rumbling laugh. "You may see hell before me, wench. If so, save me a warm spot, won't you?"

"You brought her here to spite me. Admit it," the invisible female accused shrewishly.

"*You* came without invitation. You've no room for complaint."

"'Tis the privilege of any river traveler to stop along the way and receive hospitality."

"Aye, for a day or a week, woman. You've pressed your privilege over a fortnight. Must I take you to my bed before you deem it time to go back to your man and leave me in peace?"

"It would seem your bed is occupied, sir."

Another laugh from the man. "So it is! And what a pretty piece lies there. But tell me, if that be the price I must pay for your farewell, would the floor suit you right enough?"

"Beast!" the woman screamed. "Am I no better than your plump and panting tavern wenches?"

"No better in the least, madam, and every bit as sporting, so I hear."

"Make her go!" the woman demanded. "I warn you for the last time, or I'll personally see an end to her."

"She stays," he said firmly. "*You* go!"

Julianna could feel the woman's hatred, a tangible force in the room. She twisted on the wide bed, trying not to listen to Kat's words, not to feel her contempt.

"Brom," Julianna called weakly.

"Bro-om," the woman mimicked. "She is most likely a stupid virgin. She has the frail and frightened look of one."

"You sound envious, madam. Tell me," he said in a mock-serious tone, "were you *ever* a virgin, or were you born impaled on some swollen shaft?"

"You son-of-a-sucking-whore! I'll kill you!"

"Temper, my beauty, temper! I thought ole Tom did all the killing in your household."

Julianna was becoming more agitated by the moment. She thrashed about on the bed, calling Brom's name over and over again.

"The little strumpet!" the woman hissed.

"Be still, wench," the man cautioned. "You've upset her. Look how her breasts heave with alarm." His voice softened. "Ah, yes! So pale and round and soft. Lovely, truly lovely. Ripe, too, and trembling to be kissed. Perhaps I'll just . . ."

Julianna moaned softly and her breasts quivered and ached as a light breeze caressed her flesh.

"Why should you crave a taste of that tart's little plums when you could savor these ripe melons?" the woman cooed invitingly. "Come here," she ordered in a coy tone. "Try my wares."

He laughed. "I? Feast on spoiled fruit? I have no longing for the bitter taste left after so many men have fed before me."

A sharp crack, like flesh striking flesh followed his words. Then the woman screamed, "Bastard-d-d-d-d!" The word drifted on for a long time, seeming to echo off the walls. Finally, it faded into nothingness.


It seemed only an instant later that Julianna threw a hand over her eyes, squinting against the bright morning light. Where was she? What had happened?

Someone was banging frantically at the front door down below.

"Julianna!" The familiar voice boomed up through her open window.

"Elliot?" she cried with sudden recognition, sitting bolt upright in bed.

He shouted her name again as if in answer.

Juli leaped off the bed, staggering drunkenly as her feet hit the floor. She caught the bedpost to steady herself.

"Lord," she moaned, holding her head, "what happened last night?"

When she felt steady, she ran to the window. The sun was just up, but there stood Elliot Creighton, pounding away.

"I'll be down in a moment," she called.

"Juli! Thank God! Are you all right?" he shouted up to her.

"Of course," she replied, wondering why he'd asked. "And, Elliot, I'm *very* glad to see you."

"Well then, how about letting me in?"

"Immediately!" she called down. "I'm on my way now."

Actually, she wasn't on her way. She meant to change out of the antique gown and into something more sensible. But the fastenings, which Maeyken had done up for her the night before, were too stubborn for her to manage alone.

"Oh, bother!" she fumed, heading for the stairs still dressed in amber silk and creamy lace.

She glanced toward the kitchen as she reached the bottom stair. No one was about. Maeyken was probably still sleeping at this early hour and hadn't heard Elliot, even though he'd almost battered the door down.

Julianna felt her heart swell with excitement as she neared the front door. Elliot, dear Elliot! Flesh-and-blood, here-and-now Elliot! She experienced a pang of guilt at her own joy. She'd hardly thought of him since her first night here. It seemed almost as if she had exited the real world to enter another the moment she'd arrived at Netherwood. But she intended to make up immediately for any lapses in the past weeks.

She threw the door wide, ready to rush into her lover's arms, but the look on his face stopped her dead in her tracks.

"Elliot, what's wrong?"

"Why are you dressed like that?" he demanded in a surly tone. "Have you been entertaining someone, Juli?" There was no way to miss the jealous accusation in his voice.

"Of course not," she answered, drawing slightly away from him. "I put this old gown on last night and now I can't get out of it by myself."

He was staring at her nearly bare bosom. "You put that on for *whom?*"

"Never mind. It doesn't matter." She gripped his arm. "Come in, won't you?"

He came in, but still protesting. "It matters to me. I'm the man you're supposed to be in love with. Have your feelings changed in such a short time?"

"Of course not, Elliot. Why would you say such a thing?" Julianna experienced an odd sense of guilt even as she spoke the words. But why should she? She hadn't been unfaithful to him, even if she hadn't spent her every waking moment thinking of him or her nights dreaming about him.

Shifting the guilt, Julianna felt totally outdone with him suddenly. She'd been so surprised and so glad to see him. Now all he wanted to do was accuse her unjustly. Why couldn't he just kiss her and be as happy to see her as she was to see him?

She led him into the parlor. "Sit down. I'll get you a cup of tea and you can tell me what you're doing on my doorstep at this early hour." She smiled and touched his cheek, feeling her fingertips tingle on contact. "Actually, it doesn't really matter why you've come, darling. I'm too happy to see you to waste time asking questions.''

He caught her hand and smiled back apologetically. ''Oh, my Juli . . . my sweet darlin'! I'm sorry I was gruff. I've had one helluva night. Do you have something stronger than tea?''

''First thing in the morning?'' Julianna stared at him. Elliot, as far as she knew, hardly drank at all.

''I think I need it,'' he replied, his handsome face still wearing a haggard expression.

''Elliot, really, there's been no one here.'' She sat beside him and took both his hands in hers, trying to soothe him. ''I've dreamed of when we could be together again, but I never dared hope that you'd drop in unexpectedly this way.''

''And you'd rather I hadn't?''

''Don't be silly.'' She kissed him quickly. ''You're always welcome at Netherwood.''

A door slammed loudly upstairs as if some spoiled child were having a sudden tantrum. Julianna glanced toward the ceiling and frowned. Probably a gust of wind, she thought.

Elliot pulled away from her. He leaned forward and put his face in his hands. A deep sigh escaped him. A shudder ran through his whole tense body.

''Darling, what's wrong?'' Julianna asked, putting an arm around his shoulders.

He looked up at her, his slate-gray eyes grave and intense. ''Don't *you* know, Juli?'' he asked. ''You're the one who called me here.''

''I?'' she asked, puzzled. ''Please, Elliot, you must tell me what's going on.''

# Chapter Four

Elliot relaxed to some degree after taking a few sips of brandy. His body still seemed tense, but Julianna noted that the lines had begun to ease from his face. He turned to her and managed a shaky smile.

"You'll never know how scared I was," he told her.

Before taking time to explain, he drew Julianna into his arms. The next moment he was kissing her with such fervent intensity that the fierceness of his passion actually took her breath away. When he released her, Julianna reached for his brandy.

"I think I could use a sip of this, too," she said, smiling into his storm-gray eyes. "I'm not used to this sort of activity first thing in the morning, darling." She took the drink, then turned back to Elliot. "Now, why don't you tell me what this is all about?"

An interval of silence filled the room while Elliot pondered what to say—how to explain last night's strange occurrence. His gaze wandered the sunlit room, finally returning to rest on Juli.

"As you know, the play moved to New York City a few days ago," he began. "I'd meant to wait, send you a letter, and let you know I would come up next weekend, if that was convenient."

Elliot paused. He took both Julianna's hands in his and gripped them tightly. She could feel his fingers still trembling. When he looked up into her face, his own was pale.

"Juli, you simply don't realize what you put me through last night."

"Me? But I was here. Tell me, Elliot," she urged gently. "What happened?"

He shook his head. "That's just it. I'm not sure. Maybe I'm going crazy. By the light of day, it all sounds too bizarre to believe, I'm afraid. You'll probably laugh at me."

"Tell me, Elliot," Juli begged. "I've had a few bizarre experiences of my own lately. I *won't* laugh, believe me."

"All right, darlin'. But I'm warning you, it all sounds insane." He took a deep breath before he began. "The performance last night started off well enough; nothing out of the ordinary. But the further I got into the evening, the more jittery I became. It was the damnedest thing! You know I never get stage fright. Midway through last night's performance, though, I was overcome by a first-class case of butterflies in the belly. A whole army of the creatures, beating my insides to a pulp. And I got this eerie feeling that someone was standing behind me, threatening me." He turned a sheepish look on Julianna. "Am I making any sense at all, darlin'?"

Julianna, grave now, nodded. "I've had similar experiences in the past couple of weeks. But what else, Elliot? You said I called you here."

"That you did!" He paused and shook his head as if he

71

could hardly believe his own words, much less expect Julianna to believe them. "Shortly after the beginning of the second act, I heard your voice as clearly as if you were right there on stage beside me. You were crying out for help, calling my name. And you kept muttering something about a cat. Does that mean anything to you?"

Juli's mind went blank for a moment. She could make no connection. She'd had an old cat that stayed around the farm, but he'd disappeared long before she left. "You don't think I was talking about old Long-Tom, the yellow mouser?"

Elliot waved his hands to dismiss the thought. "No, no! This cat was female and you were afraid of her. I remember distinctly hearing you say something like, 'Keep *her* away from me. Cat hates me. She'll hurt me.' "

"Oh!" Juli gasped softly. "You mean *Kat*!"

"Yes, that's what I said. Cat!" Elliot repeated in a slightly bewildered tone. "But you were never afraid of any animals that I know of, Juli. So why would I imagine such a thing?"

Julianna tried to look perfectly innocent as she replied, "There's no cat here, Elliot. And I wasn't afraid. I slept like a baby. Really!"

He turned to Julianna, a deep frown marring his dark good looks. "You're sure nothing happened here last night, darlin'?"

Julianna decided not to mention the Ouija board. Elliot probably would think she was the one who'd gone crazy. But, actually, nothing had happened that she could recall in any detail. Her attempts with the board had failed. She remembered clearly sitting down at the table at midnight, then waking up with Elliot shouting her name. She wasn't sure when she'd gotten into bed. She must have been exhausted, though, to sleep in the uncomfortable antique gown.

72

Suddenly she blinked, and behind her closed lids she saw the words "B-E-G-O-N-E . . . K-A-T." A shiver ran through her. Something *had* happened last night. But she dared not tell Elliot.

She tried to laugh off his fears. "Really, Elliot, I think your imagination has been working overtime. You've probably been pushing yourself too hard—those long rehearsals and so many performances each week. It's no wonder you're hearing things. I was fine last night." She paused and gave him a radiant smile. "And I'm even better this morning, now that you're here."

He drew her into his arms once more, burying his face in her bright hair. "Oh, darlin', you don't know what a relief that is to me. I was half crazed all the way here. It seemed that milk train would never arrive. I watched every one of those twenty-seven miles creep by."

"Elliot Creighton, do you mean to tell me that you sat up all night wide awake on a train? My poor darling! I'm going to put you right to bed."

He grinned at her in a boyish fashion, his fears laid to rest. "Another brandy first?"

A half-hour later, Elliot followed Julianna up to the comfortable master suite, across the hall from her room. The Worthingtons' former bedroom, which they had added some years ago, was typically Victorian, with its papered walls of lilies on a field of mauve and violet, its lace curtains, and its rosewood furniture from the best cabinetmaker in the state. A bath, a dressing room, and a sitting room adjoined the main chamber.

"Nice!" Elliot remarked appreciatively. Then, glancing about, he noticed that the suite appeared unoccupied. "But isn't this your room, Juli?"

"No, I'm in the old nursery across the hall." She laughed

softly at his surprised expression. "Somehow it didn't seem right for me to take my aunt and uncle's room. It's bad enough that I've invaded the sanctity of the parlor. I'm sure if I took Aunt Martha's bedroom, too, her ghost would have a fit. She'd probably haunt me so, I'd have to move out of Netherwood altogether."

Elliot reached out for Juli, coaxing her back into his arms. As he slipped one hand about her waist, the other went to the low-cut bodice of her gown. She trembled with pleasure as his fingertips traced the line of lace.

"I don't know who's making your clothes these days, darlin', but I approve." His head dipped down and he drew a damp trail over her quivering bosom with his tongue.

"I thought you were exhausted," Julianna whispered, trying to rein in her suddenly raging desires.

"Hm-m-m," he sighed lazily. "Maybe it's the brandy or maybe it's you, but I feel a lot better now, darlin'."

Elliot pressed her close to his body. Julianna could feel his heat and it stirred her own longings almost to the boiling point.

"Why don't you take that dress off?" he murmured into her ear.

"I can't."

Elliot drew back and stared at her, frowning deeply. "What do you mean, you can't? Of course you can. You don't have to be shy with me, darlin'. And we have hours before I have to catch my train back. Let's not waste a minute of that time."

Julianna laughed. "No, I really mean it, Elliot. I can't! That's why I'm still wearing it. The fastenings in back are too tight."

She turned to show him. Immediately, she felt his fingers busy at the difficult task. Moments later, cool air, then Elliot's lips, touched her bare back. He maneuvered her toward the bed.

Any form of protest was the farthest thing from Julianna's mind. Granted, she'd been unable to recall the full details of their previous loving encounter, but now she was more than willing to relive those forgotten pleasures. She had a moment's pause at the thought of Maeyken downstairs. But the woman would simply think that Julianna was still asleep in her own room. Maeyken certainly wouldn't disturb them. As for Zeke, he almost never came upstairs.

They lay down, side by side, Elliot still clothed while Julianna was half in, half out of her gown. He seemed to like it that way as it gave him a certain masterful advantage over her shy vulnerability. Slowly, kissing every inch of her as he uncovered it, Elliot slipped the long sleeves down until her shoulders and breasts were bare.

"Ah, darlin', it's been *so* long."

Julianna caught her breath as his mouth closed over her nipple. Fire raced through her as his tongue probed at the tender flesh. She moaned his name and twined her fingers through his thick brown hair.

"Elliot, I do love you so. I wish we could be together all the time. I've missed you. I've needed you. You have no idea . . ."

Julianna realized suddenly that, though his mouth was still at her breast, Elliot was no longer kissing her. Instead, his breath was deep and even upon her skin. A wave of disappointment flooded through her. But, after all, he had had a long and exhausting night.

She remained where she was for a time, taking pleasure in watching him sleep, not wanting to disturb him. His face was relaxed now, his lips, slightly puckered, still touching her breast. She caressed his hair, his shoulder, his thigh. The swell in his breeches felt hot to her fingertips. He stirred in his sleep when she touched him and she quickly withdrew her hand.

With a wistful sigh, Julianna eased away from him and

off the bed. Let him rest, she thought. There would be time for their loving, later in the day.

She tiptoed out of the room and crossed the hall. At least now, thanks to Elliot, she could get out of the old silk gown. When she returned to her room, oddly enough the heavy drapes at the windows were drawn shut. The room lay in thick shadow. Maybe Maeyken had been in to close the curtains so that the sun wouldn't fade the carpet.

Julianna sat down on the side of the bed and slipped the gown down over her hips. She glanced at herself. Elliot's kisses had left her nipples peaked with unassuaged desire.

"*Plums*, indeed!" she exclaimed.

What on earth? Why had she said such a thing? Shaking her head, Julianna stood and stepped out of the dress. Carefully, she draped it over a chair, then glanced at her naked body in the mirror. Seldom did she look at herself this way. It seemed indecent somehow. Her mother had always taught her that modesty was one of the true signs of a lady. But now other forces were at work, guiding her life constantly in new and surprising directions. She felt no qualms as she ran her hands over her hips and smooth belly, down to the fiery triangle of tight curls at the junction of her thighs. Then she lifted her breasts with her palms, staring at the pale flesh and dark-rose nipples.

"Plums?" she repeated, pursing her lips as she tried to remember some elusive fragment of dream from the night before.

Shaking her head, she turned from the mirror. She stretched and yawned. It was still quite early. Perhaps she'd just lie down for a few more minutes before she got dressed.

She threw back the counterpane, slipping between the cool sheets. For what reason—she hadn't a notion why— she pulled the bed curtains, closing herself into total privacy. Her heavy lids fell shut in an instant, warm, thick darkness embracing her totally.

Suddenly, a man's voice whispered to her out of the silence. "If they are but plums, madam, they are the sweetest and ripest on earth."

Julianna sat bolt upright, her eyes wide. "What?"

All was quiet. No phantom voice answered her question. She must have been dreaming, she decided, rubbing her eyes with her knuckles.

Unnerved, Juli threw open the bed curtains and dressed quickly, glancing over her shoulder now and again. Once more, the all-too-familiar presence seemed to be with her. Gooseflesh rose on her arms and tingled along her spine. As quickly as she could manage it, she was out of the room and seeking company.

She tiptoed across the hall and opened the door to the master suite. Elliot was still sound asleep, still in the same position as when she had left him. She quelled a sudden, desperate urge to wake him, to beg him to hold her and love her.

"Work!" she told herself firmly. "That will make the morning pass quickly."

Julianna turned and hurried down the stairs. She could hear the rattle of pots and pans from below. Netherwood was coming alive for another full and active day. She smiled with anticipation. If she kept herself busy, all these strange sensations would vanish. She was sure of it. Elliot was here now—her anchor to reality.

The moment Julianna entered the kitchen, Maeyken, hands on hips and pale eyes gleaming, demanded, "Well?"

Guiltily, Julianna imagined that the woman knew she had been in the room with Elliot and what their intent had been.

"He is a close friend of mine," Julianna explained, trying to fight back a blush. "Elliot Creighton. He arrived very early on a train from New York and I helped him get settled in the master suite. He's sleeping now."

"We've a guest?" asked Maeyken, surprised. "You

should have told me right off. I'll cook him up a fine meal while he's resting. *Zult, kool slaa*, and *hutspot.*"

Julianna couldn't help smiling at the thought of such an extravagant meal—sausage, cole slaw, *and* Maeyken's famous stew of carrots, onions, and potatoes cooked together in her great black pot.

"What?" Juli teased. "No spiced red cabbage, Maeyken?"

The old woman threw up her hands in feigned exasperation, but the twinkle in her eyes told Julianna that she was secretly pleased. "You want *rood kool*, you get *rood kool.*" Then she leaned closer and her voice lowered as she spoke. "But what about last night? The Ouija board and the captain? Tell me, Miss Juli."

Julianna shrugged. "There's nothing to tell. I fell asleep too soon, I suppose."

Maeyken's eyes narrowed suspiciously. *"Nothing?"*

"Not that I remember," Julianna answered almost honestly. No need to tell Maeyken about Kat, Juli decided. Mere mention of the Rhinehart woman's name seemed to upset the old nurse.

"*Oh!* Nothing that you *remember*," Maeyken replied. "That's different, then."

Ignoring the implication, Juli continued. "I really am beginning to think this is all a waste of time, Maeyken. It was fine fun when I was a child, thinking up this imaginary man to make life more exciting. But . . ." She paused and smiled. "If you want to know the truth of the matter, the only man I want in my life now is sleeping upstairs. Brom Vanderzee can go find his own woman."

Just then, a plate clattered from the cupboard and smashed to the kitchen floor. Both women started.

"Tell Zeke he'd better fix that loose shelf," Julianna said.

"It ain't loose!" Maeyken answered emphatically.

Julianna stooped to pick up the pieces of the shattered

78

dish. When she'd cleaned up the mess, she glanced around, wondering what to do next to fill the long morning.

She was about to head for the attic when suddenly her mind changed, seemingly of its own accord. "I think I'll go down to the cellar this morning and have a look around before Mr. Creighton wakes up."

"There ain't nothing down there," Maeyken said quickly. "Nothing worth fooling with anyway."

Julianna was tempted to take Maeyken's word for it. She hated damp, gloomy places. And there was that stack of old letters she'd left untouched in the attic. Maeyken was right; the cellar could wait. But when Juli opened her mouth to tell Maeyken her change in plans, other words tumbled out unbidden. "All the same, I want to see for myself what's down there."

Maeyken caught Julianna's arm as she started for the cellar door at the far side of the cavernous kitchen. "What about your gentleman friend, Miss Juli? He could wake up any time."

Julianna's desire to go to the cellar had suddenly become a raging passion. She would brook no further delays. "If he wakes, just call down. I'll come right up."

Refusing to allow Maeyken to interfere a moment longer, Julianna headed straight for the door to the cellar stairs. Lighting a lantern, she started down the creaking steps, wondering why she suddenly had this great urge to explore the dank place. Carefully, she eased down the narrow stairs.

The cellar was damp and musty. Spiderwebs, probably undisturbed for generations, hung like transparent curtains on every side. No windows marred the gloom. A few rotted baskets sat in one corner of the first room. Julianna held her lantern lower. Mouse tracks created zigzag patterns across the dirt floor. She experienced a sense of disappointment mingled with relief. Still, her urge to explore drove her on.

The second room was smaller than the first. Some rope,

a few rusted tools, nothing more. Julianna turned up the wick of her lantern to see into the shadowy corners, half expecting to discover a pile of bones or something equally gruesome in this eerie place. She glanced about and gasped. There in the far wall was a wooden door—a small, arched door with a shiny glass knob. She hurried toward it, her heart beating frantically.

Setting her lamp aside, Julianna turned the knob and pushed. The rusty hinges refused to budge. She strained and groaned, broke a fingernail, hurt her toes when she tried to kick it open. Finally, a great, painful heave of her shoulder against the old wood forced the stubborn hinges to move. The door swung in.

At that instant, Julianna imagined all sorts of things hidden in the room beyond. Maybe a fortune in pirate treasure. A secret passageway. Or would she step over the threshold to find herself once again face-to-face with Captain Brom Vanderzee?

The light from her lantern brought a crushing wave of disappointment. The room was barely large enough to turn around in. The walls were hewn from the formation of limestone on which Netherwood had been built so long ago. A spring bubbled up through a crevice in the the rocks at the very center of the uneven floor.

Exhausted and perspiring after working so strenuously to gain entrance, Julianna sank down and dipped her fingers in the water. It was cold and clear with a slight effervescence. She cupped her right palm and brought some to her mouth. It tasted fresh and sweet. She took another drink. Suddenly, her lantern light turned eerily green before her eyes.

In the next instant, the confines of the little room vanished. The spring still bubbled beside her, but she was sitting in a clearing in the woods. Birds sang in the branches over her head. The bunch of wildflowers in her lap told her it was springtime, not autumn as it had been a moment before.

Where was she? What on earth was happening?

She stared down into the mirrored surface of the pool. She saw herself—her wind-tousled red-gold hair a riot about her face. She was still Julianna, it seemed. Then with a start, she noticed the second image in the water. A man stood behind her, the stiff breeze off the river whipping his shoulder-length black hair. He was smiling at her reflection, his dark mustache cocked up by his lopsided grin.

"Aye, it's a pretty woman you are, Julianna," he said in a deep, foreign-accented voice.

She turned to confirm that he was really there. When she did, he reached down and took her hand, helping her to her feet. He pulled her against his broad chest and smiled down into her eyes, his own glittering like twin beads of jet. A moment later, his lips pressed hers. Frightened, Julianna tried to pull away, but he held her close.

This couldn't be happening . . . could it?

"Ah, love," the man whispered, gentling her with soft words, "don't be afraid. You think I don't know how young and innocent you be? Do I look like a man who would take unfair advantage?"

Julianna stared up at him. Yes, he did, as a matter of fact. Wild hair, bearded face, a golden earring glinting in the sun. Yet her heart softened toward him. He was beautiful in a savage way, his dark eyes clouded with some secret sadness. She felt her heart flutter as she gazed at him.

"Brom?" she whispered, almost fearing his answer.

"Aye! Would I allow any other to hold you so closely? Why, I'd take my cutlass to any man who tried! He'd soon be wearing his manly jewels in a pouch round his neck, by God!"

Turning from fierce to tender in an instant, he lifted his hand to brush the hair out of her eyes. A green flash blinded her as the noon sun hit his emerald ring. Julianna stared at the odd piece of jewelry.

81

"You like this, eh?" He waggled his finger to make the ring's stones dance with flashing green fire. The golden dragon, set with emerald scales. "Well, my dearest heart, you'll wear this someday." Holding her tucked under one arm, Brom made a broad sweep with his other. "I've purchased all this for the two of us. A place with a certain magic about it, don't you agree? I mean to build you the finest manse on the river, right here where we stand. And when it's done, you'll be my bride and wear this ring so every man knows to keep away from Brom Vanderzee's woman."

Julianna glanced about. She recognized this place, and Brom was right about its magical quality. Here was the bubbling spring and the outcropping of blue limestone that would someday be locked away in the cellar of Netherwood. Over there was the ancient apple orchard. But now the gnarled limbs she had climbed as a girl were young and strong and green. Out there lay the broad Hudson River, and riding at anchor was the tall-masted ship she'd seen once before, on her first evening back at Netherwood.

"Come now, love," he begged. "Show a poor sailing man a bit of gratitude, won't you?"

He sprawled out on the soft grass, pulling Julianna down next to him. They stretched out, using his scarlet cloak as a pillow. For a long time, he lay staring up, his arm under her shoulders.

"'Tis so peaceful here," he said with a sigh. "What say you, Julianna? Could you live in this place and be my love?"

"Yes," she heard herself answer, wondering even as she spoke what spell he had cast over her.

"Happily?" he asked. "Forevermore?"

"Happily and forevermore." Again the words, spoken with strong conviction, seemed to come from someone else. But Julianna realized she meant them with a passion.

Brom turned on his side, staring into her face. His smile

was gone. His black eyes shone with some deep and secret emotion.

Julianna trembled when he traced her brow with one finger and the cool gold of his dragon ring grazed her flesh.

"If I were the blackguard they claim me to be, I'd be in your skirts by now and congratulating myself on a morning well spent. I doubt I could think of anything, dearest heart, that would please me more. Please you as well, I vow."

Julianna stiffened, an untried maiden's reaction to his bold words.

"There, there, love," he soothed, rubbing his big hand along her bare arm. "I be saying what I'd like, not what I mean to do. There's time enough for that. But a kiss for your captain, mayhap?"

Julianna closed her eyes, waiting to feel his mouth cover hers. She parted her lips, letting the tip of her tongue glide out to moisten them.

"Ah, pretty wench, how you tempt me!" He sighed.

Then his lips met hers—a gentle kiss at first. But Julianna felt the flames scorch them both. Soon her arms encircled his neck and her slender body moved under his big, hard frame. His tongue flicked at the inner softness of her lips and his hand crept to her breast.

She'd seen when she looked into the pool that she still wore her high-necked blue work dress, the bodice closed from the waist by tiny bows of braid. Now she felt his fingers on the tie at her neck. Several tugs and her breasts were free. Her flesh quivered as his fingertips played over her with light strokes. He drew his mouth away from hers, letting his lips trail down to the pulse at the side on her throat, then on to her aching breasts.

The next instant, an explosion of sensations raged through her body as he sucked one nipple into his mouth and tongued it lazily for a time.

"Ah, you've breasts as sweet and soft as ripe plums," he murmured against her flesh.

She smiled when he looked down at her. The sun was warm, the blue, blue sky littered with puffy white clouds. And there, with his arms around her, his body covering hers, his eyes devouring her, was her beloved. The man she had searched for all these years—Captain Brom Vanderzee.

"You'll wed me then?" he begged gently.

"I will!" Julianna words were more than an answer. They were a promise and, at the same time, a warning of what was to come.


"Miss Juli? Miss Juli, are you still down there?" It was Maeyken's voice.

Julianna started. When her eyes flew open, she was staring down at the pool of water—the clear, cold spring in the damp cellar. Everything seemed the same. The lantern was there, the water still bubbled out of the rocks, the door stood open as she had left it. Nothing had changed. Nothing but Julianna herself.

She shook her head, trying to clear it. Had she dozed off for a moment? She felt so strange, so disoriented. She felt something else, too. Such a burning need she wanted to cry. She stared at her hands. Had they really touched *him*? No! It couldn't be! Surely she had imagined the whole scene.

Julianna covered her chest with her hands, trying to quiet her racing heart. Only then did she noticed her high-necked gown. The tie closings were all undone. Her bare breasts strained at the opening, the nipples peaked with arousal.

"Oh, dear God!" she moaned. "Oh, what's happened? Brom!"

"Miss Juli, you better come on up here. Mr. Creighton wants you."

"Elliot!" she cried. She'd forgotten all about him. Suddenly, she had a sense of being rudely jerked back into reality. How long had she been down in the cellar? And how could she explain what had happened? Even to herself!

Quickly, she tied her bodice, grabbed the lantern, and headed for the stairs. She met Elliot halfway up.

"Darlin', what are doing down in this damp cellar? You'll catch your death." He touched her cold arms. "Why, you're trembling all over."

"I'm all right," she assured him, wishing she could reassure herself as easily. "I wanted to look around since I hadn't been down here before. But Maeyken was right. She told me there wasn't anything much to see. Just a few mice."

Elliot laughed and touched her nose. "And dirt," he added. "You have a big smudge just there."

Julianna didn't want to ask what time it was, but she was relieved to see the sun still high when they got upstairs.

"Did you have a good nap?" she asked, trying to sound natural.

"A *disappointing* nap," he answered, pouting as his gray eyes flashed a meaningful look into hers. "You left me, darlin'."

She smiled. "You needed your rest. We'll have another nap after you've had something to eat."

Elliot slipped his arm about her waist, then leaned down and gave her a quick kiss—oddly enough, a kiss that Julianna didn't even feel. How puzzling!

"Sounds good to me," he said. "Mighty good!"

Maeyken had the table set and food—sausage, cole slaw, vegetable stew, *and* spiced red cabbage—ready for them when they reached the dining room. Elliot filled his plate, then cleaned it in record time, never taking his eyes off Julianna. He was obviously eager for the naptime she had promised.

"You're making me nervous," she told him. "I can't even chew properly with you staring at me that way."

"I can think of better things to do with your mouth, darlin'," Elliot answered, first glancing over his shoulder to make sure Maeyken wasn't listening.

"Elliot Creighton! Not at the dinner table!" She tried to force a light tone, but she was still too shaken by what had happened—or what she had imagined—to carry it off well.

"No, darlin', not at the table." He gave her an absolutely seductive grin. "But, come to think of it, that might be fun. We'll have to try it sometime when we're all alone in the house."

Julianna started to tell Elliot that she had a feeling they would never be truly alone in *this* house. But she thought better of it and held her silence through the rest of the meal.

By the time they finished and got upstairs, Julianna was as nervous as a cat. She was sure Maeyken and Zeke knew exactly what they were up to, but her disturbed feelings were caused by more than simple embarrassment. Suddenly, she didn't feel quite comfortable with Elliot. Was he different, or was she? And, too, there was this odd sensation of someone watching their every move—someone who disapproved of Elliot's being here. She kept glancing over her shoulder, sure that she would catch some intruder spying on them. But of course, no one was there.

Elliot didn't wait to get into the bedroom. He took Julianna into his arms for a deep kiss the moment they reached the upstairs hall. At the same time, his hand went to the ties of her bodice, undoing them quickly.

"Elliot, wait!" she whispered, frantic now. "At least let's get behind a closed door."

She had meant to take him back to the master suite, but instead he headed for her bedroom.

"No, not in there!" She sounded horrified.

"Yes, in here," Elliot insisted in a husky whisper, tug-

86

ging her toward Brom's room. "Then when I'm gone, dar-lin', you can lie in bed at night and remember how it was when we were together."

He hurried her into the room and onto Brom's bed. They had no sooner settled into an intimate embrace than a knock at the door shattered their romantic mood. Julianna, un-nerved and feeling disoriented once more, leaped off the bed. Quickly, she put her clothes in order.

"Yes?" she called, her voice and her whole body shak-ing.

"I need to talk to Mr. Creighton," Zeke answered.

"Not now!" Elliot groaned, motioning Julianna back to the bed.

"It's important, sir. Train schedule's been changed. If you figure on getting back to New York tonight, you got to be at the station in the next few minutes. That train'll be the last one out till tomorrow."

"Damn!" Elliot cursed, already rising from the bed.

"Do you have to go?" Julianna sounded disappointed, but unaccountably she felt relieved.

"I've no other choice. There's a performance tonight," he told her. He kissed her again. "Juli, come with me," he pleaded. "Stay with me while I'm in New York. We'll be there only a few more days before we head west."

She stared hard, right into his eyes. Feeling mesmerized by his gaze, she could almost remember the delicious ecstasy of their lovemaking. A warm thrill passed through her. She sighed and smiled.

*Yes!* her heart cried joyously.

Of course! she decided in that instant. It was a fine idea. She could throw a few things in a bag, take the train with him, stay at his hotel. They'd have a wonderful time to-gether. Maeyken and Zeke could easily take care of things here.

Julianna opened her mouth to voice her enthusiastic approval of the plan, but to her utter horror and amazement, she heard herself answer instead, "I'm sorry, Elliot, but there's so much I still have to do here. Winter's almost upon us. I can't just up and leave, not even for a few days. Please understand."

Another knock at the door. "Mr. Creighton, you best hurry. I'll drive you to the station, but if we don't leave right off, you ain't going to make that train."

Still staring at Julianna, his eyes gone dark with disappointment, Elliot called, "Coming right now, Zeke."

He started to turn, but Julianna caught his hand and tugged him back for one last kiss.

"Elliot, I do love you," she whispered, feeling tears near the surface. "I *really* do!"

When he left without saying the words to her, Julianna fell back on her pillows, sobbing. Why hadn't she gone with him? What could she be thinking? What had come over her? It was almost as if someone else was controlling her every thought, word, and action.

She sat up suddenly, her teary eyes wide. "*Brom!*" she exclaimed, sudden realization clearing her vision. "Blast it all! You made me stay here when I wanted to go."

Somewhere in the distance, she heard a deep, rumbling laugh. Then a man's voice said, "Do I look like one who would take unfair advantage, pretty wench?"

Julianna threw a pillow across the room, hoping she'd hit the scheming ghost.

"How dare you meddle in my life?" she cried.

# *Chapter Five*

By some quirk of time and fate, some tiny rip in the fabric of the universe, past, present, and future coexisted on the very spot where Netherwood's Captain Brom Vanderzee chose to build his Hudson River retreat. This was the magic that he had sensed about the place when first he saw it.

Only mildly annoying at times, this state of things could prove exasperating at others to Netherwood's residents. Captain Vanderzee preferred sleeping on his ship to enduring the strange dreams that invaded his sleep during nights spent under Netherwood's newly tiled roof. Even in daylight hours, he was not immune to forces from the distant future. Sometimes it seemed to him that only the thinnest curtain separated age from age inside this great house that he had erected over the bubbling spring on the hill.

So, it was only natural that the lusty, iron-willed Dutchman should take umbrage at having his premises invaded by a strange man. Though Brom hadn't actually seen the fellow, he had felt his presence in another part of the house. Who this stranger was mattered little, only that he and his disrupting influence be gone posthaste. Away from Netherwood. More importantly, away from Julianna!

Brom Vanderzee stood in the center of his bedroom, thoughtfully puffing his long-stemmed clay pipe and feeling utter relief at having the trespasser dispatched back to wherever he'd come from. But disturbing currents of air still marred the peace of his quarters.

*Am I going mad?* Brom wondered. Then he chuckled and said aloud, "If this be madness, it is indeed a sweet state I've come to."

The outline of the woman in his bed grew dimmer as he watched. She'd been in tears moments before. Her unspoken agony had called him upstairs from the library where he'd been working on his charts. Her pain had summoned him to the bedroom as surely as if she had urgently and repeatedly cried out his name. But the moment he had come to her, she'd begun hurling curses at his head. Even as she began to fade, she ordered him to stop meddling in her life.

"I?" he responded in all innocence. "'Tis *my* life, young woman! How you came into it, I have no notion. But since you have, and since you've made me love you besides, I won't allow you to order me away."

She seemed not to hear him, even though her green eyes—bright with tears and wide with anger—stared right at him. As her final, defiant act before she disappeared, she raised her nearly transparent arm to hurl a pillow directly at his head. He dodged, but it struck him a glancing blow.

"Damn!" he muttered with a grin. "I'll have to remember to keep pistols and cutlasses out of the wench's reach."

Brom went to touch the place where she had been. The sheets were still warm. The other pillow was damp with her tears. He stared down at the rumpled bed, pulling thoughtfully at his beard.

"What kind of phantom weeps real tears?" he asked himself.

For a long time he stood there, his pipe clutched in his fist, his arms crossed over his chest. *Julianna*. Her name was really all he knew of her. Her name, and that he loved her. When had she first appeared in his life? he mused. Where had she come from . . . and where did she go?

He strode across the room and sank down into the Russian leather chair beside his desk. Glancing out the window, he caught sight of his ship, *Bachelor's Delight*, riding high in the water. But the sun gleaming on the tall mast and the trim line of his vessel failed to bring the usual swell of pride to his broad chest. Other concerns clouded his mind and pained his heart this morning.

"And Julianna heads that list of concerns," he murmured aloud.

Laying his pipe aside, he closed his eyes and buried his face in his hands. Why did she remain so elusive, flitting in and out of his life like some bright butterfly? He wanted her here, now and forevermore. He longed to make her his wife, but how could that ever be possible? It seemed he could never hold her long enough to wed her.

Brom sifted back through his memory, trying to sort out the times he had been with Julianna, trying to make all the pieces fit in some logical order. When was the very first time? It seemed now as if she had been a part of his life forever, though in and out of it with disturbing regularity.

"Aye!" he said suddenly. Looking out toward the river, his eyes half closed, he focused on the blurred image of his handsome sailing vessel. "'Twas the night at sea when the fever came on me as I battled the storm." He shook his head in wonder. "I never thought to see the break of dawn. Had it not been for Julianna . . ."

He closed his eyes again, remembering, or trying to remember, as much as he could of that night. It had seemed more dream than reality at the time and so it remained in his memory.

The voyage had been going well—well enough, in fact, that the captain had gone below to sleep, leaving his first mate in charge. Brom was deep in dreams when the man burst in upon him.

"Captain Vanderzee, you'd best come on deck at once." First Mate Hawkins woke Brom abruptly from his sound sleep. The ship's second in command wore a worried expression on his face that matched the anxious tone in his voice. "The weather's turned dirty on us, sir. I've had the men rig lifelines, and I've ordered the sheets shortened. But that may not be enough to save us. This storm's a killer, sir."

The year had been 1689. They were returning to New Amsterdam from a run to the Indies, their hold loaded with rum, sugar, and mahogany wood. *Bachelor's Delight* had been flying up the coast all day, pushed by a miraculous wind. Now it seemed the fierce source of that amazing breeze—a West Indian cyclone—was bearing down on them with all its life-threatening fury.

Brom was out of the cabin door before his first mate finished speaking. He glanced about. Waves that seemed as tall as Storm King Mountain crashed over the pitching deck. The sturdy vessel wallowed drunkenly in the troughs before being dashed this way and that by the angry sea. His sailors looked like wary ghosts as they moved about in the eerie, dingy yellow light of the storm, clinging desperately to the lifelines in order to maintain their footing on deck.

"Haul down the rest of the sail!" the captain yelled to Hawkins, trying to make himself heard over the hurricane's banshee wail. "Then order all hands below when their tasks are completed."

92

"*All hands*, sir?" the first mate shouted back, incredulous.

"Aye! You heard me, Mr. Hawkins. *All*—yourself included," Captain Vanderzee replied. "I'll man the wheel."

Before the men finished their tasks and went below, the captain had himself lashed to the helm. He doubted any of them would be alive come morning, but he meant to do battle with this monster storm before he allowed it to take his ship and the lives of all his crew.

The hours crept past. The night grew blacker than the inside of a pharaoh's tomb. Brom's body ached as if every bone were broken. The wind tore at him ruthlessly and the sea battered him like a drunken bully in a barroom brawl. His hands bled from gripping the wheel. Each new blast of salt water burned like bloody hell.

He squinted up at the sky for so long, trying to spot a break in the boiling clouds, that his eyes began to play tricks on him. The gaunt masts, illumined by flashes of silvery-white lightning, became three crosses. He heard the moans and cries of the crucified victims. Suddenly, Saint Elmo's Fire danced across the spars and masts and crackled through the rigging. It seemed the devilish blue-green flames touched Captain Vanderzee's very soul. He felt himself shiver in the grips of a raging fever. Everything about him became surreal. Only the storm and his determination to best it remained in his consciousness. Soaked through, weak with exhaustion, a broken, sick, seemingly defeated man, Brom Vanderzee battled on alone through the long night.

"God save us," he moaned near dawn, feverish and almost delirious from his hours of torture, "for surely I cannot."

He slumped against the wheel, the last of his strength and his spirit drained. His clothes, whipped to shreds by the driving rain and wind, hung in sorry tatters on his limp frame. His last sight before his eyes closed was the bare deck

93

awash with spindrift from the storm. Nothing remained, not even hope. It was then that she had appeared before him for the very first time.

Brom had felt a light touch on his shoulder. Battling his way back through the dizzy waves of blackness that threatened to overtake him, he forced his eyes open against the stinging torrents of rain. At first he thought that his ship had broken up, that she was a mermaid from deep in the sea come to welcome him to his watery grave. But, no! He could still feel his stubborn heart beating. Mayhap they had been rammed by another vessel during the storm, for surely this was a masterfully carved ship's figurehead that stood before him. Then she moved as no woman carved of wood could ever do. The gale whipped her burnished hair while her long white gown billowed out around her. When she smiled at him, her full red lips parted. She reached one slender hand toward him and stroked his fevered brow.

"You can't go," she said simply. "Your time has not yet come. And our time is yet to be."

She came to his side and slipped a supportive arm about his trembling body. Her strength and spirit seemed to flow into him, recharging his very soul. The pain and cold vanished. He steadied the wheel and, with a glance heavenward, dared the fierce storm to another round.

Through the rest of the night she stayed with him. She remained still and silent until his eyes closed in exhaustion. Then she murmured his name and kissed him—the light, sweet kiss of a virgin, but with more power than a thousand hurricanes. Each time he felt the touch of her lips, he revived to fight on once again.

At dawn, the storm subsided. She stood beside him for a time, both of them staring out at the becalmed, pink-pearl sea.

"Farewell for now," she whispered, already fading before his weary, salt-stung eyes.

"Wait!" he called, reaching out but touching only thin air. "Your name. For God's sake, tell me your name!"

"Julianna."

Had she said the name or had the restless waves whispered it to him? His eyes closed. He slumped forward and slept.

The next he knew, First Mate Hawkins and several of his sailors were slashing at the ropes that still bound him to the helm.

"Is he dead, sir?" the captain heard one of the sailors ask of the first mate.

"Could any man have survived such a night up here on the open deck?" Hawkins replied sadly. "But by giving his life, he saved his ship and the lives of every man on board. It's a hero's burial at sea Captain Vanderzee deserves."

"Aye!" Brom heard his men agree solemnly.

"And so shall we give him," First Mate Hawkins declared.

Brom smiled now, remembering how he'd shocked them all mindless when he roused and exclaimed, "I'll not accept such a burial! Thank you all the same, maties. I mean to sail the full course of my life before this able body is deep-sixed for all eternity."


A similar shock jolted Brom out of his reverie when he heard Julianna's voice again in the bedroom. She had vanished only moments before. Now she was back, and still furious with him, it seemed.

"Brom Vanderzee, if you are near and can hear my words, you had better take heed!"

He swung around in the chair. There she sat in his bed, only slightly transparent, her hair tousled adorably, her hands on her tiny waist with elbows akimbo, those great green eyes flashing a dire warning.

"I wanted to go to New York with Elliot Creighton," she said, looking away from where he sat, but with a determined stare that she obviously hoped was directed straight at him. "I don't know what this is all about, but the game is up, sir. I love Elliot and I will not have our relationship ruined by your ghostly shenanigans."

The moment Julianna declared her love for Elliot, a deep, rumbling rage took possession of Brom. He had sensed the man's presence earlier while Creighton was sleeping. But then the stranger had been somewhere that was not a part of the present house—Netherwood, as Brom had designed and built it. Julianna had taken her uninvited guest to a room that existed only in the far-distant future. Brom could do nothing then, other than will Julianna away from this trespasser.

But when Julianna brought the stranger into Brom's own bed, that was a different matter entirely. What was his was *his*! To Brom Vanderzee's way of thinking, not only the bed belonged to him, but Julianna as well. Oddly, Brom had been unable to enter his own bedroom while the man was there, but he'd had no qualms about imposing his will on Julianna to change her mind. His scheme had worked beautifully. Julianna was still here—well, partially here—but now the man was gone. He had his room, his bed, and his woman back. If only she would stay here with him where she belonged.

"Elliot's gone and left me again," Julianna moaned.

"Good riddance!" Brom boomed angrily. From the change of expression on Julianna's face, he knew she had heard him.

"You *are* here!" She darted her eyes this way and that, trying to locate him. Other than a faint hint of tobacco smoke in the room, everything looked and seemed normal. "Brom, you have to stop doing this. You can't play with my life this way."

"Play with *your* life? Were you only jesting when we met beside the spring and you said you could be happy with me forevermore?"

He watched as she shook her head, then put her face down in her hands and whimpered softly.

"Well, madam? Do you remember that promise or not?"

She looked up, tears glistening in her eyes now. It broke his heart to see her weep.

"Yes, I remember. But it was a dream. That's all it was," she whispered. "There was nothing real about it."

"I beg to differ!" Brom boomed. Then his tone softened, making Julianna ache with his pain as he said, "My breaking heart feels very real to me at the moment. Tell me you meant what you said at the spring and that you've come to me this time to stay."

She made a pleading sound and whispered, "Where was I then? Where are you now? None of this makes any sense to me."

"You were here with me, Julianna," he answered gently. "It was the day I first showed you the magical glen by the spring. You must remember how happy you were, and how happy that made me. As for where you are now— Look around you. You're in *my* bed, in *my* room, in *my* house. That would seem to make your intentions clear enough."

Julianna shook her head. "It doesn't make anything clear. Netherwood belongs to *me*. And my heart belongs to Elliot Creighton! What are you doing here? Why did you come into my life in the first place? All these years I've been waiting to find out."

"You, madam, barged into *my* life!" Brom answered in a huff. "What sort of game are you playing? You make me love you, then tell me you want another? Even Kat plays by fairer rules."

"Kat?" Julianna's image wavered and almost disappeared before Brom's eyes.

"Don't go," he begged. "We've things to talk over. Stay here with me, Julianna."

"Here?" she murmured in a tone lacking all hope.

"Where is here? What time and place? What year is this, Brom Vanderzee?"

She heard his mocking laugh. "Has that fellow addled your brain, girl? The year is 1696, of course."

Julianna gasped. "It wasn't a while ago."

"What year did you think it was?" he asked suspiciously.

"The year of 1899. At least it was this morning when I woke up."

Again his laugh echoed in the room. "If you'll step to the window, you'll have your proof of the actual date."

Julianna, still glancing about, felt slightly foolish. Try as she might to find Brom with her eyes, she could catch not the slightest glimmer of his shade. Still, she did as he instructed. Even if she couldn't see him, she could hear him all too plainly.

"There. What do you see?" Brom asked when she stood before the window with the bright sun shining through her shimmering form.

"A ship," she murmured. "The same ship I saw before."

"*Bachelor's Delight*," he said with pride, "built in 1689, and a worthy vessel she be. But I doubt she'll hold up for two hundred years. That would be asking a lot, don't you think?"

Julianna covered her lips with the tips of her fingers as she stared out at Brom's ship. Confused thoughts whirled through her brain. "Oh, my! Oh, dear! This can't be!"

"This *can* be," Brom whispered very close to her ear. "In fact, this was meant to be. I'm sure of it, dearest heart."

A moment later, Julianna experienced the oddest sensation. The air about her turned warm and caressing. Her lips trembled as she felt the pressure of his mouth. Her eyes, wide and staring, told her that she was alone in the room. But the fire racing through her blood, the ache of her breasts, the lightness in her heart, all told her that Brom was here . . . that Brom was holding her and kissing her and making

98

her feel this way. How could such a thing be happening? She had to be imagining this entire, insane conversation. She was simply overwrought because Elliot had left.

Brom, too, was confused. Even as he took Julianna into his arms and kissed her deeply, it was clear she couldn't see him. Life seemed so maddeningly contrary these days, and Julianna seemed to be at the very core of all the chaos. She popped in and out of his life with no rhyme nor reason. He could never tell when she might turn up and he couldn't seem ever to keep her with him long enough to find out what was happening. Even now, as he held her close, she was taking on a certain distressing transparency again.

"Julianna, don't go, please," he begged her. "Stay and talk to me. Tell me what you feel."

"I feel strange. Dizzy . . . so very sleepy . . ."

She drifted out of his arms and back to the bed. No sooner had she stretched out than she was gone—vanished to thin air.

"Damnation!" he muttered, slamming his clenched fist down on the desk.


"Damnation!"

Julianna awoke with the oath reverberating in her head and the smell of burning tobacco still tickling her nose.

She sat up and glanced about. "Brom?"

Only the syncopated ticking of the antique clock disturbed the silence.

"No answer," she said with a sigh. Then she shook herself all over. "Of course there's no answer," she scolded herself. "What did you expect? *Whom* did you expect?"

She looked toward the clock on the chest. Two hours had passed since Elliot's departure. She must have dozed off after her fit of hysterics. Her emotional upset had caused all manner of strange dreams. At least this time, though, they were *only* dreams. That she was sure of. Certainly, there was no way that she could have carried on a conversation with an invisible Brom Vanderzee in this very room.

Julianna rose and went to the windows, staring out as if she were searching for something. What? She couldn't think. Everything looked as it should—the drive, the elms, the rose garden below. Through the dense branches of the trees, she caught the faintest glimmer of the sun sparkling off the river's smooth surface. She shrugged and started to move away. But her eyes focused on a curious object on the desk: a white clay pipe with a long stem. She frowned.

"Where on earth did that come from?"

Julianna reached out and touched it. The mouthpiece was damp. The bowl was warm, with smoldering ashes inside. She sniffed.

"The burning tobacco smell!"

Suddenly, all that had happened came rushing back to her. Brom had been here. She closed her eyes and concentrated. No! She had been there—wherever *there* was. He had told her it was 1696. The ship . . . Yes, his ship had been anchored in the river. She glanced back out the window. She couldn't see the spot now for the trees.

She sat down at the desk, cradling his pipe in her hands. A single tear made a silver trail down her cheek. Whatever was happening to her? Perhaps she'd been working too hard. She was quite obviously overwrought to be imagining such strange things. She sighed and closed her eyes, but she was still very conscious of the warm clay of the pipe clutched in her hands.

Brom stood beside his chair, one hand gripping its back until his knuckles turned white. He could still feel her presence. If only he could see her, talk to her, hold her.

A knock at the door distracted him.

"Come!" he called.

His peg-legged butler thumped into the room. "You've visitors, sir. Captain Kidd and his wife and daughter."

Brom's face broke into a broad grin. "By damn, man, show them in, and tell Cook to prepare a feast for a king. Bring up my best wines from Madeira. Nothing's too good for my friends."

"Aye, sir," the butler replied. "They be waiting for you in the library even now."

Brom, forcing all thoughts of Julianna from his mind, hurried down to greet his guests. The moment he spied William Kidd, Brom could tell by the gleam in his friend's dark eyes that he had. news—good news. The two men shook hands, slapped backs, and poured wine.

Mrs. Kidd stood by, silent but glowing. She adored Brom Vanderzee; all women did. Her patience was rewarded when he caught her at the waist and planted a brotherly kiss on her plump, rosy cheek.

"Ah, my dear lady, you're looking pretty as can be. That blue frock—French, isn't it?—brings out the sapphire sparkle in your eyes. You should wear no other color."

She flushed with pleasure and giggled behind her dainty hand. Lord, when a woman finally snagged Captain Brom Vanderzee, the young Mrs. Kidd mused, what a prize that lucky lady would have!

"And how's my pretty Miss Sally?" Brom asked, sweeping up the fair-haired five-year-old in his arms. "You'll be breaking every heart in New-York soon with that flirtatious smile, little girl."

Sally Kidd, wide-eyed with adoration, hugged Brom's neck soundly.

William Kidd nodded toward his wife, indicating that she should leave them alone to talk business. She smiled at both men, took Sally by the hand, and excused herself to go walk in the rose garden.

"Well?" Brom said, once they were alone. "What news do you bring, William?"

Captain Kidd's ruddy cheeks glowed with pleasure as he answered, "The best! Lord Bellomont plans to outfit his own private navy to sail against the bloody pirates Governor Fletcher welcomes so readily to New York. Our lord governor will sign on any of us who are willing to accept his British letter of marque. The sailors will work for no pay, only a share of the take. That alone should be considerable. Any enemy of the British Crown will be fair game. I myself will soon be sailing to England to finalize plans, handpick my crew, and take command of my new ship, *Adventure Galley*. She's a beauty, Brom!"

"Tell me more!" Brom demanded eagerly.

The rough-faced Scots captain grinned like a child describing a new toy. "She's 287 tons, and mounts thirty-four guns, well equipped for taking on any and all freebooting adversaries. What say you, Captain Vanderzee, are you ready to join our force? May I count you and *Bachelor's Delight* in when we go to sea early next year?"

Brom clinked his glass to Captain Kidd's as his pleased laughter erupted in the quiet room. "Aye, I'm in, sir. Just try to keep me out of a good fight, especially one with such enticing rewards."


Julianna, still sitting in Brom's chair at his desk, tried to force her thoughts back to Elliot, but his image blurred in her mind. His brief visit seemed like an illusion—more so than her confrontation with Brom Vanderzee moments before. She stared down at the pipe in her hands. It couldn't be, but it was.

Laughter—Brom's laughter, she realized—rang through the open widow, coming from below. Juli started at the sound. He was talking to someone, but his voice seemed different now. It was not as loud as when he'd been in the room with her. It seemed to come from far away in distance and time. Something about his tone chilled her through.

"No, Brom," she whispered. "Please, no! Whatever you're planning, don't do it!"

She felt foolish. Why on earth had she said that? And why did she have this feeling of foreboding suddenly? Somehow, she had to reach Brom. She had to find out what he was planning. She sensed disaster on a head-on collision course with them both.

Julianna stood and went to the windows, staring out. How peaceful everything looked. Tall elms, no ship. Why should she be worried about a man who had lived two hundred years ago?

As she stared out, she noted a peculiar mist drifting in from the river. It came like a cloud—thick and cottony and opaque—obscuring the hill, the woods, the elm-lined drive. A shiver ran through her. She looked to the front garden, untouched yet by the fog. There she saw a blond woman and a small child walking among the roses. Neighbors, no doubt. She couldn't blame them for trespassing. The flowers were in full bloom now and as beautiful as any she had ever seen.

On sudden impulse, Julianna decided to go down and introduce herself to the stranger. It was time she met her neighbors. She hurried out of the room and down the stairs. In moments, she was at the front door. The fog was growing ever thicker. She ran to the garden, calling, "Hello?" But no one answered. It seemed the flaxen-haired woman and her little girl were gone.

Julianna sighed. She had hoped that meeting her neighbors might take her mind off Brom, might put an end to these strange dreams and visions of hers. But, alas, she had missed her chance.

She lingered in the garden, hoping the fog might yet lift in time for her to find the woman and her child.

Over dinner, Mrs. Kidd said to Brom, "Won't your lovely, bright-haired lady friend be joining us, Captain?"

Brom frowned, puzzled by the woman's words. "I don't know who you mean, ma'am."

She blushed deeply. When would she ever learn to hold her tongue? Obviously, the woman she'd seen staring down at her and Sally from Brom's bedroom window was meant to be kept a secret. Then she smiled. She couldn't blame the captain for wanting to keep such a beauty all to himself.

Odd, though, the pretty young woman had looked familiar, even from a distance. At first she had thought it might be Katrina Rhinehart. There had been some talk about town that Kat had set her bonnet for Brom. But she knew that sluttish wench was warming the bed of another of Captain Kidd's mates at present. So who could this flame-tressed beauty be? And why was Brom loath to share her company with his best friends?

*Never mind*, Mrs. Kidd told herself. The gossips of New-York would know all about Captain Vanderzee's latest love affair before too long. No one could keep a secret in the close-knit society of seafaring men.

A thought struck her suddenly. "Captain, you will be bringing someone to the governor's next reception, won't you?"

Brom cocked one dark eyebrow, chuckled, and nodded. "*Someone*, aye" was all he said.

Satisfied, Mrs. Kidd smiled happily. All in good time, she told herself. She would meet Brom's special lady soon enough.

# Chapter Six

Julianna lingered at the front door, gazing out into the garden. How could the woman and child have disappeared so quickly and so completely?

Stepping outside, Juli walked over to the rosebushes. She glanced down. Odd! There were no footprints in the soft earth. Still, she knew they had been standing right here by the bush of red roses. She'd seen them with her own eyes.

"Miss Juli?" Maeyken called from the door. "Will you be wanting your supper soon?"

Food was the last thing on Julianna's mind at the moment. "Not right away," she called back. "I think I'll take a stroll down to the post road, then maybe on toward the river."

"Don't be staying out there after dark," Maeyken warned, sounding much like an overprotective mother. "And mind you don't lose your way in this fog. Stay to the path."

"I won't stray far, Maeyken. I'll be back in a short while."

Julianna headed down the curved drive. If she hurried, she might yet catch sight of the woman. She and the little girl couldn't have gone far.

The golden leaves of the tall elms sighing overhead, the eerie stillness of the thick fog, and the encroaching darkness all worked on Julianna's frazzled nerves, making her jump at the slightest sound from the woods. Several times she thought about turning back, but she forced herself on, eager to reach the main road. When she did, she glanced both ways, but saw no sign of the woman from her garden.

"Ah, well," she said with a sigh, "the brisk walk's done me good. I'll meet her another day."

Turning, she looked back up the hill toward Netherwood. She could just make out the ghostly outline of its stepped gables and twin chimneys. The dark windowpanes seemed to gaze down on her like so many blind eyes. She shivered and clutched her shawl closer around her shoulders.

A sudden gust of cold wind off the river parted the enshrouding mists for an instant. Through the thick ivy covering Netherwood's facade, Julianna could make out the lines of the original dwelling—four rooms below, two bedrooms above, and the attic. Her aunt and uncle had added the master suite on the back of the house over a porch on the ground floor. She wondered how Netherwood had looked when it was newly constructed, when Captain Brom Vanderzee was master of the manor.

She stood for a long time, staring back up the hill and thinking of Brom—trying to visualize him in his suit of purple velvet and plumed hat, taking the steep slope in long, powerful strides. Who had lived here with him? A woman? She frowned suddenly at her next thought: Perhaps *many* women over the years? Brom Vanderzee had obviously never been the sort of man to lead the life of a monk. Pirates, she reminded herself, seldom were, if the stories she had read were true.

Darkness was coming on fast. Julianna glanced toward the river, wondering if she might find *Bachelor's Delight* anchored there in a shroud of fog. She brushed the thought aside. She'd never make it down to the water and back before full dark. So she turned, starting back up the hill. While kicking through the drifts of yellow leaves paving her way, she noticed a narrow path off the drive that led into the deep woods. Curious, she decided to investigate.

Carefully, she wound and twisted through the woods until she became quite dizzy trying to follow the maze. Dead limbs fallen to earth slowed her progress. Obviously, it had been a long time since anyone had come this way. She had almost decided to turn back when, finally, she broke out of the dense forest into a small clearing. She froze, shock quickly replacing relief.

There before her stood a low stone wall, dark green with moss. Inside the enclosure she spied a single, lichen-encrusted tombstone. A shudder ran through her. The air felt cold suddenly.

Forcing herself to stay calm, Juli tried the old iron gate set into the stones. The rusty hinges gave way the moment she touched it and the gate came off in her hands. Setting it aside, she stepped carefully through the opening.

The large tomb loomed up taller than she. Though worn by the elements, the etched words in the stone were plainly visible even in the fading light. She moved toward it, her heart pounding. Slowly, she let her fingers trace the words on the monument.

The tombstone was carved in the shape of a tree trunk, cut down while still in leaf—the universal symbol of a man whose life had ended abruptly during its prime. The cold granite quickly warmed under her hand. She leaned close to peer at the inscription: "BROM VANDERZEE—Born 1660—Died 1699—Born of the sea, but died of treachery before his time. God have mercy, for no man did."

107

The words chilled Julianna through. Dead! Dead all these years. Yet the man seemed as alive to her as any person she had ever met. She refused to allow herself to think of him lying there under that cold stone. Not the magnificent Captain Vanderzee!

"Not my Brom," she murmured, bowing her head.

"Miss Juli! Where are you?" Maeyken's frantic cries, drifting through the woods, gave Julianna a start.

She stood silently before the tomb a moment longer before she answered. Tears coursed down her cheeks. She was shivering convulsively. She had to get control of herself before she faced Maeyken. The woman would think she was crazy, sobbing in mourning here at Brom's tomb.

But that was not to be. When Julianna turned, the old woman stood at the stone fence staring at her with a stern and level gaze. Maeyken's lined face looked as ancient and chilling as the grave marker.

"How'd you find this place?" Maeyken demanded.

Feeling guilty for no apparent reason, Julianna shook her head. "I don't know. I just wandered down the path and here it was. Maeyken, he's *buried* here!" she cried. Julianna knew she didn't have to say who for Maeyken to understand.

"Aye," Maeyken whispered. "And you're the first to visit his grave in many a year, Miss Juli."

Still at a loss to control her emotions, Julianna blurted out, "But he told me only this afternoon that the year is 1696. His tomb says he died in 1699. That's only three years away. I have to do something!"

Maeyken gasped in horror and clasped her gnarled fingers under her chin as if in prayer. *"This afternoon?"* Her voice was harsh with accusation. "You've been with him this very day? Miss Juli, what are you doing? Why are you meddling in what's passed and done and can't be undone?"

"Can't it?" Julianna's question was punctuated by a

108

barely suppressed sob. "Is there no hope, Maeyken? Oh, please! Tell me there's something I can do."

Maeyken took Julianna in her arms, trying to soothe her. "There, there, child. Come back with me now to the house. Have some supper and you'll fell better. You're over-wrought from working so hard. You should have gone with your Mr. Creighton to New York like you meant to do."

Julianna looked at the old woman suspiciously. "How did you know I even thought of that?"

Maeyken chuckled. "There's not much that goes on at Netherwood that I don't know, Miss Juli."

By the time the two women reached the house, Julianna had her emotions under control. But still, finding Brom's grave had left a deep and lasting scar on her heart. It almost seemed as if she hadn't really believed that he was dead until she read that inscription. But now . . .


Long before Julianna finished supper, she had made up her mind what she must do. As Maeyken was clearing the table, Juli said casually, "I hear there's a town fair at Greenburg tomorrow. You and Zeke have both worked so hard, why don't you take a day off and go enjoy your-selves?"

Maeyken's wrinkled face broke into a grin. Then she sobered. "We couldn't leave you alone here after what's happened, Miss Juli."

Julianna forced a laugh. "Of course you can. You'll be gone only a few hours and home before dark. I have letters to write, some mending to do, and a new book to read. A quiet day alone might do me a world of good."

Maeyken frowned again, but it was obvious she longed desperately to go to the fair. "Well, a day at the *kermis*— or fair, as you English call it,—does sound tempting. If you're sure, Miss Juli."

109

"I am," Julianna assured her. "Now, go tell Zeke, then both of you get to bed early so you'll be good and rested for your big day tomorrow."

Juli's mind was made up about what she planned to do the following day while Maeyken and Zeke were gone. She slept soundly that night. No dreams, no phantom voices, no further regrets for not having gone with Elliot to New York.

She was convinced now that it was no mere happenstance of fate that had brought her back to Netherwood, back to Brom Vanderzee. She had been sent to warn him against whatever cruel fate lay in wait for him three years in his future. Only she could save him.

"And save him I will!" she vowed.


By the time Julianna awoke at dawn, Maeyken and Zeke had long been on the road to the *kermis* at Greenburg. She sighed with relief to have Netherwood all to herself, although she did feel quite lonely and just a touch nervous, she had to admit. But now she was used to the specter of Brom Vanderzee hovering always near. In fact, she welcomed his ghostly company.

Leaping out of bed, she pulled on her wrapper, then sped downstairs. She stopped briefly in the kitchen, but only to get a large blue-banded ironstone pitcher. Her true task awaited her in the cellar. Quickly, she lit a lantern and hurried down the narrow stairs. She paid little attention this time to the two outer rooms, but moved single-mindedly toward the arched doorway.

Julianna smiled when the sound of bubbling water greeted her ears. Kneeling at the pool, she set her lantern aside and dipped the pitcher into the cool, clear water. Then she closed the door and headed back to the bedroom.

Not a drop of the precious liquid did she spill on her way upstairs. She placed the pitcher on the bedside stand as

110

carefully as if it contained holy water from the Vatican. Then she breathed a deep sigh of relief. Soon all would be ready for her great adventure. She realized now that the magical powers of the spring water were her ticket back to Brom's time.

Julianna looked down at herself. Since she had no idea where she might pop up or with whom, she could hardly go dressed in her nightgown. A sudden delightful thought struck her. She ran to the old Dutch *kas* where Maeyken had hung her clothes. There in the very front of the huge pine armoire she spied what she sought—brand new and all hers, the first truly fine, store-bought gown she had ever owned.

"Perfect!" she whispered.

Julianna would wear her new French traveling costume, the one she had purchased at John Daniell & Sons, Haberdashers, on Broadway. She had bought the outfit during her stop in New York City on her way to Tarrytown from the farm in Pennsylvania. It was a truly fashionable ensemble, and since she planned to go visiting, she meant to dress in proper style.

Over her best cambric drawers, corset of jersey webbing, and hair-cloth bustle, she donned the gown of silver-gray camel's hair trimmed with soft velvet of a deeper shade. The outfit looked more coat than dress with its high collar and inset of velvet at the deep-V opening to the waist. The lighter fabric came only as low as the elbows, simulating a form-fitting overcoat, with the dark velvet in tight cuffs to the wrists. As a final touch, Julianna wound the Empire sash three times about her cinched waist and let the draped knot hang low and slightly to one side in front. She braided her hair, then pinned it in a knot at the nape of her neck. She set her matching gray felt hat with its ostrich plume at a saucy angle on her head, then pulled on her new suede gloves.

111

"Ready!" Julianna said with a pleased sigh. Then, glancing into the mirror, she smiled her approval.

"Well, my girl, you certainly look fashionable enough to turn a few heads while strolling along the finest streets of New York in the 1890's. I only hope you'll look presentable in old New Amsterdam of the 1690's."

Glancing toward the desk, Julianna spied Brom's clay pipe. "I'll take it to him," she said, easing it into her reticule and pulling the drawstrings tight.

The moment she realized she had nothing left to do, an attack of nerves overcame her. Getting ready to go was one thing. Actually drinking the spring water in order to take the leap was quite another. Her palms grew sweaty, her head felt light, and she found her adventurous self in pitched battle with her more sober and sensible side.

"Calm down!" she said aloud. "It's not as if you haven't done this before."

*But never while you've been totally alone in the house*, her wary side reminded her.

"It's a simple matter of taking a drink of water and waiting for something to happen," she said reasonably.

*Waiting for* what *to happen is the question*! her timidity argued.

"I know it will work," she insisted. "I'll drink the water and I'll go straight to Brom, exactly as it happened the last time I sipped from the spring."

*Ah, but how will you get back?* reason interjected.

"Oh, be still, won't you?" she snapped at her own frowning image in the mirror. "I'm going to take a drink. *Now!*"

She poured some of the fizzy water into a glass, but found that she could not bring her hand—paralyzed with indecision—to her lips. She was shaking so that she spilled a few precious drops down the front of her new gown.

"Oh, bother!" she muttered, brushing at the damp stain.

Finally, she set the glass back on the table and paced the

floor, trying to gather her courage. The room felt warm with the morning sun beaming in and the windows all closed. She opened one and stared out toward the little graveyard in the forest that she'd visited the day before. Tears sprang to her eyes as she thought of Brom lying out there all alone.

"Oh, Brom," she whispered, "what good is all this? It's only a dream. Some kind of fantasy. It's no use." She wiped at her tears and shook her head sadly. "You're gone . . . gone forever."

Her spirits at a low ebb, Julianna went back to the bed and lay down, letting her tears flow at will. By the time she had cried herself out, her throat felt sore and parched. Not even thinking about what she was doing, she reached for the glass beside the bed. The water tasted cool and sweet.

Closing her eyes, she pulled the bed curtains against the strong morning light. She felt spent, emotionally exhausted. Perhaps she'd just nap for a bit.

But sleep was not to be.

Suddenly, laughter seemed to shake the bed, the whole house. Julianna's eyes shot open.

"Well, bless me, madam, if that isn't the silliest-looking get-up I've ever seen in all my days!"

Julianna found herself standing in a strange room with Brom Vanderzee before her, laughing his head off at her new Paris gown.

"Tell me, how does one sit with that outrageous growth protruding behind?" He reached around and patted her horsehair bustle.

"If you don't mind?" she scolded, switching her derrière out of patting range.

His laughter softened to a chuckle. "But I do mind, dearest heart. I like your true shape—all smooth curves and soft mounds. Come here to me."

Julianna had no intention of obeying his command after he'd laughed at her. But she found she had little choice in

113

the matter as he took her hands in his and pulled her close to his chest.

"What manner of torture chamber is this and who shut you away from me inside such a thing?" he grumbled, letting his fingers slide over her tightly-bound waist and breasts. "I'll give the one responsible for this a taste of my cat-o'-nine."

"You don't like my clothes?" In spite of the fact that she was in a strange place with a man she knew had been dead for two hundred years, her feminine instincts reacted most strongly to his disapproval of her new ensemble. "Brom, I wore it just for you."

"Then perhaps you'll take it off just for me?" he suggested, letting his mustache tickle the narrow margin of bare flesh above her high, tight collar.

Julianna pushed out of his arms. "No!" she cried. "I will not! I've gone to a great deal of trouble to find you, but I didn't come here to be seduced."

Brom backed away, his palms up, shoulders hunched, and an innocent look on his darkly handsome face. "But why else does a woman come to the captain's cabin uninvited? Not that I mind in the least, of course. I've had this happen in many a port and always the lady's intentions are the same. It is the law of the sea, Julianna."

"Well, I happen not to live by your law of the sea, sir."

"Too bad," he muttered under his breath, stroking his pointed beard and looking quite disappointed.

Julianna glanced about the room with its low ceiling, narrow bunk, lanterns attached by brass brackets to the walls, books, charts, and a sextant. "Where exactly am I?"

"I told you, dearest heart. You're in my cabin on board *Bachelor's Delight*."

She narrowed her eyes at him. "And I can just guess how it got that name."

Brom grinned sheepishly and twitched his mustache.

"I'm glad you came," he said, trying to make up for angering her. "And the gown, it will do, I suppose. But I'd rather you wear the things in the trunk I left in our bedroom."

Julianna rounded on him. "*Our* bedroom?"

He shrugged and reached for her hand. "Dearest heart, why are you angry with me? Yes, it is our bedroom. I have slept there and you have slept there. Perhaps soon you will agree to marry me and then we can both sleep there— *together*."

"*Marry* you?" Julianna's head was spinning. How could she marry a dead man? Which one of them was crazy? Perhaps both, she decided.

"You promised," he reminded her.

Julianna shook her head. "The man I mean to marry left Netherwood yesterday for New York City. *You* sent him away, didn't you?"

"I?" Again there was that boyish note of innocence in his voice.

"Yes, you!" she cried. "I would have gone with him, but you made me refuse. Why, you changed the train schedule, too, didn't you?"

"*Train schedule?*" Brom looked as if she were suddenly speaking a foreign tongue. "I have no idea what you're talking about." He was the injured party now, matching her anger and then some. "What is this that you accuse me of, wench? Tell me or get off my ship!"

It was Julianna's turn to try to defend herself. What would she do if he sent her away? Where would she go? It wasn't as if she could stalk off his ship and take herself home. She had no idea how to get home from here. If she was truly in the seventeenth century, she would be totally alone without Brom. No home, no family, nowhere to go. Fear had a calming influence on her quick temper.

"Of course," she murmured, her eyes downcast. "I

115

should have realized. There were no trains from New York to Tarrytown in your day. No trains at all. I'm sorry, Brom. Please forgive me for being so suspicious."

He moved toward her immediately, taking her in his arms to acknowledge her apology. His mouth came down over hers before she could protest. Not that she wanted to. He had a way of kissing her that chased all else from her mind. She clung to him, wanting never to let go.

When, finally, he released her, he whispered, "Ah, my dearest heart, why must we fight when there are so many other lovely things we could do together?"

Still holding her with one arm about her waist, Brom drew the long pin from her hat and removed the plumed nuisance. Then he pulled out the hairpins that held her braid.

"So soft and beautiful," he murmured, fingering her bright tresses. "I like to see it flowing all about you with the sunlight turning it to fire."

Julianna held her breath, feeling every touch of his fingers in her hair a thousand times over. Slowly, he undid the braid, granting her riot of curls the freedom they sought from confinement.

He led her to his bunk and motioned for her to sit. Then with slow, careful strokes of his fingers, he combed out her hair full and long.

"That's better," he whispered. "So shiny, like Oriental silk."

When his lips touched her temple at the hairline, Julianna thought she might faint. A shiver, hot and intense, ran through her at his light fondling. The feel of his breath on her face, the press of his hard thigh against hers, his soft words and softer caresses all wove a web of magic about her.

"Ah, dearest heart," he said, "how wonderful it will be when I can love you. I dream of that time—of stripping away all barriers between us . . . of taking you into my arms and kissing those secret places no other man has yet explored. I try to imagine what you will taste like. Warm honey? Crushed mint? Sweet ambrosia?'' He paused and sighed. ''I try to think how you will feel. Will your skin be like satin, silk, or warm velvet?''

His hand moved up her arm. He touched her breast, seeking flesh. He could find none.

Julianna, so overwrought by his words that she felt she might burn up alive, thrust his hand away. ''Please, Brom, don't,'' she begged.

He caught her face between his hard palms and made her look directly into his dark, smoldering eyes. ''You don't want this as much as I, Julianna? Tell me truthfully.''

Truthfully, she could not deny that she wanted him— wanted him with such a driving passion that she thought she must go mad. But she could not bring herself to profess such wanton feelings.

Still staring at her, unsmiling, he touched his lips gently to hers, then said, ''You need not say a word. Your heart and soul lie naked in your eyes, dearest heart. I will wait, if you wish. But, in time, I will know all the things I can only dream of now. You will know them as well.''

He kissed her again, his hands still holding her prisoner. But she was a willing captive as his mouth opened over hers and his rough tongue made intimate love to her, turning her blood to fire.

Blazing green light met her eyes a moment later when the cabin door flew open and the sun struck Brom's emerald ring. They both looked up to see a man standing just outside.

''Oh, I beg your pardon, sir,'' the embarrassed first mate muttered. ''I had no idea . . . I mean, I thought you were alone.''

''Hardly!'' Brom growled, rising from the bunk. ''What is it, Hawkins?''

When Brom rose, Julianna noticed for the first time that

he was dressed differently from when she had seen him before. Now he wore his working clothes. His full-sleeved linen shirt was open almost to the waist, showing his magnificent chest. His breeches, rather than velvet, were of soft leather, molded skintight to his form. The tan hide exposed every rippling muscle in his legs and buttocks. And, most astounding of all, was the front view. The leather strained almost to bursting over his obvious erection. Julianna averted her eyes, embarrassed.

Her unbidden thought at the sight brought a smile to her lips: *Well, at least I know for certain that this Brom Vanderzee is very much alive!*

Brom and the man named Hawkins exchanged only a few quiet words—something about the ship's workings—then the captain closed the door and they were once more alone.

He grinned at her. "Now that I've taken care of the ship's business for the afternoon, why don't you and I stroll up to Netherwood? I hear the last of the carpenters finished only yesterday. I'm eager to see the new furnishings and how you've had them placed."

Julianna's confusion lasted only a moment. Obviously, they weren't married. Apparently, they were not living together, either. Brom was staying on his ship and he seemed to assume that she was already installed at Netherwood. She shook her head to clear it. She was living there, yes, but in another time. At any rate, the thought of seeing Netherwood as it had been in the seventeenth century delighted Julianna.

"Oh, Brom, that's a wonderful idea!" she cried. "Can we go right now?"

He smiled broadly at her enthusiasm. "I don't see why not. After all, it will be our home someday, dearest heart. It's time we began sharing it."

In her excitement, Julianna forgot that she had come back to Brom's time to warn him of some approaching danger, some danger she couldn't even put a name to. As she stared

118

up into his wonderfully savage face, all she could think of was how dear he was to her this very moment and how she longed to be with him forever. But what about Elliot and her other life and time?

Brom leaned down once more and kissed her softly. When Julianna opened her eyes, she was staring directly into his. The oddest feeling overtook her. She knew these dark, brooding eyes. She had stared into them many times before. She had seen the lovelight shining from them just as it was this very moment. As she remained mesmerized, his eyes seemed to go from black to silver to gun-metal gray. With a jolt, she realized that she was staring not into Brom's eyes, but into Elliot's. How could that be?

Julianna turned slightly away, trying to fight the confusion she felt. When she looked again, Brom was frowning and his eyes were as dark as a moonless night at sea.

"Is something wrong, dearest heart?" he asked softly.

She shook her head and forced a smile. "Nothing. Not a thing in the world, Brom."

Brom was no more convinced by Julianna's words than she was herself. There was something about this relationship that was far more mysterious and uncanny than could be accounted for by the mere two centuries that separated them. Until now, Julianna had seen Brom in a fascinating light. She had hardly taken him seriously as a genuine part of her life. One didn't contemplate marriage to a ghost, after all, no matter what she might say under duress to such a charming phantom.

Suddenly, all that had changed. The object of her childhood obsession seemed now disturbingly real to her for the very first time. No longer was he a shadow of a flesh-and-blood man, a shade to be summoned at her whim through thoughts and dreams. No! Brom Vanderźee—this fiercely passionate man—was truly alive and truly in love with her.

*And I?* Julianna asked herself silently, gazing still at the

119

swarthy Dutchman. She nodded almost imperceptibly. There was no denying her feelings for him. They were identical to the deep passions she felt for Elliot—identical in every way.

*But how can that be?* she asked herself again.

Julianna had fancied herself in love on two occasions before she ever met Elliot: once to a neighboring farmer, another time to a shy young minister. Both those loves had been different from each other and far different from what she felt for Brom and Elliot. Yet the deep emotions she harbored for her pirate and her actor mirrored each other in every regard and degree. It seemed as if her love were split between them, but with each man receiving the full measure.

Only a tart would love two men at the same time, she reminded herself. A blush crept to Julianna's cheeks at the very thought until reason soothed her shame. She might love both men, but certainly not at the same time. At this moment, when she had to admit to herself that Brom Vanderzee owned her heart, Elliot Creighton had yet to be born. However, the instant she returned to her own time—*if* she returned, she mused nervously—her affections would center once again on her handsome actor. That made the odd situation rather tidy, actually. But what a problem it would be if ever *both* men found their way into the same century!

"Total chaos," she murmured under her breath.

"Are you sure you're all right?" Brom asked.

Pushing the disturbing thought from her mind—It would never happen, she told herself—Julianna smiled at Brom and said, "Quite!"

"Then let's be off, dearest heart, to see this wondrous new home we'll share. And share it we shall before too much longer. I generally get what I want, Julianna, and you are my goal at this moment. Be warned!"

He swooped down to capture her lips again, leaving her breathless and quivering by the time he was done with her.

# *Chapter Seven*

Brom offered Julianna his arm. When she slipped her hand into the crook of his elbow, he gave her a sweeping bow, then a broad smile.

"Well, dearest heart, if nothing is wrong, then everything must be perfect with our little world. Shall we go inspect to make sure?"

"Let's!" she answered brightly.

"You cannot imagine how I've longed for this day," he said. "Remember last year—the afternoon at the spring?"

She nodded. How well she remembered! But only hours had passed for her since then.

"Netherwood is the home I promised you that day at the spring. And now it is ready. Do you know what that means, dearest heart?"

Julianna shied away from a direct answer. She had come here, to Brom's time, only for a visit. She never meant to stay. So his talk of marriage unnerved her. She answered him without actually telling him anything. "I can only imagine in my wildest dreams, Brom."

That seemed to satisfy him for the moment. He led her out on deck. A half-dozen sailors were about, performing various tasks, but the captain seemed not to see them. He hurried Julianna toward the gangway and onto the dock. Julianna noticed a few sidelong glances cast her way by the men. Perhaps they, too, thought her Paris gown and bustle odd-looking attire.

"Look!" Brom said, pointing.

Crowning the steep green hill stood Netherwood in all its glory. It was smaller than when Julianna had gazed at it the afternoon before, but it seemed to stand straighter and prouder somehow. Its paint was creamy-white with no tangle of ivy climbing the façade.

As yet there was no drive or even a path up the rise. Brom helped Julianna through the tall grass and around tangled thickets. Suddenly they came upon the narrow trail leading off toward the woods, the very one Julianna had followed the afternoon before.

"Ah, look there," Brom whispered. "We've had trespassers on our land."

"What?" Julianna asked, bewildered. Her pulse pounded with alarm at the sight of the path. She knew what lay at its end: Brom's own grave.

"Let's go investigate," he suggested.

Julianna tried to pull away. The clearing in the forest was the last place she wanted to go right now. She couldn't allow Brom to visit his own gravesite. What if something happened and they were suddenly whisked back to her time?

But he kept a firm grip on her arm and tugged her along in spite of her protests. "It's all right, Julianna. I suspect I know what we'll find in the woods."

"No, Brom, I don't think you do," she murmured, but he seemed not to hear.

As they neared the clearing, Brom slowed to a creep and put one finger to his lips to caution Julianna to silence. Her throat was so tight and dry she couldn't have uttered a sound had she wanted to. All she could do was cling to Brom's arm and try to prepare herself.

"There," he whispered. "Just as I thought."

Julianna realized suddenly that she had closed her eyes moments before, so fearful was she of coming upon Brom's tomb. But when Brom spoke to her she opened her eyes and stared at the little glen. There, nestled against their mother's side, lay two tiny spotted fawns.

"Oh, Brom," Julianna murmured, near weeping with relief. "They're so sweet . . . so beautiful. And the mother looks rightfully proud."

Brom leaned down and kissed her softly. "As proud as you will be when you bear my child, dearest heart?" he asked.

Julianna felt herself blushing, but when she looked up into his eyes—so dark and serious and loving—all embarrassment fled. She smiled and nodded, fighting sentimental tears.

Brom signaled silently that they should go and leave the little family in peace. Moments later, they stood before Netherwood's front stoop. Julianna gazed up in wonder at the clean, beautiful lines of this house Brom had designed and built for her—its rows of tall, narrow windows, the crow's-foot gables, the twin chimneys at either end.

"Isn't it wonderful, darling?" she said.

On hearing the endearment, Brom leaned down and kissed her until her cheeks flamed as bright as her hair. "Almost as wonderful as you, dearest heart."

As they toured the rooms, Julianna marveled at the elegant old furniture she knew so well. But now everything was gloriously new. The woodwork inside was a much lighter shade than she remembered. Two centuries of fires for cooking and heating would in time mellow the wood to a smoky hue. The ceilings sparkled with fresh whitewash. The brass on the stairway runners gleamed like gold. Downstairs were the library, the parlor, the dining room, and the kitchen. Gone was her aunt's haphazard china clutter from that later age, replaced by Brom's love of simplicity and order.

The long dining-room table she saw was the same. "I had it made in Spain," Brom told her proudly, "especially for this room."

What she remembered as her uncle's study, it turned out, was originally the front parlor. "Your room for entertaining lady friends," Brom told her, "while my mates and I conduct business in the library."

Suddenly, a picture came to mind of Brom and his pirate cohorts swilling rum and smoking their long-stemmed pipes in the library while they planned their next daring raid. Julianna laughed softly.

"You find something amusing?"

"I was only thinking of your odd profession," she told him. "Do pirates actually conduct true business, other than making poor unfortunates walk the plank?"

He turned her toward him, a frown on his face as he stared into her eyes. "You think I'm a *pirate*?"

She felt at a loss. Her words seemed truly to have offended him. "That's what I've been told, Brom. You've never said otherwise. Your ship . . . your clothes . . ." she stammered.

"Who told you such a thing?" he demanded.

Before thinking, she blurted out, "Maeyken said it."

His eyes narrowed. "And you believed her?"

Not until much later would Julianna find it odd that Brom knew Maeyken's name.

"I may have been in a few minor, unsavory scrapes when I first set to sea as a lad, but now I am a legitimate merchant captain,'' Brom explained. "I will admit that my own father was one of the infamous pirates of New Amsterdam, but I have never been nor will I ever be one of those brigands who roam the seas preying on unarmed vessels. I loathe the cowardly bastards! Do you understand that, Julianna?''

She nodded, anxious to get off the subject. She'd had no idea it would anger him so.

"A merchant, of course,'' she replied. "I shouldn't have listened to idle gossip.''

Seemingly satisfied, Brom dropped the subject and ushered Julianna into the kitchen, the proud gleam back in his night-black eyes.

"You see, we have running water,'' he told her proudly.

Julianna stared, aghast. A large black pump loomed over the deep sink. Her arms ached just looking at the monstrous thing. She glanced out the window. There beyond the main house stood a small wooden structure. A privy. Her heart sank. No doubt this, along with the antique pump, were considered modern conveniences in Brom's time.

She remembered then that her uncle had installed the first true plumbing at Netherwood, the bathroom with a cooper tub and a flush toilet. The cistern installed on the roof provided running water. He had planned to bring in electricity, too, but had died before the wiring was completed. Already, New York City and some smaller towns boasted light at the flick of a switch.

"Well, aren't you pleased with such a modern kitchen?'' Brom prompted. "I've also purchased a goodly supply of woolen cooking skirts for you, dearest heart.''

"Cooking skirts?'' Julianna countered, having no idea what he was talking about.

"Aye!'' His face fell with a sudden sad expression. "My own mother was lost in a cook fire. Had she been wearing wool instead of light cotton that hot summer day, she would

125

have smelled her skirt afire and put it out before she was engulfed. I fear fire more than the swift swipe of a cutlass blade.'' He turned to Julianna, his voice stern. ''If you must cook with our servants, as most wives do, you will promise me now that you will always wear wool in the kitchen, no matter the season.''

He paused, obviously waiting for her answer.

''I promise,'' Julianna answered, recalling suddenly what Maeyken had told her about Brom's mother losing her life in a tragic fire.

She glanced about hopelessly in search of Maeyken's big black stove. Obviously, any cooking in Brom's kitchen would be done in the heavy iron pots that hung in the massive fireplace and the Dutch oven built into its side wall.

''Good!'' he answered, smiling again. ''So you like your kitchen well enough?''

''Quite'' was all Julianna could think to say.

Julianna felt relieved when they headed upstairs. When they reached the hallway landing, she noted with keen interest that only a solid wall stood where the door to her aunt and uncle's master suite would be built onto the house someday.

Brom's bedroom was the place she was most eager to see. She was curious to find out if her re-creation of that chamber was true in every detail.

First, however, they went into the smaller guest room. It was furnished nicely, but not as luxuriously as Brom's.

''We're likely to have many guests,'' Brom explained, ''being right on the river as we are. This room is for them. Friend or stranger, no one is ever turned away from the hospitality of a Hudson River house.''

His words seemed to cast a ray of light into a darkened corner of Julianna's memory. The term ''privilege of a river traveler'' echoed in her thoughts. A woman had said that to her. No, not to *her*, to *Brom*. But when? She couldn't quite

126

remember. However, the words gave her an uneasy feeling. Then it came to her in a flash.

"Brom, do you know a woman named Kat?" she asked.

Her question caught him totally off guard. For a long moment, he only stared at her, looking puzzled. "You mean Katrina Rhinehart? What do you know of her?"

"Nothing really," she answered truthfully. "I thought she was a friend of yours."

An angry growl escaped his throat. "You really must stop listening to gossips, Julianna."

"Then you don't know her personally?" she pressed.

He drew himself up as if ready to do defensive battle. "I know her, aye," he admitted. "But knowing the wench and doing some of the things with her that I've been accused of are hardly one and the same."

She recalled then what Maeyken had told her about Katrina, that the red-haired woman had meant nothing to Brom, but Julianna realized suddenly that she wasn't quite convinced. Without knowing why, she harbored a feeling of jealousy and suspicion toward the woman.

"Are you coming in or not?" Brom asked, holding the bedroom door open. "Close your eyes. I have a surprise for you."

He took her hand and led her across the room.

"Now you may look," he told her. "As I promised, a trunk full of the latest Paris gowns."

He lifted the lid and Julianna saw a profusion of silks, taffetas, and laces in rainbow colors.

"Oh, Brom! How beautiful!" she cried. "I want to take them all out and look at them."

"Later," he answered. "Right now, what about the room? Is it to your liking?"

Julianna immediately put aside all thoughts of the latest styles of 1696 in her eagerness to inspect the bedroom. When she glanced about, her eyes went wide. Something was very wrong. This was Brom's room—green walls, Persian carpet, Chinese urns—but something was not as it should be.

"The bed!" Julianna gasped.

Brom chuckled. "You like it, eh? Why don't we try it for fit?" he asked in a playfully scheming tone.

"No!" Julianna cried, shaking her head. "It's not right!"

"Oh, come, pretty wench, don't be so prudish." He hugged her. "We'll be married soon enough. Simply lying together for a moment won't sentence us to eternal damnation."

"That's not what I mean, Brom. The bed itself is wrong. This one doesn't belong in here. Look at it!"

Brom walked over and inspected the bed. Julianna could tell by the pleased expression in his eyes that he thought it a grand piece of craftsmanship. She, on the other hand, hated the grotesque gilt thing, with its carved gargoyles, satyrs, naked numphs, and ondines.

"But it came from one of Italy's most famous craftsmen," he said, as if that explained everything. "I have it on good authority that this bed is a work of art."

Julianna could tell from the way his fingers traced its garish carvings that he did not share her distaste for the piece of furniture. He turned back to her, his face plainly showing his disappointment at her reaction. "I thought it would please you."

How could she explain to him? "It's not that I don't like it," she began, skirting her true feelings, "it's just *wrong* for this room, Brom. I thought something in oak, more sedately carved, with bed curtains for privacy and warmth."

He shook his head, then glanced up and smiled at her. "Women!" he muttered. "A man should never try to outguess a female. Come with me."

He reached out and took Julianna's hand.

"Where are we going, Brom?"

128

"To the attic," he told her.

"Why?"

"You'll see."

The attic proved a wonder to Julianna. It looked huge, almost empty as it was now. The wood planking was shiny and bare. No spiders had had time to settle in and weave their homes. Sun streamed through the clean dormer windows, lighting the farthest reaches of the cavernous storage area that she knew someday would be piled high with generations of discarded treasures.

"Well, there it is," Brom told her. "The very bed you've described. It belonged to my mother and father. I was born in that bed, but I haven't slept in it since I was a child. On bitter cold nights my parents used to tuck me in between them to keep me warm. I don't know why, but I could never bring myself to get rid of it. Something of a family heirloom." He paused and turned to her. "Actually, you've guessed my boyhood dream, Julianna. I always imagined that when I took a wife, she and I would share the same bed where my parents conceived me and where my mother bore me. They brought the frame with them when they crossed the ocean from Holland." He smiled and drew her into his arms. "Thank you, dearest heart."

"For what?" Julianna asked.

He laughed. "For hating that gilded Italian monstrosity downstairs. I should have realized myself that it was a horror instead of listening to the opinion of another."

Julianna was about to ask whose opinion he had trusted so, but Brom never gave her a chance. Tugging her along with him, he hurried back to the bedroom and called out the window to some men in the yard who were clearing brush. "Come up here, won't you, and lend a hand?"

A short time later, the proper bed stood in its proper place, while the golden "whore's bed," as Julianna thought of the thing, had been relegated to a far corner of the attic.

129

"You are absolutely correct, Julianna. This old bed looks perfect in the room. Now it truly feels like home."

"Yes," Julianna murmured, smiling, "doesn't it?"

Brom moved about the room, eyeing the bed from all angles. For a moment, he propped against the desk, his head tilted to one side.

While he remained silent and absorbed, Julianna reached into her reticule and brought out the clay pipe he had left in her room the day before. She laid it on the desk beside him.

He glanced down. "Aha!" he cried out. "My favorite pipe!"

Julianna watched a puzzled look replace his smile of discovery.

"But how did it get here? This is the first time I've been in this room for nearly a fortnight. I had this pipe only yesterday, but couldn't find it this morning."

"You really don't know, Brom?" Julianna asked seriously.

He stared at her, obviously at a loss.

"You left it in this very room only yesterday," she told him.

"No! I did not! Are you trying to make me think I'm losing my mind?"

"Well, I suppose it wasn't really yesterday—not as *you* count time."

"Julianna, why must you talk in riddles? Say what you have to say plainly."

She paused, trying to figure out how and where to begin. "Yesterday—*my yesterday*, that is—you came to me in this very room. It was all so strange because I couldn't see you."

"There you are, then," he snapped. "If you couldn't see me, I was never here."

"Oh, yes, you were!" she answered vehemently. "I'm not sure when you came. I think you arrived before Elliot Creighton left. I still think you somehow willed me not to go with him to New York City. After he left, I heard your voice. I threw a pillow at the sound of it.''

A light of recollection kindled in Brom's dark eyes. ''Aye! Two weeks ago I came to the house to do some work on my charts in the library. I thought I heard your voice, too. It seemed you were calling me, that you were in great distress. I rushed up here, but found no one. I looked to the bed.'' He paused, glancing about in confusion. ''It was this bed, in fact, not the one from Italy, and it seemed I saw your outline there. I sat for a long time, smoking here at the desk, remembering the times we've been together and how you saved my life.''

''I saved your life?'' Julianna was incredulous. ''I don't remember that.''

Brom told her of his vision—the night she had first appeared before him on the deck of his ship during the killer hurricane. Oddly enough, Julianna vaguely remembered having had just such a dream many years earlier, before she ever came to Netherwood to visit her cousins. She was going to tell him all about it, but, without giving her a chance to speak, he abruptly returned the subject to their most recent encounter in the bedroom.

''I recall that you seemed angry with me over something—another man, I think. This Elliot Creighton. And, yes, dear wench, you flung a pillow at my head.'' He laughed. ''Thinking it all through later, I assumed I'd drunk too much the night before and was paying for my sins by imagining all manner of unpleasant things. I was enormously happy when Captain and Mrs. Kidd paid a surprise visit and tore me away from my torment.''

Sudden realization forced Julianna to ask, ''Did they bring a young girl with them?''

''Aye, their daughter Sally.''

The woman and child in the garden, Julianna thought. ''You did not imagine me, Brom. I was here. And something that happened during that time disturbed me greatly. Actually, that's why I've come to you now. I have to warn you of some danger.''

"What danger?''

Julianna shook her head. "I don't know, but I think it has something to do with Captain Kidd. I'm sure it is something life-threatening. Are you involved in some scheme, some dangerous plan with him, perhaps?'' She sighed hopelessly and looked to Brom for help. "Do you have any idea what I'm talking about?''

"The only plan discussed that day was the formation of a fleet to sail against the pirates. Captain Kidd asked me to join the force.''

Julianna's heart fluttered anxiously at this news. "You won't do it, will you?''

"Of course I will,'' he answered firmly. "I must!''

"But, Brom, it will be so dangerous, and you'll have to go away. I want you here.''

A half-smile cocked his mustache to one side. "Can you tell me, my dearest heart, where exactly *here* is? Where do you come from? Are you some sort of witch? You come to me, you say you'll marry me, then you disappear. I never know what the next day will bring. Julianna, I cannot go on this way.''

"Nor can I,'' she answered softly. "But what can we do? I live at Netherwood, but, as I told you before, I come from the year 1899.''

"Then how did you get here today?''

"I drank water from the spring.''

"The spring in the cellar, you mean?''

She nodded.

Brom strode over to her and pinched her arm.

"Ow!'' she cried.

"You are no phantom,'' he said. "You really are here.''

"Yes, really, for now." She pushed up her sleeve to show him her arm. "I even bruise like a real person."

"I'm sorry." He bent to kiss the red spot on her arm.

"Quite all right," she answered stiffly.

"Will you stay?" he asked hopefully.

She shrugged. "I don't know."

"How can I convince you to remain with me?"

"It seems it's not up to either of us," she answered in a dismal tone. "I may stay simply because I don't know how to go back. I found out quite by accident that drinking the spring water would bring me to you."

He closed his arms around her. "Stay!" he pleaded.

Suddenly, the sight of Brom's tombstone flashed through her mind and a thought came to her. "It would be better, safer, if you could come with me, back to my time."

"I have no idea how to do that."

"You did it yesterday," she insisted.

He looked flustered. "Not really. You yourself said you couldn't see me. Even if I could travel into the future, why would I want to?" he argued.

Indeed, why would he? Julianna wondered. Why would she want him to? What would she do if he and Elliot were in the same time and she had to choose between them? The very thought was dizzying. She loved them both. She actually wanted to marry them both. But polygamy did not sit well with her.

Brom took Julianna's hand in his and drew off her glove, coaxing the soft leather one finger at a time. When he had denuded her hand, he leaned down and pressed his lips against her flesh. Looking up, his eyes met hers and he offered her a seductive smile.

"Perhaps if I can make you wish with all your heart to remain here, it will happen. Let me try, my dearest."

Julianna felt herself yielding to his tender persuasion.

133

When he drew her into his arms and kissed her deeply, all thoughts of her real life fled her mind. Brom Vanderzee seemed more flesh and blood, more real to her than ever before. No ghost could enflame her this way. She had seen the graveyard for herself only a short while before. It contained life, not death. Brom was alive this minute. If she stayed, perhaps she could keep him that way.

"Will you stay here and love me?" he pleaded. "Will you fall asleep in my arms each night and awake beside me to soothe my morning passion? Will you marry me, Julianna?"

As he talked, Brom had maneuvered her toward the waiting bed. She never knew exactly how it happened, but suddenly they were lying together. Brom's hands were at her throat, loosening the tight collar, stripping away the deep V of velvet that shielded her aching breasts from his kisses. His strong but gentle hands played over her bare flesh, sending hot tremors through her whole body. Julianna could no longer think, she could only feel. Yet he was demanding answers to his persistent questions.

"You want to stay with me, don't you?"

"Hm-m-m" was all she could manage by way of an answer as his fingers loosened the front fastenings of her corset.

"Have you so much to leave behind in that other time?"

She shook her head slowly, watching wide-eyed as he gently stroked one of her breasts, then leaned down to kiss her. He nibbled tenderly at its crest.

"Would it be such a terrible life here with me?"

This time, her body gave him his answer as she thrashed about, deliciously tormented by the feel of his rough tongue dragging ever so slowly over her nipple.

"We would make wonderful children, you and I, my dearest heart. Flame-haired, black-eyed beauties. Don't you agree?"

"Yes!" she gasped as he sucked her nipple into his mouth and tongued it ever so lazily. Releasing her, he drew in a shuddering breath.

"You want me as much as I want you. Admit it," he demanded softly.

His hands moved lower, freeing more of her flesh to his loving touch, searing Julianna through and through with a desire so deep it was painful.

"I do," she moaned. "Oh, yes, Brom, I do."

He buried his face between her breasts so that his voice was muffled when he sighed and said, "Then this Creighton fellow is of no further consequence. He will come between us no more. I cannot live with half your heart. I must have it all."

His words had the effect of a dash of cold water. Julianna returned to her senses, ragged and abused as they were by his gentle loving.

"Brom, please, give me time to think," she begged, pushing out of his arms. "How can I do this? To simply vanish from the face of the earth into another time . . . to try to live another way, with other people. And what will become of me in 1699?

The moment she said that date, a flash of green light seared her eyes. She gasped and turned away. When she looked back, Brom was gone.

For a time, she lay very still, fighting waves of dizziness and nausea. When she could bear to open her eyes again, she glanced at the clock. If this was the same day, and she assumed that it was, only an hour had passed. She remembered lying down on the bed, torn between whether or not to drink the glass of spring water.

"I drank it. Yes!" she recalled. "By accident, but I did drink it."

Still, perhaps she'd simply dreamed everything. After all, she had been on the bed and she was still on the bed—on

135

the oak four-poster, not that gilded horror from Italy she had imagined.

"That was more nightmare than dream." She laughed weakly.

She had almost convinced herself that nothing had happened, when her hand touched her breast. She cried out when looked down at herself. The velvet V from her bodice lay rumpled on the bed beside her. Her corset was undone and her bare breasts gleamed like alabaster in the noon sun, the nipples still peaked with desire.

"Oh, no," she moaned, throwing an arm over her eyes. "This can't be!"

Again, she tried to make herself believe that it had all been a dream, albeit an extremely erotic one. In her imagined, passionate state, she reasoned, she had started undressing for her phantom lover. Yes, that was it! Embarrassing, yes, but there were worse things that could have happened. Suppose Maeyken had returned home and come in to find her this way.

She rose from the bed quickly and began fastening her corset. Only then did she spy undeniable proof.

Cautiously, as if she were approaching a viper ready to strike, she moved toward the trunk. Dreading what she knew she would see inside, she slowly opened the lid. A blaze of color greeted her eyes.

"Oh, Brom," she murmured. "Brom, what have you done? There's a king's ransom in gowns and jewels here."

Her recent gray camel's hair purchase from New York paled by comparison to these fabulous creations. Quickly, she skinned off the hot traveling costume, then unhooked her corset again. She held up a silk gown the color of the most brilliant sunset, eyeing it in the mirror. The sheer fabric felt cool and inviting against her bare breasts.

A moment later, she slithered into the gown. It barely caressed her shoulders, nestling so low on her breasts that the deep valley between them showed plainly above the neckline. The full skirt belled out around her—yards of filmy silk billowing like waves of a coral-tinted sea. An apron of delicate gold lace fell from the waist.

She dug deeper into the trunk. There she discovered soft, golden slippers and a velvet jewel box. She spied a necklace inside that obviously went with this gown—a fine web of gold, set with fire opals and pearls. She fastened it at her neck and cried out with pure joy when she looked at her blazing image in the mirror.

Julianna Doran was transformed. " 'God knows, I'm not myself'," she quoted, remembering Mr. Irving's character, Rip Van Winkle, and his statement of surprise he when awoke so changed after his long sleep and his visions of another time.

"Maybe," she mused, "old Rip drank from Netherwood's spring, too."

But unlike poor Rip, Julianna's transformation was glorious. Her bright hair hung free and wild to her waist. She remembered the feel of Brom's fingers undoing her braid. She shivered with pleasure and closed her eyes for a moment. Looking back at herself, she saw that the sunset silk did ever so much more for her than the dull grays of her traveling costume. And the cut of the gown! It was scandalous and breathtaking at the same time. Never in this day and age could she wear such a daring creation in public.

Suddenly, she felt quite embarrassed, staring in the mirror at herself. What if Maeyken and Zeke should return right now? It would never do to have them see her dressed this way. Quickly, she started to slip out of the gown.

"Please! A moment longer," Brom's voice begged from somewhere and nowhere in the room. "You are so lovely, my dearest heart."

Julianna glanced about and smiled. "Thank you," she murmured, "for everything, Brom."

# *Chapter Eight*

Julianna stood in the center of the room—*her* room at Netherwood in the year 1899. As the echo of Brom's voice had faded away, she experienced a deep ache of loneliness. She had a sense of being not quite herself. She felt like two separate people, torn between two different times and two different lives. Most distressing of all, she felt torn between Brom and Elliot. How could she love them both? But it seemed that she did. "Julianna, dearest heart" adored Brom Vanderzee, while "Juli darlin'" would give her very soul to spend the rest of her life with Elliot Creighton.

Guilt added its aching load to the other distressing emotions weighing her down. She felt unfaithful to both men since she was incapable of giving either of them her undivided devotion. She paced the room for several moments, trying to sort out her confusion. If she couldn't make some sense of all this, she feared she'd go mad.

"But this is so crazy," she moaned. "How can I be in love with a vision?"

*A vision?* Was that all Brom and his time were to her? No, there had to be more. His pipe, the trunk, his blood on her nightgown. Weren't those things proof enough for her?

Julianna shook her head sadly. "No," she murmured. Thinking everything through, she finally had to admit to herself that nothing she had seen or heard was true proof that any of this was real.

The blood on her gown the night of the séance? Perhaps her pricked finger had bled without her knowing it. Brom's pipe? Zeke might have found it in the attic, tried it, then left it there for her, knowing how she loved old things. The same could be true of the very gown she was wearing and the rest of the articles in the trunk. They could all be newly-discovered treasures from the still-cluttered attic—surprises that Maeyken and Zeke hoped would delight their mistress.

She finished undressing, feeling less interest now in the elegant gown and jewels. She tossed the coral silk onto a chair. It slithered to the floor and out of sight. She never even noticed. If these weren't gifts from Brom, were they so special, after all?

Julianna continued to argue with herself as she pulled on her work dress. What about his voice? What about the way he made her feel when he held her and touched her and kissed her?

*"You've a bizarre imagination, my girl."* Suddenly, Julianna remembered her aunt Martha's parting words to her the morning she was expelled from Netherwood after the Ouija board incident. *"You'll come to no good because of it, mark my words. And I won't have you tainting the minds of my innocent daughters."*

"Maybe you were right, Aunt Martha," Julianna murmured. "What good is it doing to tear myself apart this way?"

140

Julianna made a decision at that moment. Difficult as it was for her, she knew she must do it. Her sanity and her future depended upon it. Quickly, she began gathering her things and carrying them across the hall. She would take everything that belonged to her, but leave anything that reminded her of Brom. She would move into the master suite, closing the door on Brom's room and on the man himself forever.

An hour later, Julianna had all her clothes moved out of the old Dutch *kas* and put away in her aunt's huge cedar-lined, rosewood armoire. She set her scent bottles, her pin tray, and her comb and hairbrush on the vanity. She even went down to the garden and cut the last fall roses, arranging them in a hand-painted china vase to try to brighten the rather gloomy chamber.

Finished, she sank down on the bed with a sigh. The place still felt empty and cold and foreign to her, not warm and welcoming as Brom's room had seemed from the very first. But she remained determined to stay in this room and in this time. Enough of what Aunt Martha had called her "bizarre imagination"!

A wave of relief flooded through her when she heard the back door open and Maeyken's call. "We're home, Miss Juli."

She spent what little was left of the afternoon in the kitchen with Maeyken and Zeke, hearing all about the cattle show, the hog judging, and the horse races while she gorged herself with deliciously sticky pastries and equally sugary fruit pies that Maeyken had bought at the fair.

"I tell you, Miss Juli, it was a wonder!" Zeke exclaimed, beaming at her over the wire rims of his spectacles. "They had this newfangled contraption they called a telly-phone. Me and Maeyken went in two different buildings, the man turned the crank, and right soon we was talking back and forth just as if we was standing next to one another."

141

"Black magic! That's what it was," Maeyken added warily, through a mouthful of rhubarb pie.

Julianna grinned at them. They looked, talked, and acted like two happy children after their day at the fair.

"I've heard of Mr. Bell's marvelous invention," Julianna told them. "Maybe someday we'll get a telephone here at Netherwood."

Maeyken laughed and shook her head. "Won't do no good, Miss Juli. Who'd we call? Ain't nobody hereabouts got one we could talk to."

"I could ring up Mr. Creighton when he's off in some big city."

"Bless me!" Maeyken cried. "You mean to tell me you could call him up all the way to New York City?"

"So they say," Julianna answered. "They've got telephones there already."

"I swan!" Maeyken breathed in wonder.

After stuffing themselves with sweets, they decided to skip supper. Maeyken and Zeke, both worn out from their exciting adventure, expressed their desire to turn in early.

Julianna rose from the kitchen table, stretched, and said, "I could use a good night's sleep. I think I'll go to bed now, too."

They were all about to leave the kitchen and go their separate ways—Juli to her aunt and uncle's former chamber, Maeyken to her room off the kitchen, and Zeke to his cabin down the road—when Julianna said, "Oh, Maeyken, I changed rooms while you were gone today. I'll be sleeping in the master suite from now on."

Maeyken's wise old eyes narrowed. "How come, Miss Juli?"

Julianna had anticipated this question and had an answer ready. "It's more convenient to the bath and there's more space."

"Zeke, you go on," Maeyken ordered, obviously want-

142

ing to talk to her mistress alone. Once he left, she demanded, "What happened here today while we were gone to make you do such a thing?"

Julianna waved her hand in the air as if trying to brush the question aside. "It's all too complicated and far too confusing to go into, Maeyken. I simply think I'll be more comfortable in the master suite."

Maeyken was not to be put off so easily. "I seen my big pitcher is gone from the kitchen. Where is it, Miss Juli?"

"In Brom's bedroom," she answered before giving herself time to consider.

"*His* bedroom?" Maeyken said. "How come all of a sudden you call it that?"

"Well, now that I've changed rooms . . ."

Maeyken cut her off. "Are you saying you been sharing that bedroom with Brom Vanderzee and it's getting a mite small for the both of you?"

Julianna tried to laugh. Little did Maeyken suspect how close she'd come to the truth. "What a ridiculous thing to say, Maeyken! One doesn't *share* a bedroom with a man who's been dead for two centuries."

Out of the blue, Maeyken asked, "What did you have in the pitcher?"

Caught totally off guard, Julianna admitted, "Spring water."

"From the cellar?" Maeyken's eyes were narrow slits as she leaned close to Julianna, awaiting her answer.

"Yes, it tastes better than the well water."

The old woman sighed and sat back in her chair. "So you found out on your own, then you went ahead and did it. You went off half-cocked trying to find him is my guess. And after I warned you, Miss Juli, to leave them people alone."

It seemed Julianna could keep no secrets from Maeyken. She might as well confess all.

143

"I don't understand about the spring, Maeyken, but its water has strange properties. When I drink it, I have the oddest visions." She smiled. "Some quite lovely, actually."

"It's them lovely ones you better watch out for." Maeyken clucked her tongue and scowled at the younger woman. "My advice to you, Miss Juli, is stay out of the cellar and don't you never drink none of that water ever again."

"Do you know what's happening to me, Maeyken?" Julianna was deadly serious now, pleading for some explanation. She had a feeling that if anyone could tell her, Maeyken could.

"Don't know as I understand all of it, Miss Juli. That bubbly water, though, is best left alone. You know I told you about the Indian stories of a spring where folks used to go and just vanish into thin air?"

"You mean that's *our* spring?"

Maeyken nodded. "And I didn't tell you all of Katrina Rhinehart's tale."

Julianna leaned closer, all attention now. The red-haired woman was high on her curiosity list.

"I told you about her man making her get rid of her baby daughter. Well, they say that evil wench brought her infant to the spring when she was only hours old. She laid the poor little thing down in that water and just stood there a-laughing as it disappeared from view, glad to be shed of it."

Julianna gasped in horror. "You mean Katrina drowned her own child?"

"I didn't say that," Maeyken answered. "That baby didn't drown. It just purely vanished. Nobody ever seen that child again. But there's some that say that Kat's daughter got sent off to another time. There's those that believed she never returned, others that vow she went back somehow to take her revenge on her hateful ma. You mess around with

144

that spring, Miss Juli, and there's no telling what might happen to you."

"But if the baby was real and alive, what could have happened to it?" Julianna shook her head, trying to comprehend. "Where could it have gone?"

"Like I said, nobody knew for sure back then, and we're not likely to find out after all this time. The best you can do is stay out of it, Miss Juli."

Shaken, Julianna rose from the table. "I intend to, Maeyken. That's why I've moved out of his room. And you can rest assured I *won't* be drinking any more spring water!"

The two women headed for bed. As Julianna climbed the stairs, she felt weary to the bone. She'd have no trouble sleeping tonight, even if she was in a strange bed.

She cast a momentary, longing glance toward Brom's closed door as she went into the bedroom across the hall. When she entered the master suite, it felt oddly cold to her. Quickly, she undressed, donned her nightgown, and snuggled under the covers. Her uneasiness lasted only moments. Soon she was sleeping soundly.


Brom paced the bedroom, wringing his hands and wishing desperately that he could find some way to bring Julianna back. She had done it to him again. They'd been right there on the bed, embracing, his lips at her breast, when as suddenly as she had appeared in his cabin aboard the ship earlier, she had dissolved in his arms. He had tried desperately to hold on to her, but it was no use. They had exchanged a few parting words across time and space and then she was gone, leaving only the coral silk gown behind.

Now, he was beside himself—angry and frustrated. Perhaps if he hadn't pressed her so . . . He'd frightened her away. She'd thought he meant to force himself upon her before she was ready.

Brom stood in the center of the room and cursed, winding up with an oath that turned into a wail of despair. Glancing toward the shimmering silk gown on the floor behind the chair, he reached down and picked it up, rubbing the soft fabric against his face. It smelled of Julianna—a warm woman-scent, mingled with the lingering essence of her rosewater cologne. The last he'd seen of her, she had been wearing this gown. It was all very befuddling. She hadn't been with him at the time. She had been in this room, but somewhere else. A fragile image bathed in glowing coral silk, looking as if she were suspended between his time and her own. She had been almost transparent and not quite real, but, oh, so lovely. He had begged her to stay. Then she had vanished totally. Moments later, however, he had turned back to find the discarded gown on the floor by the chair, as if she had rejected it and him.

He threw back his head and wailed, "Julianna! Where are you?"

No answer, yet he felt a stirring in the air. He sensed her presence very near. He walked to the windows and glanced out. Down the hill, he could see the watch lamps of *Bachelor's Delight* reflected in the water. All was quiet and calm.

Still clutching her gown, Brom sank down on the bed. He closed his eyes and visualized her face. He murmured her name over and over to himself. For nearly an hour he stayed there, until he felt mesmerized with wanting her and trying to call her back. Then a thought struck him. Actually, it had been her idea. If she wouldn't come to him, perhaps he could find his way to her. He closed his eyes again, concentrating so hard that he blocked everything else from his mind. Her murmured her name until his mouth went dry and his throat ached.

"Thirsty," he muttered, reaching to the bedside stand for the salt-glazed stoneware pitcher he always kept filled with water. He grasped the handle, not bothering with the squat tumbler beside it. Tipping the spout up to his lips, he drank deeply. The water was cool and sweet, with a slight effervescence.

Brom lay back on the bed. "Julianna," he moaned. "Ah, dearest heart, where are you now?" He waited, listening, hoping against all hope to see her image take shape before him once more.

Suddenly, the hair prickled at the back of his neck. A shudder ran through him. He couldn't see her, but he could sense her near. Just barely—but she was there, somewhere. Something had changed. He felt an odd dizziness and a sense of unreality.

"Julianna?" he whispered. "Are you here?"

No answer. Something stood between them. More than time and space—some barrier that hadn't been there before.

Rising from the bed, he went to the door and looked out. The house was dark and quiet. He stole out of the bedroom, alert to the slightest sound he might hear. Slowly, holding the railing, he made his way downstairs. Halfway down, he had to stop for a moment when an attack of vertigo overtook him. The walls seemed to swim about him. He heard a sound like the rush of water. He sank down on the stairs, waiting for the sensation to pass. A moment later, he regained his equilibrium. The bothersome noise in his head faded away. Only the tick of the clock from the library below disturbed the deep silence around him. Hurrying to the main floor, he moved from room to room, searching. Searching for what? he wondered.

"For Julianna," he reminded himself.

Embers glowed on the kitchen hearth. Brom frowned.

"Odd," he mused. "I don't remember kindling a fire."

By the dim light, he noticed a plate on the table. Lifting the tin cover, he found a single slice of pie.

"Rhubarb," he murmured. "My favorite."

As he ate the pie, he glanced about him. Something was

wrong here. The pump! Had some thief broken in and stolen it? An odd-looking spout stood in its place. This was wrong—all wrong!

A noise from above drew his attention away from the sink. He turned quickly and headed back up the stairs. Suddenly, he felt weary beyond words. What was the use of searching for her? It seemed he had no control over her comings and goings. All he could do was wait and hope for her return. Still, it seemed now that he could feel Julianna's presence more strongly than ever.

The first light of dawn was creeping in through the windows. When he reached the upstairs landing, the eerie sight that greeted his eyes left him shaken and confused. Directly across the hall from his room, where only the wall had been earlier, he saw Julianna. But it was as if she were suspended in some time or place beyond his grasp. She was sleeping in a strange bed in a strange room—a room that was not a part of the Netherwood he knew. He went to the wall that now seemed transparent. With a great sense of relief, he realized that all he had to do was open the door and step over the threshold. In an instant, he would have Julianna in his arms once more.

He smiled to himself, savoring his sense of triumph. Now that she was right there, within his reach, perhaps he'd watch her sleep for a time before he disturbed her. She looked so peaceful, so lovely, with her bright hair fanned out over the pillows.

"Brom?" Julianna turned on her side and murmured his name in her sleep.

"I'm here, dearest heart," he answered.

"Oh, Brom, *please*," she moaned, turning and tossing fitfully. But he could tell she was not responding to his voice, only to her own disturbing dreams.

Wanting to put an immediate end to her distress, Brom reached for the doorknob. He would go to her now, take her into his arms, and kiss away all her fears. But when he reached out to grasp the knob, his hand slammed into the solid wall. He cursed softly and shook his bruised fist.

"What in hell is this?" he growled.

He could see Julianna. He could see the whole room as if there were no partition at all. Yet the wall was as solid and impenetrable as the day it was built, as if the room he could see so plainly were not actually there at all.

"Julianna!" he shouted, striding up and down the hall-way, pounding on the wall. "Julianna, let me in!"

The more he shouted for her, the more agitated she became. Still, she did not awake. Still, he could not go to her.

Giving the wall one final kick for good measure, Brom cursed and gave up the battle. With a sinking heart, he realized that he could never reach Julianna as long as she remained locked away in this strange room—a room that he had not built and consequently was forbidden from entering.

He went back to his own room, storming about in a fury, knocking books off the desk and toppling a chair. His noise alone should have awakened her. Finally, he grabbed her silk gown from the bed and stormed back out into the hall-way. She was still there, still sleeping. He slumped down to the floor, holding her gown close, and vowed he would wait as long as it took. Sooner or later she had to open that door—a door that wasn't there, to a room that didn't exist.

Exhausted, physically and emtionally, he nodded off.


Julianna awoke early. Thunder had disturbed her dreams. The very walls had seemed to shake during the night. But the sun, barely up, was unmarred by storm clouds.

She glanced about, disoriented, until she realized where she was. She yawned and stretched. Her first night in the master suite had been anything but restful. She had slept, but not well. It seemed the whole house had shuddered

149

around her during the night, and she kept dreaming that Brom was calling her name.

Aching all over, she decided a hot bath was what she needed. Going into the bathroom, she lit the gas jets under the pipes to heat the water from the cistern. When the tub was half filled, she eased herself in with a gratified sigh.

When Brom awoke, he felt stiff from sleeping propped up against the wall. Again, slight vertigo clouded his vision for a moment. He shook his head, hoping to snap himself out of it.

His first clear vision was Julianna's coral silk gown in his lap. He caressed the soft fabric with his fingers, then brought it to his lips.

"Ah, dearest heart, where are you?"

A moment later when he looked up, he dropped the gown to the floor, forgotten. His heart sank. The strange room on the other side of the solid but transparent wall lay empty before his horrified eyes. Julianna was gone!

"Blast it all!" he cursed. "She must have left while I was sleeping."

He was still pondering his next move when he caught a slight movement out of the corner of his eye. He expelled a long breath of relief. She was there after all. Another door, he saw now, led out of the bedroom on the far side. Julianna was in there, out of his direct line of vision.

A moment later, she returned to the bedroom, toweling her wet hair. Brom purred his approval. What she'd been doing in that other room, he had no idea. But when she walked back into view, he saw her for the first time in all her naked glory.

Lounging against the wall, Brom smiled as he watched her move about the room. Her proud breasts bobbed slightly as she walked around the bed. Her waist was small, her hips pleasingly rounded. His gaze locked hungrily on the fiery patch of curls at the top of her long, slender legs.

"What a beauty!" he breathed, aching to hold her, to love her.

Julianna walked out of the bathroom, feeling relaxed and refreshed. The cool air after the hot water felt so good, in fact, that she didn't bother to cover herself. She wandered about, brushing her hair dry as she thought about plans for her day. Brom, or thoughts of Brom, had filled so much of her time lately that she felt somewhat at a loss this morning. But she was determined to go on with her life in spite of him. The first thing she would do, she decided, was write a long-overdue letter to Elliot, inviting him back to Netherwood. His last visit had been less than satisfactory.

As she stood, naked, in the middle of the room, Julianna suddenly caught her breath and glanced about. The oddest feeling had come over her, as if someone were staring at her.

Quickly, she dashed back into the bathroom and slipped into her dressing gown. More comfortable now that she was covered, she went to the armoire and took out a becoming morning dress of red-and-green plaid wool, then, scooping up her underthings, she went into the dressing room to get ready for her day.

"Another door," Brom groaned when Julianna disappeared.

Again he pushed against the stubborn wall, but it was no use. Until Julianna decided to open this door and come out into the hallway, there was no way he could reach her. He settled in to wait, scowling at the empty room before him.

Moments later, his patience was rewarded. She reappeared, turning back the white cuffs of her bright frock. She headed straight for him.

Brom positioned himself so that the instant she walked through the door she would come right into his arms. How surprised she would be! He smiled broadly and stroked his beard in anticipation.

Even as he watched Julianna reach for the doorknob, Brom experienced a wave of dizziness. His throat grew so dry suddenly that it ached. If only he could get a drink of water, but there was no time. Vertigo made his head spin. He felt sick and faint.

"Great God," he muttered, "what's happening to me?"

He realized the answer to his question the moment Julianna opened the door. She stared right at him—right *through* him. She was so close he could have seen his own reflection in her green eyes. But there was nothing to see— no image to reflect. He had come to her time, but now he was fading back into his own.

"Julianna," he wailed, reaching out toward her blurred image. "I'm here, dearest heart! Look at me! Listen to me!"

He gripped her arms, but she only shivered slightly, then walked right through him. In the next instant, Julianna and the strange, transparent room vanished before his eyes. Brom found himself standing in the hallway alone, staring at the solid, blank wall across from his bedroom at Netherwood.


"What an odd sensation!" Julianna muttered as she stood outside the door to the master suite. She shivered and rubbed her hands over her arms. "Almost as if someone touched me."

She glanced about, but she was alone in the hallway. Then she noticed the door to Brom's bedroom standing slightly ajar.

152

"I closed that," she murmured. "I'm sure I did."

Going to the door, she glanced inside. Nothing seemed amiss. She reached for the knob and pulled it shut. Only then did she spy the soft mound of coral silk lying in the shadows on the hallway floor.

"How on earth did that get out here? I know I left it in the room."

Unwilling just now to seek answers to unanswerable questions, Julianna hurried down the stairs. She found Maeyken in the kitchen, scowling at a grumpy-looking Zeke.

"I wouldn't mind had you took it, if only you didn't try to fib to me about it," Julianna heard Maeyken say in a scolding tone.

"I tell you, woman, I'm *not* lying. I ain't even partial to rhubarb pie. Apple's my own particular favorite."

"What's going on?" Julianna asked.

"Zeke here ate the last piece of my pie last night and now he won't fess up to what he done."

"I didn't eat her old pie, Miss Juli," Zeke insisted, a deep scowl on his wrinkled face. "And if this woman's going to make me out a liar, I reckon I won't be able to work alongside her no more. You'll have to find yourself another handyman. I'm sorry."

Julianna couldn't believe her ears. Zeke, ready to leave over a missing piece of pie? He couldn't go. She needed him at Netherwood. Besides, he and Maeyken were sweet on each other—any blind man could see that. How could they let a piece of rhubarb pie come between them?

"I ate the pie," Julianna lied. It was the only way she could think of to keep peace under her roof.

"You're sure about that, Miss Juli?" Maeyken asked, not happy at the prospect of having to apologize to Zeke for accusing him unjustly.

"Quite sure, Maeyken."

153

Without another word, the old woman turned back to the ham she was frying for breakfast.

"You'll stay, won't you, Zeke?" Julianna pleaded.

He glanced toward Maeyken's back, then at Julianna. "I reckon I'll stay, ma'am," he said at length. "I like it here most times. And she don't even have to apologize to me."

"I do, too," Maeyken muttered, still hunched over her skillet. "Just give me some time to work up to it."

When the three of them sat down to breakfast, Julianna had to hide her smile as Maeyken apologized to Zeke in the only way she could bring herself to do it. She spooned a huge mound of eggs and the thickest slice of ham onto his plate, along with extra butter for his bread and enough raspberry jam to choke a plow horse.

"Reckon I'll be making an *apple* pie this morning, Miss Juli," Maeyken said, still unwilling to apologize verbally, "seeing as how that's Zeke's particular favorite."

"That would be nice, Maeyken." Suddenly, Julianna was distracted by her own thoughts. If neither Maeyken nor Zeke had eaten the last slice of the rhubarb pie, then who had? Perhaps the same person who had opened Brom's door and left her silk gown in the hallway?

"Miss Juli," Zeke said suddenly, interrupting her troubled thoughts, "I almost forgot. I was down to the village earlier and this letter come for you, all the way from New York City."

"Oh, Zeke, thank you!" Julianna cried, as delighted to be distracted from the disconcerting questions of the pie and the gown as she was to have word from Elliot.

As Juli tore into the envelope, Maeyken said, "I reckon it must be from your Mr. Creighton, eh?"

"Yes," Julianna answered, scanning the page.

"Good!" Maeyken said emphatically. "High time you was hearing from him."

154

Both Maeyken and Zeke leaned close, obviously eager for Julianna to share her news. Finally, Maeyken asked in an impatient tone, "Well? What's new in the city, Miss Juli?"

Ungluing her eyes from the letter, Julianna smiled brightly at Maeyken. "Elliot wants me to take the train to New York tomorrow morning. He says he has reserved a room for me at his hotel, the Metropole. Everyone plans to celebrate after the final performance tomorrow night. He wants to take me to Rector's Champagne and Lobster Palace for supper."

"And you should go, Miss Juli," Maeyken said, nodding vigorously.

"I'll drive you to the train station," Zeke offered.

Julianna looked from one of them to the other, her smile expanding to cover her whole face. "Yes! I am going!" she cried. "I really am this time."

When Julianna went upstairs to start packing, she reread Elliot's letter in the privacy of her room, cherishing each word he had written in his bold scrawl.

One paragraph made her chuckle softly. "Darling," he wrote, "Rector's is *the* place where all theater people go to see and to be seen. I know you'll make a hit there, but won't you do me a favor? I would be *so proud* to make an entrance with you on my arm if you were dressed in that scandalous silk gown you wore the last time I saw you. Wear it for me, won't you? Believe me, no one in New York City will find it shocking."

Julianna blushed with pleasure and a touch of embarrassment. At the same time she felt a flutter of excitement at the thought of appearing in public with so much bosom displayed. Then she sighed resignedly. She hated to disappoint Elliot, but the old amber-colored silk gown was far too fragile to be trusted in public. The seams, the very fabric, could let go at any time.

Then she brightened. Crossing the hall, she slowly opened the door to Brom's room, almost afraid of what she might find, or not find.

"It's still here!" she cried, both astonished and delighted.

Hurrying across the room, she opened the lid of the trunk Brom had somehow sent to her and began sorting through the magnificent costumes. Spying one particularly elegant gown, she held it up and gazed in the mirror.

"Ah, Elliot," she said to her reflection, "I won't disappoint you, my darling."

An angry wind rose out of the clear blue sky, hurling itself at the window. It banged against the wall, breaking the recently restored pane.

Julianna stood frozen, her mouth open, staring at the shattered shards of glass gleaming on the Persian rug. Shaking herself loose from the shock, she hurried out of Brom's room, still clutching the gown. She closed the door firmly, then went back to the master suite to get on with her packing.

"Brom did *not* do that!" she told herself firmly. But the words were easier to say than to believe.

# Chapter Nine

Julianna's train to New York arrived late—too late for her to make Elliot's final performance at the Majestic. But her deep disappointment turned to a sense of awe and excitement as she traveled by hansom cab through the bustling city streets at twilight. The whole place was like a great stage show being put on for her personal benefit. She was in the very midst of the grandest adventure of her lifetime.

"New York!" Julianna exclaimed, craning her neck as she tried to see everything at once. "What a wonder!"

The two-mile strip of Broadway from Madison Avenue to Longacre Square glittered with electric lights—powered by the spidery black web of lines overhead—and the jewels of ladies in the many fancy carriages that paraded up and down the broad avenue. Everyone seemed headed for the various theaters of the district. Julianna grew quite dizzy trying to take in so many sights and so much activity after the peace and quiet of Netherwood.

"The Gay White Way, some calls it," the cabdriver informed Julianna. "I guess you can see for yourself why that is."

Too awestruck to answer, Julianna only nodded.

"About first-dark, they all comes out," her rawboned, top-hatted driver continued, "the big Wall Street movers, the Four Hundred in their fancy duds and diamonds, right alongside gamblers, pugilists, pickpockets, and ladies that don't quite deserve the name."

A clash of cymbals at that moment drew Julianna's attention to a modestly-clad band of men and women on the corner of Broadway and Fortieth Street. A trumpet blared, accompanied by the tinkling rattle of tambourines, as the group wailed out a funeral rendition of "Onward Christian Soldiers."

"Salvation Army," the driver informed her when he noticed her interest. He doffed his hat and gestured toward the band. "They'll be a long time saving all the wicked souls in this city, but I reckon somebody better try before it's too late."

The driver called his weary old horse to a stop at the southwest corner of Broadway and Forty-second Street. "Here we are, ma'am, Hotel Metropole."

A doorman in smart black-and-scarlet livery hurried to help Julianna out of the cab while a bellman took possession of her single black cardboard suitcase. A steady stream of people—some dressed in rags, some in riches—jostled her on the sidewalk as she tried to make her way to the hotel entrance. Before she had even crossed the threshold, she felt as if she'd been through a war.

The tall foreign-looking doorman smiled down at her. "Your first time in New York, miss?"

She straightened her gray felt hat and smoothed the skirt of her good traveling costume. "No," she answered, "but I've never ventured out after dark before."

158

He nodded and pursed his lips. "Wise of you, miss."

Then the doorman was forgotten as Julianna entered the lobby. Even wearing her clothes from Paris, she felt the typical country bumpkin as she stood in one spot, her mouth open, gazing about at the electrified chandeliers, the scarlet plush furniture, the mirrored walls, and the people—people everywhere—talking, laughing, hurrying to and fro.

"May I help you, ma'am?" The desk clerk smiled at her, but he was obviously eager to have her sign the register so that he could get on to other, more impatient guests—guests who had been here before and knew that one did not stand about gawking, but took care of one's business, then moved along.

"Yes," Julianna answered breathlessly. "I believe Mr. Elliot Creighton has reserved a room in my name."

Since Elliot was in the theater, Julianna assumed that the mere mention of his name would bring immediate recognition. However, Elliot's name seemed to mean nothing at all to the clerk.

"Yes, ma'am," the man answered with infinite patience. "But what is *your* name, please?"

"Oh! Oh, yes . . . of course," she stammered, accepting the offered register and pen. "I am Miss Julianna Doran."

After she signed in, the clerk breathed a sigh of relief, then motioned to the bellman. "Welcome to the Hotel Metropole, Miss Doran. Sam will show you to your room."

Julianna was ever so glad to reach the safety and quiet of her own suite. The luxury of the place all but took her breath away. When she had stopped overnight in New York on her way from the farm to Netherwood, she had stayed in a rather shabby little boardinghouse in Greenwich Village. A bed had proved its only luxury, that and an ironstone chamber pot that had prevented her from having to visit the necessary out back during the dead of night. But this suite contained a full bath, closets, a dressing room, and even a cozy sitting room with a window that overlooked the mad bustle of Broadway below.

She had hoped she might arrive in time for Elliot's evening performance, but she hadn't really counted on it. A good thing, she told herself. Her train had arrived late, and she had a feeling that, rather than taking her straight to the hotel, the cabbie had given her a tour about town, including a ride through Central Park. All very interesting, she admitted, but time-consuming as well. At any rate, she was too weary to bathe, dress, and dash to the Majestic Theater in time for the rise of the curtain.

Going to the sitting-room window, she looked down. Broadway was a sea of theatergoers' carriages, snarling the regular traffic. The sidewalks flowed with a steady, undulating river of humanity. She put her wrist to her forehead and turned away. No, she definitely did not want to enter that human race again before she had rested for a bit.

A loud jangling disturbed the silence in the suite. She glanced about, at a loss. The annoying noise—an off-and-on ringing—continued to ravage her nerves. Finally, she spotted the odd wooden box with its black fixtures on the wall beside the door.

"Why, it's a telephone!" she cried, hurrying to answer it.

She had seen pictures of the instrument before, but she had never spoken into one. Gingerly, she lifted the hearing part to her ear and waited.

"Julianna? Are you there?" She smiled. It was Elliot's voice, as clear as if he were standing right here in the room.

"Elliot!" she yelled, trying to make her voice carry all the way to the theater.

"Gently, darlin'. I can hear you fine. Thank God you finally arrived. I've been telephoning the hotel for the past two hours. I was really getting worried. But you sound wonderful. How are you?"

160

"Tired, and disappointed that I won't get to see your play tonight," she admitted, then added, "and a little unnerved just now, too." She stopped at that, deciding not to mention the unpleasant incident with the strange man on the train. "But, actually, I'm simply dazzled by all I've seen and heard since I got here."

He laughed. "You'll get used to the city's frantic pace soon enough, darlin'. Later tonight you will be the one doing the dazzling. I can hardly wait till the gang at Rector's feasts their eyes on you. You *are* going to wear that daring silk gown, aren't you?"

"No." Now it was Julianna's turn to smile. "I've brought something you'll like much better."

He sighed audibly. "Tell me!"

"I want it to be a surprise. You'll have to wait until after your performance to see it."

"I was so hoping you'd get here in time to come to the theater. You could come now. You wouldn't miss much."

"I only just arrived, Elliot," she explained. "I'm done in. I want a bath and then to rest for a while. You understand, don't you?"

"Of course you're worn out, darlin'," he answered sympathetically. "You rest. I want you to be feeling your best later on when we go to Rector's. Oh, Julianna, wait till you see the place! You'll be amazed."

She laughed. "Everything I've seen in New York so far amazes me, Elliot. I've never been this far uptown before or seen the city blazing with electric lights. And this suite! Why, it's fit for royalty."

His voice lowered to an intimate, husky tone. "That's the bridal suite, darlin'. I figured since we have only one night left together before I head out to Chicago, we'd better make the most of it. Besides, I didn't want you to have to stay in my dull, drab room."

"Elliot, you are a sweet man," she murmured. "Thank you."

"Hey, lady, there's something I forgot to tell you before old Zeke hustled me away from Netherwood."

"What?"

"I love you," he whispered. "More than you'll probably ever know."

"Oh, Elliot!" Tears sprang to her eyes and her throat ached with a need to sob. "I love you, too. I wish I could make you understand how much."

"You'll have your chance to convince me, darlin'. Later. Now, I have to ring off. I'm half in, half out of my costume, and it will be curtain time soon. I can't wait to see you," he added in a whisper.

"Am I supposed to tell you to break a leg?" Julianna quizzed playfully.

He laughed. "You'll do fine in this town, sweet lady. Now, I'm off. Meet me in the hotel lobby, won't you? We don't want to be the last ones to arrive at Rector's. Rumor has it that Diamond Jim Brady is coming with Lillian Russell tonight. Their entrance is something you *must* see!"

"Oh, Elliot!" Julianna gasped. "Really? Do you know them?"

"Not well," he admitted.

"But we'll actually get to see them?"

"Better yet, darlin', they'll get to see *you*. Must ring off now, Juli. I'll be over later."

"Yes, later," she murmured, but the telephone had gone dead in her hand.

Julianna was still staring at the amazing instrument, thinking of Elliot, when someone knocked at the door. "Yes?" she called.

No answer.

She waited for a time, thinking she might have imagined the sound. Finally, curiosity forced her to open the door a crack. There on the floor lay a long silver box. A plain white card on top read simply: "Julianna."

"What on earth?" she cried.

Juli glanced up and down the hallway. She saw Sam, her bellman, shuffling down the corridor.

"Did you deliver this?" she called.

He turned and grinned at her. "No, ma'am, Miss Doran. I don't know who did, but it sure looks like an admirer sent you flowers from some fancy florist."

"Flowers, yes," she answered distractedly, trying to think how they got there.

With Sam looking on, Julianna opened the box. Before she even had the lid off, the sweet scent of roses pervaded the hallway.

"They're sure mighty pretty, Miss Doran."

She nodded her agreement, but her attention now centered on something else tucked inside the box. Nestled in among the twelve long-stemmed red beauties, she found another surprise. A black velvet bag with a thin silver drawstring. When she pulled it open, a choker of what looked like diamonds gleamed brilliantly.

"My, my!" Sam exclaimed when he saw her draw the necklace out to examine it more closely. "A person would think your friend was Mr. Diamond Jim Brady himself, Miss Doran."

Realizing by the stern look on her face that he had offended her, Sam bowed quickly, then moved off down the hallway.

Back in the bedroom, Julianna poured the contents of the velvet bag onto the bed—choker, earrings, and a dozen hairpins, all set with the glittering gems. The jewelry would be perfect with the gown she'd brought.

The enclosed card read: "From the one who loves you more than life itself."

Now the tears Julianna had fought to hold back while she

was on the telephone won the battle. She sobbed happily while she cradled the sweet-smelling roses to her face and stared at the sparkling jewelry. The dampness of her tears turned the faux diamonds to iridescent stars.

"Oh, Elliot," she murmured, fingering the necklace. "I couldn't love these—or you—more if they were real and worth millions."

Recovered from her happy hysterics, Julianna found a crystal vase in the sitting room and put her roses in water. She unpacked her few things and hung up her gown, pressing the wrinkles out as best she could with her hands. Still not satisfied, she decided to hang the filmy dress in the bathroom while she took a steaming soak.

As she lay back in the long claw-footed porcelain tub, the weariness seemed to seep out of her bones. She closed her eyes and breathed deeply. The intoxicating perfume of the roses drifted into the bathroom.

"Dear Elliot!" She sighed, smiling. "How foolish of him to spend a fortune on this suite, the roses, the jewelry! Um-m-m, but I do love him for it."

How good it felt to be where she belonged again, with the man she was meant to love and to marry. She drifted off, euphoric with the hot steam and scent of roses enfolding her. How long she slept, she wasn't sure. But when she finally climbed out of the tub, the water had gone tepid, and someone—she assumed, the maid—had been in the room. Her gown was gone from the bathroom door where it had hung. Glancing out to the bedroom, she saw it spread out on the bed, pinched in at the waist as if it already contained her form. Lying above the low neckline was the glittering choker, with the earrings to either side and the hairpins gleaming over all.

Julianna blushed, thinking of the maid slipping in so silently and catching her asleep in the bath.

"Ah well!" She shrugged it off. "All women look much

alike. I'm sure she sees everything I have each time she looks in her mirror." Still, Maeyken, Julianna knew, would never creep into her room without permission.

"But this is New York City," she reminded herself. "A different world."

A glance at the clock told Julianna that she had less time than she'd planned to get ready. She would have to hurry or she'd be late. And she certainly didn't want to disappoint Elliot tonight, making them the last ones to arrive at Rector's because of her tardiness.

She brushed her hair out to let the natural curls dry in place. Sitting down on the bed, she carefully eased on black stockings, then fastened the frilly garters in place. Next came her underthings—long petticoat, lace-trimmed drawers, and ribbed camisole. All black silk. She had found them in the trunk and they obviously went with the gown, which was of the sheerest midnight-blue lace, shot through with silver threads. The delicate fabric looked more cobweb than cloth.

Taking great care, Julianna eased the filmy gown over her head. It slithered down her body, making her shiver. The neckline settled into place, barely touching her bare shoulders and nestling so low on her bosom that a hint of black lace from the strapless camisole peeked out daringly. The long sleeves puffed out extravagantly, ending several inches above her wrists. The bodice fell to a deep point, molding itself over her slim waist, rounded hips, and smooth stomach. From that point, petticoat and cobweb skirt swept out voluminously, forming a train behind. She stepped into silver slippers, and she was dressed—all except for the jewels.

Julianna stood before the vanity mirror and, with great skill and patience, fashioned her bright tresses into draping waves, using the diamond-studded hairpins to hold her elaborate creation on high. She pulled a few curls loose at the nape of her neck and puffed more out around her face.

165

Satisfied with the effect, she reached for the earrings. They soon gleamed at her lobes. Only when she tried to fasten the choker did she encounter any difficulty. The stubborn catch refused to slip into place.

"Oh, bother!" Julianna fumed. "I need help with this or I'm going to be late."

Brom had been sitting on the bed, smiling as he viewed the proceedings from start to finish. He had especially enjoyed the interval during which Julianna, before donning camisole or drawers, slipped on the black silk stockings, slowly and carefully, then fastened the garters in place. He'd all but gone wild when she'd pointed each toe, eyeing her black-clad legs admiringly.

"The wench has fine limbs," he'd assured himself at the time. "There is no denying it."

Brom wasn't quite sure how he had accomplished it, but he had determined to accompany Julianna to New York City from the moment he first sensed her plans. There seemed something magical about the trunk of clothes he had given her. When she wore them, touched them, or even thought about them, he was able to travel back and forth through time at his own whim. Yet this mode of transportation did not prove altogether satisfactory. He seemed to lack a certain substance upon arrival in the year 1899.

Earlier, he had cursed New York City and his own invisible state roundly. He could neither make Julianna see him nor hear him, and people, horses, carriages, everything in this odd, reeking city rolled right over him. *Through him*, actually.

Still, he mused, being invisible did have its advantages. He realized now that when he had been at Netherwood, unable to reach Julianna in the strange room, he had visited her century for the first time. Now, he was back again. He

166

had returned the moment she opened the lid to the trunk in her bedroom to search out a gown.

Since she could neither see nor hear him, it had been a simple enough task to follow along on her journey. Granted, the ride on the hissing, spitting, smoky "train," as she had called the cinder-belching iron monster, had proved a frightening experience to him at first. Most appalling of all had been the gross fellow who took the seat next to Julianna, sitting squarely on Brom. It had taken all his concentration and willpower to squirm and wiggle through the man's portly form.

Brom chuckled, remembering the incident. He had paid the fellow back right enough for sitting on him. Perhaps Julianna could not hear him, but it seemed he was able to enforce his will upon others, making them say whatever he wished. This could only be accomplished through applying full concentration, but so far it had proved well worth the effort. And quite amusing as well, he reminded himself.

The fat, bug-eyed salesman on the train, for instance. At Brom's mental insistence, he had turned to Julianna, shocking himself as much as her, when he blurted out, "You're quite a nice piece, pretty wench. Why don't you and I spend some time together in New York? No one will ever know."

Julianna had smacked the masher soundly with her reticule, calling him an amusing assortment of epithets, whereupon some ancient soul who seemed to be in charge of keeping order on the strange landgoing vessel had commanded his first mate to stop the train at the very next port. There the corpulent lecher was unceremoniously put off far short of his destination.

Brom chuckled. He had felt rather guilty about the incident at first. But, after all, how could he have known that the unsuspecting fellow would actually repeat the very words Brom had whispered in his ear?

167

As for the other things he'd done since arriving in this sinful city, in Brom's opinion, the rude people here deserved whatever they got. This had been a nice little town the last time he'd seen it. Now, just look what they'd done to New Amsterdam! Buildings so tall they threatened to tip over, noisy cars that ran on wires instead of being pulled by horses, chattering foreigners everywhere. He grinned, pulling at his beard. The ladies were nice, though, he had to admit. He glanced toward Julianna.

"One lady in particular," he mused.

"Oh, damn!" Julianna muttered, still trying to fasten the choker.

"Temper, temper, dearest heart," Brom said, knowing that she couldn't hear a word of it, nor had she any idea that he was near. "Mustn't have you talking like a sailor. Allow me to lend assistance."

Fumbling at the catch, Julianna suddenly felt it ease into place. A little shiver ran through her when something tugged at the curls on her neck. She slipped her hand back to the clasp to see if her hair was caught in the stones. No, everything was fine. She took a deep breath, watching her breasts rise proudly inside her daring bodice.

"Well, Juli, my girl," she said to herself, "it seems you're ready for anything."

"Anything?" Brom murmured, kissing his way across her bare shoulder and slipping his hands about her waist to press her back, hard against his hot crotch.

"Oh!" Julianna exclaimed. "I must be hungrier than I thought. "My stomach's pressing in upon me."

A final nibble at her diamond-studded earlobe and Brom released her.

"So, dearest heart," he said, smiling his invisible smile, "where are we going tonight?"

Julianna looked about the room. "Let's see now—purse, hankie, gloves . . . All ready, it seems. To the lobby, then

168

on to Rector's,'' she said to herself, having no idea she was answering Brom's question.

''Ah, Rector's,'' he said, nodding his approval. ''The place up the road with the blazing griffin over the entrance. I believe when I was in that vicinity earlier I heard a fellow outside the establishment mention something about champagne and lobster. Good choice, my pretty wench. Shall we be off?''

Brom offered his arm, but his lady brushed past him. Opening the door of the suite, Julianna slammed it firmly behind her, right in Brom's face. With a loud but inaudible curse, he was forced to walk through it.

The lobby was jammed with fashionably dressed people, lately arrived after the final curtain calls at various theaters in the district. It seemed to Julianna that every woman in New York City must own a trunk of diamonds, pearls, rubies, and sapphires, and that they must be wearing them all at this moment. The glitter under the bright, electrified chandeliers positively hurt her eyes.

Julianna accidentally jostled one overstuffed and bejeweled matron and excused herself politely. The woman offered her an annoyed glance, then turned to her husband and said, ''I'll only be a moment, Alfred. I must go back up to our suite and put on my hat. One mustn't be seen at Rector's during the supper hour without one's hat, you know. Why, bare-headed I might be mistaken for one of *those* women.'' As she said the last two words, she raked Julianna meaningfully with sharply disapproving eyes.

Julianna glanced about. Sure enough, all the women seemed to be wearing hats. Not small felt chapeaus like the one that went with her traveling suit, but huge, wide-brimmed satin creations, adorned with plumes, stuffed birds, elegant gardens of silk flowers, and more diamonds, more pearls, more sapphires and rubies. She had felt practically naked before, with her shoulders bare and bodice cut down to her you-know, never mind. Hatless, she certainly felt underclothed.

"Darlin'!" Hearing Elliot's voice from across the lobby, she turned. When her eyes met his, she felt ever so much better.

Paying no heed to the crowd surrounding them, Elliot swept Julianna into his arms for a long, rapturous kiss. She came up breathless, but smiling and dewy-eyed with pleasure at the sight of him and the taste of him.

Elliot held her at arm's length, measuring her with his appreciative gray eyes. "Darlin', you look magnificent!"

Several older gentlemen nearby, hearing Elliot's praise, turned and nodded their silent agreement.

Julianna laughed nervously. "Elliot, stop it," she whispered. "You're making me blush."

His gaze dropped to her barely-clad bosom and he beamed anew. "Lord, when you blush, you blush all over, don't you, darlin'?"

"I need a hat," she whispered, as if that might solve her whole problem. She repeated to him what she had overheard Alfred's wife state as a firm rule of fashion for supper at Rector's.

Elliot glanced about the lobby, noting the multitude of smartly-chapeaued ladies. "Julianna, if you haven't a hat, you haven't a hat." He shrugged and grinned. "Besides, I don't want you to cover another inch of yourself. Your hair looks wonderful with those jewels twinkling in it like a halo of stars."

She touched her hair gently with one hand and smiled at Elliot. "Thank you, darling," she whispered, meaning for his gift, not his compliment.

\* \* \*

Brom scowled down on the lobby from the landing at the top of the broad stairway.

"Blast the man!" he cursed.

He had discovered to his utter dismay that for some odd reason he could not descend the stairs. It was as if an invisible barrier barred his way. The same had been the case at Netherwood. He'd found, while Elliot Creighton was there, that he was unable to enter any room the man occupied. Since Brom could presently walk through walls, move through carriages and people, he found it highly disconcerting that Creighton's sudden appearance curtailed his activities so drastically.

He eyed the fellow closely, then sneered his disapproval. The actor, dressed all in black except for his white-boiled shirt, looked more as if he were going to a funeral than to a fancy eating establishment. Brom looked down at himself. Maybe no one else could see him, but at least he knew he was dressed properly for the occasion—purple velvet breeches and matching justaucorps with gold braid, scarlet cape, lace at his throat and wrists, silk stockings, yellow boots with golden spurs, and all of it topped off with a plumed purple hat of such enormous proportions that Julianna herself would have been proud to wear it to Rector's.

"What a waste," he said with a sigh, thinking how all of New York was being deprived of the sight of such a fashionable figure.

Brom waited on the landing until he saw Creighton usher Julianna out through the front doors. Then he moved down the stairs, pinching a few plump rumps along the way and whispering the most scandalous tidbits into the ears of select gentlemen, then roaring with silent laughter at the ladies' faces when their husbands passed his suggestive words along.

"Yes, this is going to be a marvelous evening," Brom assured himself.

Elliot Creighton sat back against the seat of the hansom cab, unable to take his eyes off Julianna. Was it possible that she grew more lovely each time he saw her? Or was he simply falling more in love with her as each day passed? She had changed somehow. There seemed a new and intriguing depth to her, a sensual heat he'd never felt from her before. And, too, she seemed so perfectly poised and sure of herself. Perhaps leading her own life the way she wished had performed this wonder. Actually, he mused, it didn't matter how or why Julianna managed to stir him so. All that mattered at the moment was that he felt a love for her so deep and sure and sweet that he never wanted to think of any other woman. Julianna was his whole life now.

"Darling, why are you staring at me with that strange expression?" Julianna asked.

Elliot took her hand and gently kissed the center of her warm-gloved palm. "You simply take my breath away, Julianna. I've never in all my life met another woman like you. And tonight . . . well, tonight, darlin', you are something beyond words. I'm very tempted to order our driver to turn around and go back to the hotel. I really don't know how I'll get through this evening, I want you so this very minute. Suddenly, I can't bear the thought of sharing you with all those others over supper."

"Elliot, you're embarrassing me," she protested in a whisper. But secretly she was delighted by his extravagant praise. "Let's talk about something else. How did the performance go tonight?"

Still devouring her with his storm-dark eyes, he shook his head and answered, "I haven't the vaguest notion. I may have been on stage in person, but my spirit was with you, darlin'. From the moment I heard your voice over the telephone, I could concentrate on nothing else."

"I'm sorry if I ruined your performance," Juli teased with a pout.

"Ha! You're not sorry in the least. I can tell!" Then a boyish smile lit his face as he confessed, slightly embarrassed, "Actually, I must have been adequate tonight, darlin', since several people who came to my dressing room afterward complimented my performance expansively. Even my leading lady went out of her way to tell me that I'd hardly bungled a line all evening. High praise from that witch! I assured her that you deserved all the credit, that each time I had to take her in my arms, I was thinking only of you, Juli darlin'."

Ignoring Julianna's mild protests that someone might see them, Elliot eased his arms around her and covered her lips with his, letting one hand creep up to caress the soft flesh of her bosom.

"I've missed you so much, darlin'," he whispered. "I've kicked myself a thousand times for falling asleep and wasting our time together while I was at Netherwood." He laughed softly. "There will be *no* sleeping tonight. Be warned!"

Julianna snuggled closer into his arms, purring with contentment and a tingling sense of anticipation.

"Would you like me to take a turn through the park before stopping at Rector's, sir?" the cabbie, aware of everything that was going on behind him, suggested.

Julianna, flustered with a mingling of desire and embarrassment, said emphatically, "No!"

"You heard the lady," Elliot answered, resignation in his tone. "Take us straight to Rector's."

The two-story yellow building loomed up on the east side of Broadway between Forty-third and Forty-fourth streets. No sign outside identified it by name, but everyone knew the electrified griffin marked the spot. Carriages jammed the street, making it impossible for their driver to weave his way through the tangle.

"Why don't we get out and walk from here, Elliot?" Julianna suggested.

"Certainly not!" he exclaimed. Then, he explained more gently, "There's only one way to do things at Rector's—the proper way. We'll wait until we can drive right up to the door."

"Whatever you say, darling."

Elliot kissed her bare shoulder, then whispered, "I hope that goes for our entire night together, Julianna. Right now, if I don't kiss you again, I'm going to die on the spot."

Elliot kissed her, all right—a long, deep, tender melding of lips, mouths, and tongues that left Julianna wondering, as Elliot had earlier, how she would ever make it through the supper hour.

She wanted him . . . *now!*

Scowling deeply, Brom stood a few yards away in the very midst of the traffic jam, but as close as he could get to Julianna with Elliot Creighton at her side.

"How dare that actor kiss the woman I love?" he growled.

Brom tried to turn away, but found himself mesmerized by the sight of the embracing lovers. And as he watched, a strange sensation came over him. His blood warmed and his loins throbbed. He could actually feel and taste Julianna's mouth on his own. Creighton might be kissing her, but Brom himself was experiencing that kiss in all its maddening sweetness.

When he saw that Elliot meant to draw away from her, Brom moaned, "Not yet, you bastard . . ."

Their kiss over, Julianna stared at Elliot, her green eyes wide with shock. She was trembling with emotion, fighting

174

for control. Sometime during the kiss, she could have sworn she was tasting not only Elliot's lips, but Brom's as well. She shook her head to clear it, feeling that both men had joined forces just now to give her a single, simultaneous, soul-shattering kiss—one that had set her body burning and her head reeling with a kaleidoscope of fanciful visions of the pair. The sensations left her breathless and trembling deliciously.

"How did you do that?" she murmured, still staring at Elliot as if she could not quite believe what had happened.

"Do what?" he asked with a throaty laugh that sounded to Julianna ever so much like Brom. Elliot reached for her again. "Do this, you mean?"

Once more, Elliot's tongue stole between her parted lips and he moaned into her open mouth while his strong, cool fingers played at her low-cut bodice. As Julianna sighed, trembled, and clung to him, visions of sailing ships, clay pipes, and golden earrings mingled with thoughts of foot-lights, stage makeup, and the waiting bed back at the hotel suite. All the exciting feelings she had ever experienced in her life seemed to converge in an instant to fan her passions to a fever pitch.

"Ah, that's good! *So* good!" Brom groaned as the after-theater crowd thronged about him and through him outside Rector's. He never noticed the crush of the mob. His whole consciousness centered on the unique sensations Elliot Creighton's actions were creating for Brom himself.

"Julianna, dearest heart, you taste of the sweetest ambro-sia," Brom moaned.

He felt too dazed with passion to try to figure out what was happening. Obviously, there existed some extraordinary link between himself and Julianna's modern-day lover. But now was not the time to try to piece together the puzzle. All that mattered at the moment was the mysterious euphoria he was experiencing.

Brom uttered a throaty laugh of pure pleasure when he sensed further passionate intentions on Elliot's part. "You're doing fine, Creighton old fellow. Kiss her again for me, won't you?"

Elliot did just that, bringing enormous pleasure not only to himself but to the phantom Dutchman as well. Still, it was Julianna who experienced the most exquisite delirium of them all. She had no idea what could be happening to her. She knew only that she never wanted the feeling to end.

# *Chapter Ten*

Brom, feeling thoroughly aroused but confused by what had just happened to him, started toward the restaurant. He glanced about, trying to pinpoint his exact location. What was this area like back in his time?

"Certainly nothing like it is today," he muttered. "Forest, a few Indian trails far north of the wall."

He noted the street signs. Here Broadway converged with Seventh Avenue where Forty-third Street crossed the way to form a broad square. Bright signs blinked on hotel façades—the Pabst, the Cadillac. And just down from his destination, "Hammerstein's New York Theater" advertised "BURLESQUE BALLET AND VARIETIES."

Brom hurried on. He walked right through the line—person by person—that was cued up outside Rector's in Longacre Square. Glancing back over his shoulder, he saw that the cab containing Creighton and Julianna was still hopelessly snarled in traffic. They would be a while.

When he reached the sidewalk, Brom checked his pace to pause and stare up for a moment. The illuminated green griffin that marked Rector's entrance reared its head and wings a full story into the air. Below the mythical creature, the peculiar front door caused him another moment's hesitation. Never had he seen anything like it in Julianna's time or his own. Made of clear glass and brass that had been polished until it looked like newly-minted gold, the door was constructed of several panels that revolved round and round, consuming customers outside, carrying them in its coffinlike enclosure, then spitting them forth inside.

He shrugged after a few moments, reminding himself that he had no need to fear the odd conveyance. Then, with ease born of invisibility, he bypassed the revolving door and the headwaiter standing guard over the dining room.

"Well, blow me down!" Brom breathed, turning in a slow circle once he'd walked through the wall and found himself in the foyer of Rector's. "What a grand place!"

Rector's was indeed dazzling—a fabulous blur of gold and green. Smokeless flames in crystal chandeliers made the ankle-deep crimson carpet blaze with a rich fire. Mirrors covered the walls, reflecting the bejeweled customers. And how did they manage to grow those trees all about inside the place? Brom wondered.

After only a moment's hesitation to gape, Brom effortlessly filched a three-pound lobster and a chilled bottle of champagne from the tray of one of the famous establishment's sixty waiters.

Having no need to tip headwaiter Paul Perret or any of owner Charles Rector's eight captains, Brom proceeded to the table of his choice—one high up in the tiers above the main floor. From this vantage point, he could see everything that happened and everyone who entered. Also, the seventy-five upper tables were practically a room apart. Perhaps the Creighton fellow's arrival wouldn't precipitate Brom's immediate departure into nothingness.

Brom settled back in the shadow of a gold curtain, munching greedily on his lobster and washing it down with fine French champagne. He relished the mingled flavors as he licked the juices from his fingers. Should he have oysters or pheasant next? he wondered. Or perhaps another of these tasty crustaceans. He couldn't decide.

A stir on the main floor caught Brom's eye. A hum of excitement, then a sudden silence fell over the club. The band of Hungarian gypsies, who had been strolling among the tables, moved toward the front entrance, turning their violins from the folk music of the Ukranian steppes they had been playing to a lively Broadway show tune. Brom craned his neck to get a better look. A lovely blond woman of admirably stately proportions—her ample bosom a jewel-bedecked prow of pale satin and lace—swept like royalty among the tables, looking neither to her right nor her left.

"It's Lillian Russel!" he heard an excited diner exclaim to her escort. "And there's Diamond Jim with her. Oh, aren't they a showy pair!"

The names meant nothing to Brom, but quite obviously they were the royalty of this day and age. He glanced back down. If the woman had looked like Cleopatra's gorgeous barge under full sail, the huge man following along in her peach satin and golden wake put Brom in mind of an entire glittering armada. Tall, round, heavy of jowl and paunch, the fellow was. Brom saw why he was called Diamond Jim. The man's ponderous physique gleamed with more jewels than his lady wore—diamond shirt studs, cuff links, rings, and pins. He was more bedazzling than the crystal chandeliers inside Rector's or the electrified griffin outside. Brom noted that the arrival of this pair of celebrities seemed to signal the true beginning of the evening's festivities. They took their places at a large table at the very center of the main floor below. Waiters hastened to bow a scrape—minions paying homage to their beloved sovereigns.

"But where is Julianna?" Brom wondered aloud, yet soundlessly.

Julianna could hardly believe her eyes. The fabulous Lillian Russell and Diamond Jim Brady himself! She gripped Elliot's arm.

"Oh, darling, I may swoon with excitement," she whispered, still gaping at the ostentatious pair as she and Elliot awaited their turn to enter Rector's shining revolving door—the first to be installed in New York City.

"I had hoped we'd be seated before they arrived, Juli darlin'. I'm sorry you missed seeing their entrance," he apologized.

"See it?" Julianna cried. "Why, I was part of it, Elliot! Miss Russell's elbow actually brushed my arm as she passed by. This was far better, darling. I never dreamed I'd get this close to either of them."

Two more couples moved into the dining room. The line inched forward.

"There's a true pecking order here and I'm afraid I'm far down on the list," Elliot explained. "Until an actor has become a recognized star, he's simply background scenery at Rector's. I have to warn you not to be too disappointed, darlin'. I'm sure they'll seat us above in the tiers, not at one of the hundred tables on the main floor."

"Elliot dearest, nothing could disappoint me tonight," she assured him, gazing up into his face with her most loving smile. "Not as long as I'm with you."

The line moved again. Suddenly, Julianna found herself miraculously whisked through the revolving door and standing in the entrance of Rector's. Her eyes went wide.

"You'll note," Elliot whispered with a chuckle, "that the decor is all the color of money."

Green and gold dazzled Julianna's eyes as she glanced about. The mirrors on every wall reflected the electrified candeliers and the even more brilliant diners. Graceful potted palms softened the glare of the lights. The main floor was a shimmering rainbow of colors and a symphony of laughter and conversation.

An army of waiters marched over the bright-red carpet as they scurried from table to table, bowing and chatting, bearing huge trays laden with delicacies—French snails, Egyptian quail, African peaches, English pheasant, and the ubiquitous lobster and champagne.

Juli glanced up to the tiers above the main floor. There she spied the inauspicious balcony tables Elliot had mentioned to her earlier. He was right—all the most exciting action seemed to be taking place below. Still, the view would be excellent from up there. It pained her, though, to think that Elliot's feelings would be hurt if he was refused one of the better tables.

"Ahem!"

Julianna looked around. A tall, arrogant-looking man dressed all in black stood directly in their path, glaring down his long, sharp nose at Elliot.

"Your name, sir?" The headwaiter's voice dripped condescension. *Obviously*, the man's tone seemed to say, *if I don't recognize you, you are no one of importance*. Julianna cringed inside and ached for Elliot, sensing his discomfort.

"Mr. Elliot Creighton and party."

"*Party*?" the captain echoed sarcastically, looking around as if searching for the rest of Elliot's guests. "You'll require a table for more than two?"

Elliot cleared his throat nervously. "Well, no, actually. I meant a party of two."

"You have reservations, of course?" The grim reaper

smiled the smile of death. *No reservations, no table*, his haughty expression warned.

"Certainly!" Elliot sounded more forceful now.

*Bravo*! Julianna thought. *Don't be intimidated by this . . . this hirling!*

"A moment, please, while I check my list." The head-waiter dismissed them totally as he went to greet one of Rector's more prominent customers—one who pressed a large bill into the captain's palm.

"This is outrageous!" Elliot said. "Why don't we just leave?"

"Absolutely not!" Julianna answered. "I'm looking forward to our evening, darling."

Actually, she'd had quite enough of the waiter's rude behavior and would have left gladly. For herself, it mattered little. But for Elliot's sake, she made up her mind what she must do. She had watched Miss Russell's entrance with more than casual interest.

"It's now or never," she murmured to herself, screwing up all her courage.

Julianna threw her shoulders back, tilted her head at a jaunty angle, and putting a smile on her lovely face that was sheer ice, she made direct eye contact with the head gypsy musician. A slight nod brought him scurrying.


Brom leaned over the railing, scanning the crowd below. He caught his breath.

There she was!

The jewels in Julianna's hair, at her ears and throat, twinkled like a constellation of stars. Brom smiled. He had made the right choice. Then his smile turned to an angry frown. What on earth was going on? What did that waiter mean, leaving her standing there while he seated someone

182

else? His Julianna deserved the finest table in the house. Immediately!

Brom was about to take matters into his own hands when he realized that Julianna had the situation well under control. Chuckling at her cleverness, he watched her go into action. In seconds, the gypsy musicians had surrounded her, leading the way to a table near the pair of glittering celebrities who had entered moments before.

He laughed. "That's my pretty wench! Give them bloody hell, my beauty!"

Julianna, her heart fluttering in her breast with a mixture of nervousness and excitement, followed the gypsies with their sighing violins. She swept by each table, head held high, eyes straight forward, breasts at a scandalously proud jut, following Miss Russell's splendid example. She brushed past the headwaiter as if he never existed. Out of the corner of her eye, she saw him step back. His jaw fell slack with surprise.

"But who is she, this beauty?" Julianna heard him ask one of the other captains. "I had no idea she was *anyone*."

"A niece of Diamond Jim, I believe" came the answer.

As Julianna approached the table where Miss Russell and Mr. Brady were already feasting on a platter of oysters on the halfshell and boiled crabs, with seven steaming lobsters waiting on the side, she smiled at them. A glittering, show-stopping, never-to-be-forgotten smile.

"Good evening," Julianna said with perfectly regal artic-ulation. "How nice to see you both again."

Diamond Jim, the enormous stone in his pinkie ring catch-ing the light and all but blinding her, stopped in midbite, sparing the lives of dozens of oysters for several moments as he gazed at Julianna appreciatively.

"My dear girl, how fetching you look tonight," Miss Russell said with a gracious smile. She hadn't a notion who the young woman might be, but guessed that her stunning appearance and queenly bearing would take her far.

Immediately, the same captain who had been so rude earlier rushed to show Julianna and Elliot to one of the best tables in the house, a table on the main floor very near the one occupied by Miss Russell and Diamond Jim. The uniformed captain almost fell over his feet hurrying to pull Julianna's chair out and motioning for waiters from all parts of the vast room to hasten their service.

Once they were seated, Elliot, grinning like a boy who'd just won a race, reached over and took Julianna's hand. He beamed at her. "Darlin', I'm not sure how you managed it, but I should have known you could. You've just acquired star status at Rector's."

Pleased by his approving words, she blushed and glanced about, nodding to other diners who smiled back at her. Her heart was still racing.

"I don't know how I managed it, either, Elliot. I'm certainly no star." She held out one hand. "Look at me! I'm trembling like a poplar in a stiff wind." Then she stared right into his eyes and confessed, "But the only place I long for star status is in your heart, my darling."

He leaned down to brush the back of her hand with his lips. "You've had that for a long time and you always will, Juli darlin'."

Further intimate conversation proved impossible as waiters clustered about their table with menus, suggestions, and a chilled bottle of *Möet & Chandon* champagne. "Compliments of Mr. George Kessler," one of the waiters told them, nodding toward a tall, dark-bearded man at a nearby table. "Wine merchant *extraordinaire*," their waiter explained. "The gentleman has just sent this bottle's twin to Miss Russell's table."

184

"We're choppin' in tall cotton now, darlin'!" Elliot sat back in his chair, grinning broadly, enormously pleased with how the evening was going as he sipped from his silver goblet.

Julianna laughed softly at Elliot's quaint southernism that seemed so totally out of place in this setting.

"Well, Juli, would you like a warm bird with your cold bubbly?" he asked. "Or would you prefer lobster?"

"A warm bird?" Julianna asked, twitching her nose from the tickle of the champagne bubbles.

"That's New Yorkese for pheasant under glass," he explained.

From somewhere and nowhere, a familiar voice seemed to whisper in Julianna's ear, "The lobster is excellent."

"Lobster, I believe," she told Elliot.

Brom smiled down from above on his balcony perch. "Good choice!" he said, tearing into his third.

Just then a disturbance broke out on the floor below. A skinny, mousy-haired woman at one of the tables was creating a scene. She rose half out of her chair, her voice pitched at a siren-screech.

"I know I'm right, Ambrose. Now, let go of me. I mean to call the police this instant."

Brom noticed the disturbance immediately and an uneasy feeling crept through his gut. Maybe it was only too much champagne and lobster, but, then again, maybe not. The light-haired, thin-faced woman looked alarmingly familiar, even though her features were now shadowed by the drooping brim of a ridiculous-looking pink satin hat. By the time he realized why she looked familiar, it was too late.

"What's going on behind me?" Julianna leaned forward and asked of Elliot. "Is it a fight?"

"I'm not sure," Elliot whispered back. "But the woman making all the racket certainly seems upset about something.

185

Her husband is trying to get her to sit down and be quiet. How embarrassing for him!''

''She's probably had too much champagne. Tell me what's happening, Elliot. I don't dare turn around to stare even though I'm dying to.''

Elliot sat back, his attention focused beyond Julianna. His smile suddenly vanished, to be replaced by a look of alarm. ''I don't think you'll have to turn around. She seems to be coming this way—right to our table.''

''Call the police!'' the irate woman yelled as she marched on Julianna and Elliot, her hat brim flopping indignantly. ''This woman stole my jewels!''

''Oh, Lord!'' Brom moaned. ''Now I remember her!'' He tried to get downstairs to help Julianna, but the barrier of Elliot's presence below repelled him. All he could do was stand and watch and curse himself roundly for getting Julianna into this mess.

Julianna's hand went to her throat. ''No!'' she gasped.

''Of course she didn't steal your jewels, madam!'' Elliot exclaimed, rising to protect Julianna if need be. ''How dare you accuse her?''

''I most certainly did not,'' Julianna replied, outraged. ''Mr. Creighton gave me these as a gift. Didn't you, darling?''

She glanced up at Elliot, expecting immediate corroboration. He only stared at her, his mouth open and an odd expression of confusion on his face—something between horror and disbelief.

''Well, tell her, Elliot,'' Julianna demanded. ''You had the jewels delivered to the hotel suite earlier this evening in the box of flowers.''

''Flowers? What flowers?'' he asked without thinking.

''You see! I told you! She stole them!'' the hysterical woman cried. ''Give me back my necklace, my earrings, my diamond hairpins.''

186

"They're *real*?" Julianna gasped.

Suddenly, the skinny woman was all over Julianna, ripping at the choker, tearing the pins from her hair. By the time the police arrived, Elliot and the woman's husband had pulled her off Julianna. But the damage was done. Poor Juli looked as if she'd been a party to a first-rate cat fight.

"I'm sorry, ma'am," a round-faced Irish policeman said to Julianna, "but you'll have to come along with us down to the station house."

"This is outrageous!" Elliot fumed. "Miss Doran is no thief!"

Julianna said nothing. Not a whimper, not a tear. She could only stare down through the hair straggling into her eyes at her ruined gown. And all around her lay the ruins of her special evening with Elliot. Nothing could be worse than disappointing him, she thought, not even going to jail for something she didn't do.

"Come along, darlin'," Elliot whispered, taking her arm gently. "We'll straighten this mess out, then go back to the hotel. Everything will be all right. You'll see."

But Julianna did not see. How on earth could she ever make them believe that she hadn't stolen the woman's jewels when she had no idea where they'd come from?

Brom followed along to the station house, calling himself a variety of names, all accursed. He reasoned, though, that it wasn't *all* his fault. He had certainly never asked to be in this invisible state, and therein lay the root of the whole problem.

He had watched Julianna pack for this trip. He'd fully approved of her choice of gowns, but he knew that she would look much more fashionable with a few diamonds sprinkled about. It had been a simple enough matter for him to watch the theatergoers in their open carriages parading

187

along Broadway, choose the jewels he wanted for Julianna, then slip into the theater and divest his victim of her diamonds while she sat snoring in the dark through a rather boring play. A quick stop at the Fifth Avenue Florist had provided him with flowers, box, and velvet bag.

He would steal it all again, Brom assured himself. Julianna's delight at seeing his gifts had warmed his heart to the core. Still, a guilty feeling gnawed at him. But how could it be *his* fault? He reasoned. He'd had no way of knowing that the woman's husband would bring her to Rector's after the show.

Suddenly, a thought struck him. A name he'd seen on a fashionable storefront window as he'd wandered about earlier flashed through his mind: "Charles Lewis Tiffany—Jeweler." He moved on toward the police station, thinking matters through.

What Brom found when he arrived at headquarters appalled him. Julianna's shrill-voiced accuser was in one room with her husband and a constable. She was still shrieking threats and accusations. Down the corridor, Julianna and Creighton were being questioned by two other officers.

Brom's heart ached for her. Julianna looked pale and ill, and tears streaked her cheeks. Her diamonds were gone, her lovely gown ruined, and her bright hair an unruly, tangled mess. Worst of all, her voice had lost all its fire and determination. The unfortunate incident had bruised her spirit and it was all his fault.

"I don't know where the jewels came from," Julianna moaned hopelessly. "How many times must I tell you that? There was a knock at the door of my hotel suite, I looked out, and there in the hall lay the box."

"You saw no one in the hallway?" a mean-faced detective asked brusquely.

Julianna brightened and sat up straighter. "Why, yes! I did see someone. Sam, the bellman who brought my bag to

188

the room. I called after him and asked if he had delivered the flowers." She paused and shook her head, once more disheartened. "But he said he knew nothing about them. He can't be of any help."

"Wrong, Miss Doran," the officer replied. He turned to the other detective in the room and ordered, "Send someone to the Hotel Metropole. Have this Sam brought in for questioning immediately."

While Brom still watched from the hallway, the two officers hurried out, leaving Julianna and the Creighton fellow alone.

"What do we do now?" Brom heard Julianna ask.

"We wait, I suppose," Elliot answered. "There seems little else we can do." He reached out and touched her hand. "Juli darlin', I'm so sorry about all this."

Brom cringed as he saw the actor take Julianna's hand in his and pat it gently but ineffectively. Elliot Creighton might be content to wait and do nothing, but Captain Brom Vanderzee was not. He'd given Mr. Tiffany's elegant shop more thought. Now he hurried out of the station house and headed toward Union Square, intent on his mission.

No one saw Brom or heard him as he walked through the locked door and into a wonderland of precious gems that included a collection of some of the crown jewels of France.

Not above pirating to save the woman he loved, Brom worked quickly, filling the deep pockets of his long-skirted justaucorps with enough sparkling gems to put the whole clientele of Rector's to shame. Burdened down by his fantastic load, he reluctantly left the rest of the treasure and hurried out into the night.

Back at the station house, the detectives were questioning Sam, whom they had awakened from a sound sleep. The poor, bleary-eyed suspect shook his head wearily.

189

"It's just exactly like Miss Doran told you," he whined. "I was passing in the hallway when she opened the door. I saw the roses. I saw the jewelry, too, but not until she opened that velvet bag and took out the necklace. I was working at the hotel all evening. How could I have gone to the theater and stole all that stuff?"

"And how could Miss Doran have done it?" Elliot pointed out to the detectives. "She told you she was in the hotel room the whole time—from the moment Sam took her up there until after the theaters closed and she met me in the lobby. Sam here is a witness to the fact that she was still at the hotel only a short time after the robbery."

Julianna smiled at Elliot and gripped his hand tighter. He noticed the first ray of hope he had seen in her eyes since they'd been hauled away from Rector's.

"I suppose you have a point, Mr. Creighton. Still . . . Are you *sure* you didn't leave the hotel at all, Miss Doran?" one of the detectives asked suspiciously.

"Of course I'm sure!" Juli cried. "Where would I have gone? I was alone. I don't know my way about this part of the city."

"I just wish we had a witness to your whereabouts the whole time," the officer persisted. "That would put an end to it."

No one heard Brom proclaim, "She was never out of my sight for a moment, you bastards!"

Julianna sighed deeply and shook her head. "I'm afraid I didn't see anyone other than Sam."

"She's lying," the woman who had been robbed screamed hysterically. "Why don't you just lock her up? She wasn't even wearing a hat at Rector's. I suppose that tells us all what sort of woman she is."

Julianna blushed to the roots of her bright, tousled hair.

For once the unpleasant detective who had been grilling her for hours came to her defense. He turned to the mousy-haired woman with a weary expression on his face. "Ma'am, I'm sorry, but we don't put ladies in jail in this city for going bare-headed."

Suddenly, an alarm went off somewhere in the building. Uniformed men scurried to and fro, calling out to each other excitedly.

"What's going on?" the detective yelled to a passing sergeant.

"All hell's broke loose, sir. Tiffany's has been robbed. It looks like an inside job—no break-in."

Brom smiled. "Don't worry, Julianna. I'll have you out of this mess in no time at all."

The invisible Dutchman moved into the empty room where Julianna's accuser had spent most of the evening. The woman's beaded reticule lay unattended on the chair where she'd been sitting moments before. Digging deep into his pockets, Brom fetched out a diamond-and-sapphire necklace that had once been worn by the mistress of a French king. He slipped that, along with several rings and other expensive baubles, into the woman's bag.

Not yet satisfied, Brom prowled the station house, bestowing other gifts on the underpaid and unsuspecting men in uniform.

"Ah, 'tis charity straight from my heart," he mused as his pockets emptied.

"Sir," one of the policemen called to Julianna's grim-faced detective, "Mr. Tiffany himself will be here soon with a list of the missing items."

Just then, the angry jeweler burst through the doors. "I want action on this robbery immediately. Otherwise, I'll have your badges!"

Julianna and Elliot, forgotten now, sat watching events unfold around them.

The woman from Rector's was every bit as passionate over her loss as Mr. Tiffany was over his. "Never mind *his* problem!'' she cried. ''I was robbed first. What are you going to do about this woman who stole my diamonds?''

''Ma'am, since your property has been recovered, I suggest you go on home and forget the whole thing.'' The detective wanted the hysterical creature out of his station house now that they had more pressing business. ''Miss Doran is no thief,'' he added with finality.

Julianna hugged Elliot's neck. ''Thank God he believes me at last!''

''I'm not leaving until justice is done!'' the woman screamed, grabbing up her purse in a fury. When she did, diamonds, sapphires, and rubies flew in all directions.

''The royal necklace!'' Charles Tiffany gasped. ''Arrest this person at once, Officer!''

''*Me*?'' squealed the woman. ''I don't know how that got in my bag!''

His nerves as raw as scraped flesh, the detective reached in his pocket for his pipe. When he did, several enormous diamond rings came out of hiding and skittered across the floor.

''Good God!'' Tiffany cried. ''The police are in on the job!''

Brom was laughing so hard he had to prop himself against the cell bars to stand up. ''Oh, glory,'' he moaned, holding his sides. ''I may die from this!''

The station house was bedlam suddenly. Charles Lewis Tiffany stormed about, threatening to call in everyone from the governor of New York to the President of the United States. Lowly policemen were grinning like boys as they pulled hidden treasures from their pockets. The woman from Rector's continued to scream at anyone and everyone.

''I believe this is our cue to leave, darlin','' Elliot said, taking Julianna's arm.

They made their way through the riot in progress. No one even noticed when they left the station house. No one but

192

# MORE PASSION AND ADVENTURE AWAIT... YOUR TRIP TO A BIG ADVENTUROUS WORLD BEGINS WHEN YOU ACCEPT YOUR FIRST 4 NOVELS ABSOLUTELY *FREE*
## (AN $18.00 VALUE)

Accept your Free gift and start to experience more of the passion and adventure you like in a historical romance novel. Each Zebra novel is filled with proud men, spirited women and tempestuous love that you'll remember long after you turn the last page.

Zebra Historical Romances are the finest novels of their kind. They are written by authors who really know how to weave tales of romance and adventure in the historical settings you love. You'll feel like you've actually gone back in time with the thrilling stories that each Zebra novel offers.

## GET YOUR FREE GIFT WITH THE START OF YOUR HOME SUBSCRIPTION

Our readers tell us that these books sell out very fast in book stores and often they miss the newest titles. So Zebra has made arrangements for you to receive the four newest novels published each month.

You'll be guaranteed that you'll never miss a title, and home delivery is so convenient. And to show you just how easy it is to get Zebra Historical Romances, we'll send you your first 4 books absolutely FREE! Our gift to you just for trying our home subscription service.

## BIG SAVINGS AND FREE HOME DELIVERY

Each month, you'll receive the four newest titles as soon as they are published. You'll probably receive them even before the bookstores do. What's more, you may preview these exciting novels free for 10 days. If you like them as much as we think you will, just pay the low preferred subscriber's price of just $3.75 each. *You'll save $3.00 each month off the publisher's price.* AND, your savings are even greater because there are never any shipping, handling or other hidden charges—FREE Home Delivery. Of course you can return any shipment within 10 days for full credit, no questions asked. There is no minimum number of books you must buy.

# 4

## TO GET YOUR 4 FREE BOOKS WORTH $18.00 — MAIL IN THE FREE BOOK CERTIFICATE T O D A Y

Fill in the Free Book Certificate below, and we'll send your FREE BOOKS to you as soon as we receive it.

If the certificate is missing below, write to: Zebra Home Subscription Service, Inc., P.O. Box 5214, 120 Brighton Road, Clifton, New Jersey 07015-5214.

---

# FREE BOOK CERTIFICATE

## 4 FREE BOOKS

### ZEBRA HOME SUBSCRIPTION SERVICE, INC.

**YES!** Please start my subscription to Zebra Historical Romances and send me my first 4 books absolutely FREE. I understand that each month I may preview four new Zebra Historical Romances free for 10 days. If I'm not satisfied with them, I may return the four books within 10 days and owe nothing. Otherwise, I will pay the low preferred subscriber's price of just $3.75 each; a total of $15.00, *a savings off the publisher's price of $3.00*. I may return any shipment and I may cancel this subscription at any time. There is no obligation to buy any shipment and there are no shipping, handling or other hidden charges. Regardless of what I decide, the four free books are mine to keep.

NAME

ADDRESS _____ APT _____

CITY _____ STATE _____ ZIP _____

( )
TELEPHONE

SIGNATURE _____ (if under 18, parent or guardian must sign)

Terms, offer and prices subject to change without notice. Subscription subject to acceptance by Zebra Books. Zebra Books reserves the right to reject any order or cancel any subscription.

GET
FOUR
FREE
BOOKS
(AN $18.00 VALUE)

Brom, that is. He decided to stay on and see the end of this madness he had started. Besides, he had a strong inkling what would transpire once Creighton got Julianna back to the hotel. Since there seemed nothing he could do to stop it, he'd just as soon not be a witness to it.

His bright spirits faded. Obviously, he'd made a mistake following Julianna to her own time. What he needed to figure out now—before it was too late—was how to return to his century, how to get Julianna to come with him, and how to convince her to stay.

Dawn was still a couple of hours away as Julianna and Elliot strolled back toward the hotel.

"Are you sure you don't want me to hire a cab, darlin'?" he asked solicitously.

Julianna clung to his arm as they strolled in the cool dampness of the night. "No, I need to clear my head. What an experience!"

He stopped on the dark street and pulled her into his arms, kissing her deeply. "I'm so sorry, darlin'. I wouldn't have put you through this for anything."

"It's not your fault, Elliot," she whispered. "I don't suppose we'll ever know what really happened." Julianna didn't want to admit it to Elliot, but already she had guessed that an uninvited companion had accompanied her to the city. She wondered where he might be at this very moment.

"Let's try to forget the past few hours," Elliot suggested, "and enjoy what's left of the night. We have so little time before I have to leave for Chicago."

Even at this late hour, carriages clogged the streets. Many people, still dressed in their fancy theater clothes, brushed past Julianna and Elliot as they embraced on the sidewalk.

"Don't New Yorkers ever sleep?" Julianna asked.

Elliot laughed. "It would seem not. At least not the patrons of the Gay White Way. These are many of the same people who ate at Rector's tonight. Others have supped at Delmonico's or Shanley's or Café de la Opéra. Now they're all headed to Jack's on Sixth Avenue for breakfast.'' He paused and turned to her. ''Would you like to go there for some scrambled eggs and Irish bacon, darlin'? You never even got your lobster.''

Julianna laughed softly. ''I couldn't eat a bite right now. Let's go back to the hotel.''

Elliot grinned at her and kissed her cheek. ''Yes, let's!'' he agreed wholeheartedly.

Julianna was glad the lobby of the Metropole was empty when they returned. She'd had to endure the curious stares of the doorman and the night clerk, but at least there were no fine-feathered ladies to lift their bulbous noses at her scandalous appearance. They hurried up the stairs, holding hands and giggling like two children sneaking in after curfew.

''A bath!'' Julianna gasped the moment they closed the door on the rest of the world. ''That's what I need most right now.''

''Me, too?'' Elliot grinned at her hopefully.

''No!'' Julianna answered firmly. ''You're starving, I'm sure. Why don't you see what you can do about getting us something from the kitchen? I promise not to fall asleep in the bathtub while you're gone, and not to accept any gifts left at the door.''

A bit crestfallen at being sent from the room, Elliot turned to go.

''Darling?'' Julianna called. ''Can you help me?''

He was back by her side in an instant. ''Anything! You have only to ask.''

''My hair is all snarled in the buttons. Can you undo my gown?''

Julianna trembled slightly as his fingers touched her neck,

easing the tangled hair out of the way. He leaned down and kissed the tender spot he'd uncovered.

"Hm-m-m," Julianna sighed. "That feels wonderful, but I think the buttons will be easier to manage if you use your hands, darling."

"Right!" he answered, all business now, at least until he had her gown undone to the waist.

Juli shuddered with pleasure when Elliot slipped his hands inside her bodice and around her body, cupping her breasts through the thin silk of her camisole.

"Oh, my darling, it's been so long," she sighed.

Julianna could tell he needed no further encouragement. An instant later, she felt the cool silk slither down the length of her body as Elliot slipped the gown off her shoulders, then shoved it and her petticoat to the floor. Blushing, Juli stood before her lover, dressed only in black silk camisole and short drawers. She knew by the smoldering look in his steel-gray eyes that the sight of her limbs enticingly encased in sheer black stockings had an immediate and powerful impact on him.

"Suddenly, I don't think I need anything from the kitchen, darlin'. I have everything I crave right here."

Juli went willingly when Elliot took her hand and led her to the bed. He motioned for her to sit. She caught her breath when she saw what he meant to do. Kneeling before her, he eased the silver slippers from her feet, massaging her toes gently as he did.

"That feels *so good*" Julianna moaned, closing her eyes.

Slippers aside, Elliot slid his hands up her right leg, forcing his fingers under one of the tight garters. Off came one and then the other.

"My bath?" Julianna asked softly.

He leaned forward and kissed her silk-clad knee. "Later," he murmured.

Julianna stared down at Elliot's face, intent as he made a

production of removing her stockings and slipping the thin silk ever so slowly down her calf. By the time his hands touched her bare legs, she was trembling all over and burning deep inside. But still he toyed with her—kissing her toes, her ankles, the backs of her knees.

"You'll drive me mad," she warned, digging her fingers into his shock of thick brown hair. "Do you know how long it's been, darling?"

"Exactly, to the minute," he answered between light, wet kisses along her right calf. "And if I'm driving you mad, you've already driven me over the brink. Only one night we spent together, and then you left me. What way is that to treat the man you say you love?"

"I don't only say it, Elliot, I mean it with all my heart and soul." She bent down, brushing his brow with her lips. His skin felt almost fevered to the touch.

When she leaned forward, Elliot gripped the strapless camisole and stripped it away. The electric lights were still burning in the room. Julianna felt odd, sitting there with Elliot's gaze focused on her bare breasts while the lights blazed around them. A smile of embarrassment quivered on her lips, but she made no move to cover herself.

"God, you're beautiful," he moaned. "Almost too beautiful to be real." As if trying to convince himself that she really existed, he reached out to tease her erect nipples with his fingertips.

"No more!" Julianna cried, throwing her arms around Elliot's neck and pressing his face to her breasts. "Love me, my darling! Oh, please!"

Even as his tongue sought and found her aching nipple, she pushed him away. A few frenzied seconds of shedding clothes and they fell into each other's arms. Too impatient to endure more of his fondling, Julianna positioned herself to receive his first thrust. When he sank deep down into her, she cried out, the pleasure came so quickly.

* * *

Brom, still at the police station, couldn't figure out what was happening to him. At first, the dizziness had made him think he was fading back to his own time. But the sensations were too sharp, too sweet for that. Something far different was going on, something similar to what he had experienced earlier in the evening as he'd watched the Creighton fellow kissing Julianna. It seemed as if he were sharing some wonderfully erotic episode and somehow Julianna was a part of it.

While he remained, out of the way and invisible, watching the continued mayhem at the police station, he suddenly experienced a languorous sensation spreading through his limbs. The heaviness was anything but unpleasant. His body tingled and throbbed. Surreptitiously, he put a hand to his crotch. All *seemed* normal enough in that vicinity.

"So how can I be feeling what I'm feeling?" he groaned.

Giving up the fight, he leaned heavily against the wall and let it happen. He could feel blood pumping through his veins at a furious, excited rate. The euphoric sensation kept building and building, driving him ever closer to the very peak of ecstasy. His hands knotted into tight fists at his sides. His brow beaded with sweat. His toes curled inside his yellow boots. Every muscle in his body strained to make it happen.

"Oh, my God!" he cried out, experiencing sweet release at last.

After a time, he slumped exhausted but satiated into an empty chair. He opened his eyes and stared down at himself in wonder. Once before, some time ago, he had experienced this same sort of magnificent, soul-rending wonderment.

"I didn't understand it then," he murmured, "and I don't understand it now. But, God, that felt like the earth moved!"

197

* * *

Julianna had never known such a night. Over and over again, Elliot brought her to the heights while guarding his own passion closely. They used the whole suite—the bed, the couch in the sitting room, the floor of the dressing room, and finally the tub.

The steaming water sloshing about their joined bodies finally proved Elliot's undoing. Gripping Julianna's trembling flesh to his, he uttered a mighty moan of release as he allowed it to happen at last.

Julianna could only cling to him, shuddering as his body heaved against hers. Never had she thought she would know such ecstasy. And never would she would let this sweet man out of her life, she vowed.

Spent at last, Elliot moaned, "God, that felt like the earth moved!"

Julianna, smiling, kissed him, then sank deeply into the waves in the tub, clinging tightly to her lover and purring with pleasure.

# Chapter Eleven

Julianna awoke the next morning smiling. By rights, she should have been exhausted, but instead she felt wonderful and renewed and exhilarated. She glanced over at Elliot, lying next to her. He was sleeping on his back. The cover had slipped down about his strong thighs. She blushed, looked away, and pulled the sheet a bit higher.

"Um-m-m," he sighed as his eyes blinked open. "Morning already?" He combed his fingers through his thick, rumpled hair, then turned toward Julianna and kissed her breast. "Lord, last night was fine!" he rasped in a husky whisper.

Julianna snuggled close, more than ready for Elliot to take her in his arms once more. She had a surprise for him this morning. First, they would make love. Then she would tell him. She had been awake for almost an hour, mulling things through, making her momentous decision. When he asked her again to marry him, her answer would be a resounding *yes*. Not weeks or months or years from now, but this very day. They could honeymoon on the train trip to Chicago.

She purred with pleasure as Elliot's hand slid beneath the covers to stroke her thighs. Aroused anew, she leaned closer and kissed him deeply, letting her tongue tease his and pressing her breasts hard against his bare chest.

"Oh, Elliot darling, last night was so marvelous! I never wanted it to end."

Her words, as she had anticipated, offered an invitation to her lover. Elliot turned to her, drawing her into his arms. His pulsing heat told her that he was as ready as she to begin their loving all over again. He clasped her close—heart-to-heart—and kissed her long and wetly. Julianna could have held that kiss all day. But Elliot brought it to an abrupt close.

"Darling?" she murmured, disappointed.

"Damn, I wish we had more time!"

Then, to her utter disappointment, Elliot rolled away from her with a sigh and stood up. Her fascinated gaze lingered of that part of him that was most awake and alive at the moment.

He turned back to Julianna, seemingly oblivious to his own aroused nakedness and his lover's appreciative stare. "Last night was more than marvelous, Juli darlin'. I only wish you'd come to New York weeks ago. We'd have had so much more time to enjoy each other's company. And, damn, I didn't mean to sleep this late!"

Julianna's heart sank while the ache of need deep within her only intensified.

Reaching for his gold pocket watch on the bedside table, Elliot flipped it open and shook his head. "I was afraid of that. Almost nine o'clock. If I don't hurry, I'll miss the train. I'm sorry, darlin'." He turned an apologetic look on Julianna and shrugged. "I hate to love and run, but . . ."

Panic flashed through Julianna. He was going to leave again. He really was! She had to do something. Quickly!

Sitting up in bed, she blurted out, "Elliot, I want to marry you!"

His head jerked toward her and his mouth dropped open. Then a smile flashed over his face, making his gray eyes dance with silver lights. "I want to marry you, too, Juli darlin'. You know that. I've certainly told you often enough."

"Well?" she demanded.

"Well, what, darlin'?" He chuckled, hardly able to believe what he had just heard. This was, indeed, his lucky day! "Do you actually mean you're finally ready to set a date?"

"Yes!" Julianna nodded vigorously. "Right now!"

Elliot tilted his head back and closed his eyes, savoring the moment. Then he frowned when he remembered the hectic schedule facing him. "Hm-m-m let's see. How about six months from today?"

Julianna felt her whole body sag with her spirits. *Six months!* That seemed an eternity.

"April the twenty-sixth, 1900. Think of it, darlin', a spring wedding. We'll begin our new lives in a new season of a new century. Sounds perfect to me. How about it, Juli?"

"But, Elliot . . ." she began in a whisper.

Caught up in his own thoughts, he never heard her, but rushed ahead with his imagined plans. "The tour out West will be over by then. You'll have time to make proper wedding preparations. We can think over where we want to live." His slate-gray eyes danced with enthusiasm. "But, consider yourself warned, wife-to-be, that when I'm on the road I want you with me. No more empty beds. No more cold, lonely nights. I mean for us to love our way across the country and back. Understood?"

Julianna, too close to tears for words, only nodded.

He leaned down and cupped her flushed cheek in one hand, kissing her parted lips ever so tenderly. "The next time we're in New York together, you will be Mrs. Elliot Creighton and I will be the proudest son-of-a-gun on earth. We'll go to Rector's to celebrate and, I promise you, darlin', that pompous headwaiter will give us the best table on the main floor. Because in the next few months, I plan to act the hell out of this new play so I can make a fortune and buy you your own diamonds. By the time I get back to this city, *everyone* will know my name and that you are my wife!"

As difficult as it was to do, Julianna kept silent. Her plan had been madness, she realized. Of course they should wait and give themselves time to do things properly. Elliot must never know how disappointed she was. After last night, she realized that she loved him far too much to take anything away from him, ever. He was the dearest man on earth and she wanted everything for him—the moon and stars, the whole universe. And, especially, his name in lights on the Gay White Way.

"I'm glad you don't want to do anything impulsive like running to a preacher this very day, Elliot," she murmured, trying to sound convincing.

"I'll admit that thought had crossed my mind," he confessed. "But it wouldn't be fair to you, Juli darlin'. I know what a great store women set by weddings, and I want you to have the best. I want to be the best husband for you, too. This tour out West will enhance my career tremendously. There's a writer I know who's hinted that if all goes well on this tour, he might write a play just for me. Imagine that! Top billing in my own production. Can you believe it, darlin'?"

"Yes," she answered quietly but emphatically. Her gaze met his and held, lovingly. "You've told me how important your career is to you, how hard you've worked to get this far.'' She gave him a positive smile. "Oh, Elliot, I know you'll go all the way!"

"But, Julianna . . ."

She watched his handsome face go solemn.

"Julianna dearest heart," he continued, "there won't be a minute while we're apart that you'll be out of my thoughts. I do love you so!"

She nodded silently, fighting back her emotions. Finally, she felt she could trust herself to speak. "When you return, my darling, I'll expect you to come bearing a suitable ring." She forced a gay laugh and reached out to stroke his bare thigh. "You bring the wedding band and I'll bring the parson. Deal?"

"Deal," he agreed, taking her hand from his thigh to place a kiss in the palm.

She extended her other hand to him. He took it in his and shook it firmly, then pulled her off the bed and into his arms. Their naked bodies clinging, he kissed the hand he'd just shook, kissed her wrist, her arm, her shoulder and neck. Finally, he captured her lips and kissed her so fiercely, so tenderly, that she could barely fight back her tears. If only they had more time.

Less than an hour later, they replayed the scene back at the farm in Pennsylvania. The farewell kiss, the scalding tears, the soul-shattering parting.

"You'd better go now, darling," Julianna whispered, pulling away from him reluctantly. "The rest of the troupe will be waiting for you."

Julianna fought a valiant battle not to beg him to stay. He kissed her a last good-bye and left. Such an emptiness closed in on her heart then that she found she was beyond weeping. Turning, dry-eyed, she packed her things quickly. Then, glancing about the luxurious suite one final time, she sighed and said, "So, he's really gone, and it's back to Netherwood with you, my girl."

203

She didn't hear Brom's silent exclamation in the room after Elliot's departure. "Thank God!"

Julianna's traveling companion had learned to behave himself properly after his near-disastrous experience of the night before. So the trip back to Tarrytown proved uneventful for Julianna. Besides, Brom was too relieved to have the actor gone and too anxious to get Julianna out of that wicked city and back to Netherwood where they both belonged to create any scenes on the way home.

Zeke was waiting in the wagon when the train arrived at the Tarrytown station. The old man helped Julianna up, then stowed her bag under the seat.

Brom climbed in and perched on the very back, ready to leap out the minute he saw his home. He had his plans all made. Certainly, he had lost ground with Julianna while she was in New York. Elliot Creighton's presence always proved distracting to her and maddening to Brom. But amazingly enough, the actor had left her again. Brom could barely believe his good fortune. With Creighton out of the picture, he would have plenty of time to remind Julianna how much they meant to each other. In fact, he'd made up his mind to use all his powers of persuasion to get her to return with him to that earlier, more peaceful time where he knew they both belonged—where they could marry and live together happily forevermore.

As Zeke touched up the horse, the wagon jerked into motion down the road. Brom abandoned his own pleasant thoughts to listen to what Julianna had to say about the trip.

"Everything go all right, Miss Juli?" the old man asked.

"Fine, Zeke. Wonderful, in fact."

"Me and Maeyken thought maybe you might be bringing that actor feller back home with you."

Julianna laughed softly. "I think he wanted to come."

"Well, then?" Zeke queried with one eyebrow arched like a tired question mark.

"He has his career to think of. I couldn't allow him to abandon his goals." Juli answered him nobly, even if she was only half convinced by her own words.

"Damn proper thinking, if you ask me," Brom put in. But, of course, no one had asked him, nor did they hear his opinion on the matter.

"I thought you were right took with Mr. Creighton," Zeke ventured.

Julianna nodded. "I am, Zeke, that's why it wouldn't have worked for him to come back here with me. Not yet. Not until he's sure that he wants me to love him even more than he wants the adoration of all those audiences all over the country. I'm not a person to take a backseat."

"Speak for yourself," Brom grumbled, angered by Julianna's profession of love for that actor. He decided he might be better off not eavesdropping on the conversation up front, but there was little he could do to avoid it.

"Well," Zeke went on, "seems to me like your Mr. Creighton's got all the signs of a lovesick pup. I reckon he'll come skidaddling back here first chance he gets." The old man gave Julianna an appreciative, sideways grin. "Can't say as I blame him none, neither, Miss Juli. You're a right fine-looking woman."

Julianna patted Zeke's arm and laughed. "He'd *better* come back! If I weren't absolutely certain of his return, I'd never have let him go."

Dejectedly, Brom stared down at his long dangling legs, and his boots that barely missed the dirt of the road. Julianna's words hurt. Had she forgotten him completely? He wished suddenly that he were somewhere else, that he didn't have to listen to her talking about her actor in such glowing terms. Easing forward, he let his heels drag along the rutted surface of the road, then uttered a dispairing sigh. Although

205

he could see and feel his feet touching earth, his heels left no marks in the dust. It was as if Captain Brom Vanderzee simply didn't exist in this day and time.

"Maybe I don't," he grumbled. "What a sorry state of affairs!"

In that moment, Brom knew he must go back. Coming to Julianna's time had been a miserable mistake. If he was to have her for his own, she must come to him in his time of her own free will. Too many obstacles stood in his way in this strange and distant century. He had sensed a sharp need to return the whole while he was in New York. But he couldn't leave Julianna in that dreadful city alone. Now, however, they were nearing Netherwood once more. She would be home and safe. She wouldn't need him, if she ever had.

He turned to glance longingly toward Julianna one last time. The late-afternoon sun gleamed down on her long hair, crowning her with a shimmering, fiery halo. Her lovely face, silhouetted against the evergreen of the forest, looked proud and calm and glowing with a new self-assurance. Brom's heart swelled with love as he stared at her. He could no longer contain his rampant emotions or his desperate need for Julianna.

"What a woman!" he shouted to the world, flinging his arms wide. "And, mark my words," he added in a quieter tone, "she *will* be mine!"

The next moment, he closed his eyes and allowed the vertigo he'd been fighting to have its way with him. For a moment, the whole world seemed to whirl inside his head. When the dizziness passed, Brom found himself alone, back in his cabin aboard *Bachelor's Delight*.

Julianna gasped softly and turned to Zeke. "Did you feel that?" she demanded.

"What, Miss Juli?"

She shivered slightly and turned around to stare at the road behind them. "I'm . . . I'm not sure. It was just a sensation, a stirring in the air like something flew past us. But I didn't see anything." She looked down and rubbed her arms frantically. "Look! I'm all goose bumps."

Zeke touched up the horse, urging it to more speed. "I ain't felt nothing," he answered. "But if there's things zooming around in these woods, I'm getting us home *fast*."

"I'm sorry, Zeke. I didn't mean to frighten you. It was only an evening breeze most likely."

Zeke made a sound of denial deep in his throat. "I wouldn't count on it, Miss Juli. You should hear some of the tales Maeyken tells of things that's happened in these darksome woods. It'd make a body's hair stand on end and his eyeballs bug out. I don't hold with being out in these parts once the sun goes down." He gave the horse's rump another tap of the whip. "Giddap, Queenie!"

Julianna tried to calm Zeke and—she was forced to admit—calm herself. She kept a steady stream of conversation going as they drew ever closer to Netherwood. But her attempts to brighten their spirits failed miserably. She couldn't imagine why she felt suddenly so alone. *Empty*, that was a better word for it.

"Has everything been running smoothly at Netherwood while I was away?" she asked.

Zeke looked at her as if she'd lost her senses. "You just left yesterday morning, Miss Juli. Me and Maeyken ain't hardly had time to make no mischief while you was gone."

Julianna sighed. "It seems like I've been away much longer. I have to admit, I'll be glad to get home."

Chuckling, Zeke replied, "That New York's some killer of a city, ain't she?"

"Oh, Zeke, it's more than I can put into words," she

answered breathlessly. "It's gay and frigtening and puzzling and dazzling. My head is still bursting with all I saw and heard. It was almost too much to take in all at one time. I think a person must have to ease into New York to feel really comfortable there."

Zeke relaxed visibly as Netherwood loomed into sight up ahead. "Hell, I've eased in and out of that city off and on ever since I was a tad, and I'm here to tell you I won't never get used to it. All them fancy-dan folks and speeding wagons and cutthroat gangs. Why, a body could get kilt in that place!"

"Or wind up in jail," Julianna murmured under her breath.

They both grew quiet as the wagon started up the long drive. The front door opened and Maeyken came bustling out to greet them.

"Well, I say, it's about time!" the old woman called. "I got supper waiting for you two. Come on in and set yourselves right down."

"Maeyken, it's good to see you," Julianna called back, feeling a rush of relief and pleasure at being home again.

Supper passed quickly. There was so much Julianna had to tell Maeyken and Zeke. She thought they would be amused by her tale of the stolen jewels, her arrest and release, and the robbery at Tiffany's. But not a chuckle came from either of them, although Julianna did notice the guarded glances they exchanged.

She saved the best for last. Just before Julianna started up to bed, she said, "Maeyken, it looks like we'd better start getting things ready for a wedding."

"Whose?" the old woman demanded with a gleam of delight in her eyes.

"Mr. Creighton will be away for six months. When he returns, I'm going to marry him faster than you can blink an eye."

"Well, mercy me!" Maeyken cried. "If that ain't the best news I've heard in a while." She hugged her mistress. "That Mr. Creighton seems like a right fine man, Miss Juli. You two will make wonderful children—flame-haired, black-eyed beauties."

Julianna frowned, trying to think why Maeyken's words sounded like an echo. Then she looked at the other woman oddly. "Elliot doesn't have black eyes, Maeyken. They're gray."

"Are they now?" Maeyken replied, avoiding Julianna's direct gaze. Then the old woman turned, heading at a near-trot for the kitchen.


As tired as she was, Julianna spent hours tossing fitfully in the bed. The night was still and cool, with a definite hint of the approach of winter in the air. Even so, perspiration glued her nightgown to her body. She rose and opened the windows of the master suite. For a long time she stood gazing out at the play of moonsilver over the dark woods. The sight only made her feel more restless and alone. Something seemed strange about Netherwood now. She couldn't quite put her finger on it. Then the word *empty* came back to mind.

"Yes," she murmured, "it's as if something is missing. But what?"

She crossed the room and opened the door. The hallway was dark and quiet. It was the very dead of night—that black hour when a solitary soul, denied the solice of rest, feels most alone. Even Maeyken and Zeke had deserted Julianna to travel into the mysterious black void where people go while they sleep. Juli shivered at the thought.

She padded across the hall on bare feet. After a moment's hesitation, she opened the door to Brom's room. A path of moonlight fell across the wide bed. Julianna looked about.

Nothing had changed since the last time she was here. Yet even this room had that empty, abandoned feeling about it.

Leaving the door open, as if that might give her some direct contact with her sleeping servants, Julianna walked slowly toward the bed. She eased herself down, feeling the familiar softness of Brom's overstuffed mattress. Her eyes closed the moment her head touched the pillow. Her mind drifted as she neared sleep.

Suddenly, she sat bolt upright, Brom's words echoing in her mind: "We would make wonderful children, you and I, my dearest heart. Flame-haired, black-eyed beauties."

"Maeyken," she whispered in the dark. "She repeated Brom's very words to me."

Julianna glanced about the room, searching for any movement in the shadows, any sign that she was not totally alone.

"Brom?" she called softly. "Are you here?"

She had felt his presence the whole time she was in New York. There was no doubt in her mind that the jewel fiasco had been his doing. But, even so, his nearness had been a comfort. It was like having a guardian angel always hovering about, even if that dark angel did on occasion cause trouble.

Now, in a flash, she realized what her empty feeling meant. Brom was gone. Somehow she knew that he was much farther away from her than Elliot would ever be. She wondered if she would see the handsome Dutchman ever again. If not, then what?

"Brom?" she whispered again. "Brom, where are you?"

The empty silence sent a shiver through Julianna. She leaped off the bed and ran back to the master suite. Pulling the covers over her head, she willed herself not to think. How long she lay there, shivering and counting backward, she didn't know. But when it seemed that sleep would never come, she finally surrendered her weary mind and body.

Her dreams were a troubling collage of Elliot and Brom. One moment she would be touching Elliot's brown hair, only to have it turn ink-black in her fingers. She would taste her fiancé lips, but then realize she was kissing the Dutchman instead. And their eyes—slate-gray, charcoal-black—ever dancing through her mind, ever different, but ever the same with their shifting, merry lights and their shared look of love only for her.

Dawn came that morning as a great relief.


If Julianna thought she had felt alone the night before, the following day would bring total solitude. As usual, Zeke was up early to go to the village for the mail. The single letter he brought back exacted an anguished cry from Maeyken when she read it.

"Lord help us!" the old woman howled. "It's my only sister's only grandchild. Six babies to tend to, her husband's run off, and the poor woman's broke her leg."

"How dreadful!" Julianna sympathized, hurrying to Maeyken's side. "What will she do?"

Maeyken shook her head until her gray braids danced. "She'll most likely go to an early grave if I don't take myself up to Saugerties to see to her and her brood. I wouldn't ask to go, Miss Juli, if there was any other way. But that poor girl has no one else in the world. Read her letter your own self. She's purely begging me to come."

Not yet grasping the full extent of the dilemma, Juliann nodded and said, "Of course you must go, Maeyken. We can get along without you for a few days."

"It may be longer than that, Miss Juli," Maeyken warned cautiously. "And I'll be needing to take Zeke along to drive me and help out. My niece lives on a hilltop farm a ways from town. Till she's fit to get around on that leg again, me and Zeke'll have to pitch in on the farm chores as well as taking care of her and the younguns. I just hope we can make it back here before first snowfall."

"Oh!" Julianna gasped. "Oh, that will be a while!"

"Several weeks, most likely. You're safe enough here, though," Maeyken assured her. "And Zeke's got the place in good shape for you. Won't be no heavy work to be done. And should an early cold snap come, Zeke's got a rightly good woodpile stacked up out back. Should get you through a month or more."

Julianna waved her hands to dismiss any doubts about her well-being. "Of course Zeke must go with you. Don't worry, Maeyken, I'll be fine. I only hope your niece recovers soon."

The rest of the morning passed in a flurry of activity. Not until the pair had packed their things in the wagon and disappeared down the drive, waving and calling good-byes as they went did the full realization of the lonely days stretching ahead of her bring a tear to Julianna's eye. With an ache in her heart, she turned back toward the big, quiet, empty house.

She closed the door, then walked from room to room—upstairs and down—her footsteps echoing lonesomely in the solitude. The place was too quiet. She could barely endure this loneliness.

"Brom?" she called at the bedroom door. "Brom, are you in there?"

No answer. No gust of wind. No flash of green light.

Julianna stamped her foot in frustration. "Where is that pesky ghost when I need him?" she sobbed, swiping angrily at the tears in her eyes.


The year was 1696. Brom found to his delight on his return that Captain William Kidd was back from England, bringing his new ship *Adventure Galley*. As soon as crews could be hired on and last-minute details set to order, they would both sail off in search of the murdering pirates that were the scourge of seven seas.

"Yes, indeed, enough of this lovesick foolishness," Brom told himself when Captain Kidd's message reached his ship. "What I need to set me back to rights is a good battle and a hold full of some bloody pirate's ill-got treasure."

He threw himself into his work for the next few days, hardly allowing time to think of Julianna at all. Still, between seeing to repairs on *Bachelor's Delight*, interviewing seamen, discussing plans with Kidd, there were those rare quiet moments. Invariably, at such times, that pretty face, those tempting lips and flashing eyes would leap uninvited into his thoughts. What was she doing now? Did she miss him? Did she think of him as often as she came to trouble his thoughts?

Every now and again he was tempted to try to return to her. *Only to say good-bye before I sail*, he told himself. When this madness took hold of him, he would curse himself with vigor and charge headlong into more work. Hadn't he learned his lesson on his last trip to that far-off century?

He had vowed *never* to go back, even if he could. Julianna belonged where she was and he belonged here. Besides, what right had he to disrupt her plans, as much as they pained him? Time would pass. She would marry her actor. And Captain Brom Vanderzee would sail into battle, perhaps never to return.

"All as it should be," he told himself.

Yet on a certain cold night, as he paced the dark, empty rooms of Netherwood, he was drawn upstairs by the heart-wrenching sound of her weeping. He stood a long time in the hallway, staring through the wall at the room that was not there—at the woman who was as far away as if the bed where she lay crying sat in far-off Cathay.

"Don't, Julianna. Please, don't!" he moaned, his own heart aching at her misery. "I know you can neither see nor hear me, love, but can't you feel me here? Can't you sense how much I care for you—how much I need you? If you'd but look my way. Leave off your sobbing, sweet woman. Come let me hold you. Let me love you."

Her weeping subsided. Blinking in the darkness and brushing the tears from her eyes, she turned in the bed toward the place where he stood.

"There. That's better, isn't it, dearest heart?" Brom soothed. "Wouldn't you be more comfortable in your old room?"

Julianna shoved the covers back and sat up cross-legged in the bed. "I can't sleep in here," she announced to herself. "I'm moving back to Brom's room."

A few minutes later, she climbed into the big wide bed in the room across the hall. She snuggled down with a sigh of sheer pleasure. The bed felt good—like coming home after a long time away.

She was asleep in little more than a moment. But even if she had stayed awake, it was unlikely she would have seen the man stretched out beside her.

Sure that her fears and her tears were gone, Brom leaned carefully over her and touched his lips to hers. Had he been one to take unfair advantage, he might have imposed himself further. Lord knows, he was tempted! But he satisfied himself for the present with holding her gently while she slept.

With the coming of dawn, he slipped away. But not before assuring his Julianna over and over again that he needed her, he wanted her, he loved her as no man ever could.

Not surprisingly, Julianna's first waking thoughts were of Brom.

# Chapter Twelve

After that first miserable night, Julianna determined to fill her waking hours with better things. Surely, that would make the time go faster. She had meant to be bold and brave while Maeyken and Zeke were away, but if last night was any example, she was certainly neither. Only a dream of Brom had finally soothed her into a deep sleep.

"Maybe it's because winter's coming on so suddenly," she told herself as she dressed in a warm woolen frock, then carefully braided her long hair. "I've always hated the sudden death of autumn's lovely colors—the gray, misty gloom of November. But I'll be fine once the first snow falls and the countryside looks fresh and clean and white."

Julianna found nothing odd about talking aloud to herself so frankly. It was a habit that had served her well back on the farm in Pennsylvania. What did bother her were the tears she had shed last night. She had to admit to herself that she had wept out of pure self-pity. And it wasn't simply because

Maeyken and Zeke had left. Until recently, both Elliot and Brom had been pursuing her ardently. Now they, too, were gone. Elliot to far-off California. And Brom? Who knew where he went or how far away it might be?

Julianna shuddered with a sudden chill and ran her hands over her arms.

"Well, no more tears and self-pity! I won't have it, do you hear?" She gave her mirrored reflection a particularly stern look. "I'll keep myself so busy that I won't have time to think."

Quickly, she pinned up her braid, making it circle the top of her head. Then she pulled on a knitted tam and matching yellow mittens before heading out of the room and downstairs. She would not spend this bright, cold day locked away within the confines of Netherwood. She needed to get out, to see people. She hurried through the front door, slamming it behind her.

A killing frost during the night had crisped the leaves and grass outside. They crunched loudly underfoot when she stepped off the front stoop. As Julianna stood at the head of the drive, surveying the countryside all around, she noticed spirals of woodsmoke drifting from various houses scattered along the old Albany Post Road. The homey scent traveled on the breeze, reminding her that Christmas was fast approaching and then a brand-new century. Her heart swelled at the thought. She loved the holidays, with their warmth and cheer and goodwill to all men.

"I'll need gifts on *San Claas*—Saint Nicholas Day—for Maeyken and Zeke," she reminded herself brightly as she hurried down the long drive.

Reaching the old post road that began as Broadway in New York City and ran clear up to Albany, she set her course due south toward the village, determined to walk the three miles to Tarrytown. If she had time, she would browse through the general store, looking for Christmas gifts. Perhaps she'd buy a new bonnet for Maeyken and a hand-carved pipe for Zeke. But first, she needed to do something she had been putting off far too long. She would stop at the old Dutch Reformed Church. It was high time she visited Sleepy Hollow Cemetery to pay her respects at the graves of her relatives. That call was long overdue.

Julianna paused for a moment and glanced down the road. In the near distance, she could see the gray roof tiles of the Philipse manor house and its nearby gristmill. A few other run-down buildings marked the once-great estate, but little else remained of the vast holdings of Frederick Philipse, who had been Brom's closest neighbor long ago. Philipse had worked his way up from a position as Governor Peter Stuyvesant's carpenter to become the wealthiest man in New-York years before the Revolution.

Maeyken had told Julianna that Philipse's two-and-a-half-story brick country house was built about the same time that Brom had erected Netherwood. She wondered absently if Philipsburg Manor had its own resident ghost. Perhaps, she mused, gregarious Dutch spirits from earlier times came with these riverine mansions built so long ago.

She walked briskly down the road, feeling invigorated by the cold air and the sun's sparkle dancing on the placid face of the Hudson River. Her spirits rose considerably with every step she took even though thick gray clouds soon obscured the bright morning light.

Crossing the bridge over the Pocantico, she turned into the churchyard. The old Dutch church, she knew, had been built by Frederick Philipse on his original land grant. It had served his family and his tenants as a place of worship and today served many of the descendants of those original settlers. She had heard, too, that Philipse and his wife, Catherine Van Cortlandt, were buried together under the church chancel.

She glanced about her. The quaint church stood in a

quiet, sequestered glen. The graves all about were shaded in spring, summer, and fall by tall locusts, cedars, and cypresses. But today the cemetery looked bleak and slightly forbidding now that the first blast of winter had denuded the trees, making them mere skeletal sentinels standing guard over the silent dead.

A weathervane spun in the wind atop the quaint bell tower that surmounted the two-hundred-year-old stone church. Its narrow-arched windows seemed to stare out over the haphazard rows of headstones in the country graveyard. Several crows perched on a bare limb lifted a raucous cry at Julianna's intrusion. Nothing in the setting seemed to welcome her to the place.

Carefully, Julianna picked her way between the old sandstone markers with their weeping willow designs. She tried not to step on any graves as she searched for the Worthington plot. But though she found tombs marked Philipse, Van Cortlandt, Hawes, and even the wrought-iron-fenced plot of Washington Irvings' family, she could locate no Worthington tombs. Finally, she stopped and glanced about, frustrated and wondering which area to search next.

"May I be of assistance, Miss Doran?" A deep male voice, seemingly out of nowhere, gave Julianna a start.

She looked up to see a short, barrel-chested, white-haired man in workclothes and heavy boots standing on the church steps. For an instant, Washington Irving's description of Henry Hudson's henchman in the story of Rip Van Winkle flashed through her mind—"a short square-built old fellow, with thick bushy hair, and a grizzled beard." Clutching at her racing heart, she laughed nervously, hoping that this was not truly another ghost of some long-dead Dutchman.

"You startled me," she said.

To her vast relief, the old man spoke quite normally. "I'm sorry," he replied, walking toward her with a lurching gait. "Do forgive me, won't you? I only meant to help. You must be looking for the stones of your aunt and uncle and cousins.''

Julianna frowned at the wizened little man with the clear blue eyes gleaming below bushy brows. "How did you know, sir? In fact, you and I have never met, so how did you even know my name?''

He chuckled softly and puffed at his well-seasoned pipe. "Being minister to the souls hereabouts, there's not much I don't get wind of, young lady. Pastor Ten Eyck, at your service, Miss Doran.'' He offered her a crisp bow and his hand in friendship. "Now, how may I assist you?''

She smiled at him, feeling a bit ashamed. If the minister knew all that went on around here, he must realize how tardy she was in making this call.

"As you said,'' she told him, "I've come—at long last— to pay my respects to my family.'' Glancing about, she spread her arms wide and shrugged. "But there are so many stones. I'm lost. I have no idea where to begin looking.''

"This way,'' he said, pointing with his pipe stem toward a newer section of the cemetery rather distant from the church.

She was relieved to see, when they reached the four plain granite tablets, that no sad willows or carved death-heads adorned her relatives' tombs. Instead, simply the names and the dates were etched into the smooth, unadorned slabs. Suddenly, Julianna frowned at the fourth grave.

"I was told that my cousin Sarah was not buried here.''

"True,'' Pastor Ten Eyck confirmed. "Naught was found for burying, I'm afraid. But Maeyken thought it proper that a place be marked to her memory.''

"Ah, Maeyken.'' Julianna nodded. "I wondered who took charge of erecting the monuments.''

"'Twas a sad time for all of us, but Maeyken is a strong woman,'' the minister said. He shook his head mournfully. "Such a pity, all of them passing in that brief span of time.

A whole family. But God has His reasons and we must not question His will,'' he intoned.

Julianna bowed her head in respect and acceptance.

His somber tone lightened as he said, ''I've been waiting for your visit, Miss Doran.''

His words flustered her. Did the minister mean that he'd had some precognition of her arrival? Stranger things had happened hereabouts.

Noting her confusion, he explained, ''The church book of records. I'd have made the entries with Maeyken as my witness, but she reminded me that it's proper to have a family member present when I record births, marriages,'' he paused, then added, ''and deaths. Maeyken said, too, that she thought you might like to have a look through the old records. If you will step into the church, we can take care of the matter right now.''

''Certainly,'' Julianna answered, wondering suddenly what might be in the records that Maeyken wanted her to see. The woman seldom did or said anything without a reason.

Following Pastor Ten Eyck into the dim interior of the church, Juli spied the huge leather-bound tome that the minister had spoken of, resting on a table just inside. She watched as he opened the book to a place marked by a thin purple ribbon.

''Ah, here we are, Miss Doran. I saved space right between the Bogardus-Wilstach marriage and the Vingboon christening.''

Julianna looked on as Pastor Ten Eyck inscribed the names of her relatives and the dates of their deaths in a graceful, old-fashioned hand. ''There! It is duly recorded,'' he said in an official tone.

''What was it Maeyken wanted me to read?'' Julianna asked.

The little minister shook his head. ''I haven't a notion,

I'm afraid. She didn't say—only that she knew you would find it of interest to peruse the entries."

"Then perhaps I should," Julianna replied, feeling more obligation than interest. Already she had spent more time here than she had planned. She did want to get on to Tarrytown to check the mail and, perhaps, do some shopping.

"I'll leave you to it, then," Pastor Ten Eyck said. "If you want me, I'll be outside, raking leaves."

Alone in the quiet church, Julianna thumbed absently through several decades of pages. From time to time, names that she glimpsed jumped out at her—more Bogarduses and Wilstaches and Vingboons, along with many Ten Eycks, Philipses, and other Dutch-sounding cognomens.

Her interest sharpened when she spied the name Washington Irving. The author had lived close by, with the Hudson River flowing past, not fifty feet from the porch of the unique Dutch-cottage-turned-Spanish-castle that he had called Sunnyside. Julianna knew the place well from her childhood excursions south of town with her cousins. One of Lettie's favorite adventures had been to sneak down the crooked lane and past the giant sycamore to the quaint house to pick the fragrant purple blossoms from the huge wisteria that made Sunnyside appear to be wearing an Easter bonnet when the vine bloomed in the spring.

She read the entry: "Washington Irving—Born in New York City, 1783, died in Tarrytown, 28 November 1859 at Sunnyside."

She sighed and started to close the book. No other names she had seen struck a familiar chord.

"Whyever did Maeyken think I would be interested in these endless recordings of names and dates?" she muttered aloud.

Suddenly, Julianna changed her mind. Before closing the book, she flipped the pages back to the earliest entries. The name, Huyberton, caught her eye, and one notation

221

galvanized her gaze. "A daughter born to Gretchen & Jacobus Huyberton, 14 October 1675, christened on the following Sabbath and given the name Maeyken."

"So that's it!" Julianna said aloud. "Without bragging openly, Maeyken wanted to let me know her heritage. Why, her family was probably here before the Philipses, certainly long before any Worthingtons! And she's named for one of those early settlers in this region."

She stared at the entry, then frowned remembering something. Brom's tombstone said he was born in 1660. This Maeyken of long ago would have lived during Brom's time.

"I wonder if they knew each other? Surely, they must have. There couldn't have been that many people in this area back then."

Intrigued by the facts she had uncovered, Julianna hurriedly flipped forward through the brittle, yellowed pages, searching for any other mention of Maeyken's ancestors. She quickly located the death notices of Gretchen Huyberton in 1698 and of her husband the following year. But, although she scanned each entry for the next hundred years, she found no further mention of Maeyken herself.

"That's odd," she murmured. "No marriage, no children, no death?"

She turned the pages to the early years of the 1800's. Perhaps she could discover the age of the present Maeyken and her parentage. Julianna paused and thought for a moment, trying to calculate Maeyken's age. She must have been born between 1820 and 1830 or thereabouts. Again, Julianna drew a blank. In fact, in the entire volume, she could locate no mention of any member of the Huyberton clan after those in the 1600's.

Flipping back to those early entries, she caught sight of another familiar name. Her heart gave a painful throb.

"Captain Brom Vanderzee, born in New Amsterdam, 11 July 1660, died 10 June 1699."

Julianna stared at the page, her eyes riveted to the date she hadn't known before, "10 June," the very day of Brom's death. Then she realized another notation followed that. Brief and to the grisly point, the additional entry proclaimed that Brom had been "Betrayed and Murdered in Boston." The words stabbed her heart with new pain.

Closing the book gently, she turned away, toward the door. Pastor Ten Eyck stood there staring at her.

"Is something wrong, Miss Doran? You look as pale as a January snow."

She shook her head, trying to find her voice. "N-no," she stammered. "I suppose I'm just a bit tired. I had a restless night."

"Would you care to join me in a cup of tea before you start back?" the man offered politely.

Julianna's first impulse was to hurry away from this place, but then she reconsidered. Perhaps she could glean more information from the friendly old parson. "That would be nice, Pastor Ten Eyck. Thank you."

He showed her proudly into his humble dwelling—an ivy-covered cottage of old yellow Dutch brick with wide plank flooring and a low ceiling. A kitchen-size fireplace took up most of one wall. He motioned her to the table and chairs near the hearth.

"Will tea do or would you prefer something else?" he asked politely.

Julianna nodded and said, "Tea will be fine. Anything hot. I'm chilled to the bone." She found that she was suddenly shivering convulsively.

"There is a nip to the air today. Feels like snow," the man answered. "I'll add a dollop of honey and a smidgen of lemon to ward off the grippe."

"Have you always lived in Tarrytown?" she asked as he poured her a steaming cup from the redware teapot.

"I have." He chuckled, and a merry light gleamed in his

sky-blue eyes. "And now I suppose your next question will be if I was here back when the first Dutch settlers planted the wheat—*tarwe*—that gave the place its name of Tarrytown. Before you ask, let me assure you that I am almost, but not quite, that old, young lady."

Julianna laughed with the man. "I always heard that Tarrytown was called that because the wheat farmers tarried so long at the taverns in the town after carrying their harvested crops of *tarwe* to the ferry."

Bringing a plate of pumpkin bread to the table and taking the chair across from Julianna, Pastor Ten Eyck nodded. "So Mr. Irving proclaimed," he told her. "He said the good Dutch wives of those farmers named the place Tarrytown for just that reason." He nodded again and pulled at his pipe. "Either explanation sounds reasonable."

"I found something in the record book that is not reasonable," Julianna told him, changing the subject abruptly.

"Really?" the pastor asked, one shaggy eyebrow arching upward. "And what might that be?"

Quickly, Julianna explained to him about the other Maeyken Huyberton and the missing facts concerning her life. "And another thing that's odd," she added. "When was our Maeyken born? I couldn't find her birth recorded in the book."

The minister paused thoughtfully before answering. "Likely, those early Huybertons moved away. That would explain the missing entries. Then 'our Maeyken,' as you call her, moved back, but after being born somewhere else. I believe she is several years older than I am." He shrugged and smiled. "At least I've known her all my life, which is a considerable amount of time."

Some of Julianna's interest in the subject faded. Why hadn't she thought of such a logical explanation? Of course, that must be it. Her thoughts moved on, away from Maeyken.

"Brom Vanderzee is listed in the book," she mused aloud.

"Aye, the pirate captain."

Julianna's head shot up and her green eyes flared. "He wasn't a pirate!" She almost added, "He told me so himself." But thinking better of such a disclosure, she said simply, "He was an honest merchant seaman."

Pastor Ten Eyck chuckled. "You know that for a fact, do you, Miss Doran?"

"Well . . . ah . . . yes," she stammered. "I mean, that's what I've heard."

He leaned closer and glanced over his shoulder as if someone might be listening. "Would you like to see something that makes me think otherwise?"

Julianna wasn't sure she did want to see anything that would cast Brom in an evil light, but her curiosity got the better of her. She nodded silently.

"Come along, then," the pastor said, motioning with one shoulder toward the closed door at the far side of the room—the man's sleeping quarters, Julianna presumed.

Sure enough, Pastor Ten Eyck opened the door to reveal his bed. Julianna gasped aloud; she couldn't help herself.

"I can't say as I blame you for that reaction," the man said with a chuckle. "It seems downright sinful for a man of God to be sleeping in such a bed, I'll agree. But then, beggars can't be choosers. Your uncle gave me this piece of furniture, right out of the attic at Netherwood. He said it was taking up too much room. And, since I'd been sleeping on a pallet on the floor after my old bedstead broke down, I accepted the offer of anything that would give me a mite more comfort of a cold night."

Julianna could not find her voice. She stood staring at the garish golden horror that Brom had meant for them to share—the very bed that she herself had relegated to Netherwood's attic. Finally, she was able to speak.

"I don't understand," she said. "Why would this bed be proof that Brom Vanderzee was a pirate?"

"The bed was his, right enough," the minister assured her. "There was this paper still attached to it." He rummaged in a drawer and drew out a brittle tag with Brom's name scrawled on it along with directions from the Philipse dock to Netherwood. "I can't rightly see an honest merchant sleeping in such a bed, can you?"

Julianna smiled sweetly at the man. "You sleep in it. Does that make you a pirate, Pastor Ten Eyck?"

He laughed and nodded. "You've got me there, Miss Doran. I suppose I may have to change my way of thinking about old Brom. Maybe, as you say, he was an honest merchant. But, if so, he must have had a lady with mighty fancy tastes."

"What?" Juli cried.

Again the old man laughed softly. "I can't see any man buying such a thing for himself, can you? Especially not such a rugged seaman as Captain Vanderzee is said to have been."

"I wish I knew more about him," Julianna said wistfully.

Ten Eyck nodded and motioned his guest back to her chair. He poured more tea for both of them, added honey and lemon.

"I can understand your interest."

Julianna eyed him suspiciously. What did he mean by that?

He answered the question before she asked. "Actually living in his house, on this land . . . well, it must make you feel sometimes as if he's right there with you. Certainly you'd be curious to find out more about the man."

Julianna smiled in spite of herself. Pastor Ten Eyck was a mind-reader.

"Do you have any idea what the entry in the record book means?" she asked.

"Ah, the reference to his betrayal and murder, you're speaking of." The minister nodded. "I know something of

226

it. Are you familiar with the story of Captain Kidd, Miss Doran?''

A rush of disturbing feelings, emotions, and fragmented sights and sounds passed over Julianna. Yes, she remembered now, Brom had mentioned plans with Captain Kidd. *Dangerous* plans, she was certain.

Fighting for composure, she replied, ''I believe he was from old New-York and that he and Captain Vanderzee were in the same line of work.''

''Aye.'' Ten Eyck nodded. ''You have that much correct. But that's the least of it. The two men shared far more than their love of the sea. They were friends, so I've heard. The very closest of friends. Almost like brothers.'' He puffed his pipe for a moment, letting his eyes scan the ceiling. ''Do you know of William Kidd's fate?''

Julianna leaned closer and shook her head, not wanting to interrupt with a single word.

''At Wapping on the shores of the Thames on the twenty-third of May in the year seventeen hundred and one, as it is written, '*infra fluxum et refluxum maris*—between the high water and low water mark,' Captain Kidd was *hanged*.''

She gasped at the minister's final, harsh word. A mental picture of Brom, his neck in a noose, swinging from a gibbet, flashed unbidden.

''And Captain Vanderzee?'' she managed breathlessly.

Pastor Ten Eyck shood his head slowly, sadly. ''Not hanged, but dead and buried before his friend's execution. Vanderzee hoped to save William Kidd, but in so doing he lost his own life.''

''What exactly happened?'' Juli was frantic to know all the facts, no matter how terrible they might be. ''Tell me everything. Please!''

The parson leaned back in his chair and crossed one boot over his other knee, clearly a man who enjoyed spinning a good yarn.

"It isn't a pretty tale, I'm afraid, but well documented," he began, stroking his wild beard. "Two hundred years ago, young New-York under English rule was already becoming a city—eight hundred and fifty families and six churches, I'm proud to say. But the two chief occupations of the place were not the sort to inspire pride in any upstanding citizen, being the sale of firewater to the Indians and the bloody pursuit of piracy. Governor Benjamin Fletcher welcomed one and all from the high seas, an especial favorite of his being one Thomas Tew, a wretched, murdering freebooter if ever there was one. But that's another tale."

Julianna thought she recognized the name, but she was too intent on hearing of Brom's fate to give much thought to anything else.

"Fletcher permitted pirates to take safe harbor in New-York," Ten Eyck went on, "to come ashore to stretch their legs, even to sell the ill-got goods they'd taken from Spanish galleons and East India merchantmen." The minister leaned toward Juli and stabbed his pipe stem for emphasis as he added, "For a *fee*, mind you, Fletcher allowed it. He required a bond of one hundred dollars a head to ensure the pirates' good behavior while in his port city. It has been written that while trade with the freebooters lasted, New-York gained an Oriental magnificence, her stores filled with rare fabrics from Teheran and Samarkand, spices, perfumes, precious woods, Persian rugs, bizarre furnishings, and rare jewels. Arabian gold became the current coin. And the gaudily-dressed pirates swaggered about town with their perfumed and bejeweled women dressed in silks from India."

Julianna's mind went immediately to Brom's purple velvet trousers and high-heeled yellow boots . . . to Katrina Rhinehart's magnificent silk gowns and expensive jewels.

"So you're telling me that Kidd really was a pirate?" Julianna interjected. "And so Brom Vanderzee must have been, too?"

228

"Not in the beginning," Ten Eyck assured her. "Kidd was an upstanding merchant with a fine house in Pearl Street during Fletcher's time. Why, the good captain even loaned his block and tackle to help with the building of the first Trinity Church. A family man, he was, with a wife and a child. But that was before he hatched a deal with a certain Richard Coote, Earl of Bellomont."

Julianna frowned, trying to remember. "I believe I've heard of him."

"As well you might," the pastor replied, arching one snowy brow. "The man's reputation preceded him to the Colonies. A lusty fellow, he married a young girl only twelve years of age. All went well as long as she remained a manageable child. But by the time she reached her third decade, Lady Bellomont had acquired an expensive taste for gambling. She traveled with London's most extravagant gaming set, while Bellomont accepted a colonial post to try to stay one jump ahead of her creditors—"

"I don't understand what all this has to do with Brom Vanderzee and his untimely death," Juli interrupted.

"It has *everything* to do with it," Ten Eyck assured her. "But let me finish the tale. You'll see."

Julianna settled back, sipping her tea and waiting for him to continue.

"Before word of Fletcher's penchant for pirates leaked back to London, causing his dismissal, Lord Bellomont struck upon a plan to make himself wealthy enough to afford his young wife's extravagant habits. He contracted with several New-Yorkers—honest men, mind you—to make up an amateur navy, their mission being to operate under letters of marque, preying on any and all pirate ships roaming the seven seas."

"Yes, yes!" Juli cried, remembering suddenly. "Captain Kidd signed on, and Brom Vanderzee as well." She stared quizzically at the teller of the tale. "But they were privateers. That's no cause for hanging."

Ten Eyck nodded. "Right you are, my girl. Honest men hired for honest work in the beginning, or so the story went. But mark my words, Miss Doran, Fletcher, Bellomont, and the privateers sailing out of New-York's harbor under a letter of marque were all tarred with the same stick—all out for whatever riches they could lay their hands on by whatever means. Captain Kidd, in my opinion, simply committed the unpardonable sin of getting himself caught when he attacked and captured the unarmed Armenian vessel, *Quedagh Merchant*, off Madagascar's coast. Then Bellomont, to save his own skin, turned on his admiral, clapped him in irons when he returned to Boston, and shipped him back to England to be tried and hanged for murder."

"And Brom?" Julianna ventured.

Pastor Ten Eyck smiled. "You speak the man's name as if you know him as a friend. Before the incident with the Armenians, Captain Vanderzee had left Madagascar, returning to Netherwood to recover from a wound taken in battle. He might have stayed safely out of it had he been a man of lesser valor. But by trying to help his old friend out of this nasty scrape, he lost his own life on the very day that Bellomont had Kidd arrested in Boston."

"I still don't understand, Pastor Ten Eyck," Juli confessed. "The entry in the book says that Captain Vanderzee was betrayed. By whom? Lord Bellomont?"

The old man shook his head. "That part of the story I cannot tell you. I don't know exactly what happened. But I can tell you this, my dear, there's some who say 'twas a woman caused his death." He glanced back over his shoulder toward the bedroom door. "Perhaps the very woman who slept in yonder golden bed."

Julianna did not go on to Tarrytown. Her conversation with Pastor Ten Eyck left her shaken, her mind in a muddle.

Who could the woman have been? And why would she have betrayed Brom Vanderzee?

A light snow began to fall as Julianna trudged back up the pike toward Netherwood. She never noticed Philipsburg Manor or the glassy calm of the river or the powdery precipitation whiting out the world. All her awareness was turned inward.

When she started up the drive toward Netherwood, some force stronger than her own will drew her off the path and into the woods. Without realizing how she got there, she found herself standing before Brom's grave. Tremors of emotion ran through her. Her throat ached with unshed tears. She wanted to scream and rave and sob at the injustice done this man so long ago. Instead, she stood quietly, reading and rereading the words on the tomb.

Finally, a strange calm settled over her. She forgot about the cold, the snowflakes clinging to her cheeks and eyelashes. Her very survival seemed centered around the survival of this man who had died, unjustly, two centuries ago.

Words formed first in her heart, then took shape in her mind. When she spoke them aloud, they came in a whisper. But that quiet breath issued forth with a depth of determination, resolve, and love.

"Now I know why you came to me the night of the séance, Brom. I won't let this happen to you. I can't. I'll find a way to stop it . . . to change the past and alter our future."

Turning slowly away, she headed toward Netherwood, picking up her pace until she was at a near-trot. There was no doubt in Julianna's mind what she must do. But this dangerous undertaking, she had to admit, would be as much for herself as for Brom.

# Chapter Thirteen

Even though Julianna was practically running, the path up to Netherwood seemed longer than usual and far more lonely. Drifting snow now locked her world in a deep silence that gave little solace. The trees, the path, the very house ahead took on a ghostly aura as she bent into the wind and hurried through the gathering gloom.

Her thoughts returned to Pastor Ten Eyck's tragic story and the sight of Brom's lonely tomb in the woods. Although she had no idea how she was connected to all this, she knew that she was. She knew, too, what she must try to do, but how to go about it remained a nagging question.

It was simple enough to assure herself—as she had done only moments before at the grave site—that she would return to Brom's time and alter the course of history. But how? How to go back? How to remain there long enough to help? And, most importantly, how to right this great wrong that had been done so long ago?

Finally, she reached the house and hurried inside out of the blowing snow. Netherwood seemed intolerably empty when she closed the door behind her. Out of habit, even though she knew no one was there, she called, "I'm home!"

Only a deep, unsettling silence answered her. She moved about, lighting lamps to dispel the gathering gloom of twilight. But chasing away the shadows helped little. Her thoughts—all disturbing—remained on Brom.

"I mustn't do anything hasty," she warned aloud. "I need to think things through thoroughly before I make a move."

She wandered into the kitchen. Listlessly, she stoked the glowing embers of the fire until they danced into orange flame.

"Food," she said. "I should eat. I *must* be hungry."

Searching the chilly interior of the zinc-lined wooden icebox, she brought out the remains of a shepherd's pie Maeyken made before she left. Juli ate it cold, her mind too filled with other things for her even to be aware of its tallowy taste. Before she finished, Julianna felt herself once more slipping away from determination and toward self-pity.

"*Enough*!" she cried, ashamed of her weakness. "Obviously, sleep is out of the question tonight. So, you'll work, my fine lady! Until you drop from exhaustion, if need be."

Although it was quite dark already, Julianna knew that she must go up to the attic. Some instinct seemed to be drawing her there. Tying on her work apron, she took broom, basket, and lantern and headed upstairs, determined to clear out the last of the papers and old letters she had left days before.

"Only one thing I know will get me through this night," she told herself sternly as she climbed to the attic. "Good, hard work. I'll worry about Brom tomorrow."

As determined as she was, the sight that greeted her brought a sigh of dismay from Julianna. Papers, papers, and

233

more papers. She was tempted to fill her wastebasket with armloads at a time. However, her curiosity wouldn't allow that. Settling herself comfortably on the floor for a long siege, she began going through the piles, one piece at a time.

Newspapers proved her greatest deterrent. She began by indiscriminately tossing years of back issues into her basket until an engraving of a familiar face gave her pause.

"Why, it's Abraham Lincoln!" she gasped.

Quickly, she pulled the paper out of the pile. The faded copy of the New York *Herald*, priced four cents, was dated Saturday, April 15, 1865. The headline of the black-bordered lead story read "**IMPORTANT**—ASSASSINATION of PRESIDENT LINCOLN."

After that amazing find, trash became treasure in an instant. Julianna decided she must save and read *all* the old papers. She would haul them downstairs to the bedroom and scan them on other nights when she couldn't sleep. There were sure to be many of those before Maeyken and Zeke returned.

Suddenly, a stack of letters, tied with a faded satin ribbon, fell out from between the folds of an early issue of the Albany *Argosy*. Julianna stared at the boldly masculine handwriting. It looked familiar.

Holding the first letter closer to her lamp, she began reading.

22 December 1696
At Sea

My Dearest Heart,

How long each hour seems without you by my side. The nights especially creep past—never-ending, black nothingness. I lie in my bunk and think of how it felt to hold you in my arms, to kiss your lips, to love you in our special way. Until you came into my life, I was no more than half alive. Without you now, I am little more than a shell of a man.

Julianna paused, frowning down at the page between her trembling fingers. Yes, she did recognize this handwriting. It was Brom's, the same bold flourishes she had read in his book of charts. She experienced a sharp pang of jealousy, then chided herself for being foolish. How could she feel such envy for a woman Brom had loved two centuries ago? Had he left a wife, then, when he sailed away? She read on, hoping to discover the truth.

I know now the secret of conquering the world. Give every man in every army a woman he can truly love as I do truly love you, dearest heart. Not one soldier, sailor, or mercenary would stir from his lover's arms to make war on his brother.

I waited so long for you to come back to me, and now to have to part from you so soon. But captains must be courageous, even in matters of the heart.

If—and I say *only* if—I should fail to return to you, know that I will seek you out wherever I go from here. I have never understood the word, *forever*. Never until now. But I will love you for that long and beyond.

Wait for me, my dearest heart. Love me, as I love you and always shall.

Forever yours,
Brom

Still clutching the stack of letters, tears blurring her eyes, Julianna rushed down to her bedroom. She dug through one of her drawers until she found what she was searching for—the note that had accompanied the roses sent to her at the Hotel Metropole.

"Yes," she murmured, holding the card close to the

235

letter to compare. It was as she suspected. "I knew it! The handwriting is the same. Brom!" she cried, glancing about the room as if he might materialize at any moment. "You sent me the flowers! You stole the jewels!"

A frown furrowed her brow. She might have solved one mystery, but what of the other? She still had no idea to whom this letter had been written. Obviously, the woman was Brom's lover. Perhaps his wife. There was certainly no doubt about the deep affection Brom had felt for her. A grim thought entered Julianna's mind. Could the love note have been written to the woman named Kat?

Trying to dismiss that troubling thought, Julianna arranged all the letters on the bed. She would put them in sequence and perhaps discover some clue. She glanced down at them. Her frown deepened. Not all the letters were written by Brom. Several of them were in another hand—a woman's tidy script. Taking up one of these, she stared at it closely. The wavering lanternlight made the handwriting seem to dance before her eyes. The ink was faded to pale-tan, almost illegible. This handwriting, too, looked familiar. Carefully, she unfolded the sheet and read.

Netherwood
October 30, 1696

My darling Brom,

As I watched your ship set sail this morning, I felt such an emptiness, such an ache in my heart. I thought: You should have kissed him one last time, you should have held him close a moment longer. But it was too late. Pardon the tears that stain this sheet, my love. Without you I am weak, with a woman's weakness for her man.

I must stop this or I will go mad with wanting you.

Julianna paused, feeling her heart sink. Certainly, this had been no one-way romance of the moment. The woman, whoever she was, had worshipped Captain Brom Vanderzee. Once again, Katrina Rhinehart crept unbidden into Julianna's thoughts. She read on hurriedly, anxious to know the truth, painful as it might be.

Have no care for Netherwood while you are at sea, my darling. I promise it will be taken care of—lovingly. As lovingly as you took care of me last night.

Oh, dear, dear Brom, how will I live now that you are gone? Until last night I was not truly alive. It seemed as if I only abided as a ghost in this time and place. You gave me life and breath with your loving. Now, I am yours for always, my darling.

I can only pray that you will return, safely and soon. Know, my dearest lover, that I will be waiting for you—the only man who has ever claimed my heart, the only one who ever will!

Always, my darling, *always*,
Your Julianna

Julianna gasped. "It can't be!" A rush of relief mingled with awe made her heart pound furiously. Tears sprang to her eyes.

She glanced back at the date. It was true. *She* had written this letter to Brom in the year *1696*!

"But how is that possible?" she murmured, still staring at the letter. "In order to write this, I had to be in that year with Brom."

True, Julianna had visited his time briefly. However, she had written no letters. And, as far as she could remember, Brom had not sailed away.

She paused, concentrating hard to remember all that had

transpired between them. Details tended to fade as dreams so often will. Suddenly, a feeling of horror immobilized her. This empty sensation she had been aware of since returning from New York City. Could that mean that Brom—wherever he was—had truly sailed away? That she had let him go without even saying good-bye? What if she was not there to answer his passionate love letters? Would these words before her eyes fade into nothingness? Would the pages crumble and dissolve? Would the love that they were meant to share never come to be?

"Then *forever* would mean nothing. Oh, please, no!" Julianna moaned, covering her face with her hands.

She looked at the letters again, her heart racing now with new hope. According to her own letter, he had sailed away on October the Thirtieth. When she had last visited his century, roses were still blooming in the garden. It could have been no later than September. Perhaps there was still time.

"Oh, God, grant me time!" Julianna begged as she began preparing mentally for her long journey.

She could not wait for morning. *Brom* could not wait for *her*!

She had promised herself earlier as she stood at his grave that she would go back. But she had thought there was plenty of time. Now she realized that was not the case.

Leaping off the bed, Julianna began readying everything for her journey. She took special pains to see that no detail was overlooked. Things must be just so for the transition.

Her gown, of emerald satin brocade stitched with threads of gold, came from the trunk Brom had given her, as did her gilt link jewelry and soft bronze kid slippers. Before dressing in her finery, however, she'd slipped down to the cellar to fill a ewer with mysterious, sparkling water from the spring. Back in Brom's bedchamber, she collected everything she knew had been dear to him—his chartbook,

238

designs for Netherwood she'd found in the attic that bore his bold signature, and, of course, the batch of letters.

Almost as an afterthought, she brought out the Ouija board and placed it on the bed. She must use every measure at hand to ensure the success of her mission.

Once she was dressed, she sighed and glanced about, her heart pounding rapidly. "Have I forgotten anything?" she asked herself. No, all was in readiness.

She sat down on the edge of the wide bed and slowly poured a glass of water. Holding it up as if to make a toast, she murmured, "I'm coming, Brom. Be there for me. Please!"

She drank it down in one smooth swallow. Then, placing her fingertips on the Ouija board's pointer, she waited to feel or to see something—anything. Closing her eyes, she willed herself to travel through time. She felt the pointer make a sudden move. A moment later, it seemed as if a strong hand pressed her down on the bed until her spinning head rested among the pillows. Dizziness overwhelmed her in that moment.

The last sounds Julianna heard were the clock striking midnight followed by the hoot of an owl as it swooped from its perch to begin its night prowlings. A sparkling purple-green mist swirled around her. Only moments later, it seemed, sounds of morning filled the room. She opened her eyes. Bright sunlight spilled across the bed, causing her to blink.

For a time, Julianna lay very still, listening, feeling. Had everything changed or would she look about her to find that she had simply fallen asleep to awake the following morning of 1899? She was almost afraid of the answer. Steeling herself, she glanced about. Immediately, disappointment engulfed her, dashing all her hopes. Everything was exactly as it had been when she lay down hours before. Her attempt to reach Brom had failed.

239

Closing her eyes again, this time against tears, she rolled over, willing sleep to once more give her solace. She felt unable to face the day ahead—all alone.

"I've failed you, Brom," she cried softly. "I'm sorry, so sorry."

Just then, she heard a noise on the stairs. The sound of boots running, nearing her chamber, sent a shiver of dread through her. Who would have brass enough to barge into her home at this early hour without even knocking? The answer seemed clear: some thief bent on dire misdeeds.

She sat up, glancing frantically about for some weapon, then leaped from the bed and ran to the big Dutch *kas*. Pulling the heavy doors of the armoire open, she slipped inside to hide from the intruder. Her heart pounded frantically. What if he found her? What would she do?

She squirmed back behind the clothes, hoping for a more secure hiding place. Settled at last and feeling almost safe, she took a deep breath. At that moment, she realized from the rough cloak scratching her cheek that she was hiding amidst a man's clothing. Garments that smelled of tobacco and leather and salt air. Clothing that smelled of *Brom*!

She heard the bedroom door crash against the wall.

"Julianna? Julianna! Aren't you ready yet? Where are you?"

"Brom!" She burst out of her cupboard hiding place, her pulses racing with excitement. "Oh, Brom! I thought you were a thief."

"I am!" he exclaimed with a broad smile, opening his arms to welcome her. "A thief come to steal your heart, pretty wench. Just look at you! Turn around." He stood back, admiring, his fingers toying with the pointed tip of his beard. "Every woman at Governor Fletcher's reception will be livid with envy and every man—pirate or no—will be trying to do me out of my treasure."

"Governor Fletcher's reception?" Julianna looked puzzled.

"Of course, dearest heart. We'll be going aboard *Bachelor's Delight* as soon as you're ready. We'll fly full sail down the river to New Amsterdam." He frowned, then laughed at his own mistake. "I cannot seem to break that old habit. I know it's been New-York since 1674, but the dear old town will always be New Amsterdam to me. Makes no difference. We still outnumber the Brits by a long shot. 'Tis *our* town, truth be told, and, God willing, she always will be. Hurry now, love." He laughed and winked at her. "Can't keep the governor waiting, can we?"

Even with Brom standing right before her, Julianna could hardly believe she was part of this miracle. She ran to the window to look out. Sure enough! The river, in full view, sparkled in the morning sunlight and Brom's great sailing schooner danced at anchor like some gallant steed pawing at the earth to be off and running.

"It's true," she breathed. "I'm *really* here!"

"And where else might you have expected to be, dearest heart?" Brom came up behind her and closed his arms about her waist.

She turned enough to look up into his handsome, weather-tanned face. Her own was solemn. "Brom, I've only just arrived from the other time. You must realize that."

The puzzlement in his dark eyes stunned her.

"Don't you remember the other times I've come to visit you?" she asked. "You've begged me to stay. I couldn't then. But I hope this time . . ."

Brom shook his head and looked down at her sternly. Then his scowl eased to a bewildered smile. "You make no more sense than a sailor who's pulled overlong at the jug. But no matter, my pretty little one. 'Tis my fault, I fear, for leaving you too much alone at Netherwood. That can't be

241

helped in my line of business. But be warned, wench, you'll be wishing to be rid of me by the time I sail. I mean to crowd your every moment till that time. You'll be thanking your lucky stars to be rid of me by the day Captain Kidd shouts his battle cry.''

Suddenly, everything came rushing back to Julianna. Battle cry! Of course. Brom and William Kidd planned to sail off to fight the pirates. She had come here, bent on stopping him. But looking at his face, beaming as he spoke of sea and ships and battle, she understood that her task would not be an easy one. Still, she had her childhood memory of the sight of Brom, pale and bleeding, and the inscription on his tombstone to give her the courage to fight his desire for adventure. *She must not let him go!*

When she looked up at him, Brom was staring at her quizzically.

"Is something wrong?" she asked, checking her gown to make sure everything was in place.

"Aye," he answered, "and it's only just come back to me. I had the strangest dreams last night."

"Tell me," Julianna urged.

"Ah, no!" he scoffed. " 'Tis pure foolishness, not worth repeating."

"Was I in your dream, Brom?"

He laughed nervously and tried to turn from her, but Julianna refused to allow him to drop the subject now that he had brought it up.

"Brom, please. Tell me about your dream," she begged.

" 'Twas such nonsense!" he insisted. "All jumbled up and disorderly. You were in the thick of it, all right, as you always are. But there was another man, or at times it seemed so. At others, it seemed I was viewing my own image, only in different garb."

"You mean this man was wearing strange clothes?" Julianna asked.

242

"No!" Brom paused thoughtfully, then belted out an embarrassed laugh. "I mean he was wearing strange *skin*. He looked nothing like me, yet I knew we were one and the same somehow."

Again he paused, this time scowling deeply and stroking his beard as if he could make neither heads nor tails of his thoughts.

"Do you know the man's name?" Julianna asked.

Brom's heavy brows drew together as he tried to think. "My memory fails me on that point. What I do recall is a confusion of other images—a strange sort of land-ship that moved on wheels and spewed fire and cinders . . . New Amsterdam with buildings so tall it seemed they would topple over upon me . . . a place all green and gold and crimson with mirrors reflecting the many people there." He looked at Julianna, his cheeks above his beard showing a stain of embarrassment. "You'll think me mad, but chasing me all through the night was a great green griffin with fiery eyes."

"I don't think you mad at all," Julianna stated quietly. She knew exactly where that griffin was and all the rest as well. But she didn't try to explain. Instead she said, "Dreams take their own shapes, often odder than reality. But you said I was in your dream. What part did I play?"

He lowered his eyelids and answered in a husky whisper, "Can't you guess, dearest heart?"

Flustered when she realized his meaning, Julianna stammered, "But we've never . . . I mean, you and I have yet to . . ."

Her gaze pleaded for confirmation that they had never made love. For, if they had, she retained no memory of it. And to forget such an occasion, she mused, staring up into his passion-filled eyes, would be a tragedy, indeed.

Brom reached out and caressed her cheek. "You speak the truth, my pretty child," he told her softly. "We have yet to know such joy together. But somehow I understand after my dreams exactly how it will be. Glorious!'' he whispered. ''Soul-rending . . . beyond human description or imagination.''

''But how . . . ?''

He shook his head. '' 'Twill do no good to ask. I understand little of it. It seemed you gave your love to that other man, but, as I stated before, curiously, he and I were one and the same. When he took you to him, I knew his ecstasy as if it were my own.'' He offered her a boyish grin. ''Not a bad night's dreaming, actually.''

Julianna was too puzzled to question Brom further. She could only stand silent and staring, gazing on him with a heart so full that he seemed to encompass her entire world at this moment. Had that other time she now remembered only vaguely ever truly existed?

''Before we leave,'' Brom's words interrupted her thoughts, ''there is something urgent I must tell you, Julianna.''

His serious tone captured her full attention. She turned to him, steeling herself for some dire news.

''What is it, Brom?'' she asked hesitantly.

As she stared up at him, his eyelids drooped to half-mast, only partly concealing his look of smoldering desire. One hand came up to cradle her cheek gently.

''This,'' he whispered. ''Words are too weak for the purpose. *This*, I have to tell you.''

Gathering Julianna into his arms, Brom bent over her, staring boldly into her eyes. ''In battle, I take no prisoners, but in love . . .''

Julianna's lips parted the instant his mouth came down on hers. With tender skill, he invaded, forcing her total surrender. As his rough velvet tongue ravaged, she knew this battle was done. She was indeed his prisoner—for now, forevermore.

By the time he released her, Julianna's senses were whirling and a warm, sweet ache had kindled deep inside her.

"Dearest heart," he murmured against her sweetly bruised lips, "I mean to ask something of you before I go."

"Don't," she begged softly.

"But I must," he insisted.

"I mean, don't *go*, Brom!"

He clutched her in his arms—a man gone desperate—and murmured against her hair, "Ah, if all of life were only as simple and as pleasurable as loving you."

"Your question?" Julianna prompted gently.

"'Tis not the time. You'll hear it soon enough, dear heart."

Suddenly, Brom seemed urgently pressed. Muttering to himself about winds and tides and ticking clocks, he shepherded Julianna out of the house and toward the shining river.

Julianna noticed that last night's snow and gloomy skies had vanished along with the elms that bordered the drive. Netherwood blazed in all its autumn glory. Fall roses lifted their full-blown blossoms to the sun. She smiled, relieved to realize she had arrived in time, before Brom sailed away.

As they walked, hand-in-hand, down the hill toward Brom's ship, Julianna realized his kisses had left her weak with longing. Something deep inside her ached with a burning so sweet that tears threatened to spring to her eyes.

She glanced up at him. The wind ruffling his long ebony hair and the happy excitement of the smile on his face made her want to touch him, to kiss him, to hold him so that nothing could ever bring him harm. But she knew she could not be his armor against the world. Only Brom could make the decision to fight or not to fight, to die or not to die. Still, Julianna meant to do everything in her limited power to sway his decision toward peace and life and love.

"I adore you, Julianna," he whispered to her.

Their eyes met and held. She could feel his gaze as if he were caressing her intimately. A smile trembled on her lips. She felt shy with him suddenly. But her heart sang in her breast at his words.

"And you, my dearest?" he begged gently. "Could you find it in your heart to love such a great, hulking Dutchman? A pirate, some say, who tends to fight too much, drink too hard, and live every day of his life as if it were his last?" His voice dropped to an intimate whisper. "Could you love me, Julianna, even for a time?"

Tears sprang to her eyes at his words and his gentle tone. "Forever," she whispered. "I could love you forever, Brom darling."

But even as Julianna spoke the words, she wondered how much time they really had left.

# Chapter Fourteen

The journey down the Hudson—or the Muhheakunnuk as the Indians had named it or the Mauritius as the Dutch called it or the North River as the English of early New-York referred to the great waterway—proved a glorious adventure for Julianna. Out of the Tappan Zee they sailed south through the reaches of the Palisades, then on toward the great bay.

Standing beside Brom on deck, she watched the misty hills roll by at water's edge. *Bachelor's Delight*, swept along by the wind in her canvas, fairly danced over the surface, speeding them ever closer to New-York. Once Julianna looked skyward to see an eagle riding the airstreams overhead. Moments later, she watched two Indians pass silently in their white birch bark canoe.

The whole scene was peaceful and quiet and soothing. Gone were the smoking, clanging steamboats she knew so well. Only the silence of nature and the softness of the wind and sun reigned over the majestic river.

From time to time she glanced toward Brom, trying to convince herself that all of this was real, that *he* was real, that she was not dreaming. He stood beside her—tall, authoritative, the master of his vessel. His very presense made her feel safe and guarded. Dressed in high fashion for the governor's reception, Brom was nonetheless ready for any danger that might threaten. He cut a gallant figure in his rich suit of dark crimson damask. Gold chains, much heavier than those Julianna wore, wound round about his neck. A broad-brimmed hat with a sweeping red plume shaded his black eyes, while a dagger with a bejeweled hilt gleamed at his waist and a pair of pistols hung from a scarlet silk sling about his shoulder.

Brom sensed Julianna staring at him and looked down. "Your thoughts, dearest heart?"

Julianna laughed softly and reached out to touch his hand. "My thoughts? Oh, Brom, my mind is so filled at the moment that I could never begin to tell you all I'm thinking."

"But they are pleasant thoughts?"

He slipped his arms about her waist and she leaned back against his broad chest.

"The most pleasant I could ever imagine," she answered softly.

"In that case, I hate to spoil them," he replied, "but I'm afraid I must. There are things you should know before we arrive at the governor's manse."

Julianna turned slightly to look up into Brom's face. His smile had vanished. He looked, if not truly grim, at the very least solemn. A stir of uneasiness passed through her.

"What is it, Brom?"

"You know of my plans with Captain Kidd—our assignment from Lord Bellomont to sail against the pirates."

Julianna's heart quickened. She knew more than he thought, thanks to Pastor Ten Eyck.

"I know something of them," she answered cautiously.

"Well, I must warn you not to speak of these things to anyone tonight. Governor Fletcher is, to put it nicely, a necessitous man, craving riches more than most. He is in the very thick of it with the pirates you'll likely meet at his home. He can be trusted no more than any of those black-hearted freebooters." Brom paused and turned Julianna around to face him to make sure she was both hearing and understanding the gravity of his warning. Confident that his words were sinking in, he continued. "And my neighbor, Frederick Philipse. Above all others, he is to be avoided when it comes to these secret plans."

Julianna frowned. She had never met Philipse, of course, but she had considered him an upstanding citizen from all she had heard about him in her own time. How could he be involved with pirates? Had history given a coat of whitewash to the man's reputation?

Before she could ask any questions aloud, Brom answered them for her. "Philipse shares in the profits of every black-flagged crew that sails into Madagascar. He financed that port of missing men off the east coast of Africa. His reputation in these parts may be spotless, but he is as bloody as the rest, providing them with shelter, then arranging the sale of their ill-got goods and taking his cut off the top. Should he get wind of our plans, failure—nay, *disaster*—is assured."

"You needn't worry about me, Brom." Julianna laughed a bit nervously. "Why would any of these men question me about your affairs? They probably won't pay the slightest attention to me."

Now it was Brom's turn to laugh long and hard. "Ah, my dearest heart, what low stock you place on your charms. Certainly not a man there would give you a glance because of your perfect face or your eyes like glittering emeralds."

His tone was affectionately mocking. "And of course they'd never notice that bonfire of tresses sweeping your alabaster shoulders." He leaned down and kissed a tender spot close to her neck. Then his hand sought her satin-clad breast. "Nor, for any reason, would these luscious mounds of delight attract a single longing male glance. Whyever should they?"

Sweeping his hat off his head, he bent over her suddenly, drawing her close. Julianna felt his moist lips, then his tongue tease the naked flesh where her gown rode low on her breasts. A staggering tremor of desire raced through her.

"Brom, no," she scolded softly. "Not in front of your men!"

He laughed and hugged her tightly. "My men are well trained to be blind to what they dare not see. I promise you, I could toss your skirts right here on the open deck and they would go about their tasks as usual, seeing nothing amiss in my actions."

Julianna pushed gently out of his embrace, her cheeks flaming at the mere suggestion of such an act. "If you don't mind, I'd rather not test that theory just now."

A flurry of activity on deck alerted them to the fact that they were nearing the harbor. Brom excused himself and went about his duties, sailing his ship right up to the government dock at the Battery before he called the order to his first mate to have the sailors furl the sheets.

Julianna's eyes were wide with her first glimpse of New-York. A dozen or more sailing ships occupied the vast port. They were similar to Brom's except that most of them flew the skull-and-crossbones on a black field. She experienced a sudden sense of dread.

"Pirates!" she gasped softly. "*Real* pirates!" Until this moment, she realized suddenly, she had not actually believed all this was true.

Julianna looked beyond the harbor, toward the town. She was hardly able to believe her eyes. Brom's New-York looked so very different from the great, sprawling city she knew. The tallest structure, except for a single windmill toward the East River that towered above all else, stood no higher than Netherwood's three floors. Each residence had its own beehive with its busy workers producing honey for sweetener and beeswax for candles, just like at home. In fact, most of the buildings along the quay looked very much like her own home, with their stone, wood, and brick construction, dormers, and stepped gables.

The neat houses, most sharing common walls, lined narrow streets that led off from the Bowling Green. She recognized the small greensward; she knew it would look very much the same two hundred years from now. The single wider street she realized must be Broadway—or at least it would be someday. Beyond the cluster of houses, she glimpsed forested hills, miles and miles of uncivilized territory.

"How strange!" she murmured under her breath. "All the trees I know are in Central Park."

Continuing to study the area, she noted that every house on the harbor had its own wooden dock. The road along the waterfront was muddy from a recent rain and rutted from wagon wheels. A small army of pigs and goats fought over refuse piles, creating a terrible racket.

The sun was setting, casting a glow of pearly-orange over the scene. In many windows candlelight winked into life while she watched, as if by magic.

Directly before them lay their destination—the English fort with its quarry stone walls and, inside those stark ramparts, the governor's residence. A nervous flutter ran through Julianna as she thought of the coming evening. How would she converse with the governor's guests? She must be careful to bring up nothing about the future with these strangers. What would she think of them? More importantly, what would they think of her?

"Ready, dearest?"

Julianna looked up. Brom was smiling down at her, offering his arm.

"As ready as I'll ever be, I suppose."

Brom threw back his head a laughed. "You sound as if I'm leading you to the gibbet."

"Don't even mention such a thing!" Julianna gasped.

Again Brom laughed. "There is really nothing to be nervous about," he assured her. "It's been my experience that Governor Fletcher provides grand entertainment. You'll no doubt find his guests fascinating."

"Pirates, Brom? Fascinating?"

"You have no idea," he whispered, leaning close to steal a kiss. "Just mind you don't let one of them whisk you away to his ship. Then, of course, I'd be forced to follow and murder the bastard." He paused and flicked an imaginary speck off his damask-clad shoulder. "And it would be a pity to ruin my new suit, don't you think?"

Moments later, they were in a cart, being hauled through the muddy street right up to the governor's door. His house was much like the others, but of only two stories. Uniformed guards in bright-red coats stood outside. One jumped to help Julianna down from the wagon. Another hurried to open the front door for them.

"Captain Brom Vanderzee and his lady!" the English soldier announced as they entered.

A great puff of blue smoke issued forth along with a babble of music and voices. Julianna also caught whiffs of strong brew and roasting meat, exotic spices and imported perfumes.

A rotund man in a powdered wig, his blue satin waistcoat

stained with food droppings, met them at the door and ushered them into the midst of the din.

"Captain Vanderzee, I am delighted to see you again." The pudgy man was forced to shout to be heard over all the noise. He pumped Brom's hand vigorously. "You keep yourself at your country place far too much these days."

"I'm delighted you invited me, Governor Fletcher," Brom replied. "I'd like you to meet my friend, Miss Julianna Doran."

The round-eyed Englishman gripped Julianna's hand in his short, plump fingers and kissed it with a wet smack. He chuckled then and glanced up at Brom. "Now I understand what keeps you in the up country, my good fellow. 'Twould be a rare delight to go into exile with such a winsome beauty, I'll admit."

Someone called to the governor from across the crowded parlor. He bowed quickly, then moved away.

Julianna clung to Brom's arm, shrinking close to his side for protection. The raucous gathering made her jittery. She didn't like Governor Fletcher very much and she wasn't sure she'd be any fonder of his rowdy assortment of guests.

The room was filled with exotically gowned women and dark-complected, foreign-looking men whose garish costumes outshone even those of their partners. If Julianna had felt the least bit self-conscious about the cut of her bodice, there was certainly no need for shame any longer. She looked positively demure beside most of the other female guests. Breasts bloomed about the room like pale white blossoms. Even as the women chose to display their lovely wares, the bold buccaneers wore trousers so tightly fit that Julianna found herself blushing, head to toe, at the sight. She vowed to keep her eyes focused above neck-level all evening.

Brom introduced her all around. So many names—English, Dutch, German—and so many faces—handsome, scarred, leering, scheming. The more people she met, the more she withdrew. She needn't have worried over meeting Brom's neighbor, Frederick Philipse. When Brom asked after him, the governor said he was off to Virginia on business. But pirate after pirate came to pay their flirtatious respects to the shy Julianna—their names escaping her as soon as she heard them. Only their faces would remain in her memory to haunt her dreams.

Not until a woman pushed her way through the crowd did any name really imprint itself on Julianna's mind.

"Brom, darling!" The words seemed to ooze from the woman's full, carmine-tinted lips. Her hair was several shades darker than Julianna's own red-gold tresses—approximately the color of the river at sunset on an evening before a killing frost, Julianna mused. The older woman's pearl-pale shoulders were shapely and completely bare. Her flame-colored gown dipped so low on her overample bosom that pink crescents peeked out from the gold lace trim.

Julianna felt Brom stiffen beside her as the striking redhead leaned quickly forward and kissed him full on the mouth.

"Well, aren't you going to introduce me to this charming child?" the brazen female asked, giving the barest nod toward Julianna, but never taking her eyes from Brom's face.

When she drew nearer, offering her limp hand, Julianna saw by the lamplight that the woman was several years older than she had assumed at first. White powder caked the tiny creases about her dark eyes and her lip rouge seeped into age cracks above her upper lip. She was surely years older than Julianna herself, and might have had as much as a decade on Brom.

Brom cleared his throat and glanced down at Julianna, an odd expression of apology in his stormy eyes.

"Katrina, I would like to present Miss Julianna Doran."

The moment Brom said her name, Juli saw the woman's eyes narrow for an instant to slits. Her wide smile faded. She quickly recovered, exclaiming over Julianna's beauty and youth to Brom as if she were truly a child or a mere plaything of sorts.

Suddenly, a cold chill gripped Julianna. "Katrina," Brom had called this woman. Katrina of her dreams, of her fears.

"Pardon me," Julianna interrupted, "but I don't believe I caught your last name."

It was Brom who answered. "You didn't catch it, dearest heart, because I'm not sure what it is at present." He turned a chilly smile on the woman. "Is it still Rhinehart, Kat, or have you finally convinced old Thomas to make an honest woman of you?"

Julianna gasped softly and squeezed Brom's arm in reproval. She had never heard him speak to anyone in such an icy manner. At the same time, she saw Katrina's face flash a look of pure hatred at her.

"You must forgive your lover," Katrina said in a syrupy voice to Julianna. "I'm afraid he's a poor loser. And, for your information, sir," she spat at Brom, "the name is still Rhinehart, as it shall remain."

"Poor Kat," Brom said sarcastically. "But then, you're better off simply warming old Thomas's bed. After all, what woman would want to be saddled with a name like Kat Tew?" He chuckled, but there was no humor in it. "Sounds like the result of a touch too much snuff."

Seething, Katrina Rhinehart turned from them, pushing several of the guests out of her way and managing to further stain the governor's waistcoat as she knocked the drink from his hand.

Julianna felt Brom's grip relax on her arm. He let out a pent-up breath. Obviously, no matter what he and Katrina Rhinehart might have once meant to each other, they were no longer even friends. Still, Julianna couldn't understand his behavior.

"Brom, you were so rude to her," she scolded gently. "What's come over you?"

"I apologize, dearest heart, for any embarrassment I may have caused you. But, believe me, Kat can be handled in no other fashion. Stay clear of that one. She is pure poison!"

*So I've heard*, Julianna reminded herself silently.

Suddenly, a loud burst of laughter from the other side of the room attracted Julianna's attention. Several of the burly, darkly-handsome pirates formed a circle around a lithe, black-tressed young woman who wore a sheer peasant blouse, a full skirt of many bright hues, and gold coins about her hips, wrists, and neck. The exotic girl showered her ogling male audience with smiles while she whirled like a dervish to the enthusiastic accompaniment of the men's clapping hands.

Fascinated, Julianna asked, "Who is that, Brom?"

A deep frown furrowed his brow and he shook his head in obvious disapproval. "That's Maeyken Huyberton, and she's letting herself in for a pile of trouble, mark my words. She shouldn't be here, and she definitely shouldn't be showing off for that pack of jackels. When her parents find out . . ."

Brom went on for several moments, listing the punishments the elder Huybertons might inflict on their wayward daughter, but Julianna wasn't listening. Her gaze remained fixed on Maeyken, who was now passing out kisses to each man in the circle. Quite obviously, the pretty, doll-like woman was a flirt and perhaps worse.

As Julianna watched, one of the pirates—a tall, mean-looking fellow with three gold rings skewering one ear—shoved all the others away. When he captured Maeyken in his arms, planted a smacking kiss on her breast, then dropped several coins into her palm, Julianna realized this

256

Maeyken Huyberton's true calling. The next instant, the pirate swept her up into his arms and toward the door, confirming Julianna's worst suspicions. She felt a pang of outrage on the other Maeyken's behalf that her ancestor should act in such a scandalous fashion.

Before making their exit, the pair paused briefly to wave good-bye to the crowd. In that instant, Julianna's eyes met the pale-blue of Maeyken's. The younger woman shuddered visibly at the impact of their locked gazes and hid her face against her pirate's neck. Julianna, too, felt a jolt to her senses. For several moments after Maeyken and her pirate disappeared, Julianna continued to stare at the doorway.

Across the room, another female was eyeing Julianna with an equal amount of interest and curiosity. The woman—short, plump, with lively sapphire eyes and pale-gold hair—recognized Brom Vanderzee's lady. She had seen her once from a distance at Netherwood. But now that she had a better chance to observe the flame-haired beauty at closer range, an uneasiness stirred deep within her. Surely it couldn't be!

"But it is," Sarah Kidd murmured to herself. "It is Julianna—right here, right now."

Sarah touched her husband's arm, drawing his attention from a serious conversation with several other men of the sea.

"What is it, pet?" he asked, his dark eyes showering love on this woman who had come into his life as if by magic.

"Look yonder," she said, nodding toward Brom. "Captain Vanderzee's just arrived. And he's brought the lovely red-haired woman I told you about. The very same one I glimpsed from the garden at Netherwood."

William Kidd glanced across the room. "Ah, good! We'll get to meet her at last. What say we ask them home to stay the night with us? I can fill Brom in on all that's happened, and you, dear Sarah, can spend all the time you like pumping the poor girl for details of the great captain's latest affair."

Sarah nodded, still staring at Julianna. "A fine idea, my love. There's much we girls have to talk about, I'm sure."

Julianna spied the couple coming toward them—a tall, wiry Scotsman and his pretty, pink-and-gold wife. The man looked most impressive in his bright velvets and silver chains, but it was the woman in her quaint Dutch dress and stiff lace hat who caught and held Julianna's attention. For the first time all evening, she felt a need and a desire to reach out to one of these strangers. The smiling little woman had dancing blue eyes and a look about her that made Julianna long suddenly for her carefree childhood days. An ache of nostalgia settled over her heart. But why should the sight of this plump Dutch matron stir such strong emotions?

"Brom, my good chap!" William Kidd hailed. "It's been too long."

"Too long, indeed!" Brom answered, clapping a big hand on the captain's shoulder.

Brom introduced Julianna to Captain and Mrs. Kidd, then the two men moved slightly away to refill their tankards with a powerful brew called Bride's Tears. Left alone with the captain's young wife, Julianna found herself overcome with strange sensations, but at a loss for words. Sarah Kidd took the dilemma out of Julianna's hands.

"I saw Kat come over here," Sarah said without preamble. "You must be careful of that one, Juli."

Julianna stared down at the woman, her eyes wide with surprise. "You called me Juli, Mrs. Kidd. No one . . . that is, no one *here* has ever called me that," she stammered.

The younger woman's smile put Julianna instantly at ease. "I hope you don't mind. It seems to fit you. And you will call me Sarah, please. Friends should not be so formal."

"Sarah?" Juli's head was spinning suddenly. "I had a cousin by that name."

"Did you now?" the young woman asked, her blue eyes sparkling with some secret light. "And were you fond of your cousin Sarah?"

"Oh, very! She was my favorite," Julianna confessed. "Much sweeter than her older sister, though I loved them both."

Suddenly, Sarah gripped Julianna's hand in both of hers. "Thank you," she murmured.

Julianna looked at the other woman, puzzled by her words.

"I mean, thank you for telling me about your family," Sarah added quickly. "Later, we'll have time to talk at length. I hope you will tell me all about yourself."

In that moment, Julianna felt extremely close to Sarah Kidd even though they had only just met. "I hope we can be friends," she said to the bright-eyed young matron. "I'm a stranger here, you see. I know no one—except Brom, of course—and the people I've met here tonight. But I must admit to you, Sarah, that out of them all, yours is the only friendship I care to cultivate."

"You're a wise girl, Juli," Sarah murmured. Then she added in a mysterious tone, "But then you always were, weren't you?"

Before Julianna could respond, Brom and Captain Kidd returned. Brom slipped his hand into Julianna's and smiled down into her eyes, offering her a secret signal of longing.

"We've been invited to stay the night with the Kidds, dearest heart. Would that please you?"

"Oh, Brom, yes!" Julianna cried, beaming back at him.

"Sarah and I have become fast friends already." Turning to Captain Kidd, she smiled and said, "Thank you for your invitation, sir. We accept with great delight."

Supper was soon announced. The two couples filled their pewter plates from the heavily laden sideboard. As they moved down the line, Brom identified the roasted meats for Julianna.

"That's wild turkey, of course," he said, pointing to an enormous, crispy-brown bird. "That thirty-pound hunk there on the huge salver is a haunch of venison. Over here we have barbecued turtle, an especial favorite of mine. Then there's the duck of your choice—mallard, canvasback, or teal—along with passenger pigeon, heath hen, goose, perch, shad, oysters."

Julianna kept eyeing a smaller platter that held the carcass of some unidentifiable creature that looked suspiciously like a cat. Sarah, noticing the direction of her gaze and her worried expression, said, "Try it, Juli. You'll find it quite delicious."

Turning a suspicious glance toward her new friend, Julianna asked, "But what *is* it? I really don't think I like its looks."

Sarah giggled girlishly. "It's not what you're thinking, Juli. We don't eat house cats here. Try it! Go ahead."

Julianna pursed her lips as a child will when being forced to taste something new. She shook her head firmly, negatively.

"Blast!" Brom exploded good-naturedly. "It's only raccoon. And one of our tastiest critters in these parts." He pulled off one leg and plopped it on Julianna's plate. Later, one tiny taste led to another and soon Julianna was enjoying this newfound delicacy that tasted like pork along with the others.

Once supper was finished, the musicians struck up a lively tune. Julianna watched the dancers, wondering how it would

260

feel to have Brom hold her in his arms and sweep her around the floor. She glanced about and her heart sank. Brom and William Kidd stood in a far corner, locked in serious conversation. Both men seemed oblivious to the music, the dancing, and the glances of their two neglected ladies.

Suddenly, a shadow fell over Julianna. She looked up, startled. Before her stood a broad, dark man with a rough sort of face that sent shivers down her spine. His eyes were set close together and were as black as the pits of hell. A thin growth of beard smudged his heavy, square jowl.

Without asking her permission, the rough-looking stranger reached down and gripped her hand. "I feel a mighty urge to dance, wench," he ordered.

Before Julianna knew what was happening, she was in the man's big, hairy arms, being whirled about the floor. She glanced toward Brom, hoping for help, but his back was turned on the dancers.

"You're a mite high-toned for a scoundrel like Vanderzee," the ruffian growled into her ear. "He don't know how to treat a lady proper. 'Tis Thomas Tew who could show you what it's like to be with a *real* man. See, I'm like Governor Fletcher's right hand. Treats me real fine, he does. You act nice and I might even get him to take you along for a ride in his fancy carriage. It's a right comfy place for wooing a ripe wench."

*Thomas Tew . . . Katrina's man!* The thought swirled in Julianna's head. Panic raced through her. She didn't want to dance with this pirate, *especially* since he belonged to the mean-tempered Rhinehart woman. Julianna wasn't sure why she should fear Kat, but enough people had warned her so that she now believed their words.

"Please let me sit down," she begged. "I'm feeling quite dizzy."

Tew only clutched her closer and bellowed a laugh. "As you should," he said in a husky whisper. "Ain't a woman alive who don't feel that way when she's rubbed up close against old Tom Tew. Did I want, I could make you swoon right here and now.''

So saying, he slipped one thick arm completely around Julianna's waist and gripped her tightly to his chest. She gasped for breath. She could feel her breasts straining to escape her bodice, so strong was his hold on her. And even through her skirts, she became alarmingly aware of the hot bulge in his tight breeches. Her soft moan of distress only encouraged the vile pirate.

Rescue came from an unexpected quarter. Suddenly, a soft hand with sharp nails gripped Juli's arm and whirled her out of Tew's embrace. A scream of outrage silenced all other sounds in the room. Then a loud smack cracked like a pistol shot in the stillness as Katrina Rhinehart delivered a mighty blow to Julianna's cheek.

"How dare you tempt my man, you little slut!" Seething, Kat raised her hand to strike again.

Brom was there instantly, catching Kat's arm and placing himself protectively between Julianna and her attacker.

"Be off with you, woman," he ordered. "And take this ruttish bastard with you. We've no wish for dealings with any of your kind."

Julianna watched the blood drain from Kat's flushed face. The Rhinehart woman's attention focused solely on Brom now. It was as if everyone else in the room had vanished.

"It wasn't always so," she whispered to Brom. "There was a time when you cared . . . when you loved me. Admit it!"

"I'll admit no such thing because it isn't true." Brom's tone was deadly.

Taking Julianna's arm, he turned from Kat without another word. Bidding a stiff good night to the governor, Brom led Julianna out the door. The Kidds followed close on their heels.

No one spoke until they were clear of the fort walls. Then Captain Kidd said, "Damn, that was close! I congratulate you, Brom. I'm not sure I could have held myself in check had that woman struck my Sarah. But a fight with Tew would have been the ruination of all our plans. How did you manage to hold on to that quick temper of yours?"

At that instant, Brom's legendary temper exploded into a stream of curses that fairly turned the air blue. Julianna covered her ears to shut out the foul sounds. When he had spent his rage verbally, Brom turned to Julianna. Oblivious to the Kidds' knowing smiles, he crushed her to him, smothering her bruised face with kisses. When finally his lips captured hers, he kissed her deeply, searching her mouth, while his big, gentle hands fondled her breasts.

If Thomas Tew's rough embrace had made her dizzy with revulsion, Brom's loving attentions came close to making her swoon with desire. She ached with wanting him. The pain of her longing was nearly unbearable. She clung to him, molding her quivering body to his strong, hard flesh. Tears sprang to her eyes. She wondered suddenly if they had ever made love . . . if they ever would.

"Julianna, Julianna," Brom murmured between kisses. "I could have torn Tew limb from limb back there. I could have gutted him where he stood. How dare he touch you? How dare he even look at you?"

Julianna tried to soothe Brom with soft words and softer kisses, but he was a man gone mad with rage and jealousy.

"And *Kat*!" he snarled. "I should have her arrested for assault . . . have the evil whore stripped and lashed in the public square. If things were bad before, they are far worse now. Stay away from her, dearest heart! While I'm gone, you must avoid her at all costs."

Brom's words—*while I'm gone*—made Julianna feel suddenly as if she was the one who had been publicly whipped. The pain was that great.

"Please, Brom, don't leave me!" she begged, her tears flowing now.

"Come along, you two," Captain Kidd called to them. "We'll have a fight yet, if we linger here much longer. Tew's mates are likely to come searching for you, Brom."

Julianna clung to Brom still, not wanting to move, never wanting their embrace to end.

Finally, it was Sarah's soft voice that urged them into action. "I hope you won't mind," she said quietly, "but I've only the one bedroom to put you in when we get home. Netherwood is far more spacious than our townhouse. But perhaps you can adjust to the inconvenience for this one night."

Brom's lips were on Julianna's as Sarah spoke. Juli felt a smile spread wide when he heard their hostess's words.

He looked up and grinned even broader. "We'll manage, Sarah." Then he stared back down into Julianna's dewy eyes. "Won't we, dearest heart?"

Julianna, her pulses racing with anticipation, nodded. She had to bite her lip to stay a sob of pure joy.

"We'll manage nicely, Brom darling. Ever so nicely, I'm sure!"

Overhearing Julianna's comment, Sarah Kidd smiled brightly and whispered to herself, "Somehow, I knew you would, dear cousin."

# Chapter Fifteen

The Kidds' home—a three-story Dutch brick residence—
stood at the northeastern edge of town, where Pearl fronted
the water at the end of Wall Street. The Water Gate at the
back of town loomed only a short distance down their lane,
set into the east-west wall that served to keep Indians out
and livestock in.

Julianna felt great relief as they climbed the stoop and a
servant opened the front door to welcome them. The governor's reception had not been the pleasant evening she had
anticipated, and their trek through the dark, narrow streets
of New-York had unnerved her further. But now all was
well. She was in the cozy home of her new friends and,
unless she had mistaken Brom's meaning, she was about to
spend her first night in the arms of the man she loved.

Captain Kidd showed them into his library, a warm room
with books and charts and comfortable furniture, much like
its counterpart at Netherwood. It was a man's room, but so

265

far as Julianna had seen, New-York was a man's world. A fast-living, hard-drinking, dangerous place to reside.

Julianna was not surprised when her hostess suggested that the two of them take to the kitchen to allow the men privacy to talk.

As she turned to leave, Brom caught her in his arms for one last kiss. "This won't take long, dearest heart. Keep that glow for me."

Julianna smiled up at him, glowing, as he had said. She wasn't used to being embraced so often, and certainly not with people looking on. Quickly, blushing slightly, she turned and followed Sarah out of the room.

"I know you want to stay close to Brom," Sarah said as she showed Julianna down the hall to the back of the house. "But since the first moment I set eyes on you this evening, I have been dying to get you alone for a good long talk."

Sarah ushered Julianna into the large kitchen with its enormous fireplace and numerous cupboards. Motioning her guest to have a seat at the square pine table, Sarah poured tea, stirring a spoonful of honey into each cup. Her duties as hostess concluded, Mrs. Kidd turned to Julianna and stared her straight in the eye.

"You *still* don't realize the truth, do you, Juli?"

"The truth?" she queried, puzzled.

"You don't recognize me, I mean."

Juli studied her new friend's face for a moment, feeling she had seen her before, but not sure where. "Should I?"

Sarah Kidd chuckled. "Perhaps not. Back when we knew each other I was plump, but not in the matronly fashion I am today. Alas, bearing a child will alter one's girlish figure. And, too, I always wore my hair down, not braided and pinned up this way. You certainly never saw me wearing these old-fashioned Dutch clothes, either."

Sarah removed her stiff lace cap, then let down her braids, fluffing out her hair about her face.

"Of course I wasn't married the last time we were together." She paused and chuckled at some memory. "I was only a frightened child of twelve."

"Frightened, you say?" Julianna was frowning now as some misplaced shard of memory struggled to fit itself to others drifting randomly about in her mind.

"Admit it, Juli. Weren't you frightened at the prospect of invading the spirit world, too? I know you tried to act brave so that Lettie wouldn't call you a 'fraidy-cat, but the very sight of that Ouija board made me shiver."

All the pieces slid into place with a mental snap. *"Sarah? Little Sarah?"* Juli cried, staring hard at Mrs. Kidd.

"One and the same," the young woman answered, opening her arms to receive Juli's hug. "Your very own cousin."

"But you . . . you drowned!" Julianna stammered.

Sarah shook her head. "No," she said quietly. "I had a bad feeling about going out in the boat that day. When Mother insisted I accompany them, I hid so she couldn't find me. Since you are here with me this very moment, I assume you can guess exactly where I concealed myself that day."

Julianna was still staring at her cousin, trying to believe all this was true. "You hid in the cellar? In the spring room?"

"That I did!" Sarah replied. "It was such a warm summer afternoon. After a time, it grew hot and stuffy down there. Afraid to venture out for fear Mother might yet spy me and drag me along with them, I drank from the spring. Almost immediately I fell asleep, and when I woke up I found myself lying on the grass under a buttonwood tree at the Battery with night coming on. Then I was *really* frightened." She chuckled and winked. "Two sailors mistook me for one of the girls who nightly make themselves available in that area. Lucky for me, William Kidd happened along just in time to save me from that amorous pair. One thing led to another, and in a few days my captain asked me to marry him. There was nothing else I could do, but I wouldn't have turned him down in any case. I think we fell in love the moment we set eyes on each other. Since then, this place has been my home. My husband and now our daughter are my whole life.''

Julianna rubbed one finger along the edge of the smooth pine table, a million thoughts warring inside her head.

"It seems much the same between Brom and me," Juli confessed. "Since that first night when I saw him on stage—"

"On stage?" Sarah interrupted. "You mean you saw him before the night with the Ouija board?"

Julianna's head shot up. What had she said? She had first seen *Elliot* on stage, not Brom. And how on earth did Sarah know about Brom's appearance the night of the séance?

"You needn't look so startled, Juli. I saw Brom, too, that night. But I could tell you were the one he had come to find.''

Julianna continued to stare at her cousin. "You and Lettie saw Brom, too?"

"No, only *I* saw him. Or at least Lettie would never admit to having seen anything.''

"But why us?" Juli wondered aloud. "Why should you and I have seen him, Sarah? What does it all mean?"

The younger woman shrugged. "Perhaps because you and I were meant to come to Brom and William, to this time, to these men.''

"It's all so confusing . . . so unreal," Juli sighed.

Sarah reached across the table and gripped her cousin's hand. "Juli, there's something I must tell you in strictest confidence. It gets even more confusing, I'm afraid. Did you see the young woman who left with that pirate tonight after dancing and flirting with all the male guests?"

Julianna nodded. "Yes, our old nursemaid's ancestor, the first Maeyken Huyberton."

"Not quite," Sarah answered, raising a dark-gold brow. "I've met the girl and talked with her. You'll think I'm daft, but I'm sure that's *our* Maeyken, the very same. Somehow, she found her way back here, too."

"No, that can't be possible, Sarah," Julianna stated with authority. "You see, I read the registry at the old Dutch Church. The woman we saw tonight was born in Tarrytown in 1675. Besides, look at the two of us. We were the same age when we arrived here that we were when we left our time. It doesn't seem possible that Maeyken could have dropped so many years along the way." Julianna thought for a moment, then added with conviction, "No! She's not our Maeyken!"

"Hm-m-m." Sarah narrowed her eyes and chewed on the end of a lock of her hair as Juli had seen her do often as a child. "This is most befuddling. You're right, of course, about her age. She must be in her early twenties now. But, as I said, I've talked with her at some length. I know the girl quite well and she's the very image of what our Maeyken must have looked like in her youth—same eyes, same smile. Even her laugh sounds familiar. Do you suppose she might someday pass into the future as easily as we traveled back to this century?"

While Sarah talked, Julianna was doing some thinking. "I suppose that could happen. And it would explain a lot to me. It seemed inordinately strange when old Maeyken told me that she had seen Brom that night the same as you and I did. And she knew so much about him. She's also warned me against Katrina Rhinehart. I found an old trunk of Kat's in the attic at Netherwood and dressed up in one of her gowns. Maeyken nearly fainted from fright when she saw me."

"With good reason!" Sarah exclaimed. "Have you heard the tale of Katrina's child?" Before giving Juli time to reply, Sarah rushed on. "Years before I got here, Kat took her newborn daughter to the spring where Netherwood would eventually be built and left the infant there. The baby disappeared. Kat has lived with the fear ever since that her child would return a grown woman, seeking revenge on such a heartless mother."

"And?" Juli asked, all attention.

"After meeting Kat tonight, don't you understand, Julianna?" Sarah asked in an exasperated tone. "Don't you even suspect?"

"Suspect *what*? Out with it, Sarah!"

"*You* are Katrina Rhinehart's daughter!" Sarah exclaimed. "It has to be! All my life I've heard the strange tale of how Aunt Ruthie found you in the woods beside the spring. Where else could you have come from? And look at you—Kat's fiery hair, Kat's eyes, her dimple in your chin. Why, even your smiles are the same, though she seldom uses hers. The first time I met her, she reminded me of someone. I studied and studied on it, but couldn't think who. Then a short time ago, something young Maeyken said made everything fall into place."

Julianna was sitting on the very edge of her chair, leaning across the table toward her cousin. "What, Sarah? What did Maeyken say?"

Sarah closed her eyes, thinking hard, trying to remember Maeyken's exact words. Finally, she shook her head and answered, "Oh, I'm not sure. Something about Kat being out for blood . . . that she wouldn't take kindly to her own daughter returning to Netherwood to steal her old lover from her, but that it was sure to happen. Then I saw you that day when William and I visited Brom. Sally and I were in the rose garden and you were up at the bedroom window, looking down at us. The thought crossed my mind then that

Kat's daughter must have returned. When I saw you tonight, I knew for sure."

Julianna leaned back, feeling as if someone had just delivered a mighty blow to her midsection. She had wanted to know who her natural parents were, but the thought of Katrina Rhinehart and that horrible Thomas Tew as her mother and father was almost too much to bear. She could only thank her stars that they hadn't wanted her, that Kat had sent her off as a castaway into another century for Ruthie Doran to find and love. But could any of this be true?

When Julianna had recovered enough to speak, she said, "Sarah, I'm not sure I can believe any of this. It simply can't be."

"Can't it? Think about it for a moment. You, a foundling. The two of us drinking from the spring, then traveling through time, back two hundred years. Surely the reverse is every bit as possible. Kat sent you forward in time where Aunt Ruthie found you, alone and abandoned. Uncle Ephraim advertised in all the papers and notified every authority, so I heard Mother say time and again. But no one came forward to claim you. Maeyken believes Kat is your mother and I believe Maeyken. She may be a tart, but she's a wise and honest tart."

Suddenly, Julianna giggled.

"You find all this funny, do you?" Sarah asked in an abrasive tone.

Juli shook her head, covering her mouth to stifle a full laugh. "Oh, Sarah, I was just thinking of Aunt Martha. Imagine her reaction if she had ever found out about Maeyken's past. Remember how your mother was always telling us that we should listen to Maeyken because we could learn so many things from her?"

Sarah joined in Juli's laughter. "Mother was certainly right about that! There aren't many tricks Maeyken doesn't know. Poor Mother! I'm glad she never knew the truth about our nursemaid. That would have killed her before the accident.''

Julianna sobered immediately. "You know about your parents, then?" she asked in a gentle tone.

"Yes." Sarah nodded. "I'm not sure how I know. But I realized before they ever left to go sailing that they wouldn't come back. I tried to stop them, but they wouldn't listen. That's why I ran and hid. When I woke up and found myself here, in this time and place, I knew they were gone forever and that I had somehow, miraculously, been saved.''

A wistful look came over Juli's face suddenly. "I don't suppose . . ." She paused and looked down at her hands, folded in her lap.

"What, Juli? What's on your mind?"

"Lettie. Is she here, too?" she asked hopefully.

Sarah shook her head. "No," she answered quietly. "I watched Lettie fall and I saw her buried. She's not here.''

"I'm sorry, Sarah," Juli replied. "I know you miss her. *I've* missed you both." She reached over and gripped Sarah's hand. "Mostly you, I must admit.''

"I've missed you, too, Juli," Sarah confided. "It's odd, but I always felt closer to you than I ever did to my sister. Lettie lived in a world all her own—apart from where you and I existed.''

Julianna rose and went to the fireplace, pouring another cup of tea from the kettle hung from the spider. With her back to her cousin, she asked, "Don't you have that the wrong way round, Sarah? You and I are the ones who existed in a world all our own. Lettie may have been the adventurous one, but we were the imaginative ones. *We* saw Brom. Lettie didn't. Perhaps that's why we are here and she isn't.''

A long silence followed before Sarah replied, "You may be right about that. Yes, indeed.''

"Have you ever thought of going back, Sarah?" Julianna

asked, taking her seat again. "I've traveled here and back several times already. I'm not sure how. But it *is* possible."

"No!" Sarah smiled and shook her head firmly. "Nothing's left for me there. Besides, I'm a part of this time now. I love William Kidd and our little Sally. I couldn't leave them. I would never try to go back. I would never want to. But what about you, Juli?"

Julianna sighed deeply, trying to think how to reply. "It's all very strange, Sarah. There is a man back there whom I love. And he loves me. I would have married him not so long ago. Actually, I think Brom somehow willed me not to wed Elliot. I felt this sudden, urgent need to find Brom, but it seemed he had deserted me. Then I found a packet of letters in the attic at Netherwood. Letters Brom had written me from sea and, more startling, love letters I had written to him. They seemed the final, positive clue that this was where I truly belonged."

"I never had such evidence," Sarah confessed. "I simply happened into this time by some odd accident of fate." She paused and her blue eyes sparkled as she smiled at Julianna. "I'm very glad that accident happened. I couldn't be happier, you see."

"Have those other times and places begun to fade in your memory, Sarah?"

"A bit," Juli's cousin admitted. "It's hard to tell how much. I almost never think of that other life I led. It seems so long ago now. Or, I should say, so far in the future. And you?"

Julianna's face went very still and solemn. "When I'm here with Brom, I forget my other life. Even Elliot Creighton, the man I meant to marry, seems only a shadow, a fragment of some dream. Yet I know that if I were there right now I would love him still. It's not that I divide my affection between Elliot and Brom . . ." She paused, trying to think of the proper words to make her cousin understand.

"It's almost as if the two men are the same—as if by loving one, my love for the other only grows and expands." She looked over at Sarah with pleading eyes. "Does that make any sense to you?"

Sarah sighed. "Love, in any form, seldom does. I believe love is a form of madness."

"I know I have a purpose here, Sarah—to save Brom from some terrible fate. Remember the night we first saw him? He'd been wounded. I think if I hadn't found a way back, he would have died from those wounds. I only hope I am equal to the task, when the time comes."

A shiver ran through Julianna as she thought of Brom with his chest bandaged and bleeding. When would it happen? Could it be that she had saved him already? Perhaps at the governor's reception, if she hadn't been there, Brom and Thomas Tew would have fought over Kat. Brom might have been mortally wounded. Juli brightened, convinced that that was the case.

"I believe the danger is past," she told Sarah. "I don't think anything dreadful will befall Brom now."

"You're probably right," Sarah said, trying to sound convincing.

Suddenly, Pastor Ten Eyck's prediction of Captain Kidd's fate flashed through Julianna's mind. Should she tell Sarah? No, she decided. Her cousin was happy. Knowledge of the future could only ruin whatever time she had left with her husband. In her present optimistic frame of mind, a new and encouraging thought struck Julianna. Perhaps between them, she and Sarah could convince their men not to undertake this dangerous venture. If the two women could do that, then surely history would be altered for the good of all. Brom, she felt, was safe, but not William Kidd. The gallows still loomed large in his future if he insisted on fighting the pirates.

However, Julianna had no time to explore the possibility

274

with Sarah. Brom and William came into the kitchen, putting an end to the women's intimate conversation. Both men wore somber expressions when they entered. Julianna felt a chill pass through her. Brom's eyes were too black, his brow too furrowed.

"Well, out with it!" Sarah demanded. "You've bad news so don't keep your womenfolk waiting and wondering."

Julianna didn't see Captain Kidd smooth his hand lovingly over his wife's soft cheek. Her eyes remained on Brom.

"'Tis not bad news, love," Kidd said quietly. "We have a mission. You know that."

"I do!" Sarah stated bravely. "What I don't know is when you mean to leave?"

"That's what we've just now decided," Brom said.

Julianna's breath caught in her throat.

"Aye, ladies," Captain Kidd added. "We sail one week from this day."

"A *week*?" Juli murmured. Her eyes went moist as she stared up at Brom. "Only seven days together?"

Brom raised her trembling hand to his lips and kissed her fingertips. "A lifetime together and then some, my dearest heart. This will be but a brief separation."

"We'll sail out of New-York and set our course straight for Madagascar," William Kidd announced. "Our prey will be any buccaneer in our path who flies the black flag. And our pay will be the treasure in their holds." He smiled down at his wife. "When we return, love, I'll drape you in diamonds and emeralds from head to toe. I'll bring rings for your fingers and pearls for your hair. You'll be the richest lady in all of New-York."

"I am that at this very moment," Sarah replied lovingly.

Sarah, long the captain's wife, took the news far better than Julianna. Or at least the younger woman seemed better able to put up a brave front.

"I suppose you'll be needing your sea chest packed, Captain," Sarah said. "We'd best get at it this minute."

"We've guests, love," Kidd replied, nodding toward Brom and Juli. "You should see to them first."

"Our guests seem to be taking care of themselves quite well," Sarah observed fondly.

The married couple watched as Julianna reached up and, placing her palms on both side of Brom's head, drew his mouth down to hers, giving him a deep, lingering kiss.

"Why don't you show Julianna to the bedroom, Sarah dear? I'll stay down here with Brom until she's settled in."

"You're an understanding man, William Kidd," his wife answered. "And a loving man, too, God be thanked!" She stood up and kissed his cheek. "Once I've settled our guest, you'll find me waiting for you upstairs. Don't tarry! We've much to see to before you sail."

"Don't worry!" Kidd answered in a voice husky with emotion, knowing exactly what his wife meant for them to see to first. As she did before every voyage he took, she would spend the next six nights plying him with more love than any man deserved. "Storing it up," she'd told him once. "So that when you're upon the sea of a dark and lonely night, you have only to close your eyes and feel your adoring woman pressed close in your arms and closer even to your heart."

Sarah put her hand on Julianna's arm. "Come. I'll show you to your room."

Without a word, only a longing glance toward Brom, Julianna followed her cousin from the kitchen. She was stunned, numb, aching with love for her man, aching with sorrow at the thought of his departure so close at hand.

Sensing her cousin's depression, Sarah gave Juli a stern lecture as they climbed the stairs.

"Chin up, Julianna! It's a sailing man you've chosen to

love and now you must face what inevitably comes with that pleasure. Our men are courageous and we must be the same," Sarah said with steel in her voice. "Show Brom no tears, only smiles. Give him no sorrow to take round the world with him, only the memory of your abiding love. The next six days will be the most glorious you've ever experienced. And the seventh day, when his ship sets sail, will be the blackest of your whole life. But you won't think of that now, do you hear me? You will live one day at the time and pack as much love and joy and happiness into every moment as is humanly possible. Now, let me look at you."

Sarah turned and caught Juli's chin in her hand. She scowled at her cousin. "Are those tears I see?" She shook her head testily. "Shame on you, Julianna Doran! But better *I* should see them than Brom. You *will* smile for him!"

Juli collapsed into her cousin's arms, weeping loudly. "Oh, Sarah, how can you expect me to smile when he's going away? My heart is breaking!"

Gripping Juli's shoulders, Sarah gave the sobbing woman a good hard shake. "Enough!" she scolded. "If you can't help your man, then go back where you came from. Now! I won't have you acting like a simpering child under my roof. Forget your dreams and your hopes and your love. Simply make yourself vanish as quickly as you appeared in our time. We don't need your tears and self-pity."

"But Brom needs me!" Juli exclaimed.

"Brom needs a brave and loving woman at his side. Your noble dreams count for naught. There's no help for Brom's fate. Don't you know that by now? What will be, will be. Do you think I came here on some righteous mission and stayed, claiming I could keep Captain William Kidd from the hangman's noose? No! I read his certain fate in a story-book when I was a child. There's no way I can change it. I accept that. I stayed here to love my man. If you can't bring yourself to accept Brom's fate and do the same, then go away, Julianna.''

Juli's tears dried in an instant. Her shock was total. How could Sarah bear knowing that her husband would die on the gallows far away in England just five years in the future? And, knowing what she did, how could she let him sail away and leave her now?

"Sarah, I'm so sorry," Julianna said in a firmer voice. "What can I do?"

"Nothing for me," her cousin replied. "I've accepted what I know I can't change. But for Brom you can do much. He's never known the true and faithful love of a good woman. Here's your room. Make yourself ready for him. You'll find nightgowns in the center drawer of the chest."

Julianna hesitated outside the door, not from any uncertainty on her part, but simply trying to find the proper words to thank her cousin. However, Sarah misconstrued Juli's inaction as an attack of conscience.

"What am I going to do with you?" Sarah shook her head firmly. "You love Brom, don't you?"

"Of course!"

"Then show him how much—the same way I showed my William that very first night we met."

"*You*, Sarah?"

"Aye! And I've never regretted it for a moment. Brom wants to marry you. I can see it every time he looks your way. You'll be his bride soon enough. Perhaps before this week is out. But a week is all you're assured of. Don't waste a moment of it playing the moral, simpering virgin."

Julianna hugged her cousin, then smiled at her. A bright, cheerful, dry-eyed smile. "Thank you, Sarah, for everything."

"That's a girl!" her cousin said with a wink. "You'll make a fine captain's lady."

Julianna went into the bedroom and closed the door softly behind her. Her emotions were in turmoil. So much had happened to her tonight, and so much was yet to come. But things were beginning to fall into place in her mind. If she was, indeed, Kat's daughter, then her return to her own time made sense. She wondered suddenly if all the foundlings in all the ages had been cast adrift in eternity by unloving parents. Assuming that was so in her own case, Katrina Rhinehart had conspired to interrupt her fate—to take away from her the most precious thing in her life—her love for Brom.

She sank down onto the edge of the bed, letting her hand smooth over the blue-and-white Storm at Sea pattern of the quilt. Glancing about the room, she examined her surroundings as her mind wandered. The walls were hung with fanciful tapestries in deep, rich hues—a unicorn and a maiden, a knight on a white charger, lovers embracing in a shady glen. Her gaze lingering on the amorous pair, she wondered how the woman felt to have her man embracing her and leaning down, ready to touch his lips to her bared breast. A shiver of anticipation trembled through Julianna. She forced her eyes away from the tapestry couple.

Light and shadow danced about the room. The bed, night tables, washstand, and chests all smelled of beeswax and gleamed a rich golden brown in the candlelight. The burning embers in the fireplace cast flickering light about the walls and illuminated the mother-of-pearl inlay in the fancifully carved teakwood screen that hid one corner.

The whole room looked warm and lived-in and welcoming, right down to the decanter of dark wine on the nightstand beside two goblets. Julianna had always imagined that she and Brom would make love for the first time in his great bed at Netherwood. But she felt no disappointment at being here. Far from it. Every nerve and sinew of her body ached with pleasant anticipation. She glanced back at the tapestry of the two lovers and realized suddenly that she would gladly surrender to Brom on the bare, muddy earth in the middle of Pearl Street at this moment if no more comfortable bower were available.

"What's keeping him?" she moaned impatiently.

She answered her own question in the next breath. "He's waiting for me to make ready for him, of course."

Going to the drawer Sarah had mentioned, Julianna opened it, smiling as the scent of crushed lavender suddenly filled the air around her. She searched through the neat stack of nightgowns until she found the perfect one, obviously a garment Captain Kidd had purchased in some faraway, exotic port. Of palest peach silk no thicker than a cobweb, the night shift was almost the color of Julianna's flesh. Delicate silver embroidery shimmered over the soft fabric, giving it the appearance of having been dusted with crushed pearls. Julianna pulled the sheer gown from the drawer and held it up before her, staring in the mirror.

"Yes!" she murmured. "This will please my lover."

A soft knock at the door made her turn.

"Brom?" she whispered.

He answered by opening the door only a crack. Beaming at her, he asked, "May I come in?"

Julianna ran to him and clasped his hand, drawing him inside and closing the door behind him.

Her breath caught as he stared down into her eyes, his own smoldering with deep-burning emotions. Julianna felt her heart beat faster. She trembled slightly. He drew her close until her full length leaned into his hard body.

"Alone at last," he whispered. "And, by God, I do want you!"

Julianna tilted her head back, closing her eyes and parting her lips to invite his kiss, letting him know without words that he was about to receive what he most desired.

# *Chapter Sixteen*

Brom felt intense heat rise from the very toes of his boots like molten lava about to blow the top off a long-dormant volcano. He couldn't believe this was actually happening, that this velvet-tongued, fiery-eyed woman was here in his arms at last, offering herself to him with the sweetest of passionate kisses.

How many nights had he dreamed of this moment? How often had he seen her in those dreams and reached out to her only to have his arms embrace thin air? But now his lips moved over soft, willing flesh. Flesh that burned with the same fire of desire as his own.

Cautiously, he let his tongue steal into her mouth. She met his thrust with a moist, silken stroke of her own. His blood rushed faster. His heart pounded as if he were in battle. This was battle, right enough, but the sweetest of them all. He drew her closer, molding his body to hers until he could feel the beat of her heart and the quiver of her cool breasts.

On and on he kissed her, almost afraid to draw away for fear she might vanish if he broke off intimate contact. If only he could hold her this way always, nothing could ever come between them. Nothing could ever tear them apart again. Not time nor space nor even death.

Julianna felt a new fierceness in Brom's embrace. She could barely breathe, he held her so tightly. His hard chest crushed her aching breasts. His arms bound her body. His hot, throbbing manhood branded her thigh even through the dense cushion of her skirts. He seemed almost desperate with longing. She realized her own need matched that desperation, perhaps even went beyond its limits.

Suddenly, Julianna felt afraid—afraid of this stranger from long ago who could make her shiver inside with a single glance. If the fire in his eyes could drive her wild, if his kiss could turn her weak as a kitten or passionate as a tigress by turns, then what would become of her when she surrendered to him totally? Would she simply melt away to nothingness when he finally entered her? Would she vanish forever if she allowed him to ride her to the very heights of sweet madness?

As if reading her fears, Brom released her suddenly. She stumbled slightly away from him, out of his reach. For a frozen moment, she stood in the center of the softly lit room trying not to let her expression betray all her doubts and her longings. She was still fully clothed, yet she felt naked and defenseless before his passionate gaze.

What were her feelings exactly? She wasn't sure herself. She only knew that when Brom held her and kissed her and fondled her, her whole body responded to him in the most marvelous, most ravenous, most scandalous manner.

As Brom stood staring at her, devouring her with his smoldering eyes, her cheeks flushed hotly just thinking how her breasts ached for his touch. She could feel desire stiffening her nipples inside her bodice. Her legs went weak with a quickening heat that made her thighs quiver and press close to each other as if her very flesh longed to capture and hold this fire raging through her blood. And where her thighs met, a hot moistness suffused her most secret places. The longer Brom held her in his obsidian gaze, the more she felt it—the ache, the quiver, the desperate longing.

"Julianna?" Her name was a soft, husky question on his lips. "Is anything wrong?"

She glanced down, avoiding the hunger in his eyes. "I'm fine, Brom." She spread a palm before her to keep him at a distance. "Give me a moment to catch my breath." She paused and breathed deeply. "I'm afraid you took it quite away."

He came toward her immediately. "Then let me give it back, dearest heart."

She had no chance to avoid this new, staggeringly intimate embrace. In less than an instant, he held her prisoner once more. Covering her mouth and parting her lips with the deft probe of his tongue, Brom breathed deeply into her mouth. A moment later, he drew the air out of her lungs. Twice, three times, he repeated the action. When he released her, the last of Julianna's strength, the last of her hesitation had fled. They had shared breath as they shared love. Somehow, Brom had made them one for a time. Julianna longed for that unity to stretch into eternity.

"A glass of wine?" Brom asked. "It will calm you, love."

Julianna touched her hot cheeks and trilled a soft, nervous laugh. "After what you just did, nothing will calm me, my darling."

Brom poured one goblet nearly full. He sank down in a chair beside the bed and sipped slowly at the rich red liquid, never taking his eyes off Julianna.

"I thought you'd have changed for bed by the time I got here," he said. "Should I have waited longer?"

Julianna glanced toward the filmy nightgown discarded on the bed. "Oh, I'm sorry. I meant to, but . . ."

A slow, lazy smile curled Brom's lips. "You needn't apologize. There's plenty of time. I don't mean to rush you. Not tonight, dearest heart. Not ever."

She glanced about. For what? she wondered. The bed? Yes, it was there—high and soft and inviting. The nightgown? Yes, there it was, lying in plain sight in all its immodest, transparent glory. She chastised herself silently for not choosing something less revealing. What would Brom think of her?

A veiled glance his way told her in an instant that no shield of modesty would be expected or even allowed tonight. She trembled inside, but more with anticipation than with any sense of dread. What had she to fear from Brom, after all? She loved him. She needed him. She wanted him. There it began and there it ended.

Brom rose and strode toward her. It almost seemed to Julianna that his every move was in slow motion, as if they were caught in one of her dreams. Without thinking, she took a step back, away from him. He stopped and gave her a reproving look.

"You aren't afraid of me?" His voice sounded deep and husky, flowing over her like a warm stream of honey mixed with the sunshine of a hot July afternoon.

She shook her head. "No." But at the same time she crossed her arms over her bodice as if shielding her breasts from him.

"*I'm* afraid," he admitted. "A little. Afraid that I won't please you. Afraid that in my eagerness I might hurt you."

Her head tilted to one side and she cast a glance at him through lowered lashes. "Don't be," she whispered. "You

284

please me every time I'm near you. As for your hurting me, I know you never would . . . not on purpose."

Brom reached out and slowly swept the hair from across her forehead. His touch was as gentle as the flutter of a thousand butterfly wings.

"I only want to love you . . . to make you happy, Julianna." He paused, leaned down, and brushed her lips with his. "Here and now for a start. Forevermore, if I have my way. You are my very life, dearest heart."

Once again his words stirred her deeply. She pressed her thighs tightly together, savoring the fleeting sense of pleasure the action brought.

"If I am life to you, Brom Vanderzee, then I surrender to your pleasure. I *will* be yours this night!"

"And I will be yours *forever*, dearest heart." He took a sip of wine, then pressed her lips, letting the sweet, intoxicating vintage flow from his mouth into hers. His tongue followed the stream, mingling the taste of desire with the flavor of the grape.

When they had drained the glass, sharing it to the very last drop, and Julianna's head—her whole body—felt light as a cloud, she eased out of Brom's arms. He made no protest, but watched her every graceful move with longing eyes as she caught up the filmy gown and slipped behind the Oriental screen to change.

"If you need any help . . ." Brom offered.

"I can manage," she assured him.

Brom took his seat again, poured more wine, and leaned back with a sigh of appreciation. He offered up silent thanks to the Oriental artisan who had fashioned the wonderful screen with its open latticework that offered such a tantalizing view. He watched, smiling all the while, as Julianna's dainty hands worked slowly at the laces of her bodice. What was hidden from view made the scene before him all the more titillating. A glimpse of creamy throat . . . a peek at rosy nipple . . . a brief view of long, tapered legs . . . a flash of snowy buttocks . . . a momentary shadow of tight red curls between her thighs.

Brom shifted in his chair, easing the ever-increasing tightness of his britches. Again he sipped his wine, savoring the rich flavor. His mouth, he noted with pleasure, still tasted of Julianna. Would that he could retain her essence forever.

A flutter of something shiny behind the screen drew his attention. Brom sat forward, straining to see more. A moment later, Julianna stepped into full view. Brom cleared his throat and wiped his hand roughly over his eyes, hardly able to believe the vision before him.

Julianna stood tall and straight beside the bed. A candle on the table behind her cast a halo of gold about her long russet tresses. The gown she wore seemed more vision than reality. The flesh-colored fabric clung softly to her shoulders before falling into long, flowing sleeves. The high neck all but disappeared against the flushed flesh of her slender neck, then traveled snugly over her breasts, hiding all but the outline of her distended nipples in a flash of delicate silver embroidery.

Brom's eyes moved ever lower. He realized he was holding his breath. He swallowed deeply as his gaze drifted down from the tie bound just below her breasts to the wave of sheer silk billowing below. The candlelight flickered in a gentle breeze, silhouetting Julianna's softly rounded hips and long, shapely legs. More of the shining design fanned out to shimmer across the tops of her thighs, making the very center of his longing seem to beckon with gleaming silvery fire.

Brom rose and pulled off his red damask coat. Impatiently, he jerked his shirt open to the waist. Julianna stared at the profusion of gold chains flashing against the coarse ebony hair on his chest. He made no move to come to her. No smile lit his darkly handsome countenance.

"'Tis unfair," he growled, still piercing her with his smoldering black eyes.

Julianna frowned slightly, not understanding.

"Finally, after searching the world over, I find the perfect woman to love." He paused and drew in a deep, shuddering breath. "And she turns out to be not real at all. Only a vision. Only a piece of a dream, too delicate to hold, too fragile to embrace, too lovely to be real."

Julianna swayed toward him, her bare feet brushing softly against the floor as her silk gown whispered against her thighs. When she reached Brom, she lifted a hand to his face, framing his cheeks with her palms.

"I *am* real, Brom," she said softly. "Were I not, could I ache for you so?"

He covered her hands and his and stared into her misty green eyes. "You aren't a dream? You won't disappear if I try to show you how much I love you?"

She shook her head slowly and smiled. "No." Her lips formed the word, though the sound seemed more like a sigh.

Brom brought her hand to his lips, kissing her palm, then stroking it slowly with the tip of his tongue. Julianna slid her other hand down his neck to his chest, fingering the heavy gold chains. She felt Brom tremble at her delicate touch.

"You be a witch, a mermaid, a siren from the depths of the sea sent here to lure me to ruin, pretty wench." He growled the words close to her ear. "But there's no man who could refuse you."

Julianna caught his chains in her fingers and gave them a twist, drawing him closer to her. When she had him where she wanted him, she tugged gently at his earring with her teeth.

287

"Arrgh!" he groaned. "Bent on stealing me gold, is it, wench? Then—all being fair in this war—I'll help meself to your silver."

Brom's big hand came up and closed over her breast. A moan escaped Julianna as his thumb made rough circles over the shining embroidery, over her aching nipple. For a time, she let him play his games with her. Then she stepped back, out of his grasp.

Aware of Brom's eyes focused on her, Julianna raised her arms as if she meant to yawn and stretch. Her breasts strained against their imprisoning silver tracery as she reached back and lifted her hair off her neck. Turning, she said not a word, but her actions commanded her lover. A single bow at the back of her neck held her filmy gown in place.

She heard something close to a moan escape Brom. Then his fingers touched her neck.

"Aye, the key that unlocks the treasure chest," he whispered. "But not just yet, dearest heart. A man likes to savor his triumph once he knows for sure that all those precious jewels are truly within his grasp."

Brom's hands slipped forward around Julianna's hips to her belly. His fingers now gripped that lower span of silver as he drew her hard against him. She could feel his pulsing heat pressed against her buttocks. A scant trace of damask and the barest hint of silk were all that kept them from giving in instantly to their longing. Feeling his fingers glide over her, Julianna looked down, but all she could see were her breasts, straining with the aching desire to be touched. His hands inched ever lower, toward that region of her body that now felt the most wonderful, licking heat.

He kissed her back, her shoulders, her neck. She let her head fall back against him and closed her eyes, luxuriating in this feeling of building passion. But how much longer could she stand it? How much longer before she would weaken and start to whimper and beg for him to take her?

"Don't move!" he ordered in a husky whisper. "Stand just where you are."

A wave of disappointment passed through Julianna when Brom's hands slid away and he stepped back, breaking their intimate contact. But she did as ordered, still facing away from him, wondering what could be happening behind her. She had little time to ponder the question. A rustling noise, a thud of cast-off boots, and then she felt him—long and hard and hot—his full length pressed to her back once more as his hands gripped her waist. Nothing separated them now except the cobweb gown. Julianna could feel him almost as if they were flesh to flesh.

She made a sound like purring as he held her, his strong fingers splayed over her belly, pressing her hard against his male heat.

Brom laughed softly. "The feel of a naked man brings far more pleasure to his woman than the sight of him, I've heard."

Silently, Julianna agreed that the feel of him was something extraordinary indeed. But she dared not try to speak for fear she might gasp aloud as waves of pleasure simmered through her blood.

"On the other hand, the sight of a woman in nature's own is a beauteous thing to behold, dearest heart."

With those words, Brom gave up his teasing caresses. His hand went at last to the tie at her neck. Slowly, he undid the bow. Julianna could hear the slow whisper of silk sliding against silk. She held her breath, willing herself not to move. Then Brom's hands slipped over her shoulders, casting the ties away and slithering the sheer fabric down over her breasts. From there, he let the gown fall at its own rate while he cupped the smooth mounds in his palms, his thumbs kneading her aching nipples.

Slowly, Julianna turned in Brom's arms until she was facing him. His hands now rested lightly on her bare hips.

She stared up into his eyes, too embarrassed suddenly to glance down at his nakedness. But he raked hers boldly with his gaze.

"Ah!" he sighed. "As I knew you would be. Perfect! And perfectly lovely." He looked back at her face, noting that she still had her gaze focused on his bearded chin. "'Tis all right, love. Fair is fair. I'll allow you a peek at this loathsome body, if you like."

"Loathsome" proved a ridiculous word for what Julianna saw when she finally forced her gaze down. *Fascinating*, perhaps, *enticingly male*, but never, ever loathsome.

Her hands soon followed the trail her eyes had taken. Starting at his muscle-thickened neck, her fingers moved down over his dark-forested chest. He uttered a deep moan as her palms passed lightly over his nipples. She spread her fingers to span the taut, tanned flesh over his ribs. His hips were sharp blades of bone. His belly felt smooth, hot, and flat. Then her fingertips twined through more coarse hair, closing at last on his throbbing, satin-skinned shaft.

Her touch seemed to melt his bones as if they were made of beeswax. Brom crumpled against her, sweeping her up into his arms. Holding her high, one hand gripping her buttocks while the other formed a cradle for her back, he bent down and captured her lips. While his tongue stroked, his strong fingers kneaded her flesh. By the time he ended the deep kiss, Julianna lay quivering uncontrollably in his arms.

"You could drive a man to madness, Julianna Doran," he rasped. "Do you know that?"

Julianna clung to his neck, burying her face against his shoulder. "Oh, Brom, don't ask me questions right now. I haven't the sense left to give you answers."

"There's only one answer I need. Do you love me, dearest heart? Will you *always* love me, no matter what happens?"

"Yes, Brom! Oh, yes, I love you!" she cried. "Now and always!"

He turned her in his arms, allowing her body to slide down his until she was once more standing before him. His hands came up, cupped as if in prayer. Then they fanned. He spread his fingers over her breasts.

"You are *so* beautiful, my Julianna!"

Again he leaned down, barely touching his lips to hers. His tongue teased at one corner of her mouth, sending new thrills through her. Then he bent his head down until his mouth touched one breast. His tongue drew invisible circles around her nipple. Julianna drew in a sharp breath. Her breasts strained forward, begging him for more, while liquid fire raged through her veins, pooling and intensifying in the lower regions of her belly.

"Brom!" she gasped against his lips. "Oh, Brom, I . . ."

"Sh-h-h!" he whispered back. "Say nothing. Only listen to your heart . . . *our* hearts, beating as one."

It was true. In the stillness, she could actually hear their hearts beating together. Again she experienced the sensation that they had somehow, miraculously, become one single entity with loving each other their sole purpose in life.

Brom's hands slipped down to her waist, almost spanning its width. For several moments, he stood, holding her at arm's length, staring down at her proud breasts. Slowly, he shook his head, a look of wonder and desire glazing his black eyes.

"Never!" he murmured. "Never had I imagined such a prize as you, Julianna. And to think that I will be your first—the one to teach you the mysteries of love. It is far more than I deserve."

Julianna felt a sharp pang of guilt. She should correct this misunderstanding before it was too late. There had been another before Brom—sometime, somewhere. At the moment, her mind was too dizzy with desire to recall the details. She knew there had been another time, another place, another lover. But for the moment, it seemed to

Julianna that she had always existed here with Brom, trembling on the very brink of ecstasy.

Before she could confess anything to him, Brom eased her toward the bed. In the blink of an eye, he was there beside her, his hands stroking her thighs. Then he was over her, pressing her down until they were truly flesh-to-flesh— mouth-to-mouth, chest-to-breasts . . .

Julianna burned. Brom's tongue fondled hers with long, sensual strokes. His hands slipped from her back to her sides, smoothing up and down from her underarms to her waist. She let her own hands stray over his strong body, feeling him tense against her when she imitated his fondling of her nipples by touching his.

"Easy, love, you've found my weakness," he gasped against her mouth.

"You have no weakness," she moaned. "Every inch of you is solid and strong and hard. But my flesh is shamefully weak." She must tell him he was not her first. "Oh, Brom, my darling . . ."

Her moment of confession came too late. She had meant to tell him that even though he was not her first lover, he would surely be her last. However, the words died in her throat, drowned by the most exquisite mingling of pain and ecstasy she had ever know. With a sudden, deep thrust Brom crashed through the tender barrier Julianna had thought broken long ago. Any wonder at this miracle was lost in the moment's soul-rending pleasure as, clinging to his lover, Brom rode with her up the mounting crest of a wave of passion higher than any she had ever known. The world seemed filled with clashing, crashing, shattering sound as the enormous climax of their loving built to its peak.

Julianna's fingers dug into Brom's back. His arms threatened to crush her. They gasped for breath as one, marveling at what they had shared.

Suddenly, the miraculous clamor ceased. Soft, sweet silence enfolded the lovers. Gasps turned to sighs. Satiny afterglow chased the fire from their souls. For a long time they lay in each other's arms in silent wonder. Brom suckled gently at Julianna's still-quivering breast while her hands stroked his damp belly. Total contentment soothed them and cradled them in the still night.

Finally, Brom moved until his mouth was so close to her ear that his warm words sent a shiver through her. "I never knew," he said in an awed tone. "This might have been my first time as well. Can you imagine, dearest heart, what it will be like to love this way for the rest of our lives? For the duration of all eternity?"

"Is it possible to love that long, Brom?" Julianna's voice was an awed whisper that pleaded for his answer to be yes.

"You'll see," he replied. "Go where you will, when you will. I'll find you. A love like ours is as strong and solid as any mountain, as relentless as the rolling sea. *Nothing* can destroy it! Neither time nor distance nor even the grave."

The candle beside the bed flickered brightly for an instant, casting its light on Brom's ring. A green flash seemed to enfold them. Slowly, Brom slipped the emerald dragon off his finger. Taking Julianna's hand in his, he placed it on her hand.

"So long as you wear my ring, I will be with you, dearest heart." He kissed her hand and then her lips.

As Julianna drifted off into a lovely sleep, she was aware of the warm weight of Brom's ring on her finger and the warmer weight of his body pressed close to hers.

Everything seemed right at last; her love was beside her.


Sometime later, Julianna awoke with a start. She lay perfectly still, staring but seeing nothing. The room—wherever she was—was locked in blackness. Her mind reeled for a moment. She couldn't think where she was or where she had been when she fell asleep.

This sort of thing had happened to her for as long as she could remember—the sudden awakening, the confusion over place and time, the terror of darkness. But this time the fear seemed far more intense. Not only was she uncertain where she was, but she had no idea if she was now in Brom's time or her own. Suddenly she remembered that Brom's time *was* her own.

She shifted slightly in the bed. Out of the darkness, a warm hand reached out the clasp hers.

"Brom?" she whispered hesitantly.

"You can't sleep, either, love?"

Along with a deep sense of relief, his voice brought a rush of feelings flooding over her—wonderful, delicious feelings of the love they had shared, the sweet wholeness they had created by joining their bodies—their very souls— in ecstasy. She turned toward him, snuggling close, longing to be held.

"I was sleeping until a moment ago." She kissed his shoulder and sighed. "Something woke me. I'm glad. It's ever so much nicer to be awake and with you, my darling."

Brom made no reply. She sensed a tenseness in his body. His breathing grew deep and raspy.

"What's wrong, Brom?" She felt his agitation as if it were her own.

Another long silence followed before he finally answered. Squeezing her hand more tightly, he said at length, "I haven't slept at all, Julianna. There's been too much to think about—too much to worry over. You, of course, are at the center of it all."

"I'm sorry, Brom." Julianna sensed her euphoric feelings slipping away, to be replaced by dread. "Have I done something to displease you?"

294

He clasped her to him. "Never!" he said emphatically. "Not in this lifetime or a dozen others could you ever displease me, dearest heart. As long as we're together, I'll never have a care in the world." He paused and kissed her deeply. "But soon the time will come for me to leave. I'd give anything I own to stay with you, but I *must* go; I've given my word. I fear for your safety after I've sailed away."

Julianna felt tears gathering in her eyes. "Oh, please, Brom, let's not talk about it. I don't know how I can bear your leaving when the time comes. I know can't bear thinking about it now."

His rough hand smoothed over her cheek, wiping away her tears. His voice was so quiet now, so gentle. "It breaks my heart to think of going. But, Julianna, we must talk about it. You can't stay here once I'm gone."

"But why? I would enjoy Sarah's company and I'm sure she would be happy for me to stay."

"I'm sure Sarah would be most grateful for your company," Brom agreed, "but it simply isn't safe."

Suddenly, realization struck Julianna like a dash of cold water in the face. She sat up in bed, staring at him through the gloom. "Oh, no, Brom! I couldn't return to that other time. You mustn't ask me to."

He reached out and drew her back to him. "Of course I'd never ask you to go back there, dearest. We've found each other at last. The right time, the right place. I don't think I could live without you now." He kissed her deeply before going on. "But I won't feel easy leaving you in New-York. want you safely back at Netherwood before I sail."

"I know what's behind all this, Brom," Julianna said quietly. "Kat! But, you see, I'm not afraid of her. Now that realize she's a threat, I'll be on guard. She can't harm me. doubt she would even try."

He buried his face in her hair and sighed. "Julianna, what

am I going to do with you? You're a stubborn wench, you are! But this is one time you must heed my warning. The situation with Katrina Rhinehart is more complicated than you suspect. You think we were lovers, don't you? You guess that's my only reason for wanting you away from her. Admit it.''

"No, Brom.'' Julianna was totally in control of her emotions now. This situation was far too serious to give way to female hysterics. "I *know* that you and Kat were never lovers.''

He laughed softly, humorlessly. "Then you're the only one who knows it. The fair Katrina has spread her lies far and wide. But, if you don't believe that, what do you think of her?''

"That she is a scheming and heartless woman—a woman who would rid herself of an unwanted child as easily as she would cast off an unfashionable gown. A woman who would turn desperate if she were ever forced to wear that gown again—even more desperate if her child returned to haunt her.''

"Then you do know the truth,'' Brom stated flatly. "But I don't think you understand how vicious a foe she can be.''

Julianna found she was trembling. All this talk of Kat set her nerves on edge. She did fear the woman, she realized. But her love for Brom ran much deeper than her fear of Katrina Rhinehart.

"Why would she wish me harm, Brom? I didn't return to threaten her in any way. I came back to find you. It's as simple as that.''

He smoothed his hand along her arm, letting it come to rest on her breast. "You're a woman with kindness and love in your heart. How could you ever understand what evils motivate a witch like Kat? First, there's the very fact that she and I were never lovers. She wanted it to be so, not out of any great affection for me, but simply because of my disinterest. Kat has always desired most what she knew she could never have. Then, as her daughter, you are a serious threat. You are young and lovely and vibrant, and you look so much like your mother did years ago. Having you here is like having a ruthless mirror held up to reflect her once-beautiful face. Vanity was ever Kat's center of gravity. Your arrival has yanked her false mask away so that all can see her now as she truly is. Then, too, there's the mother's guilt she must face. She threw you away. To Kat's way of thinking, why else would you come back, if not to have your revenge?''

"But I didn't know the truth until this very night!" Julianna exclaimed.

"Ah, but Kat knew. She's always feared you might return. Now that you have . . ." Brom let his words trail off.

Julianna slipped her arms around him and pressed her lips to his chest. "I'll do as you wish," she said. "I'll go back to Netherwood, but that's as far as I'll go. I mean to be here when you return."

A long silence followed her words. She could feel him staring at her, although it was still too dark for her to actually see.

"I want you here when I return," he whispered. "Oh, Julianna, if only I didn't have to go. I'm so afraid that you'll . . ."

"What, Brom?" she coaxed gently. "Afraid that I'll *what*?"

"I fear you'll grow tired of waiting for me and go away again."

"Never!" Julianna gasped, "Why would I leave?"

"Perhaps out of loneliness," he suggested. "You see, I know of your other love."

"What?" she cried.

"Elliot Creighton," he said quietly. "I know, too, that you are a woman who needs to be loved. What if you sense

297

his return and his need for you. Won't you be drawn back to him?''

"What if *you* return and I'm not *here*? I couldn't stand that, Brom. It breaks my heart to think about it. No! You have nothing to fear, my darling. As you said, we've found each other now. This is our time, and I mean to live it to its fullest. Even now, it's as if I only dreamed that other life, that other love. I was born into your time. I was meant to be here to love you. My own mother tried to disrupt my fate, but her scheme failed. Nothing . . . *no one* could ever lure me back.''

He drew her close. The next instant, he slipped, hot and throbbing, into her warm nest. "You will be here, then? Always? Forevermore?''

"Always,'' she whispered. "Forevermore, my darling.''

Brom gathered her to him. Their discussion ended abruptly. Within moments, Julianna was lost—swimming in a velvet sea of passion, ecstasy, and love.

But even as Brom held her and loved her, some sense of dread lurked in a dark part of Julianna's heart.

# Chapter Seventeen

The next six days were to fly by faster than any Julianna had ever known. Her nights were as filled with love as her days were with adventure. Parties, picnics, strolls along the Battery—each hour seemed to bring some new delight. It was, as Sarah had told her, a week she would long remember.

Together with the Kidds, Julianna and Brom explored every inch of old New-York, not that there was much territory to cover in that early day and age.

Modern New York, as Julianna remembered it, stretched many blocks to the north. In fact, as the planners of Central Park had feared might happen when they purchased the rocky squatters' den on the outskirts of town in 1856, the New York skyline was already encroaching on the verge of the park by late in the nineteenth century. First came the Dakota Apartments in 1881, looming over the lake and trees to the west side, and then all of New York seemed to march north, crowding in on Central Park. But in the late seventeenth century, with the hills and forests of Manhattan stretching north as far as the eye could see, the citizens had yet to imagine a day when the creation of a great public park might be the only way for New York to retain any of its early sylvan splendor.

In Brom's day, the rough log wall—built to keep pigs in and warring savages out—marked the town's northern extremity. A few farms, or *bouwerij* as the Dutch called their country estates, stretched beyond the wall, but most of civilization lived within the confines that ran from the Hudson to the East rivers and from the Battery to the wall.

So much was different here in Brom's time—her own time, really, Julianna had to keep reminding herself. What she had known as Broad Street was now no street at all, but a canal. Names, too, were different. The Dutch even had the gall to call the beginnings of Broadway "Bloomingdale Road." Many thoroughfares Julianna knew were missing entirely, having been laid out on land that built up along the rivers over the years.

Along Petticoat Lane, housewives hung their linens out to dry in the sun. In the middle of Wall Street near Water stood the Meal Market where black slaves were auctioned off right in the shadow of the first Trinity Church, now under construction.

The people of old New-York hadn't changed the least. Granted, they wore different fashions, but just as in the sprawling city of the late nineteenth century, they were a polyglot society, made up of people from many lands, speaking many tongues, and worshipping each in his own way. As for the brash and flashy pirates who roamed the unpaved streets, Julianna had to admit that pirates abounded in the city in the late 1890's as well, although they might call themselves by other names.

* * *

One of Julianna's favorite places, the White Horse Tavern, was a frequent haunt of Brom's, owing to the fact that it was the most convenient place to post letters. With his departure imminent, Brom had to settle his business affairs before he sailed. To Julianna's surprise, she found that he had merchant associates all along the coast, from Maine to Virginia, as well as in England, Holland, and the Indies. He bought and sold goods of every sort—pelts, timber, rum, sugar, even slaves on one occasion, his first and last venture into that dark trade, he vowed.

The mail pouch at the rustic tavern drew many customers and proved a lucrative business. Customers would inevitably order a drink as they handed over their parcels or wax-sealed missives to the barkeep with the suitable amount in gold to see them on their way. The tavern keeper would then send a boy to deliver the mail to the appropriate ship waiting in the East River.

The combination tavern and mailroom in Peck Slip north of the wall was housed in a narrow two-and-one-half-story log building that sat jammed between two large warehouses close to the East River docks. In the common room a large fieldstone fireplace dominated the dark interior, covering the end wall opposite the bar. Rough plank tables and benches littered the central area of the hard-packed dirt floor. Sprawled before their tankards at any hour of the day or night, one might find the governor himself elbow-to-elbow with lowly seamen, ship's captains, pirates, and prostitutes. The air was always thick with smoke and profanity. But something about the very baseness of the establishment amused and fascinated Julianna. The tavern was so different from anything she had ever known. The very sense of danger she enjoyed made Julianna draw closer to Brom for protection.

They sat together at a table near the fire one cold, snowy evening, Brom guzzling a fiery Kill Devil while Julianna sipped a more sedate Mimbo, a concoction of rum, loaf sugar, and water. Suddenly, the door flew open, sending a chilling blast through the warm room. All eyes turned to scowl at the lone figure whose arrival had caused this invasion of snowflakes and icy wind. The many sour expressions around the room quickly turned to interest when they saw that this new customer was a woman, alone.

"Blast!" Brom muttered. "What's *she* doing here?"

Julianna, half afraid Katrina had arrived on the scene, turned to watch the woman pull off her hooded cloak. So far, they had managed to avoid Kat since the governor's reception that first night, but Julianna knew it was only a matter of time before her erstwhile mother crossed their path again. This, however, was not the Rhinehart woman.

"Maeyken!" Julianna said too loudly.

The girl, hearing her name called, turned toward Brom and Julianna with a broad smile. Taking recognition for invitation, she hurried to their table and helped herself to part of the bench.

"God, it's cold out there!" she gasped through chattering teeth. "Buy me a Kill Devil, won't you, Captain Vanderzee?"

"I will not!" Brom exclaimed. "'Tis a man's drink, not fit for a girl."

"Not even if the girl's been kicked out of her house to wander through a blizzard for hours and is half froze?" Maeyken pleaded.

"You poor child!" Julianna cried, patting Maeyken's icy hand.

The young woman smiled at Julianna, then turned again to Brom. "Your lady's right nice, Captain. Why can't you act the same?"

"What I ought to do, Maeyken Huyberton, is turn you

over my knee and wale the daylights out of you. What are you doing here? And what do you mean, you've been kicked out?"

Julianna noted that Brom's face had gone dark as a thunderhead. She didn't understand. The girl was shivering, probably hungry, and certainly needed compassion far more than she needed a tongue-lashing.

"Ease off, won't you, Captain?" Maeyken begged. "'Tis not one of my better days."

"And whose fault is that?" Brom growled, his eyes flashing black fire. "Haven't I warned you time and again to mend your ways, girl? I don't know what you've done now, but my guess is you're lucky your parents *only* threw you out. Were you my brat, I'd cane you to within an inch of your life for some of the stunts you've pulled."

Maeyken turned to Julianna and laughed in spite of Brom's harsh words. "He don't mean that, ma'am. Pay him no mind."

"You'd better pay me some mind, girl. I mean every last word of it!" Brom countered. But even as he spoke, he motioned to the tavern keeper to bring two more Kill Devils—one for himself and one for the shivering little tart.

Julianna sat silently, watching and listening to Brom and Maeyken go back and forth at each other, hoping she might get some inkling as to what was going on.

Finally, Maeyken, after several gulps of her hot drink, turned to Julianna and said, "We ain't been introduced. I reckon you know who I am." She paused and rolled her pale-blue eyes. "There ain't many hereabouts that don't know me by reputation and some by sight . . ." Maeyken broke off suddenly and leaned close, staring right into Julianna's face. "Lord help us!" she cried, turning back to Brom. "She can't be! But she is, ain't she? Kat's baby girl, all growed up."

Brom shushed Maeyken and glanced about the room to

303

see if anyone was listening. Turning back to the women, he whispered, "'Tis so, Maeyken, but keep it to yourself. I mean to take Julianna back to Netherwood before I sail to keep her out of harm's way. I don't want any more trouble with that woman before we leave New-York."

Maeyken looked Julianna up and down with a keen eye. "Going to Netherwood, are you? How'd you like some company? Gets mighty lonely, I'll bet, up in them woodsy regions. And there's some that would welcome a roof over their heads right about now."

Before Brom could say a word, Julianna cried, "Why, that's a wonderful idea! Yes, Maeyken, do come. The time will go so much faster if I have someone with me."

Brom groaned. "Dearest heart, you don't know what you're letting yourself in for. Maeyken is trouble spelled with a capital 'T.' Tell us, Maeyken dear," Brom went on in a falsely sweet tone, "just why did your pa see fit to throw you out on such a cold night? Did you drink all his rum? Did you steal his gold? Did you sass your long-suffering mother? What was your crime *this* time?"

Maeyken shrugged and glanced up at the ceiling. "I ain't done none of those things. I told you, Captain Vanderzee, I reformed. Last week. I been keeping my nose clean and acting like a genuine lady."

"And that's why Jacobus threw you out—for acting like a lady?" Brom demanded.

"Well, sort of. I had a gentleman friend call for me while Pa was still at work. When my fellow brought me home, Pa pitched one of his royal fits. Claimed he didn't approve and called me some real bad names. We was just gone a little while and I figured I'd be home before Pa got there."

"So you never expected your father to approve of this man," Brom accused. "You were slipping around behind his back."

Maeyken shrugged and gave Brom a helpless, childlike glance. "Pa don't approve of much I do these days."

"Maeyken, can you blame him?" Brom asked, exasperated.

She toyed with the frayed sleeve of her red satin gown. "I reckon not. But he ought'n to have throwed me out like that. Pa tossed me right down the stoop and told me to get out and don't never come back! 'I got no daughter from now on!' he said."

Julianna's heart went out to the pitiful girl, who seemed on the very verge of tears. But Brom, who knew Maeyken well, was not taken in by her ploy for sympathy.

"Aha!" Brom exclaimed as if some light had just dawned. "Might I ask the name of this gentleman friend?"

Maeyken's pale cheeks flushed and she stared down into her tankard, her fingers stroking nervously at the pewter handle. "You might ask and I might tell," she replied quietly but defiantly. "His name was Tom."

Brom's mouth fell open. He seemed struck dumb, but fierce anger kindled deep in his eyes.

"Never mind!" Maeyken cried before he could reply. Tears welled up in her eyes and spilled down her flaming cheeks. "You don't have to tell me I'm crazy. I know that now. But Tom Tew offered to take me for a ride in the governor's pretty carriage." Sobs of remorse were now punctuating every other word. "He promised he wouldn't do nothing to me. He said I was so pretty and young and all that he just wanted to sit next to me and hold my hand while we drove about town." She gulped down several hiccoughing sobs, then finished in a nasal whine, "But that ole Tom, he lied to me, Brom! And when I wouldn't give him what he wanted, he treated me *real* bad!"

Maeyken slipped her gown off her shoulder to show Brom and Julianna the bruises on her throat and chest.

Julianna gasped, "Oh, you poor dear!"

"Damn the bastard!" Brom seethed.

"And he said I hadn't seen the last of him—that he always got what he wanted and he wanted *me*!" Maeyken told them, real fear making her voice tremble.

Julianna reached out and drew Maeyken into her arms, murmuring soothing words over her. Suddenly, it dawned on Juli what an odd situation this was. How often when she was growing up Maeyken had given her the same sort of comfort. A skinned knee, a dead bird found in the forest, a harsh scolding from Aunt Martha and she had fled immediately to Maeyken's sheltering embrace. Now their roles were reversed by time, place, and circumstances.

"This settles it, Brom," Julianna stated firmly. "Maeyken *is* going to Netherwood with me!"

"Very well," he relented. "Perhaps it's all for the best. Maybe you can teach her how to be a *real* lady while she's there."

Maeyken smiled up at Julianna, her misty blue eyes gleaming. "Yes, Juli can teach me," she said. "I'll do whatever she says."

"I think I'd better be getting you ladies home," Brom said when another customer entered and the blast of cold wind and swirling snow showered everyone in the room. "This storm's not letting up."

The three finished their drinks quickly and in silence. Brom was on his feet already, and Julianna and Maeyken were pulling on their coats when the door flew open yet again. A sudden stillness settled over the room.

Julianna glanced toward the door, curious as to the crowd's reaction. A tall woman in a flowing fur cape stood just inside the door. She shrugged off her heavy wrap and tossed it to her driver, who stood nearby. The woman stood in deep shadow, but Julianna had no need to see her face to recognize her.

306

"Kat!" she breathed.

"Never mind," Brom said in a rasping whisper. "We were just leaving and so we shall."

Julianna felt Maeyken's cold fingers dig into her arm. The girl was obviously terrified of Thomas Tew's woman. As well she might be, since she had been with him this very night. Julianna could feel Maeyken trembling and those shivers of fear proved contagious.

"Ladies?" Brom prompted, motioning toward the door.

But Katrina Rhinehart stood between them and the single exit. Neither Julianna nor Maeyken moved a step.

Given this advantage, Katrina stalked directly toward them. When she reached the table, she stood before the other two women, glowering at first one and then the other, her green eyes flashing pure hatred.

"Well," she purred. "Isn't this a delight for you, Brom? I always believed that it would take two women to satisfy you after you left me. Now it's finally come to that, has it?"

"I never left you before, Kat, but I'm leaving you now." Gripping Julianna and Maeyken each by an arm, he tried to move them, but they seemed frozen to the spot.

"Why such haste?" Kat asked in a sugary tone. "I've hardly had a chance to speak with your Julianna."

Juli felt Kat's eyes rake her with a cold and calculating look. Then, quickly, Kat turned her menacing gaze on poor, trembling Maeyken. "As for *you*," she hissed. "I think we have something to discuss, you panting little bitch!"

Maeyken cringed closer to Brom and whimpered like a whipped pup.

"I'd watch how I throw names around, if I were you, Kat," Brom warned.

Katrina leveled her gaze at Brom and her eyes narrowed malevolently. "She was with my Tom tonight. Did she tell you that? And did she also tell you that she tried to seduce

307

him?'' Kat laughed aloud. ''Can you imagine? *My* Tom with a girl so pitifully in need of anything she can get that she regularly strolls the Battery each evening, picking up sailors, vagrants, and God-knows-what-else?''

'''Twas Tom's idea!'' Maeyken shot back with an unexpected burst of spunk. ''He told me you were *too old* for his tastes.''

''Why, you little . . .'' Kat's voice was the scream of a banshee. She came at Maeyken with her long-nailed fingers crimped into claws, spitting and hissing like an infuriated alley cat.

Before Brom could react, Julianna stepped protectively in front of Maeyken and gave Kat a mighty shove. Caught off balance, the Rhinehart woman stumbled backward, tripped on a chair, and toppled to the dirt floor in a tangle of silk skirts.

Coolly, Julianna smiled and said, ''You really should learn to mind your manners when you're in a public place, Katrina.'' Then, turning to Brom, Juli took his arm and suggested, ''Shall we go home now, darling? I'm feeling quite weary of the drab company in this place and I'm sure Maeyken is as well.''

They started for the door, but Kat struggled to her feet, seething with rage. She leaped on Brom's back, clutching him about the throat, truly trying to strangle him.

''I'll see you in hell before I let you go with *her*!'' she screamed at Brom.

Loosening her fingers from their death-grip, Brom shrugged her off. He swung around, one hand rubbing his throat, the other clutched into a fist. Julianna, terrified that Brom meant to kill Kat here and now, gripped his arm with all her strength.

''Don't, Brom!'' she cried. ''She's not worth it!''

Katrina—her hair in disarray, her dress torn, and her face paint smeared—smiled a deadly smile at Julianna. ''I'm worth a lot more than you will ever know. Someday you will all understand that. *You* in particular, Miss-High-And-Mighty-Julianna! Your fate is in *my* hands. You realize that, don't you? It has been since the first moment you arrived here. I have only to bide my time, to decide my course, and then to act.'' She laughed—horribly. ''You might call this a cat-and-mouse game and, unfortunately for you, I am the Kat!''

Brom hurried Julianna and Maeyken through the door. Kat's harsh laughter followed them. They could hear the sickening sound even over the wail of the wind.

By the time they climbed into Brom's coach and sped off, Maeyken was clutching Julianna, sobbing and trembling uncontrollably.

''Oh, Lord, what's to become of me?'' the girl wailed. 'That woman means to kill me . . . to kill us both!''

''Hush now,'' Julianna soothed. ''Kat isn't going to kill anyone. She's all talk. She's only trying to frighten you.''

''And doing a damn fine job of it, she is!'' Maeyken wailed.

Brom rode in silence back to the Kidds' house on Pearl Street. His mind was too cluttered with dark thoughts to lend itself to casual conversation. He'd dreaded leaving Julianna before. Now the very thought terrified him. If Kat were a man, this would be so easy. He would quickly eliminate the threat before he sailed away. But one simply did not go about killing women—not even a woman of soul-deep evil like Kat. He had to do something to assure Julianna's safety while he was away. But what?

An answer finally came to him as they were passing through the Water Gate. But if this was truly the only answer, it caused him as much concern as leaving Julianna unprotected within Kat's clutches.

Sarah and William Kidd were still awake, trying to soothe their fretful child, when the carriage drove up.

Peeking out the front window, Sarah cried, "Mercy, William, they've brought someone home with them. Quick! Help me tidy up the parlor."

A moment later, the three tired, cold, troubled travelers stamped snow into the entry. Sarah bustled about, taking cloaks, asking questions, and offering food and drink.

"I thought you'd decided to spend the night at the White Horse with this weather so nasty," Sarah said. "But I'm glad you're home. You know how I worry when I don't know where you are." She cast an accusing glance at Brom. "Sometimes I think it's easier when you men are at sea. We women don't go gadding about at all hours in all sorts of weather. We stay home where a body's supposed to be in a blizzard."

Brom wasn't listening to Sarah's chatter. His mind was still working at more serious pursuits.

"I'm sorry if you worried about us," Julianna apologized. "And I hope it won't be any trouble to put Maeyken up."

"Maeyken?" Sarah did little to disguise her shock. She knew a third party had arrived with them, but she hadn't recognized the girl in the shadowy hallway. She recovered quickly. "Maeyken, is that really you? What on earth are you doing out on a night like this? But never mind, my dear. Of course we can find a place for you. Mercy me, your mother must be beside herself, not knowing where you are. Come in here by the kitchen fire, all of you. You're frozen near-stiff."

Soon the five of them were settled in Sarah's cozy kitchen, sipping mugs of honeyed cider and nibbling at fresh-baked cruellers just out of Sarah's Dutch oven.

It took Sarah and William little time to sense the ominous mood of the three.

"What's happened, Brom?" Kidd asked. "You didn't run afoul of some pirate tonight?"

310

Brom shook his head. "Worse," he muttered. "Kat!"

"Oh, Lord!" Sarah moaned. "*That* woman!"

"'Tis all my fault," Maeyken admitted in a small voice. "I let Thomas Tew take me for a carriage ride this evening. he found out and came after me."

"Oh, *Lord!*" Sarah gasped. "Maeyken, what could you ave been thinking, child?"

Maeyken only hung her head, at a loss to explain her ighty behavior.

"Kat's threatened Maeyken, right enough," Brom explained to the Kidds, "but it's really Julianna she has it in or. I've been mulling over the problem all the way home." Ie shook his head and shrugged. "I don't know what to lo. But I can't leave the woman I love all alone at Kat's nercy."

Julianna gripped Brom's hand and tried to give him a onfident smile. "Don't worry, darling. Maeyken and I will e safe at Netherwood."

"Oh?" Sarah said, disappointed. "I had so hoped you vould stay here with me, Juli."

"I can't," Julianna said firmly. "Not after tonight. I'd only bring trouble down on you, Sarah. We'll all be better ff if I'm away from New-York."

"*Far* away," Brom muttered.

"What's that, darling?" Julianna asked.

"I've been thinking, as I said," he answered. "There's ne place you could go that she'd never find you. She'd ever even look for you there. Somewhere much farther way, much safer than Netherwood."

The gleam in Sarah's bright blue eyes showed that she understood and agreed. But Julianna only stared at Brom, a rown of confusion creasing her smooth brow.

"Brom's right, Juli," Sarah seconded. "You could go back vhere it's safe, then return here when Brom gets home."

"*Go back*? I don't understand, Sarah." But Julianna was beginning to understand and she didn't like it one bit. She didn't even want to think about it.

"I'll take you to Netherwood tomorrow, as we planned. You and Maeyken. You know what you must do when you get there. Then when I'm ready to return to New-York, you can go to the spring and . . ."

"No!" Julianna cried. "I *won't* leave you, Brom. I can't! Not now. Not after . . ." Gathering tears stopped her words. She must not give way to emotions now. This was too important. This was her whole life!

William Kidd, too, knew of the strange powers of Netherwood's spring. At first, he hadn't believed Sarah when she'd told him how she came to his time. Finally, she had made him see the truth, strange as it seemed. Now, he rallied behind Brom and his wife to convince Julianna.

"It won't be safe for you here, Julianna. We'll be gone a long time," William explained. "Two years, maybe more."

"I know that, William," Julianna said calmly. "I'm willing to wait however long it takes for Brom to come back to me. But I am *not* willing to put even more distance between us. Two years is one thing. Two *hundred* years is quite another."

Maeyken had remained still and quiet through the whole discussion, her sharp eyes darting from one face to another. Now she could keep silent no longer. "What in the world are you people talking about?" she demanded with a burst of passion. "A place that's safe from Kat? A spring at Netherwood? Two hundred years? I know I'm an outsider, but you best explain what you're talking about or I'll go crazy, wondering."

Julianna and Sarah took turns telling the stunned girl all about the place they came from and their odd mode of travel.

312

Maeyken's pale eyes grew wider and wider. By the time they finished, her mouth was wide open, too.

"I know it's difficult to believe," Julianna finished, "but it's really true, Maeyken, all of it."

For several moments, Maeyken only stared at Julianna. Then slowly a smile spread over her pretty young face. "A place that's safe from Kat," she murmured. "'Tis close to heaven, no doubt."

Julianna bit her lip to hold back a tear. "Not very close when Brom is so far away," she whispered.

Nothing was settled when Brom and Julianna climbed into bed that night. Julianna lay stiffly on the down mattress. Her whole body was tense. She was sure that Brom would once again try to change her mind. And how could she fend off his persuasiveness in bed?

When the mattress sagged under his weight, Julianna turned her back to him. Maybe he would think she was asleep already and give up the battle, at least for the night. She huddled on the far side, chastising herself for wearing only Brom's ring to bed. The barrier of a thick linen gown might have discouraged him.

"Julianna?" Brom said quietly. "Are you asleep, dearest heart?"

She lay very still, breathing deeply, hoping that he would be fooled. He uttered a heavy sigh—a sound of disappointment. Relieved, Julianna settled in, willing herself to go to sleep quickly.

But a warm hand stole up her thigh, then to her waist, finally coming to rest cupped around a breast. Now it was Julianna's turn to sigh. How foolish she had been to think she could deceive this man when his slightest touch awoke fire in her blood. Her body, seemingly of its own accord, slithered across the sheets, fitting itself to Brom's warm, hard form.

"Ah!" he whispered against her hair. "I could tell a lie and say I'm sorry I woke you. But I'm not."

Brom turned her in his arms and sought her lips. The kiss was total and all-encompassing. Their whole bodies—mouths to toes—took part in the passionate embrace. For those rapturous moments, Julianna almost forgot that Brom was going away in only two days and that he wanted to send her even farther away.

"Julianna, I want to ask you something," he whispered. "Please think it over carefully before you answer."

Before waiting to find out what he meant to ask, Julianna blurted out, "No, Brom! I won't go back. Please, don't beg me to."

Brom placed one finger over her lips. "Sh-h-h!" he warned. "Don't answer until I have asked." His finger trailed from her lips down over her chin, from the dimple in her chin to her throat, then down between her breasts and lower, lower, ever lower until it was stroking that one pulsing point of all longing.

"What, Brom?" Her voice quivered; her whole body quivered.

"When we go back to Netherwood, will you marry me, Julianna? I've thought it over and I can't wait until I return. I want you to be my wife now. I want to know while I'm gone that you'll be here waiting for my return."

Wave after wave of perfect pleasure washed over Julianna—the pleasure of relief that he hadn't tried once more to convince her to leave him and go back, the pleasure that his touch was turning quickly to pure ecstasy, and most of all, the deep, heartfelt pleasure that came with the knowledge that Brom wanted to marry her, not someday, but *now*.

"Oh, yes, Brom! Yes!" she cried, twisting under his sweetly torturing hand as it brought her to the heights.

"Julianna, my dearest, dearest heart," he moaned against her breast, "I may never be able to tell you how much I love you. But I can tell you how long. *Forever!*"

Brom slid over her and found his way to her aching depths. Long into the night, they made love with a new and glowing intensity. When exhaustion finally forced sleep, Julianna knew no sadness or fear in her dreams. The colors of her nightworld shone with silver linings as she and Brom shared a lifetime—many lifetimes—of living and laughing and loving.

But deep down, Julianna sensed that those silver linings might soon be tarnished by Kat's evil cunning.

# *Chapter Eighteen*

The riotous light of the autumn sunset filtered through the frosted windows of the transom, casting a red-gold glow about the captain's cabin aboard *Bachelor's Delight*. Julianna, dressed in ivory damask, trembled slightly as she stood staring up into the dark, loving eyes of the man who would be her husband. She was bàrely conscious of the others in the cabin—Sarah and Maeyken standing to her right side, Captain Kidd in full dress uniform before her, a Bible open in his hands.

Try as she might, Julianna could not convince herself that this was all real. She'd had lovely dreams last night. This day seemed only an extension of those silver-lininged musings.

Everything had happened so fast. Brom had tugged her gently from their bed at dawn, insisting on a need for haste. Over breakfast, they had broken their happy news to the Kidds and Maeyken. Sarah Kidd had refused to be left out of the elopement, insisting that all the plans be left up to her. In little over an hour, she had produced her own wedding gown and altered it to fit her taller, slimmer cousin. Ordering servants hither and yon, Sarah soon had a proper wedding feast stuffed in a stout hamper and a bag packed with clothes enough for her and her husband to stay overnight on *Bachelor's Delight* after the wedding.

"You and Brom won't be needing any guests up at Netherwood on your honeymoon night," Sarah had insisted.

Almost before Julianna had realized what was happening, they were all on board Brom's ship, heading up the Hudson. Sarah and Maeyken had helped Julianna dress for her wedding in the captain's cabin while the men were sent to the first mate's quarters to prepare.

Now Julianna glanced up at Brom. He looked darkly dashing in a suit of midnight velvet with a gold sash, the ever-present dagger with its bejeweled hilt resting against his thigh.

An expectant silence descended over the gathering. Captain Kidd cleared his throat, then nodded to Brom. "If you will take her right hand in yours, we can begin."

As shyly and tentatively as a bashful boy, Brom touched his fingertips to his bride's. She looked into his face. His features were grave, but a look of overwhelming love and passion lay buried deep in his coal-black eyes. Julianna felt suddenly overcome with soul-rending emotions. Right here, right now, they were touching—she and Brom. In moments, through the words Captain Kidd was about to speak over them, they would be joined for life. Then, after only one night together as man and wife, Brom would sail out of her life. Could she bear to see him go?

"Julianna?" Captain Kidd prompted gently. "Your response. Will you take this man to be your husband?"

Brom offered her an encouraging smile. Tears brimmed in Julianna's eyes. "Yes!" she whispered. Then much louder, "Oh, yes, I will!"

"The ring," Kidd said, nodding to Brom.

Once again, he slipped the emerald-studded dragon on Julianna's finger. But this time it seemed different to her somehow, even though she had worn it up until an hour before the ceremony. It was as if the ring fit better and felt more permanent because of the vows they had exchanged.

Captain Kidd closed the Bible with a soft plop. "There's naught left but to kiss your wife, Captain Vanderzee," he announced with a broad smile.

Not yet touching Julianna, Brom leaned down and pressed a soft kiss to her lips. Then his arms slipped about her waist and hers about his neck. They clung together, savoring a long, deep first kiss as husband and wife.

"Lordy, much more of this and we'll have to call out the whole crew to pry them apart," Maeyken said with a shrill giggle.

Everyone laughed, including the bride and groom. Hugs, kisses, and handshakes were passed out all around. Soon, Maeyken and Sarah were spreading the wedding feast while some of the sailors tuned their instruments—fiddles, hornpipes, and mouth harps—to play for jigging on deck.

The next two hours passed in a blur for Julianna as she was passed from one eager man to the next to be whirled and twirled to the sailors' joyous songs. Never too long went by, though, before she was back in her husband's arms. Brom seemed hungry for the sight of her, for the feel of her. Nor was she totally happy when he was out of her sight.

Finally, it was Sarah who broke up the wedding party. Shoving a wicker basket into Brom's arms, she ordered, "Take your bride and this wine up to Netherwood now. We've some serious celebrating to do here on board, and you two, mooning over each other the way you are, would only be in the way. Off with you now!"

"We're going! We're going!" Brom growled, but with a broad grin splitting his face and a devilish twinkle in his night-dark eyes.

Hanging the basket over one arm, he whisked Julianna up and held her tightly as he crossed the gunwale to the dock. He set her gently in their waiting buggy, climbed in himself, then clicked to the horse. Everyone on the ship waved them away, cheering and encouraging them to get on with the business of making a family.

Julianna waved until the ship was lost in darkness. Then, clinging to Brom's arm, she hid her face against his sleeve in a sudden fit of overwhelming shyness.

"What's wrong, dearest heart?" Brom asked gently.

"Everything's happened so fast!" she exclaimed. "I'm breathless with it all."

Brom chuckled. "So, Mrs. Vanderzee has been struck breathless."

She sat up and smiled at him, then hugged him so tightly that her actions caused him to jerk the reins. The horse whinnied its objections.

"Yes!" she cried. "Mrs. Vanderzee! I love the sound of it, Brom. Julianna Vanderzee. Mrs. Captain Vanderzee." She tried out various forms of her new name, smiling her wholehearted approval at each one.

As they drew up before Netherwood, Brom threw back his head and laughed out loud, pleased by her sheer pleasure in her new name and status as his wife.

Servants had been sent up to Netherwood from the ship to light fires and lamps before they hurried back to the vessel for the night. A stablehand waited in the drive to take care of the horse. Then he, too, would slip away, leaving the newlyweds all to themselves.

Brom climbed out, tossed the reins to the waiting man, then gathered his bride in his strong arms. Holding her, he leaned down to kiss her once before he headed for the front stoop.

"And now, Mrs. Vanderzee," he whispered, "your husband is about to take you home for the first time. Only a wife and children can make a home of any house."

"*Children*," Julianna repeated with a sigh, visualizing daring little dark-haired boys and cunning, bright-tressed girls.

"A dozen at least, I should think," he added.

"Oh, Brom! A *dozen*?"

They were inside now. He kicked the door soundly shut and nodded. "If we start right away. Then every time I return to port, I'll leave you with another before I sail again. It's a seaman's way, don't you know?"

Julianna laughed with him, but her heart was not in it. Why did he have to mention going away just now? Another name popped unbidden into her mind: "Widow Vanderzee." She reached up and clasped her hands behind Brom's neck, bringing his lips down to hers. She kissed him long and hard.

"Well," he breathed when she finally released him. "I think we'd better get you up to bed right now."

"Yes, please," she murmured, snuggling even closer in his arms.

A fire glowed, shedding rich golden light over their bedroom. Brom placed Julianna gently on the bed, staring at her suddenly as if he were seeing her for the first time.

"Do you know how beautiful you really are, Mrs. Vanderzee?"

Julianna lowered her lashes and gave him a modest smile. "'Tis all in the eyes of the beholder," she whispered.

"If you're hinting that I see you through the eyes of love, you're right. But were I a blind man, I would know your charms just as well."

Brom closed his eyes and moved toward her. He reached out to touch her face as a sightless person might do. "Ah, such smooth skin, such long lashes. Nose? A bit impudent in its tilt, but pretty enough." His fingertips moved on, seeing her—making her tremble. "Lips, full and soft and begging to be kissed."

He leaned down and did just that, letting his tongue see her even better than his fingers had. Julianna caught her breath as his hands moved down her bare throat.

"Such a slender neck," he murmured, "so long and erect." His fingers twined through the curls at her shoulders. "Hair like silk." Then a hand eased inside her bodice, finding her breasts. He sighed deeply, but said nothing.

Julianna, her voice no more than a quivering whisper, spoke the words for him. "And aching breasts, their nipples straining for your touch . . . your kiss, my darling."

His hands still on her warm flesh, Brom opened his eyes and found himself staring directly into hers. They glittered with dancing, reflected lights from the fire and glistened with happy tears.

"Julianna!" Her name on his lips was half moan, half prayer. "*My* Julianna!"

His hands came to the pearl buttons at the front of her wedding gown. Nimbly, he undid them, then pressed the fabric away from her breasts and back off her shoulders. Going to his knees before her, Brom gripped her waist and eased her toward him. She stared down at her own naked breasts, watching as Brom kissed each nipple in its turn, then teased each one with the tip of his tongue. When he covered one aching peak with his mouth, gently suckling her, a tremor of sizzling pleasure raced through her whole body. Twining her long, slender fingers through his riot of dark curls, she held him close, crooning his name as he continued this delicious, tender torture.

After a long, sweet time, Brom rose, leaving Julianna sitting, half naked, on the side of the bed. He went to the wicker basket and took out the bottle of sparkling wine that Sarah Kidd had provided. He popped the cork with ease. Pouring two glasses, Brom handed one to Julianna. They clinked a silent toast, then drank to each other. Julianna could hardly swallow, aware as she was of Brom's eyes still examining her with such loving desire.

Made bold by the wine, she stood, set her glass on the bedside table, and stripped off the rest of her clothes. Firelight danced warmly over her pearly-white flesh.

"My God!" Brom groaned. "Oh, my God, Julianna! You mean to bewitch me for certain."

"Would that please you, my darling?" Her voice was low, husky with desire and invitation.

In answer to her question, Brom came to her and wrapped his arms about her, letting his big hands play over her flesh until she tingled and burned with his touch. When he shed his own clothes at last and drew her down to the Persian rug before the fire, it was only the first of many times that he would pleasure her that night. The silver lining of Julianna's earlier dreams took on a sheen of pure molten gold. Her body, her very soul, came alive. And she lived and breathed only for this man—her husband.


The first light of dawn brought grim reality. The reality of Brom's leaving. A bride of only one night, Julianna now had to face the dark, lonely months—perhaps years—stretching ahead. She awoke, euphoric, reaching for her husband before she even opened her eyes. He came to her and loved her well, one last time. As they lay in each other's arms afterward, savoring their lingering passions, a booming sound out over the river made Brom sit bolt upright.

He ruffled his hand through his tousled hair and groaned. "How can it be that late?"

Julianna glanced toward the windows. Dawn was only now tinting the sky with its misty-pink and lavender hues.

"What do you mean, Brom?" Julianna knew well enough. The ache in her heart answered her own question.

She tried to coax her husband back into her waiting arms. "It's early yet, darling. Love me again."

He shook his head sadly, already rising from bed and pulling on his britches. "There's no time, dearest heart. I'm afraid it only seems early. I told William to give me a cannon blast if I wasn't back on the ship by time to set sail."

Everything from then on happened so quickly that Julianna barely had time to acknowledge her pain. She stood by watching as Brom dressed hurriedly and gathered his things to leave. An aching silence hung between them for a moment when he turned to her. Without a word, he bent to kiss his wife farewell.

"It may be a year, even two, but I will return," Brom promised. "Trust me, dearest heart. I know this separation will be difficult for you. If you choose to go back where you came from while I'm away, I'll understand."

Julianna shook her head furiously, fighting back tears. "Never, my darling! I'm your wife. I belong here."

"Then take this," he insisted, thrusting the jewel-hilted dagger into her hands. "If Kat comes, you must be ready to defend yourself."

"No! I couldn't," she protested.

Brom stood firm. "I won't know a moment's peace while I'm at sea as it is. At least let me rest in the knowledge that you'll always have a weapon close at hand. Just in case, dearest heart."

Reluctantly, Julianna took the evil-looking dagger, though she never intended to use it.

Brom caught her in his arms then and kissed her deeply one last time. Neither of them could bear to say good-bye. Their parting, therefore, proved a silent ordeal.

A moment later, he was gone. The slam of the door below was like prison bars closing on Julianna's heart.

Gazing from the window, tears streaking her cheeks, Julianna watched her husband stride down the hill to board his ship. As *Bachelor's Delight* cast off her lines for the sail back to New-York, the ship's captain fired a volley to salute his weeping bride.

With the sound of cannon fire still echoing in the distance, Julianna brought her left hand to her her lips and kissed Brom's dragon ring. As long as it remained on her finger, her husband would remain in her heart.

"And I will *never* take it off!" she vowed.


A short while later, Maeyken arrived, to drag Julianna out of her misery with her whirlwind activity and constant chatter.

"Lord, it was so romantic!" the girl cried the minute Julianna met her at the door. "You and Brom, getting married on his ship, then coming up here to this fancy house for one night together. I would have married me one of them sailors yesterday had any asked just so's I could be a party to such a romance."

Julianna, her tears dry now, laughed in spite of herself. "Maeyken, that's not exactly how it works. You have to love the man you marry for it to be that romantic."

"Tell me what you did last night," Maeyken pleaded. "Everything, from start to finish, so's I'll know how to act when I do fall in love and get married."

Julianna felt a blush creep to her cheeks as her mind wandered through those dark, passionate hours of her wedding night. Never, not in a million years, would she ever tell Maeyken or anyone else how she had cast aside all modesty and inhibitions last night to play the wanton for her passionate husband.

"You won't need advice on your wedding night, Maeyken. Believe me, you'll know exactly what to do."

Maeyken laughed and gave Julianna a sly look. "But I bet my man won't know how to do it half as good as your husband did it. From the looks of your glow this morning, I'd say Brom Vanderzee knows right well how to pleasure his woman.'' Then she leaned close and whispered, ''My guess is your man's got a stallion's fittings and a jockey's seat.''

''Maeyken!'' Julianna cried, mortified by the girl's frank words. ''You just never mind. What we did and how we did it is our business. Now, let's stop all this chatter and go fix some breakfast.''

''I'll bet you did work up a powerful appetite last night,'' Maeyken said with a giggle.

Julianna hurried out of the door so Maeyken wouldn't see the scarlet flaming her cheeks.

Even though Julianna missed Brom terribly, the days and weeks seemed to rush by for her. There was so much for the two women to do at Netherwood—firewood to haul in, meals to be cooked, animals to care for. And then there was Maeyken herself to divert Julianna's thoughts. The girl was always up to something, always good for a laugh and a bit of fun.

Together they whiled away the short winter days. During the long evenings, Maeyken invariably worked the conversation around to the things she had overheard in New-York about Sarah and Julianna and the strange way they had happened into this time and place. The young woman's curiosity was insatiable. She wanted to know everything about Julianna's other life. Still fearful that Kat might turn up, Maeyken insisted they go down to the cellar and fetch spring water up to their bedrooms.

''Should anything threaten us, Juli, we can just drink some water and''—she snapped her fingers—''disappear quick as you please.''

Julianna feared no threats that serious, but she was willing to humor the girl's high spirits and fantastic imagination.

She allowed Maeyken to place a jug of spring water beside each of their beds.

Only the nights were long and lonely for Julianna. Then the black silence seemed to close in, trying to smother her. She ached for Brom. She would awake with a start sometimes, sure that she had heard him call her name. If only she *could* truly hear his dear voice again.

Several hard freezes in late February had turned the river into a solid block of ice, stopping even the hope of mail coming in to the dock. It seemed winter's long silence would go on forever.

Finally, when Julianna had all but given up on ever seeing a fine, warm day again, she awoke one morning to see the first sure sign of spring on the river—a boat pulled in at the Netherwood pier.

"Maeyken!" she cried. "Come quick! We've a visitor."

But Julianna had slept later than the younger woman. Even as she stood at the window, gazing out at the river, she saw Maeyken dashing at top speed up the hill. Obviously excited, she was waving something over her head. Julianna pulled on her wrapper, then hurried downstairs to open the front door.

"Mail, Julianna!" Maeyken gasped, out of breath. "Mail from Captain Vanderzee!"

Julianna could hardly contain her happiness. During the long months Brom had been gone, she had written to him faithfully every day. The letters were all stacked neatly beside her bed with Brom's jeweled dagger placed atop them. There had been no mail coming in and none going out. Now, at long last, she had a letter from her husband, and the boat at the dock could carry hers to New-York to be forwarded to Brom, wherever he was.

When Maeyken put the letter into Julianna's hands, she kissed the parchment, then hugged it to her heart for a moment.

"Well, open it!" Maeyken ordered with an impatient stamp of her foot.

Julianna did, tearing off the wax seal and scanning the page with tear-blurred eyes. The words sounded vaguely familiar to her.

My Dearest Heart,

How long each hour seems without you by my side. The nights especially creep past—never-ending black nothingness. I lie in my bunk and think of how it felt to hold you in my arms, to kiss your lips, to love you in our special way. Until you came into my life, I was no more than half alive. Without you now, I am little more than a shell of a man.

Julianna shook her head, trying to clear her thoughts. It almost seemed as if she had read this letter—word for word—many times before. But, of course, that wasn't possible, was it? Perhaps she had only dreamed of hearing these loving words from her husband for so long that she imagined she knew them by heart.

"Well?" Maeyken begged. "What does he say?"

Julianna smiled at her, once more clutching the letter to her heart. "He says he loves me, Maeyken. Isn't that wonderful?"

"Shoot! You already knew that," the girl answered, disappointed. "What's he say about the pirates?"

That first letter didn't mention pirates, but the ones that arrived in the following weeks spoke much of battles and wounded sailors, captured treasure, nights at sea, and that faraway isle called Madagascar. It almost seemed to Julianna that Brom had sailed off into a different world. How would he find his way back to her? And when could she expect him? The questions nagged at her day and night.

# Chapter Nineteen

By early May the trees were budding out. The last patche of snow had melted, encouraging spring flowers to bloom All of Netherwood and the surrounding countryside took o a new air of promise. The long winter behind her, Juliann. felt renewed hope with the advent of the season.

One particularly bright morning, Julianna hurried dow to meet the mail boat. She was delighted when the captai handed her a letter from Sarah Kidd. Juli scanned it quickly

Her cousin wrote that she hoped Julianna and Maeyke would come down to New-York for a visit soon, the weathe being fine and no stifling heat in sight yet. Sarah mentione cryptically that "the woman who might cause you concer is out of our hair for a time—off to Albany with her man.'

Julianna had to stop and think for a moment who Sara could mean—Katrina Rhinehart had been that far from he thoughts these past months. Any threat from the woma seemed lost in some distant time and place.

While strolling back up the hill from the dock, Julianna reread Sarah's letter. William had written to his wife that all was well. Little Sally was feeling much better now that the cold winter had passed and she could play out of doors in the sunshine. New-York, according to Sarah, was all a-dither with the news that Governor Fletcher was about to be replaced—the Crown finally having got wind of his purse-lining dealings with pirates—and that Lord Bellomont, it was rumored about town, seemed a likely choice to be his successor. How cozy that would be for their husbands, Sarah remarked, having their protector as head of the colony. If the guard did change, Sarah went on, Julianna certainly wouldn't want to miss all the celebrations and parties that the arrival of the new governor was sure to spawn.

When Julianna returned to the lawn, she found Maeyken—her dark hair tousled and dirt smudging on her cheeks—tussling with a stray puppy she'd adopted.

"You look a sight!" Julianna called, laughing. "Watch out! Here he comes again."

Maeyken, down on hands and knees, snarled at the playful pup, who dashed at her, snatching the blue ribbon from her hair. Maeyken tumbled over and over on the new grass, yapping and growling at the frisky brown hound.

"I declare, Maeyken, you act more like a tomboy than a young lady," Julianna scolded, still laughing. "What would Brom say if he could see you now? He asked me to teach you some manners. I suppose I'll simply have to take you to New-York and reintroduce you to society to make you behave."

Maeyken sat up, quickly trying to straighten her hair and her rumpled frock. "I have manners. I just don't use them always," she said, beaming. "I promise, I'd be a real lady if we was in New-York, Julianna."

"If we *were* in New-York," Julianna corrected. "Why must you slaughter the king's English so?"

329

"I'll talk proper, Julianna. I promise that, too. If only you'll take me to the city. I do miss all the excitement there. Netherwood is pretty and quiet and I love it here." She whirled around in a circle, holding out her skirt as if she were at a ball. "But, oh, to have a man say sweet things to me again! To be admired and fought over and whispered about."

"Maeyken," Julianna warned, "if I do take you back for a visit to New-York it won't be so you can go strolling along the Battery, collecting unsuitable beaus. You'll have to act as well as speak properly."

Maeyken bobbed a curtsy. "I promise, Julianna."

Julianna returned to the vessel at the dock a short time later with her letters for Brom and a note to Sarah, promising to take the next week's boat downriver.

The rest of that week, Julianna and Maeyken cleaned house, sewed new frocks for their trip, and packed their bags. It would have been difficult to guess which woman was more excited over their coming adventure.

But the day before the expected arrival of the mail boat, another sloop moored within sight of the house on the hill. Peering out through the bedroom window, Julianna called, "Maeyken, come look. It seems we have a surprise guest. I wonder who it could be."

"Could be anyone," Maeyken commented, leaning over Juli's shoulder for a better look. "Some stranger, taking advantage of river hospitality, most likely."

The phrase sent a shiver through Julianna. Why? she wondered. Brom had explained to her that any and all comers were welcomed into the homes along the water's edge. But her dread of the term seemed long buried in her subconscious.

"Let's hurry down and put the kettle on for tea," Maeyken suggested. "And some of those sky-berry tarts would go good, don't you think?"

Julianna followed the younger woman down the stairs, still mulling over her unaccountable sense of dread. She hadn't long to wonder over its meaning. A knock came at the door and she hurried to open it. When she did, that bud of uncertainty sprang to full blossom in an instant.

"Katrina Rhinehart!" she gasped.

The tall, fire-haired woman in a handsome purple traveling costume stood planted on Netherwood's stoop. The carpetbag in her hand confirmed her plans to stay.

"Well, well!" Kat said, her cold smile not reaching her eyes. "If it isn't Julianna Doran. I saw the smoke from the chimney and wondered who I'd find to welcome me to Brom's house."

"You haven't heard then?" Julianna could have bitten off her tongue, but it was too late now to keep the cat in the bag. Still, maybe a tiny lie wouldn't hurt and might be far better than the truth at the moment. She would just tell Kat that she was minding Netherwood while Brom was away.

"Heard what?" Katrina demanded when Julianna hesitated.

"That Julianna is now Captain Vanderzee's wife—mistress of Netherwood," Maeyken announced, coming down the hall with the tea tray.

For a moment, Katrina paled and all expression faded from her face. Then that cold tightening of lips that passed for a smile returned. Her bag slipped from her hand, landing with a thud on the stoop.

"Congratulations," Kat said curtly. "I only hope you won't be disappointed in the man."

A sudden rush of almost maternal rage filled Julianna. "Oh, I assure you, Kat, Brom has never disappointed me."

The woman chuckled and stroked a single, dangling curl of her long red hair. "Give him time. He will."

Without waiting to be asked, the univited guest swept into the house as if she owned the place. "Tea. How nice!" she crooned. "Do get my bag and fetch it upstairs, won't you, girl?" This to Maeyken, who stuck out her tongue at the woman the minute Kat turned her back.

Julianna cast a pleading glance toward Maeyken, who grumbled under her breath, but brought the carpetbag inside.

Katrina gazed around the front parlor, shook her head, and clucked her tongue disparagingly. "Poor, dear Brom. I told him he needed a woman's touch when it came to decorating his house. These tacky old tapestries and those tiles around the hearth . . ." She looked at Julianna frostily and sighed again. "Oh well, I suppose there's no help for it now."

"I love the house the way Brom decorated it!" Julianna cried in his defense.

Again Kat chuckled deep in her throat—a patronizing sound. "You would, of course."

A strange day followed. Katrina was by turns rude, haughty, falsely kind, apologetic—but mostly Julianna found her simply infuriating. As for Maeyken, it soon became clear that the young woman was terrified of Katrina Rhinehart.

Getting Juli alone in the kitchen for a moment, Maeyken confided, wide-eyed, "She's come to do me in, Juli. I know she has. She's just biding her time, torturing me. A woman like that one never forgives if you mess with her man. Oh, I was such a fool to go with Thomas Tew! He only wanted to make her jealous and he did that. Now, I'll have to pay."

"Don't be silly," Julianna whispered back. "If she's come after anyone, it's me. My guess is she heard that Brom and I were married." Suddenly, a shudder trembled through her body. "Then there's that tale about my being her daughter."

"You best watch her close, Juli," Maeyken warned. "Don't dare turn your back on her for a minute."

332

Julianna nodded her agreement before returning to her less-than-welcome guest. She almost ran over Katrina in the shadowed hallway.

"Tell your girl she may bring my bag upstairs now," Kat ordered. "I believe I'd like to freshen up and rest for a bit before supper. Oh, there you are," she said, spying Maeyken at the kitchen door. "Put it in the room with the golden bed. At least I know Brom has one fine piece in his home, since I picked it out."

"There ain't no gold bed upstairs," Maeyken said with an indignant sniff.

"But of course there is," Kat insisted. "I should know. He bought if for me."

The hair on the back of Julianna's neck rose like the hackles on a cur. "Maeyken is correct. I had the golden bed banished to the attic. I found the piece tasteless and vulgar. To be quite blunt, I hated the thing."

Katrina said nothing. She gave Julianna a cold look of disdain, then started up the stairs, her silk skirt swishing as she walked.

Julianna and Maeyken followed along behind, exchanging silent signals with their eyes. On the floor above, they parted, Maeyken following Kat into the guest room to deposit her bag while Juli turned into the room she shared with Brom, anxious to be where she felt closest to him and even more eager to shut a door between herself and the Rhinehart woman.

Juli had no sooner done that than she heard a sharp smack—flesh cracking flesh—followed by a piercing cry from Maeyken. Julianna hurried back out into the hallway in time to see Maeyken burst from the guest room, tears in her wide eyes and the blistery-red imprint of a hand marking her cheek.

"What in the world, Maeyken?"

"I'm leaving!" the hysterical girl cried. "I ain't staying another minute under the same roof with that high-priced whore!"

"Maeyken, wait!" Julianna called. "What happened? Where are you going?"

Maeyken turned back long enough to say, "She slapped me right in the face is what happened. But more than that, she told me—smiling all the while—that she reckoned I wasn't fit for this world . . . that any woman that fooled with her Tom should get what she deserved."

"But that doesn't mean that she'll really harm you, Maeyken. She's all talk."

"Oh, yeah?" Maeyken shook her head until her dark curls bounced crazily. "You wasn't in there to hear her—to see that killing meanness in her eyes. She said she had plans for me . . . that she wouldn't tell me what or when, but that she'd get me before leaving Netherwood. You think I'm staying after hearing that? No, Juli. Not me! And you best be thinking how you'll get by her, too. Without me around to spend her wrath on, she'll likely turn on you. You told me the way out of here and I'm taking it. *Now!*"

Maeyken sped into her room and slammed the door. Julianna tried to followed, but found the bolt slipped tight. She banged with her fists, begging Maeyken to open up. When the girl refused her request or even to answer, Juli leaned her ear against the thick wood. Only silence. Then she heard something smash to the floor. That sound was soon followed by a rush of wind on the other side of the door, then more silence. An emptiness curled through the pit of her stomach.

"Oh, no, Maeyken! You didn't! Not the spring water!"

Her shoulders sagging, Julianna walked back to her room. She fell on the bed and threw an arm over her eyes. What in the world was she going to do? She made up her mind quickly. She would confront the Rhinehart woman and send

334

her packing. A forceful knock at the door interrupted Juli's thoughts. She leaped up, relieved.

"Maeyken didn't drink the spring water, after all." Juli was sure she would find the girl standing out in the hallway, a sheepish grin on her face.

Julianna was wrong. A hard knot formed in her stomach when she found Katrina Rhinehart there instead.

"Oh, Julianna dear, I've come to apologize for striking your girl." She even hung her head as if she were truly sorry. Or perhaps—the thought flashed through Julianna's mind—Kat was only trying to hide her insincere expression.

"Maeyken is not my 'girl,' as you put it. She is my friend, my very *dear* friend. How could you be so cruel to her?"

Katrina swept past Julianna into the bedroom, her eyes fixed on the big, curtained bed. "The golden one looked much better in here, you know." She glanced at Julianna and shrugged. "No, I don't suppose you would know. Raised on a farm, weren't you? Dirt-poor and totally unsophisticated. Ah, well, we can't all be blessed with superb taste."

"Did you come in here to apologize or to insult me?" Julianna demanded, the fire in her green eyes leaping dangerously.

Katrina smiled her icy smile, then glanced about. "Actually, I simply wanted to visit Brom's room *again*."

Kat's emphasis on her final word rang in Juli's ears like a bell tolling a death in the family.

"You see, Brom and I were *very* close for a quite some time."

"Brom told me all about it," Julianna replied, displaying amazing calm. "He said the two of you weren't nearly as close as you would have liked everyone to believe."

Kat chuckled. "Of course he would have to tell you that,

wouldn't he? What else could a man like Brom say to his jealous little snippet of a wife?"

Julianna clamped her lips tightly shut to keep in the curses that were curling angrily on her tongue. She stood beside the table near the bed, her whole body rigid with unuttered venom for this—what was it Maeyken had called her?—this *high-priced whore*. Juli allowed herself a smile. Yes, she mused, that was exactly what Katrina Rhinehart was.

Kat moved about the room, her fingertips caressing Brom's things. She drew in a deep breath and closed her eyes. "Ah, it's almost as if he's right here. The very maleness of him lingers in the air."

"I believe you'd better leave," Julianna said, having heard quite enough.

"Very well." Kat shrugged. "I only wanted a moment here to remember the way things were not so long ago. What time will supper be served?"

The woman was insufferable. She could not take a hint. She could not even understand plain English. "I don't mean that I want you to leave my bedroom," Julianna said evenly, through teeth that ground between words as she spoke. "I mean leave Netherwood . . . *now* . . . *forever*!"

Kat swung around, her eyes blazing, her lips twisted in a snarl. "How rude of you, you beastly little waif! I'll stay here as long as I please. I am *Brom's* guest, under *his* roof!"

"*My* roof!" Julianna countered, advancing on the woman, ready to throw her out bodily if need be.

"You shouldn't even be here," Kat hissed. "I sent you away, I thought, for good. How dare you return to bedevil me?"

Julianna felt a cold smile touch her face. "So, you admit it! It was beastly of you to cast me away, but I can't say I'm sorry you did. You'd have been some fine mother! My only regret was that you interrupted my fate and Brom's.

But we've put things to rights now. You'll never come between us again.''

Julianna heard an animal-like snarl. When she looked up, she saw Kat advancing on her with Brom's jewel-hilted dagger raised, ready to strike.

"I should have drowned you in the spring," Kat spat, "instead of leaving you there for the wolves. I won't make that mistake this time. I mean to see an end to you once and for all.''

With a blood-curdling scream, Kat lunged at her unwanted daughter. Julianna caught her wrist, managing to stop the needle-sharp point of the dagger a bare inch from her breast. The force of Kat's movement, however, threw Julianna off balance. She crashed into the bedside table, then to the floor. The Rhinehart woman stood over her, smiling, almost purring with evil pleasure.

"I have you now. I won't make the same mistake I made years ago. And once you're gone for good, I'll have Brom.''

Julianna felt the broken shards of her pitcher jabbing into her back, the water that Maeyken had drawn from the spring seeping through her gown. The next thing she felt was the sharp stab of the dagger's point piercing the flesh of her breast.

She screamed in pain. Her eyes closed. Bright dots swam beneath her lids, then blackness closed in. A sound like rushing water and wind filled her ears. The searing pain vanished as a green mist wrapped her in comforting warmth.

Kat's horrified cry filled the bedroom. She stared at the dagger, its sharp tip dripping Julianna's blood. But even as she watched, the red stain disappeared. And where her victim had lain mere seconds before, only a pool of water drenched the Persian rug.

"She's gone!" Kat cried, her eyes wide with a mingling

of shock and horror. Then she threw back her head and laughed long and hard. "Yes, *gone*! At last!"


Julianna felt as if she were floating among the clouds. Green clouds, lined with shimmering flecks of silver. Warm wind wrapped round and round her, cradling her as gently as a calm sea. After what seemed the longest time—Days? Months? Years?—she felt herself losing the sense of motion.

In the back of her mind, a tiny voice—her own—kept repeating, "No, Brom, no! Don't send me back. Let me stay with you." When all the motion stopped, she realized she was saying words aloud.

Someone tapped her shoulder. "Pardon, lady, but it's getting a mite late. Shall I call you a hack to take you home?"

Julianna opened her eyes and looked up into a round face, stubbled with beard, and the gleaming bald pate above it. She had never seen the man before in her life.

She blinked several times, then asked, "Where am I?"

The man frowned. He could get in a wicked lot of trouble for serving a decent women too much liquor, and by the look of her he guessed she wasn't a common whore. Then, too, he was expecting a big crowd in to celebrate tonight. He didn't want a lone woman taking up valuable table space.

"You're at the White Horse Tavern, ma'am. And been here some time, you have. I reckon your gentleman forgot he was to meet you."

"My gentleman, that is, my *husband*, is at sea." Julianna put a hand to her forehead as a wave of dizziness spun the room around before her eyes. "I wasn't expecting him to meet me."

Now the barkeep was even more anxious to hustle her out of the place. Being an old sailing man himself, he didn't hold with seamen's wives frequenting taverns alone, looking to pick up any man who could satisfy the itch 'tween their thighs.

"Let me hail you a cab," the stranger offered again. "You'd best be getting home. This part of town ain't safe for a lady come full dark."

Rising slowly, Julianna tested her legs. She still felt weak and shaky. She glanced about her, the man's words suddenly registering. "The White Horse Tavern, did you say?"

"Aye," he answered, holding the door for her.

A sudden rush of relief filled Julianna. She knew this place. She knew the rough tables and benches, the long bar, the fireplace, and there—yes, there over the bar—hung the leather mail pouch. She hadn't been thrust suddenly away from Brom's time after all. But how had she gotten here? What had happened?

"Come along, ma'am," the barkeep urged. "There's a cab just outside."

Julianna followed in a daze. She saw the burly tavernkeeper confer with the tall, lanky driver, but she didn't hear what passed between them—the bald-headed man telling the cabbie that she had had a nip too many and for him to take her wherever she wanted to go, so long as it was a good piece away from the White Horse. He gave the driver the fare since his tipsy female patron hadn't even a purse in evidence.

Not until Julianna was inside the carriage, calling up to tell the cabbie to take her to Captain Kidd's house, did her head truly begin to clear. But that clearing was little consolation. Brom was still gone. And now she was back in New-York, many miles from Netherwood.

"But many miles from Katrina Rhinehart as well," she reminded herself with a relieved sigh. "At least for now . . ."

# Chapter Twenty

"Cap'n Kidd, you say?" the driver called down to her before leaving his spot outside the White Horse Tavern. "I don't believe I know the gent. Whereabouts might he live?"

Julianna could hardly believe her ears. Not know Captain Kidd? *Everyone* in New-York knew him!

"Captain *William* Kidd," she emphasized. "Surely you've heard of him. His house is in Pearl Street."

"Ah," the man answered, "that I know well." He clucked at his tired-looking horse and the cab jerked ahead.

Julianna leaned back in the closed carriage. She had never felt so tired in her life. Her lids ached to close, but she dared not give in to that luxury for fear she would fall asleep. And if she slept, she might dream. Her encounter with Kat had been nightmare enough. So she sat back, trying to relax but still stay awake, trying not to think of what had happened. She knew she would be safe once she reached Sarah's. At least for the time being.

Julianna twisted her head to one side suddenly, staring out the open window in the door of the cab. Something wasn't right. But what? The sound of the horse's plodding hooves. That was it. Instead of the dull thud of hoof on packed dirt she was used to, the old gray's shoes rang on cobbles. But the town of New-York itself wasn't paved and certainly the oft-used trail up to the White Horse, which was well outside the wall, was little more than a wide rut of dust or mud depending upon the weather.

She sat forward, gazing out the window in the gathering twilight. On both sides of them, tall buildings crowded the road and each other. Where were the thick woods she remembered? As they rode on, she spied nothing that told her where they might be. What on earth was going on? This wasn't Brom's New-York!

"Here we be, ma'am," the driver called to her. "Pearl Street. What number?"

"Oh," Julianna fretted, "I can't remember. But it's very near the Water Gate."

"Beg pardon, ma'am? The old Water Gate was tore down years before my time."

Julianna leaned out of the window, glancing up and down the street, sure that she would spot the Kidds' tall brick home. But nothing looked familiar. Nothing even looked Dutch. All of the houses she remembered from her days with Brom were gone. She glanced toward where the windmill should be. It, too, was gone.

"Are you *sure* this is Pearl Street?" she inquired, politely, but with panic rising. Something told her—White Horse Tavern or no—she was far from Brom's time.

"Onliest one in town," the man assured her. "Now, where do you want I should take you?"

With a sinking heart, Julianna leaned back and sighed. This was New York, all right, but not the one she had hoped it would be. For a moment she remained silent, thinking

341

through her situation. She had only assumed she was still in 1697—that she had been transported, not through time on this occasion, but from one place to another in the same century. Apparently, her assumption was incorrect. She remembered the wetness seeping through her clothes, the broken jug. *The spring water*, of course!

"What year is this?" she asked the driver, dreading his answer.

He shook his head and rolled his rheumy eyes. The barkeep was right; the woman certainly had been at the jug too long if she couldn't even remember the date. How could anyone in his right mind forget what *this* day was?

"Today's the very last day of the nineteenth century, ma'am. December 31, 1899."

Julianna gasped. She was back in her own time—at least the time she had known for most of her life. She wanted to scream with frustration, to rant at the driver to convince him that he was wrong. Either course she decided would be wasted effort. But what would she do now? Where could she go? She knew no one in New York.

"Elliot Creighton!" she said suddenly. For months his name had crossed neither her mind nor her lips. It seemed as if her long stay in Brom's time had wiped away all memory of this time. But now everything came flooding back. Elliot might be in the city. If he was, she knew she could count on his help.

On sudden impulse, she called up, "Do you know the Hotel Metropole?"

"I do, but it ain't likely they'll have a vacant room this late, tonight of all nights."

"Never mind," Julianna answered. "Just take me there, please."

The man clucked up his horse once more, turning north.

It was just a chance, of course, but Elliot Creighton should be back in New York by now. She had no money, no clothes except what she was wearing, no way to get back to Netherwood. As the cab crawled through the bustling traffic along Broadway, she prayed silently that Elliot would be there. She would simply explain to him what had happened. He wouldn't be pleased, but he would help her. If Elliot wasn't in town, she hadn't a clue where to turn.

The dazzle of the Gay White Way gave her some comfort. At least it looked familiar. Throngs of people crowded the street, some hurrying toward supper before the theaters opened, others out bent on celebrating the birth of the new century.

"Oh, Elliot, be here!" she murmured. "Please!"

As if in answer to her prayer, they passed the brightly lit front of the Majestic Theater and she spied a silver-on-white banner over the entrance that announced, "Opening Night—ELLIOT CREIGHTON in *SAILOR'S LAMENT*."

"Thank God!" she cried.

"What's that, ma'am?" the driver called down.

"Nothing. Just get me to the Hotel Metropole as fast as you can."

The minutes crept past as they inched through traffic. The whole town seemed turned out to celebrate tonight. Finally, they pulled up in front of the hotel's familiar façade.

Julianna leaped out, reaching into her skirt pocket, only to find it empty. She looked up at the driver, panic in her eyes as she remembered her penniless state. "I haven't any money."

He doffed his shapeless hat and grinned down at her. "No problem. The barkeep gave me your fare." Then he flicked the reins and melted into traffic, happy to be rid of his strange, confused, and likely drunken passenger.

Elbowing her way through the milling crowd, Julianna rushed inside and straight to the front desk. The hotel guests—all of them turned out in finery and jewels—stared at her shabbily old-fashioned frock.

343

Ignoring their disdainful glances, she demanded of the hotel clerk, "Is Mr. Creighton registered here? Mr. *Elliot* Creighton?"

The thin fellow, black hair slicked close to his head, smiled brightly. "No need to tell me which Mr. Creighton, ma'am. Everyone knows his name nowadays. Best actor on the Gay White Way. Certainly, he has a suite here! Mr Creighton would settle for none but the best." He looked her up and down, but seemed to find nothing amiss with her sorry attire. "And you must be Miss Doran. Mr. Creighton told me before he left for the theater that he wasn't sure, but he hoped you might arrive sometime this evening."

"He did?" Julianna asked, puzzled.

The man made no reply, but, turning slightly, reached into a cubbyhole behind him and drew out a key. He handed it to her. "Mr. Creighton said to tell you your ticket for tonight's performance would be waiting for you at the theater box office."

Julianna thanked the man, then hurried up the stairs. A million questions were swimming in her head. Why had Elliot thought she might arrive tonight? When had this new play come about? She'd never heard of it. But, apparently, Elliot's status in theater circles had risen several notches since the last time he played New York.

She stopped outside the door and looked down at herself with a sinking heart. Her clothes really were a mess, still slightly damp with spring water, rumpled, and meant for the kitchen more than for a night out in New York. The faded woolen gown would never do for opening night at the Majectic.

"Oh," she moaned, "what am I going to do?"

Inside the suite—the same one she and Elliot had occupied on her previous visit to New York—she found a huge pot of hothouse gardenias, a note from Elliot propped against it.

344

Darling,

I feel a bit foolish writing this, not knowing if you'll turn up or not. But, surely, you'll come tonight. I can't believe you'd miss my opening in this new play that was written especially for me. I've been wild, searching for you! *Were have you been?* I went to Netherwood. Maeyken and Zeke are taking your disappearance with a good bit more grace than I've been able to manage. I left word with them that I'd be at the Metropole. I only hope they've had a chance to tell you. There is so much we have to discuss. Assuming you arrive to read this, we'll talk after the show. I hope you approve of the things I bought you. I want us both to shine tonight!

I love you, Juli!

Always,
Elliot

Julianna sank down to the bed, staring at the note, her emotions at war within her. Reading Elliot's words, she'd felt a spark of the old love between them. But it all seemed so long ago . . . so far away. Now she was married—Brom's wife. She would simply have to do her best to make Elliot understand.

A coldness closed around her heart. "No," she murmured. "I'm Brom's *widow*." At this point in time, she reminded herself, Captain Brom Vanderzee had been dead for two hundred years.

She glanced down at her hand and a soft gasp escaped her. Brom's ring was gone. He had said that she would be his wife for as long as she wore his ring. But sometime during her strange transition after Kat's attempt to murder her, the emerald-studded dragon had vanished. She closed her eyes, trying to summon up Brom's dear face. Only a blurred reflection of his image materialized. She sighed, a shuddering sense of loss filling her. It seemed her whole world had been turned inside out once more.

What could she do? Where could she go? She hadn't a notion. She would simply have to take things one step at the time.

"Very well!" She stood and glanced warily at the wrapped packages on the vanity. Thoughts of the gifts she'd received the last time she was here crossed her mind. Stolen jewels. But she had no reason to fear these presents. Elliot had stated plainly that he had bought them for her. Besides, neither Brom nor his ghost was in New York at present. He might have been a million light years away; her sense of him seemed that vague.

She opened the packages. At another time, she would have been all smiles, delighted by Elliot's surprises for her. He had thought of everything. She no longer had to worry about what she would wear to the theater. And she would, indeed, shine, as Elliot wished.

Julianna stared off in the distance, trying to ignore her nervousness. Stars were twinkling like sharp, frozen diamonds in the blue velvet sky, and she could just make out the dark outline of some of the buildings that bordered Central Park. It was a cold but brilliant night. So why couldn't she feel its magic?

"Don't stand there daydreaming, young woman. Can't you see the line has moved forward?"

Julianna, standing outside the Majestic Theater, waiting to pick up her ticket, glanced over her shoulder at the surly man behind her. A head shorter than she and three times as wide, the dapper fellow sported bristling muttonchop whiskers. His dark eyes, too small for his round face, glared at her. When she failed to moved immediately, he tapped his ebony walking stick impatiently on the sidewalk.

She gave him a haughty stare before she took a step forward, feeling he deserved no less for his rudeness. After all, it wasn't as if she were still dressed like a scullery maid in the old woolen frock—a nobody who could be ordered about at will. No! Thanks to Elliot, she wore a ruby velvet cape over a magnificent, daringly-cut cloth-of-gold gown. No jewels at all this time—only one of Elliot's fragrant gardenias in her hair. Although she might not feel like one, she looked like a queen.

The ill-mannered fellow grumbled a few more words under his breath. Finally, a couple of more steps and Julianna arrived at the ticket window.

"Yes? How many?" the clerk asked, not looking up.

"I believe Mr. Elliot Creighton left a ticket for me. The name is Julianna Vanderz—She stammered for a moment, then remembered. "*Doran*," she finished emphatically.

The ticket clerk quickly located an envelope with her name on it. "I hope you enjoy the play, Miss Doran," he said with a smile.

She hurried inside, glancing down at the ticket to locate the number of her seat. As usual, Elliot had her seated on the front row at the very center of the stage. Without help from an usher, she found her place and quickly sank down into the red plush seat, relieved to have arrived in place before curtain time.

She wondered what the play was about since she'd never heard of it before. But, then, of course she wouldn't have. Elliot had told her in his note that it had been written especially for him. And this was opening night. Probably a letter from him was waiting at Netherwood, telling her everything from start to finish. If this was truly the last night of 1899, she had been away for some time.

As if on silent cue, a hush fell suddenly over the audience. All talking, coughing, and boot-shuffling ceased. A moment later, the curtain rose. Julianna caught her breath, her eyes going wide.

The scenery before her was a recreation of Brom's New-York. She recognized it even though the artist's conception only vaguely resembled the early port town. But there were the quaint Dutch houses, the windmill, and the Water Gate, with a pair of buttonwood trees in the far background.

Her attention turned to the actors parading before the colorful scenery. It seemed a Dutch *kermis* was in progress, or perhaps a wedding celebration. Brightly-dressed pirates and their gold-bangled women strolled about while the narrator, an old woman who looked not unlike Maeyken, began her tale of magic and mystery and ghosts of sailors gone down with their ships. Although Julianna searched every face, Elliot's was nowhere to be seen.

Then the old hag of a storyteller moved back to the shadows upstage, while the bowsprit of a sailing ship eased into view from the wings. A tall, dark actor in leather britches, high boots, and a flowing shirt strode on stage to thunderous applause from the audience. He was forced to take a bow even before he delivered his first line of dialogue.

"Elliot!" Julianna whispered, feeling a sharp tug of familiar emotions. Even in costume he looked the same to her, except that he had let his hair grow for this part. It hung long and straight to his shoulders, while a new beard and mustache added the look of a sailing man to his usually smooth face.

As if he had heard her small whisper over all the rest of the sound and fury in the theater, Elliot looked directly at Julianna, his gray eyes sending a private message even as they had that first night she saw him on stage. She smiled back, feeling none too settled by the intensity of his gaze.

The other actors on stage had frozen in position at the sight of him, as if they were seeing a ghost.

Finally, the audience quieted enough for Elliot to utter his opening line. "Fair Margrit, keeper of my heart, I have

348

returned to you at last. Come here to welcome me, my dearest love!'' His voice boomed in an agony of unrequited passion. ''Fly, sweet wench, into my arms and kiss away my pain . . . soothe my breaking heart.''

Elliot moved about the stage, going from one woman to the next, searching for the well-loved face of his Margrit. But, alas! She was not amidst the crowd. The poor sailor bent his forehead to his forearm to shield the sight of his pain from the other actors, but he projected his bitter emotions to the audience so plainly that Juli wept.

Julianna sat transfixed through the entire performance— the tale of a Dutch sailor presumed lost at sea. His Margrit, giving up hope after many years of waiting, consented under pressure to wed, all the while knowing she could never love another. The poor sailor—Abraham by name—having fought off hurricanes, savages, wild beasts, and pirates to return to his one and only love, arrived to find her about to marry another. Margrit flew to her Abraham's arms and would have called a halt to the nuptial proceedings, but her father, greedy to the very soul, refused to allow his daughter's love of a destitute sailor to interfere with her marriage to a wealthy patroon.

Julianna wept until she thought she could not possibly squeeze out another tear. Elliot was brilliant, playing the role of tender lover so convincingly that it made Juli tremble with deep emotions, while he handled Margrit's villainous fiancé and her scheming father with a strength and dominance that left Julianna feeling swelled up with pride and passion for Abraham and for Elliot.

Deafening silence followed the fall of the final curtain. Only a bit of self-conscious sniffling could be heard here and there. Then, suddenly, the theater exploded with applause. As a unit, the audience rose to its feet, chanting first, ''Bravo! Bravo!'' and then, ''Creigh-ton! Creigh-ton! Creigh-ton!''

Julianna could feel the applause for Elliot thundering in her chest. She became a part of it and it a part of her. She realized she was crying again. But this time her tears were happy ones for Elliot and his success, not sad ones for poor, love-starved Abraham. However, Elliot had indeed made Abraham come to life for her in the past two hours.

"Bravo!" she cheered again, trying to make Elliot hear her above the others.

Did he hear her or was he simply drawn by the shimmering golden gleam of her gown? Julianna decided that it didn't matter. All that mattered was that Elliot's name was on every pair of lips and that his fame was assured. The bold look and half-smile he bestowed on her made her blush. People on either side of her turned to stare, no doubt wondering who she was, but realizing full well that this evening's star had singled her out.

Julianna heard a woman behind her whisper to someone, "Lucky girl! I wouldn't mind having Elliot Creighton smile at me that way. Better yet, I wouldn't mind having his tall black boots under my bedstead as she obviously will before this night's done."

Giggles followed. Juli's cheeks flamed scarlet. She wanted to turn and tell the gossipy woman that she was mistaken, that Elliot would certainly not be sharing her bed tonight or any other night because she was a married woman. Then the foolishness of such a move dawned on her. Quickly, she fled from her seat. She would wait for Elliot backstage, in his dressing room. She would explain everything to him the moment he came through the door. She wanted no misunderstandings about why she was here.

—

Julianna moved about the small dressing room, marveling at Elliot's costumes, the pots of greasepaint on the table, and the other more familiar things that reminded her so of

350

him—his favorite books, his offstage clothes, and finally a small portrait of herself in a velvet-lined, gutta-percha case. Elliot had insisted that she go to the daguerreotype studio for a sitting once when she was in New York. She stared at the picture, smiling. She had not smiled that day, feeling stiff and uncomfortable with her neck held in place by a metal clamp so she wouldn't move and spoil the plate. Elliot had clowned about, trying to make her composure slip— making silly faces, blowing kisses, taking exaggerated bows as if he were on stage and she were the sole recipient of his outrageous performance.

Her back to the door, she didn't see him slip in. Not until Elliot's hands gripped her shoulders and his warm lips kissed her neck did she know he was there. She turned, staring into his bearded but familiar face.

"You came," he breathed, a hesitant smile trembling on his lips.

Julianna felt her throat tighten. She'd meant to tell him everything the moment he came to her so that there could be no misunderstanding as to why she was here or what was or was not between them any longer. But words failed her. Fighting for control, she simply nodded and returned his uncertain smile. Surely, any moment now she would find her voice again.

He looked down at her, his smoke-gray eyes loving but troubled. "God, I've been so worried about you! Where have you been, Juli darlin'?" Before she could answer, he waved a hand to dismiss his question. "No! Not now! I don't need explanations. I only need this."

Slipping his arms about her waist to draw her close, he leaned down, covering her lips with his.

The "no" on Juli's lips was swallowed up in Elliot's burst of pure passion. She pressed the heels of her palms hard against his shoulders, trying to shove him away, but he would have none of it. He held her, helpless, in his arms, crushing his lips to her mouth, pressing the hot swell of his body to her gold-encased thighs.

When Elliot finally released her, Julianna stumbled back, stunned. He started toward her again, but she extended her arms to hold him at bay. "No, wait, Elliot! Give me a moment, won't you?"

*A moment for what*? she wondered wildly. She was dizzy and trembling and felt flushed all over. She needn't try to tell herself that there was nothing left between them—that her love for Brom had erased her feelings for Elliot. Once again, it occurred to her that she loved both men with the same passion.

"I don't want to wait." Elliot, his eyes smoldering, took another step toward her.

"You have to listen to me," she said in a rush. "Hear me out. Please!"

Her frantic tone stopped him more than any words she might have spoken. He gave her a curt nod and began stripping his shirt off over his head. Julianna almost groaned aloud. How could she talk to him when he was undressing before her very eyes. But to her relief, he quickly reached for a silk robe and pulled it on, the air in the room being quite chilly.

"All right, Juli, what is it that can't wait to be told?"

She opened her mouth to speak, then closed it abruptly. What, after all, had she been about to tell him? That she'd been gone so long because she had moved? Moved from the nineteenth century back to the seventeenth? Or she might tell him that while he'd been away, she'd married someone else. Of course, he would want to know who, and when she answered Brom Vanderzee, a cohort of Captain Kidd's, Elliot would likely have her committed. She could simply lie and tell him that it was all over between them and that they would now have to go their separate ways. But then how would she explain the fact that she had checked into his hotel suite, was wearing the gown and cape he'd bought

352

her, and was at this moment backstage in his dressing room, aching for him to kiss her again?

"Well?" Elliot prompted. "What is it, Juli?"

In spite of the cool air in the room, she fanned her face with her fingertips. Then she took a deep breath, gathering her courage. "This isn't easy for me, Elliot," she began tentatively, having no idea where she was going from there.

Elliot reached out and touched her flushed cheek. "Darlin', you can tell me anything. You know that."

She smiled, her mind racing suddenly. "It's just . . . just that you are such a huge star now. You were magnificent on stage tonight. I wept until I thought my heart would break. Why, even now, it's almost as if I'm standing here talking to Abraham instead of to you, Elliot. And I feel odd somehow, as if you're a stranger to me suddenly. You were still Abraham when you walked through the door just now. Abraham when you kissed me." She shook her head and laughed nervously. "I don't know. It all sounds crazy, doesn't it?"

Elliot leaned down close to her face. "Abraham kissed you, did he? Then I suppose that means it's my turn next."

So slowly, so tenderly, so thoroughly did he kiss her this time that Juli felt herself weak and breathless when he drew away. She couldn't let this happen, she told herself. She had to remember Brom . . . that he loved her . . . that he was coming back to her . . . that she meant to return to him.

Quickly, she moved away from Elliot again, making sure to put enough space between them so that he couldn't reach out and touch her. If he did, all was lost.

"Elliot, I need your help."

Her serious tone had its effect on the twinkle in his gray eyes. He stood staring at her now, not making a move.

"Are you in some kind of trouble, Juli? God, I should have guessed by the odd way you've been acting. What is it, darlin'?"

"Money," she said quickly, not giving herself time to lose her nerve. "I need some money to get back to Netherwood. I've lost my purse, everything I had with me."

He grinned. "Is that all? I thought you were in real trouble. Don't you worry another minute, darlin'. I'll see that you get back to Netherwood in high style. But first, we're going to celebrate tonight. I've reserved a table at Rector's for their big New Year's Eve party and I've invited some guests to join us. Now, don't press me to find out who they are. I want to surprise you. It won't take me long to change, then we'll be on our way." He paused and reached into the pocket of his robe, then grinned at her as he produced a black velvet bag with silver drawstrings and offered it to her. "But first . . ."

"Another gift?" Hesitantly, Julianna took the soft little jewel bag that he held out to her. "Oh, Elliot, you shouldn't have," she said, wishing sincerely that he hadn't.

"I made you a promise, darlin'. Remember? You were to get the parson and I was to get the ring. I know it's not April yet, but I can't wait to make you my bride."

Julianna slipped the ring out of the bag. The size of the single pear-shaped diamond dazzled her. Tears sprang to her eyes. "Oh, Elliot!" she cried. "You *really* shouldn't have!"

He leaned down, kissed her, then slipped the huge diamond on her finger. "You and I, we're going to get married just as soon we can," he whispered. "I love you, darlin', with all my heart, and I don't mean to let you slip away again."

Julianna felt perfectly faint. Why couldn't she force herself to tell him the truth? She had to do something and do it fast. If not, they'd soon be on their way to Rector's and then back to the hotel suite. She couldn't let that happen. She had to find out what was going on before she let this go any further. She really did need to get back to Netherwood with all haste. Maybe Maeyken could explain all this to her.

She knew now that Maeyken had first come to the nineteenth century with Kat's arrival at Netherwood. No doubt, the woman had moved back and forth at will through time. She must know what Julianna's true fate was meant to be. Julianna meant to find out.

Elliot sat down and began tugging off his boots. "It won't take me long to change, darlin'."

Seizing her one chance for escape, Julianna smiled and said, "I'll step outside in the hallway until you're ready."

Elliot threw back his head and laughed. "Bashful still at the sight of a man without his trousers, eh, darlin'?"

She nodded. Moments later, she was gone, not only from his dressing room, but from the theater.

A long line of cabs waited out front to take the theatergoers on to supper. Julianna dashed to the head of the line and leaped into the cab, stealing it from a surprised couple who had been making their way at a regally slow pace toward their conveyance.

"Take me to the nearest pawnshop," Julianna called up to the driver, "and *hurry!*" She had to do the deed quickly, before she lost her nerve; it was the only way.

They were in the lower part of the city—a rough-looking area near the Battery—before the driver found a pawnshop open this time of night on New Year's Eve. Steeling herself for the unpleasant but necessary task, Julianna told the driver to wait while she went into the dingey place.

"Help ya?" the short, grizzled faced pawnbroker mumbled, squinting up at her through dirty eyeglasses.

"Yes," she answered, careful to keep her voice steady, although her heart was pounding frantically. "How much can you give me for this ring?"

Guilt riddled Julianna as she slipped Elliot's large diamond from her finger. The pear-shaped stone flashed brilliantly in the dim lamplight. She had the man's full attention now.

355

Moments later, with far more than enough cash in hand to buy a train ticket to Netherwood, Julianna was back in the cab.

"Where to now, miss?"

Julianna barely heard his question. Suddenly, there was a ringing in her ears and a fluttering all about her as if invisible wings were beating the air. She felt a pain in her chest, similar to what she'd experienced when Kat had stabbed her, but different, too. This was more like the sharp twinge she remembered from the first night she'd seen Brom—the night of the Ouija board.

"Miss? Where do you want to go now?" the driver said in a louder voice.

She had meant to tell him to take her straight to the train station, but when she opened her mouth, she ordered instead, "To the White Horse Tavern." Maybe that would be an even quicker way home.

The old horse clopped along the Battery at such a slow pace that it seemed to Julianna they were barely moving at all. She stared out over New York Harbor. Steamships crowded the water, their stacks black against the lighter night sky. She watched a heavy fog drifting in, obscuring even the largest of the vessels. The fast-advancing haze took on a greenish tint from the lights of the city. Julianna watched, mesmerized.

Suddenly, she gasped. Out of the thick fog, another ship emerged. A tall sailing ship with ghostly shrouds hanging limp, untouched by the wind. At the same instant, she heard Brom's voice in her head as clearly as if he were sitting next to her.

"Where are you, dearest heart?" he moaned. "I need you. Come back . . . come back to me."

Julianna closed her eyes, concentrating on Brom with all her might, repeating over and over a litany of willpower, "I'm coming, my love, I'm coming . . . I'm coming!"

# *Chapter Twenty-One*

"I'm coming! I'm coming!"

Julianna was still murmuring the words to herself as she mounted the stoop at Netherwood. But would she find Brom there waiting for her? That was the question that had nagged her all through the long train ride from New York and during the long wait at the halfway point when the train broke down on the track.

Now it was late afternoon. She glanced about. To her dismay, Netherwood looked exactly the way it had when she first visited the place as a child—as it had when she'd inherited it from the Worthingtons. Tall elms along the drive. New wing and porch. A single, malformed lilac bush that had never recovered from her cousin's fatal fall into the heart of it.

She opened the door cautiously. "Maeyken?" she called. "Are you here?"

Twilight had claimed the interior of the house already.

No lamps glowed to chase away the gathering gloom. And no fires burned, Julianna noticed, gripping her cloak more closely about her and shivering in the chill.

She checked the kitchen. Empty. Lighting a candle on the windowsill, she headed for the stairs. Slowly, she climbed, trying not to think how alone she felt in the old house. Halfway up, she had to pause a moment as a wave of dizziness made her stumble.

"It's hunger pangs," she said, taking some comfort from the sound of her own voice. She couldn't remember when she had last eaten, or in which century.

She would rest for a while in her room, then go back to the kitchen to see if Maeyken had left any food in the icebox. But at this moment, the very thought of eating made her stomach clutch itself in horror.

Staring down at the floor, she inched her way through the chill darkness to the bedroom door, intent on nothing more than lying down and letting sleep claim her. Her disappointment was overwhelming. All during the trip, she had truly believed that somehow Brom would be here when she returned. She reached out for the knob to open the door to the master suite, but her hand met only smooth wall.

She looked at it, bringing the flickering candle up, her eyes wide and staring. No knob! No door! No master suite!

"Brom!" she cried, flying across the hall to fling his door wide.

Before her eyes had time to adjust to the darkly-draped room, she heard his voice. "Julianna! Thank God you've come!"

Setting her guttering candle on the table, Julianna stared down at the figure on the bed. He was dressed in purple velvet breeches and yellow leather boots, his bare chest swathed in a bloody bandage. This was exactly the way she had seen him on that long ago night of the séance.

Julianna reached out to him. "You're hurt."

"Wounded, yes, but not mortally, dearest heart. I had my men bring me home, sure that you'd come to take care of me."

She flung herself on the bed, covering his face with kisses. When her exuberance brought a moan of pain from her husband, she sat back, stricken.

"I'm sorry, love," she murmured.

He chuckled and gripped her hand. "No matter. I can endure more than a small twinge to have you in my arms again. It's been *so long*, dearest heart."

As Julianna redressed the stab wound in his chest, Brom recounted all that had happened. He and Captain Kidd had sailed their separate ships all the way to Madagascar. Then in a battle with some especially fierce pirates, Brom had taken a dagger slash near the heart.

"Lucky for me the bastard's aim wasn't better." He gritted his teeth as Julianna poured a few drops of whiskey into the ugly wound. "I'd not be here today. But he won't be tearing any other flesh. I fed the ugly son-of-a-whore to the sharks when I was done with him."

Kidd had insisted that Brom sail for home with all haste, saying that he would return soon to New-York himself. But word had reached Brom on the way home from a ship they passed at sea that William had run into trouble before he had finished his business. Some of his crew had rebelled when their captain refused to fire on an unarmed ship. The ensuing battle had resulted in Kidd's flagship burning to the waterline. He'd taken another vessel, the *Quedagh Merchant*, and was sailing her at present. But there was talk that Kidd had helped himself to the wrong cargo. Word had spread quickly across the seas that the Crown had declared Kidd himself a pirate.

"The charges are pure rubbish, of course," Brom told Julianna, "clearly trumped up by someone in the government who covets the rich prizes William's taken."

Julianna's thoughts went immediately to Sarah. "Where is Captain Kidd now?"

"Running for the Caribbean the last I heard." Brom eased himself into a more comfortable position on the pillows, glancing down to inspect his new bandage. "He'll be safe there until he can find out the full story on the charges."

"And you?" Julianna asked, searching the face of the man she loved so dearly.

He drew her close and kissed her. "I'll stay here for a time, dearest heart. I need to recover—not so much from this mosquito bite of a wound as from those long, lonely nights at sea. God, how I've missed you, Julianna!"

He bent down to cover her lips again, fondling her breast at the same time. Julianna trembled at the impact of his tender caresses. She hadn't realized how much she'd missed him until this very moment. True, her days without her husband had seemed overly long—the clock ticking in slow motion, the sun creeping across the sky. But now, tasting him, feeling his sheltering arms around her, she knew with a certainly that she could not have lived if he hadn't returned to her.

After a time, Brom leaned up on one elbow, looking at her as if seeing her for the first time. His black eyes devoured the sight of her form, still gowned in glittering gold.

"You went away, didn't you?" His voice was soft and understanding, not the least accusing. Still, Julianna felt that her actions needed some defense.

"I had to, Brom."

"Kat?" he asked.

Julianna nodded, her eyes focused on his face, memorizing every plane and angle. "She came here. She tried to kill me." Julianna glanced down at her own chest, where the wound had been before it miraculously vanished. She caught her breath. There it was. Healed, only a tiny dent in the flesh above her breast, but now quite visible.

"Blast the woman to hell!" Brom cried, drawing Julianna to him protectively. "How did you manage to escape that vicious bitch?"

"Maeyken saved me," she replied after a moment. "She guessed that Kat might come here to make trouble, so she put pitchers of spring water in each of our rooms. Maeyken left first, after Kat threatened her. Then she came in here and attacked me. I stumbled into the pitcher, spilled the water, and took a good drenching. A lucky soaking, I'm happy to say! Another moment and . . ."

She looked away, not wanting Brom to see the fear in her eyes. Kat was still out there somewhere and would likely strike again.

"And?" Brom prompted gently.

Julianna shrugged. "When I awoke I was in the White Horse Tavern."

"A safe place compared to anywhere that Kat is," Brom said. "And which of my old drinking cronies was there to see to my bride's welfare?"

"No, you don't understand," Julianna said, shaking her head. "It was the same place, but in another century. It seems the White Horse will have a long and prosperous life. When I came around, I was in the year 1899."

Brom frowned, shaking his head in wonder. "So far into the future! What did you do while you were there? Where did you stay?"

Desperately trying to evade his questions, Julianna answered simply, "I wasn't there very long. Only a few hours. I went to the theater; that's why I'm dressed this way. I was trying to get back to Netherwood all the while." She paused and searched his face, her own troubled. "Then I saw your ship sail in and I heard you calling me. I knew I had to return to you at once."

He nodded as if he understood everything perfectly. "What about Maeyken? Wasn't she with you?"

"No," Julianna answered. "I don't know where she is. Perhaps she didn't travel as far as I did." Sudden realization dawned. "That must be why her death was never recorded at the church, Brom. There aren't *two* Maeykens; there's only one. Of course! I know her both as the girl and as the old woman, my childhood nurse."

At that moment, many things came clear in Julianna's mind. Just as Sarah had guessed, that had to be how old Maeyken knew so much about Brom and Kat and Netherwood itself.

Brom's gentle touch soon brought Julianna out of her reverie. "Never mind all that," he whispered. "Your husband's home, wife. I think it's time I had a proper welcome."

They had to be careful because of Brom's injury. But any pain their lovemaking might have cost him was more than compensated by the pleasure, he declared. He was especially gentle with Julianna, leaving her breathless and glowing by the time he took her to the heights with him. And this time, Julianna knew, something had been different between them. Something had happened. Something wonderful!

Afterward, as they lay in each other's arms, Julianna touched his cheek with her fingertips.

"Darling," she whispered. "Remember once that you said we would have beautiful children—red-haired, black-eyed sons and daughters?"

"I do." He said the words as if he were holding his breath, waiting for her to continue.

She took his hand and pressed it firmly to her belly, smiling.

"Why didn't you tell me?" he demanded.

"Because I think it's just now happened. I'm not certain how I know, but I'm sure of it, darling."

"God, what a woman!" he exclaimed, rubbing a hand roughly over his face as if he could hardly believe his good fortune in finding Julianna, in having her for his wife and the mother of his child.

"I love you so much, Brom," she whispered.

Gathering her into his arms—carefully, because of his wound and his newly-planted seed—he held her as tightly as he dared. "Words don't even begin to express how I feel about you, dearest heart. I'd give you the moon and the sun and the world, if I could. You are more precious than the most dazzling diamond."

Julianna felt a sudden twinge of guilt at his mention of a diamond. But she soothed herself, remembering that she had mailed the pawn ticket to Elliot from the White Horse Tavern before she left New York. She'd wanted to write a note, explaining why she couldn't marry him. But she had decided that any such attempt to explain would meet with miserable failure.

She glanced down at the finger where Elliot's diamond had been for such a short time. A smile warmed her face. There was the glittering green-scaled dragon. It had reappeared as suddenly and inexplicably as it had disappeared earlier.

"I am, indeed, Brom's wife again," she whispered, smiling.

Brom and Julianna whiled away the next weeks and months in blissful solitude. They took long rambles through the woods, picnicked by the river, made love every night, and slept late every morning. Julianna's shape began its gradual change—her breasts swelling and her belly rounding just enough for Brom to pronounce her figure "pleasingly plump."

Only two things proved unsettling to Julianna: the distressing news of further charges against William Kidd and the date. During her travels back and forth, time for Julianna had become distorted. Brom had not been gone the few months she had first assumed, but two full years. Now the seventeenth century was fast drawing to a close, and the date on Brom's tombstone loomed large in Julianna's memory. Who would betray him? And how could she keep it from happening in order to save his life?

Spring had turned the world into a pastel riot of tender new grass and budding wildflowers on the fateful day when the news arrived. Sarah wrote that Lord Bellomont, now governor of New-York, had sent an envoy to the Caribbean to entreat her husband to return. Bellomont, who had been William Kidd's mentor, promised that he would press no charges—that all talk of piracy and murder would be dismissed if only Captain Kidd would meet him for a friendly chat in Boston.

Julianna was in the kitchen, rolling dough for a dewberry pie, when Brom strode in, holding Sarah's latest letter and grinning like a boy.

"I knew it!" he declared, striking his fist on the table for emphasis. "All the charges were trumped up from the start. William's no more a pirate than I am, and he's certainly no murderer. Bellomont has stood behind him all along and will continue to do so."

The hair on the back of Julianna's arms stood up suddenly. "Are you sure this isn't a trick?" she asked for no reason she could think of.

"A *trick*?" Brom roared. "Blast it, love, you are ever the suspicious one! Why would you ask such a thing? Isn't the governor's word good enough for you?"

She turned and tried to smile at him. "I suppose. If it's good enough for you, Brom. It's just that I've worried so about Sarah."

"Well, don't you waste another minute worrying about anything, Julianna." He leaned down and kissed her, deeply and tenderly. "The only thing you need bother your mind

364

with is our baby.'' He patted her slightly rounded belly. 'Sarah says William is sailing to Gardiner's Island at the eastern end of Long Island. She plans to meet him there. I'll be there, too, then sail on to Boston with him just to lend my support.''

His words struck Julianna like a blow. She whirled back toward him, her reply fierce. "You must *not* go!"

He frowned and touched her bright hair. "Of course I must, dearest heart," he answered gently.

"But, Brom . . ."

"No buts, Julianna! William has always been a good and faithful friend—someone to stand beside me through the worst of times as well as the best. Now I mean to show him the same loyalty."

Julianna knew there was no use begging him to stay. "What should I do, then?" she asked, trying to sound much calmer than she felt at the moment.

Brom smiled at her, his eyes glistening like obsidian. "You can go to New-York with me. Then after our meeting on Gardiner Island, you can wait for me at the Kidds' home. I'm sure Sarah would be glad of the company, and you two can do some shopping or whatever you please. William and I will be back before you know it. I promise!"

He sealed his promise with another kiss, but Julianna still felt that painful tug at her heart and a certain sense of doom closing in.

The date was June 5, 1699. As much as she tried not to think about it, Julianna was unable to force her mind to more pleasant things. *Five more days!* The words kept ringing in her head like a death knell tolling—tolling for Brom.

They had come to New-York the day before. Then with Sarah and little Sally, they'd sailed on to Gardiner's Island. Now Brom and Julianna stood a short distance away from

365

the Kidd family, saying their farewells before the men set off for Boston.

Brom cradled Julianna in his strong arms, nuzzling her hair with his cheek. "You aren't going to cry, are you, love? You promised last night."

In spite of her feelings of doom, Julianna smiled when he mentioned the night before. How well he had loved her during those wonderful dark hours! How well he had *always* loved her!

"I'm trying not to, Brom," she whispered, "but it isn't easy to keep such a promise." Blinking back the tears that threatened, Julianna looked up into his face, memorizing every line. "You will be careful, won't you, Brom? If anything happened to you, I don't know if I could go on."

He chuckled softly and hugged her closer. "Dearest heart, I'll be back before you know it. As for anything happening to me, you needn't worry about that. I lived through my battles with the pirates, didn't I?"

She reached up and touched his still-tender scar. "Barely," she whispered.

"But I did survive. If I could come through that alive, I have little to fear from the governor and his men. This won't be a battle, dearest, only a meeting among civilized men."

Remembering what she had heard, Julianna asked, "Will there be any women there?"

Brom cocked one dark eyebrow and grinned down at her. "So that's what you're worrying about. Not that I'll be killed, but that I'll be lured away by some female." He drew his pregnant wife close and kissed her deeply, so deeply that heat curled like a glowing flame inside her.

"Brom, please don't tease me," she begged. "You know I'm not worried about any other woman taking you away from me. I *am* worried about Kat, though. What's happened to her? Where is she? What if she turns up in Boston and causes trouble?"

366

Suddenly, the full weight of Julianna's fear threatened to crush her. Of course! Why hadn't it dawned on her before? Katrina Rhinehart was the woman who would betray Brom, who would cause his death. She had tried once to disrupt their fate; she would try again.

"Who knows where Kat might be?" Brom said offhandedly. "And who cares? I doubt she'll force another confrontation with you, dearest heart."

"But if she can't get at me, she might go after you, Brom."

He laughed. "Let her try!"

Another long, tender kiss, and then the men went aboard Captain Kidd's ship. Brom waved to Julianna from the gangplank one last time. She blew him a kiss and allowed her pent-up tears to flow freely.

Back in New-York Sarah Kidd did everything in her power to try to cheer Julianna. She took her visiting and shopping, insisting that if they kept busy the time would go faster. But nothing could chase the gloomy fear from Julianna's heart.

After the men had been gone four days, Sarah all but gave up on her cousin. As they were eating supper that night—just the two of them in the kitchen—Sarah said, "I simply don't understand, Juli. They should be home in less than a week. You weren't this upset when they left to go after the pirates." She glanced at Julianna with a knowing smile. "But then you weren't pregnant at that time."

Julianna shook her head and continued toying with her untouched food. "The baby has nothing to do with the way I feel, Sarah. Something terrible is going to happen. I just know it."

"*How* do you know it, Julianna?" her cousin asked indulgently.

Juli looked her squarely in the eye. "Because I've seen Brom's grave."

Sarah tossed her head and clucked her tongue. "You mean you've had a bad dream? Well, that doesn't mean anything. Oh, the horrible things I dreamed when I was carrying Sally!" She shuddered, remembering.

"This was no dream, Sarah. I saw Brom's tombstone in the forest at Netherwood."

Sarah's smile faded and she turned thoughtful. "But that doesn't mean anything, you see. Of course Brom is going to die; we all will eventually."

"Not tomorrow, we won't!" Brom's distraught wife answered tonelessly.

*"Tomorrow?"*

Julianna nodded. "That's also the date in the church record book. June 10, 1699."

"Oh, Juli!" Sarah cried. "You should have told me earlier. What can I do to help . . . to make you feel better?"

"Nothing," Julianna whispered. "There's nothing anyone can do." Suddenly, she was in her cousin's arms and both women where sobbing. But the more she wept, the emptier Julianna felt.


By the time Julianna went to bed, she felt emotionally drained. She knew she should never have told Sarah. Why make her cousin suffer? Now neither of them would sleep all night.

But, amazingly enough, Julianna dropped off to sleep the moment her head touched the pillow. As she slept, she wandered the pathways of her entire life, seeing everything in sharp detail. She remembered being left at the spring by her mother, Katrina Rhinehart. She recalled the sweet face of Ruth Doran smiling down at her, the tender arms cradling

368

her. All her years on the farm, all her childhood summers at Netherwood returned for her review. Again, she lay in Brom's arms, feeling his sheltering love, feeling his passions kindle hers to bright flame. She relived the exact instant when their child had taken hold inside her body and the deep ache of joy and pride and wonder. Finally, she was forced to say good-bye to Brom again, but oddly enough, as they shared that final farewell kiss, Brom changed before her eyes. She watched herself kissing Elliot, then Brom, then Elliot again.

Near dawn Julianna stirred and moaned in her sleep. Then she slipped deeper than ever into her dream world. She could hear Brom calling her name, not frantically, but softly and tenderly, as if he lay next to her, coaxing her to love him.

It seemed she opened her eyes and came fully awake. "Brom?" she murmured. But her subconscious told her that she was still only dreaming as a new scene unfolded in her mind's eye.

She was on a busy dock, in some unfamiliar place. Soldiers stood guard all about—their bright red jackets crossed by white cartridge belts, their muskets at the ready. A man in a powdered wig and a black damask suit seemed the center of all attention.

"Governor Bellomont!" It was Brom's voice she heard hailing the man.

At that moment, Brom and William Kidd stepped into view, coming off one of the ships at the quay. Julianna tried to call to her husband, but found she had no voice in this matter.

"Good to see you both," the governor said. "Captain Vanderzee, you're looking fit after that wicked slash you took. But, Captain Kidd, you've a gaunt and haunted look about you." The man smiled cordially and slapped Kidd on the shoulder. "We'll see if we can't put an end to your worries this very morning. Come along with me, both of you. We'll meet in yonder counting house since it's close."

As the dream unfolded, Julianna turned and twisted in the bed. There seemed nothing ominous about the scene, yet her feeling of foreboding only intensified as the moments ticked by.

One of the soldiers advanced on Brom and Kidd. "Your weapons, please," he demanded. "A courtesy to the governor, sirs."

Julianna watched Brom hand over his cutlass and William give up his two pistols. They entered the two-story building and Julianna followed, it seemed. The moment they were inside, her heart all but stopped. There, next to the chair reserved the governor, sat a woman.

"Brom! Look out! It's Kat!" Julianna's scream was only silent anguish.

As soon as Brom entered the room, Kat rose and ran to him. "Oh, love, I've prayed you'd come!" she cried, flinging her arms around his neck.

Brom tried to thrust her away, but she clung like a thorny vine. Only Julianna saw what happened next. Kat slipped one hand among the folds of her purple silk skirt and drew out a dagger—the very same jewel-hilted weapon with which she had tried to murder Julianna. In a swift, secret move, she slipped it into Brom's hand.

The next instant, Kat screamed, "Captain Vanderzee has a weapon! He's come to kill Governor Bellomont!"

She stepped away from Brom then, far enough away so that when the governor's bodyguard fired his musket, she was out of harm's way.

Julianna felt the hot lead enter her own breast even as she watched the crimson stain spread over the front of Brom's shirt. The dagger still in his hand, he staggered forward, his eyes glazed. Then, in his final moments, he plunged the

370

glittering weapon—point to bejeweled hilt—into Katrina Rhinehart's breast. The two of them collapsed in a bloody heap.

Julianna awoke trembling and sobbing. She wailed Brom's name to the rafters. Suddenly, she felt a hand on her shoulder. She cried and looked up. Brom stood beside the bed, smiling down at her.

"Don't weep for me, dearest heart. You promised you wouldn't."

"Brom, you're here!" she cried, reaching out, but touching nothing. "What's happened?" she begged. "Why did I see those terrible things?"

"Never mind," he told her gently. "None of that matters. What's important is for you to know that I still love you, Julianna. That I will *always* love you. But now you must go back. Return to your own time."

"No, Brom!" she cried. "I can't leave you!"

He shook his head and bent down to kiss her—a deep, soul-rending kiss. "You won't leave me. Not ever. Nor will I leave you, dearest heart. As long as you wear my ring, I will be your husband. Go now. I'll be waiting. I love you, Julianna. *Forever!*"

The vision faded in a swirl of greenish light. Feeling as if she'd been drugged, Julianna lay back on the pillows.

"Brom," she murmured over and over again. "Brom, don't go! Please! I love you. I need you."

She had a sense of drifting, of flying through fog. Try as she might, she could not clear her senses. At last, Julianna gave up fighting and let her whole body relax. Blackness closed out all else.

# Chapter Twenty-Two

"I'll be waiting," Brom's voice whispered to Julianna's heart. "Go back, Julianna. Go back."

Suddenly, dreams, fog, and blackness vanished. Julianna's eyes shot open as a surly voice—certainly not Brom's—shouted near her ear, "Don't stand there daydreaming, young woman. Can't you see the line has moved forward?"

She could only stare at the blustering fellow—the same man who had spoken those very words to her once before. His muttonchop whiskers quivered with impatience as he glared at her with beady eyes and tapped his ebony walking stick on the sidewalk in front of the Majestic Theater.

As Julianna stepped quickly along, she glanced up at the marquee. "ELLIOT CREIGHTON in *SAILOR'S LAMENT*," it read. A large silver-on-white banner over the theater's entrance proclaimed this to be Opening Night.

"It can't be!" Julianna gasped. Could all that had hap-

pened to her in the past weeks and months have been only
a dream? She glanced down at herself. She was wearing the
same golden gown, the same hooded cape of ruby velvet,
even the gardenia from Elliot in her hair that she had worn
that other night. She glanced about. The weather was the
same, with the brilliant stars and the last faint tints of sunset
fading in the sky over Central Park.

"Central Park!" she murmured aloud, realizing with a
sudden sense of awe that she had once more traveled through
time and space to reach the here and now.

The ill-tempered man behind her urged her on once more
with a few grumpy words. Two more steps and she was
standing at the box-office window.

"Yes?" prompted the ticket seller. "How many,
please?"

Julianna was trembling so, she could hardly bring herself
to speak. "I believe Mr. Elliot Creighton left a ticket for
me. The name is Julianna Doran."

The man shuffled through a stack of envelopes and shoved
one toward Julianna, smiling as he did. "I hope you enjoy
the play, Miss Doran."

"Thank you," she murmured, knowing since she had
seen it once before on Opening Night that she would. As
she hurried toward the door, she looked at her ticket—the
very same seat, of course.

Julianna hardly noticed the glittering crowd gathered for
Elliot's premier performance. Her mind was whirling with
a million thoughts. How could this be possible? Things like
this didn't happen in a sane world.

She almost laughed aloud at the thought. Since when
had her life been sane? She seemed forever caught up in
madness.

Settling in the soft red plush seat, front row center, Julianna tried to calm her nerves. She had literally run out on
Elliot the last time she saw him. How would he feel toward

her now? How could she face him again? Would she ever be able to explain?

"Of course not!" she muttered under her breath. "I don't believe what's happened, so I certainly can't hope to make Elliot understand."

She sighed hopelessly, but refused to allow herself to think about it any longer. She would stay for the play, then slip out afterward. Elliot would never have to know she was there. *Ridiculous*! she reminded herself. He could practically reach down and touch her from the stage. Of course he would know she was there!

The curtain rose on the first act. Julianna forced herself to concentrate on the actors and the story. Elliot had yet to appear on stage. At present, the Dutch *kermis* was taking place on the waterfront in old New Amsterdam. A half dozen "pirates" and their gaudily-dressed women strolled about as an old hag, the narrator who looked like Maeyken, began her tale of ancient spells and long-lost seamen.

Examining the set, Julianna smiled again at the artist's conception of the quaint old houses, the windmill, and the Water Gate at the east end of the town's wall that only vaguely resembled the place she knew so well. Memories of old New-York came rushing back.

Suddenly, the bowsprit of Abraham's sailing ship eased into sight from the wings. This was Elliot's cue to appear. When he strode on from stage right, the audience erupted in thunderous applause. Julianna did not join in. Her hands remained frozen in her lap. She felt numb, paralyzed, unable to believe her eyes.

Until this very moment, everything about the evening had been identical to that other opening night that seemed so long ago. But Elliot was different—*totally* different. He had let his hair grow long as before, but it was much darker than she had ever seen it, and a gold earring gleamed through his flowing locks. Gone were the tight leather breeches and full

374

white linen shirt he had worn before. He was dressed in purple velvet trousers and his yellow boots were of finely tooled leather. His chest was bare save for a bloodied bandage.

When he moved to center stage to deliver his first line, his eyes met Julianna's. She tried to look away, afraid of the hurt and resentment she expected to see in his face. But she found herself unable to shift her gaze. His gray eyes— one almost black with some deep-smoldering emotion— fixed hers with such a look of desire and passion and love that Julianna felt her heart leap in her breast. A new realization dawned. For the first time she understood.

Someone else very dear to her—long ago and far away— had looked at her through those same eyes, the very soul shining through. Brom! Brom and Elliot . . . Elliot and Brom! They were one and the same to her now. They had always been but she had been too blind to see it before this very moment. Brom had promised he would never leave her. She knew now that he had kept that vow.

Julianna never took her eyes off Elliot for the rest of the play. She remained oblivious to the story, caught up in her own life's tale. By casting off her daughter into another time, Katrina Rhinehart had unwittingly disrupted Julianna's fate. Brom and Julianna had been meant to be together as if it were written in the stars. But it could not be. Not in that lifetime. Brom had died in 1699. Julianna had witnessed the sad end of his body. But his soul lived on. Driven by love, her wondrous Dutchman had found her again. She smiled up at Elliot, *dear* Elliot—her one and only love. The same love who had made a prisoner of her heart two centuries ago.

The curtain fell. The audience rose to its feet as one, shaking the rafters with applause.

"Bravo!" rang out on all sides. Then the theatergoers set up a chant. "Creigh-ton! Creigh-ton! Creigh-ton!"

Time and again Elliot returned for curtain calls. Julianna felt herself bursting with pride and happiness. All his life Elliot had longed for this night. Now, at last, he had the adulation he craved.

*And I?* she mused. *I have the man of my dreams.*

She rose with the others, cheering him until her throat ached and her gloved hands smarted painfully. Before the joyous uproar subsided, she slipped out of her seat, eager to be in his dressing room when he arrived from the stage. If the rest of the evening went as it had previously, Elliot would offer her a ring and marriage and a long, sweet life with him.

"Yes, yes, *yes!*" she cried as she hurried backstage.

Suddenly, with his dressing-room door in sight, Julianna stopped dead in her tracks. Suppose Elliot, too, remembered that other night. Suppose he had taken her flight as refusal, firm and final. How could she explain her sudden change of heart?

Tossing her cape back over her shoulders, determined to the core to make things right, Julianna forcibly cast off her doubts and entered his dressing room. Nothing inside had changed.

Julianna determined not to have Elliot catch her with her back turned this time. She wanted to see him the moment he entered the room, to assure herself that she was right about him. She would stare into his eyes and she would know for certain.

After what seemed an eternity, the door opened. The man who stepped inside could have been Brom himself. Not just the clothes, the hair, the golden earring. Brom Vanderzee's very soul shone through Elliot Creighton's dark eyes with a look of love so powerful that it almost took Julianna's breath away.

"I came back," she whispered.

"I've been waiting, dearest heart."

No other words passed between them for a time. Elliot crossed the room in three long strides and took Julianna into his arms. He pressed her close and captured her lips, parting them, searching her mouth with his tongue. He slipped the cape from her shoulders to caress her soft flesh.

"Elliot! Oh, Elliot, my dearest," she murmured.

"Sh-h-h, Juli darlin'. I don't want to talk. I only want to hold you . . . to kiss you. I'm so glad you're here. I'm never letting you go again. I mean to keep you with me *forever*!"

*Forever!* The word swirled through Julianna's head, creating a firestorm within her. Brom had promised to love her for exactly that long, and through Elliot he would be able to keep his vow.

By the time Elliot released Julianna, she was dizzy with desire. Dizzy from another cause, too, she realized suddenly. Morning sickness always visited her in the evening. Now her hand went to her barely-rounded belly. She smiled. She was still carrying Brom's child. She almost laughed aloud, wondering how in the world she would calculate the date of its coming birth.

"You're happy. I'm glad, dearest heart," Elliot said.

"You'll never know how happy, darling!" she exclaimed, hugging his neck and laughing. "I was so afraid I'd lost you. After I left so suddenly last time . . ."

He pulled slightly away and frowned. "I was the one who left you, fool that I was! I'm just glad you could come tonight. When I returned to New York and went to Netherwood, Maeyken said you'd had to go see to a sick relative in Saugerties. She assured me, though, that you would be back in time for the opening tonight."

*Bless you, Maeyken!* Julianna said silently.

"Wait till you hear the fantastic night I have planned for us," Elliot enthused. "We're going to Rector's for their big New Year's Eve celebration and I've invited a few guests

377

to join us." He beamed at her. "Don't ask me who. I want it to be a surprise, darlin'."

"Oh, Elliot, it sounds marvelous!" She laughed and touched her hair. "But I haven't a hat."

He reached into a huge box sitting on the table and brought out an enormous confection of gold tulle and silk roses. "Oh, yes, you have!"

"You thought of everything, my darling!" Juli cried with glee.

"Just you wait," he said, drawing her back into his arms. "After midnight, we'll go back to the hotel and bring in the new century in our own special way. Lord, I wish we were there right now! It's been so long, darlin'."

"I'd like that, too," Juli agreed, "but we have to celebrate your opening first. I insist we go to Rector's. Now, change your clothes."

"Don't you dare leave the room," he warned.

She laughed softly. "I won't."

"Oh, hell, I can't wait any longer!" Elliot burst out.

Julianna glanced about, frowning. If he meant what she thought he meant, they would certainly find things cramped here in his dressing room. The closest thing to a bed available was a narrow, hard cot.

Seeing her expression, Elliot laughed again—a deep-throated laugh that sounded so much like Brom's. "No, I mean I can't wait to give you this," he said, handing her a black velvet jewelry bag with silver drawstrings. "Before you open it, I must tell you that I really had my eye on an enormous pear-shaped diamond. But then I spied this in the window of a pawnshop and I had to buy it. I really tried not to, Juli darlin', but somehow I knew it was meant for you. I hope you like it."

Julianna took the bag and opened it with trembling fingers. A flash like green lightning struck her eyes when the ring tumbled out into her hand.

"Oh, Elliot!" she gasped, tears spilling from her eyes. "It's magnificent!"

He slipped the emerald-studded golden dragon on her finger and kissed her hand tenderly. "As long as you wear this you'll be my wife," he whispered.

"We aren't married yet, are we?" Julianna wasn't quite sure at the moment.

"The parson's only a detail, darlin'. I feel like I've been married to you for the longest time. As if we've belonged to each other since before time began."


An hour later, Julianna arrived on Elliot's arm at Rector's Champagne and Lobster Palace. Their situation was totally different this time. Elliot's star had risen. He was the toast of the Gay White Way. Julianna beamed with pride and love as the crowd outside the stylish eating establishment parted like a wave to make way for Elliot Creighton and his future bride.

Charles Rector himself was waiting just inside the revolving door to welcome his star customer. The former horsecar conductor turned restaurateur bowed deeply before them.

"Your table for six is ready, Mr. Creighton. If you will please follow me . . ."

Just then the gypsy musicians spied Julianna, who was hard to miss in her glittering gold gown and fabulous hat. Their leader smiled and nodded his recognition. The Hungarian musicians surrounded Juli and struck up a romantic tune to accompany her entrance. Elliot, not the least bit disappointed at having the limelight stolen from him by his lady, beamed broadly as he followed along in her shining wake. Every head in the place turned to admire the tall, flame-haired beauty dressed all in gold. Nor was Elliot ignored this time. As they passed through the crowded dining room, the other customers renewed their chant from the theater. The vast room resounded with calls of "Creigh-ton! Creigh-ton! Creigh-ton!"

Before seating Juli, Elliot took her left hand in his, presenting her to the restaurant's patrons and at the same time showing them her unique engagement ring. Julianna curtsied and smiled.

A new burst of applause rang out, then a resounding chorus of "Bravo!" Elliot bowed to his audience, then took his place at the best table in the house.

"My word!" said Juli breathlessly. "I believe you've made it, Elliot darling!"

He leaned over and kissed her flushed cheek. "I would say we've both made it, dearest heart."

Julianna was still smiling, but her expression turned quizzical. When had Elliot started calling her by that particular endearment? That had always been Brom's favorite name for her. But then, so many things about Elliot now reminded Julianna of Brom—certain mannerisms, the tone of his laugh, the soul-deep gleam in his dark eyes.

She reached over and took his hand, smiling into those eyes. "I love you, darling, more than ever. At least twice as much as I did before."

He kissed her fingers just below where the dragon ring rested. "You'll find out exactly how much I love you before this night is over."

Just then the gypsy musicians struck up a wildly lilting tune and the customers broke into more applause, clapping with the rhythm of the fiddles. Julianna turned to see who was arriving. Her eyes went wide.

Whirling and dancing her way toward the table came a small figure with coins jingling at her wrists, neck, and waist. Her gray hair flew in riotous curls about her wizened face, and she was dressed in the costume of a pirate wench. Behind her, a little old man came hobbling along, looking lightly uncomfortable in his high-heeled boots and buccaneer's garb.

"Can it be?" Juli cried. "Can it really be?"

Elliot laughed aloud and stood to welcome the couple to their table. "Maeyken and Zeke were both in the play," the actor explained. "Didn't you recognize the narrator, Juli?"

Julianna didn't answer. She was on her feet, hugging her old friend from so long ago.

"Well, bless me, if you ain't a sight for sore eyes, Miss Juli!" Maeyken cried. Then she caught sight of the dragon ring on Julianna's finger and her lips moved silently as if in prayer. "You finally got your man, eh?" she whispered for Juli's ears alone.

"Oh, Maeyken, so much has happened. There's so much I have to tell you."

The old nursemaid winked. "There's quite a bit I can tell you now, too. Couldn't have before. It wouldn't have done no good. But I reckon everything's come round now to where it ought to be."

Zeke hugged Julianna, too. He was too overcome with emotion and the excitement of the evening to say more than hello.

There was little time for conversation anyway as the musicians once more struck up a special tune. A wave of admiring whispers passed from table to table.

"Well, finally you'll get to see Miss Russell's entrance," Elliot told Julianna.

She watched as the lovely blond woman strutted toward them, her spring-green gown glittering all over with crystal beads, the wide brim of her hat fluttering over her blue-blue eyes. Lillian Russell almost, but not quite, outshone her escort, Diamond Jim. They came straight for Elliot's table. He rose, accepting the lady's hand.

"Elliot, my dear chap," she said, "you outdid yourself tonight. Mere words cannot express what your performance made me feel."

"Quite so, Creighton!" Diamond Jim seconded. "But it seems your crowning achievement this evening is your choice of partners for the New Year's celebration." He turned an admiring look on Julianna.

"I'd like to present my fiancée, Miss Julianna Doran."

Before many minutes passed, the six people at the table were deep in lobsters, champagne, and witty conversation. The evening flowed by in a steady stream of goodwill.

Julianna felt as if she had been transported into a new and magical world. Mirrored balls revolved about the ceiling, casting flickering lights around the room. When Elliot danced with her, she felt as light as one of those flickers. At midnight, a beautiful young woman gowned in a drape of gossamer silver burst through the face of the huge clock by the stairs. Champagne corks popped, voices raised in song, and tears flowed.

"It's a new century," Elliot whispered, then kissed her soundly.

"And I feel like a new life is unfolding before me," Juli added.

"Are you ready to begin that life this minute, dearest heart?"

"More than ready, my darling!"


The new century was barely an hour old by the time Elliot unlocked the door to their suite at the Hotel Metropole. Julianna leaned on his arm, feeling slightly drunk. Not on champagne, but on the gay time they had had, the good friends they had spent the evening with, and, she mused, on life and love in general.

Surprising her with his sudden move, Elliot swept Juli up

her arms and carried her across the threshold of their hotel
suite.

"It may be a bit premature," he explained, "but I might
well rehearse being married. I feel as if we are already.
And, darlin'," he whispered, nuzzling her neck, "I mean
for us to share star billing in this honeymoon suite tonight."

Elliot Creighton promised no more than he was capable
of delivering. He played his best role ever as lover, using
the entire suite as his stage. He stripped away Juli's glittering
gown, wanting to play opposite her gleaming flesh. He
teased it to a warm, rich glow, fondling her until she moaned
with desire, kissing her until her head felt as light and as
hot as the rest of her body.

When Elliot finally shed his evening clothes, Julianna
smoothed her palms over his naked chest. Her hand rubbed
a scar just above his heart.

"Oh!" she cried. "What happened, darling? That wasn't
there before."

He shook his head. "Damned if I know," he confessed.
"I woke up one morning and there it was. I wish I could
explain it."

Juli leaned and kissed the mark. "It doesn't matter. I love
you, scar and all."

"All?" he teased. "Every last inch of me?" His hands
slid around her, cupping her buttocks and drawing her so
close that she felt him slip—hot and ready—between her
thighs. She was ready, too.

"The bed," she purred.

"No need, darlin'."

So saying, he lifted her up, guiding himself into place. Juli
clung to him—her arms around his neck, her legs around his
hips. He moved with her, slowly, careful to make each
stroke deep and sure. When she shuddered against him,
overcome with pleasure, Elliot eased her to the floor for
more amorous play.

383

The window seat, the library table, and the bed. Elliot took full advantage of all the suite's possibilities. As Julianna lay back in the bed sighing his name, wondering how she could live through such exquisite pleasure one more time, Elliot rose from her side.

"A bath," he said. "Wait for me, dearest heart."

Julianna snuggled against the satin sheets, her whole body throbbing deliciously. Far off, it seemed, she heard the splash of water. The scent of gardenias intensified in the room. She stretched and purred. She felt so wonderful, so relaxed, so loved.

Then Elliot was there, lifting her in his arms again, leaning down to suckle at her breast. When he carried her through the bedroom and into the bath, she opened her eyes.

"Elliot! Another surprise?"

"Um-hum," he murmured softly. He lowered her into the tub through the mass of fragrant gardenias floating on the surface of the steaming water. The sweet scent of the hot, crushed blossoms rose about Julianna's face. Intoxicating and arousing. She held her arms out to Elliot.

He slipped into the water with her, crushing more delicate blooms. Then he found the one perfect flower he sought. As he thrust gently but deeply, his passions rose to a fever pitch. Beneath the fragrant waves, they met once more for that night's final, earth-moving leap to the heavens.

"Happy New Year, dearest heart," Elliot moaned close to her ear.

"Happy *forever*!" she answered, clinging to the one and only man she would ever love—through this and many lifetimes yet to come.